HEROES

A Novel by

David Shields

SIMON AND SCHUSTER   NEW YORK

Designed by Eve Kirch
Manufactured in the United States of America

10   9   8   7   6   5   4   3   2   1

Library of Congress Cataloging in Publication Data
Shields, David.
   Heroes.
   I. Title.
PS3569.H4834H4   1984   813'.54   84–13956
ISBN: 0-671-52564-6

The author gratefully acknowledges permission to quote from the following:

"Rapper's Delight" by the Sugarhill Gang, copyright © 1979
Chic Music Organization, Ltd. Used by permission.

"A Love Supreme" by John Coltrane, copyright © 1973 Jowcol
Music. Used by permission.

I would like to express my gratitude to the National Endowment for the Arts and the Ingram Merrill Foundation for fiction grants, the Iowa Writers' Workshop for a James Michener Fellowship, the San Francisco Foundation for the James D. Phelan Award, PEN and the Carnegie Fund for Authors for emergency grants, and the Authors League for an emergency loan. I would also like to thank MacDowell Colony, the Yaddo Corporation, the Virginia Center for the Creative Arts, Millay Colony, and Ragdale Foundation for offering me the time and space in which to write this book.

For Adrienne

The process of living means that we are all only temporarily able-bodied persons.
—SULLIVAN COUNTY YELLOW PAGES

ONE

I STOOD in the middle of downtown renovation, watching frat boys push their sorority sisters around the only block the Refurbishment Project hadn't turned into rubble. Greeks were dressed in green doctors' gowns while the sweethearts of Alpha Omega, pretending to be patients, lay under blankets in beds that had wheels the size of my headache. It certainly wasn't my idea to spend Thanksgiving Day covering the third annual Bed Races as a sports event. That brainstorm belonged to my editor, Marty, who assured me the effect would be funnier than hell. Marty was wrong. A KRNA deejay called each heat live, then jumped off the sound stage to interview the winners like they'd just won Preakness.

I suppose I should have been in a better mood, should have tried to ask the racers how they took that last corner at hairpin speed, but my seven-year-old son, Barry, is a diabetic who devotes the majority of his waking hours to staying out of the hospital, so the sick humor of the whole charade didn't do a whole lot for me. Also, "Iowa" is an old Indian word meaning "beautiful land," not "urban renewal." The college kids are in one long stupor the four years they're here. They couldn't care less about the trashing of River City. I live here, though. The pedestrian greenway and Sycamore Mall and Plaza Center One have ruined this town, and now the Old Capitol Center promises to bury it under eight feet of cement.

The students were celebrating Happy Hour and everyone seemed to be having a fine time and it was all for a good cause, since the prize money was going straight to Mercy Hospital's cystic fibrosis fund. *Race Beds So Others Might Leave Beds.* The Stallion mascot whickered at anyone who wasn't decked out in River State roan-and-gray in honor of the first basketball game of the season later tonight. Most stores boast a Stallion Medallion department, where everything from key chains to lounge chairs are available in red roan-and-gray. A couple of cheerleaders, delectable girls with too much makeup, let me kiss the tiny Stallions painted on their cheeks.

"What's your prediction?" the Stallion asked me. The mascot never appears in public without his horse costume because he suffers from the Midwest's worst case of acne. I inevitably feel like I'm conducting a conversation with Mr. Ed.

"Take Omaha and the points."

"No, really, come on."

"River State in a romp," I said. "Menkus'll be sky-high."

Mr. Ed danced in place, hooves flying.

The Stallions used to be called the Indians. There used to be a shoe repairman who, if you weren't careful, would talk winter boots with you until closing; a café where regulars lingered over lunch, reading the paper I write for and getting free refills; a laundromat owned by a guy so pasty and roly-poly that I suspected he'd gotten tossed into the rinse cycle once too often; a sporting-goods dealer who knew more about goose down than geese do. They're gone, all of them, all the friendly stores run out of town or onto rural route 6 by what my wife, Deborah, calls chichi shops. I now know why the Amish refuse to drive their black-box buggies in from Kalona.

Water taps belch sludge, the air smells sooty, and we feel the tremor of drill presses all day long. It wasn't always like this, I keep trying to tell people, but they don't believe me or don't especially care. A few years ago the Old Capitol Building, the first state capitol, was named a national historical site, which locked up the past in a nice neat mausoleum and gave carte blanche to development boys bent on turning downtown into a rock quarry. The unfinished malls and parking lots and abandoned foundations make me feel my life isn't being lived so much as put on hold, traded even-up for an urban planner's dream of the entire business district as a quiche dispensary. They've seen the future, these boys, and it takes place in a plastic bubble.

> *Kappa Kappa Gamma*
> *Is number one.*
> *First we'll win,*
> *Then have fun.*
> *Go, you guys, go!*

Kappa Kappa girls rooted home their housemates. The contestants the deejay interviewed said how thankful they were they could do something to help people who had cystic fibrosis. The sky had the Astrodome quality it gets when snow is working its way south from the Great Lakes. The wind picked up as dusk darkened, making it difficult to want to stay here. Some kids had stopwatches and actually timed the bed racers as they skirted the edge of building demolition and street repair.

This was a slightly worse assignment than usual, but I'm assistant sports editor on a two-man staff. Marty sticks close by the office, doing layout and only the major articles, while I cover bowling tourneys and Tae Kwon Do seminars and the dog races in Cedar Rapids. I wanted out and that out took 80 east to Chicago, then 94 north to Milwaukee, where I was still in the running for a job at the *Journal*, an employee-owned paper that gives reporters a lot more leeway to free-lance. Milwaukee: I yearned to chart a sailboat on Lake Michigan and go to Marquette games and Bucks games and Brewers games at County Stadium and get sloshed in German beer halls. I was on the lookout for a solid story to dig my claws into because so far the piece of mine the *Journal* brass like best was a Where-Are-They-Now? thing on Bob Pettit, which was less a transcript of my telephone conversation with the ex-All-Pro than an ode to my youth, when the game of basketball ran deepest and loudest and clearest in my soul.

As a kid I worshiped Pettit because he had a perfect jump shot and kept track of how many points he scored, and those were my main problems, too. My father was always away on the tennis circuit, and, until she became an alcoholic, my mother was always out showing houses; I needed something I could practice nonstop to prove my significance, and I found it in bombs from top of the key. Once, when Pettit played valiantly in a lost cause, the radio announcer said he had the guts of a cat burglar. I felt the force of truth, cried into the couch, and wanted to be his partner in crime. The summer between my junior and senior year of high school I attended the Bob Pettit Coaching Camp in St. Louis. After watching me throw behind-the-back passes during a weave drill, he lifted me off the burning asphalt and said, "Stop fartin' around like you're Cousy. Work on your jumper." His voice had the sound of a train horn and he resembled a balding giraffe.

Now, though, pushing forty, I was going all out for Belvyn Menkus, who is as different from Bob Pettit as I am from my wife, a scholar. The first time I saw Menkus' name was three years ago at the bottom of a recruiting list under the heading "Best of the Rest" in the *Midwest Basketball Monthly:* a six-foot-three guard averaging twenty points and ten assists for Franklin Vocational, a Chicago sports factory River State has plundered ever since I've been in town. I'd read glowing scouting reports on him, but I learned long ago that blue-chip high school seniors with flashy stats are a dime a dozen. His Sioux City highlight film portrayed him as one more community college gunner, which completely misses the picture, since he is above all a giver, a point guard with great court sense. Preseason practice was closed to the press, so I wrote the usual puff for the *Register.*

Halfway through the first game, I started believing every word of the hyperbole I'd been writing about Menkus most of November. Even now I would gladly trade a year of my life or the slow side of my brain for two hours inside his skin because,

14

although he looks like lead alto in an Oak Park choir, he plays basketball like he just invented jazz. This winter I was so madly in love with what his body can do in a gymnasium, so obsessed and depressed and driven nuts by daydreams, that sometimes I thought the only relief would be to plant a kiss in the middle of his mug or at least squeeze his immense right hand, to show my awe but also to make sure he wasn't a ghost. It's a long story.

Before going to the gym, I bought an orange plate of cholesterol at Arby's and wrote a fingernail-thin story about the Bed Races while catching clips from football games on a television sitting on top of the cigarette machine. Then I had to call Deborah at her chairman's house in North Liberty and tell her I wasn't going to have time to get out there for Thanksgiving dinner.

It was difficult to hear over the crash of academic bullshit at her end, but I think she said, "Well, won't you at least tell Richard that you deeply regret being unable to clink sherry glasses and wax witty with him over this year's bounty?"

Richard Tolliver is her department chairman. Deborah actually talks like this. I said no.

The River State field house was built in 1926 with metal and brick and a very low ceiling to create beautifully bad acoustics. Chairs are packed close together on top of the court and the balcony seats are all benches: when one person cheers, that cheer flows into the bloodstream of the next person, and you get a cumulative effect. Every sound echoes and re-echoes; every ovation is shared with your neighbor. It's such a great gym, with so much energy and character, that Coach Hinselwood wants the athletic director to declare it a firetrap and build him an oval sports complex with perfectly regular dimensions. The old barn can come alive in the cold, and even tonight, on this chilly Thanksgiving, when wiser heads would have been watching the game at home, adding kindling to the fire, a capacity crowd wearing gray slacks and roan shirts

15

stampeded to its seats. The Stallion Battalion, rowdy students who sit together in the northeast bleachers, was out in full force.

Menkus was the only person on either team not goofing off during warm-ups. He paced the time line, cradling the ball in his humongous hands like he was trying to read *Spalding* on the leather. It was the goddamndest sight, this skinny junior college transfer standing alone at midcourt, oblivious to ushers and vendors wandering courtside, kids wanting autographs, klieg lights burning in his face, and Hinselwood shouting at him to get some shots in along with the rest of the team. Hinselwood's assistant coaches, Ott and Nagel, scribbled on clipboards. The managers got water ready and folded towels. Happy, a deaf-mute who always carries his Instamatic and a sandwich board of Stallion buttons, tried to get Menkus to say cheese.

Anyone else stomping around the center circle I would have dismissed as a head case, but there was something immediately, absolutely serious about Menkus that made me leave the press balcony to go watch him from the scorer's table. Twenty minutes before game time, Menkus was already stripped down to his uniform. Under his jersey he wore a ludicrous gray sweatshirt that had been through a thousand washings and made him look twelve years old. He worked strenuously on a pack of bubblegum.

"Belvyn, how's it going?" I heard myself ask. "Ready to run? Omaha'll be a piece of cake."

He didn't say anything. He was so far gone into his own voodoo I doubt he even heard me. I couldn't expect him to remember who I was on the basis of a couple of media sessions. He jogged while moving the ball between his feet and behind his back and around his waist—coaching-camp clichés, but you could barely follow the ball and he controlled it like he was playing a private round of Atari.

Nonchalant, he popped a few line-drive jumpers from straightaway. All of them went in, and on all of them he jumped at least a foot and a half off the floor, cradling the air in

16

his hand until the net lifted. Then he whipped the ball off the arms of empty chairs and the legs of tables; it kept rebounding into his hands. The Stallion Battalion, ensconsed in the safety of the first tier, razzed him a little, but I don't think he was hotdogging it. He was just doing what he loved doing, and, in this age of glory hogs and tally counters, it was probably difficult for the drunken idiots in the northeast bleachers to comprehend that there was one poor kid left whose main passion was still passing.

His right leg was lightly bandaged, he needed a shave, and his birch-white face carried absolutely no expression. From a distance, his profile might make you think you were watching a lummox. Up close, he awakened terror. In Menkus' eyes was that typical athletic meanness which my junior varsity coach at West Des Moines said separated the wheat from the chaff, and which he also said I lacked and would always lack. Menkus' green eyes looked everywhere and nowhere, telling you everything and nothing at all. He had bushy sideburns halfway down his cheeks and a blond Afro that was about to come uncurled any minute now.

Tuning up in the west bleachers, the pep band sounded like they still had a couple of numbers to rehearse. The Stallions' trainer retaped Cliffie Davis' black piano-key fingers. Omaha finished warming up with sloppy lay-up drills and sat down. River State ran to the bench to the roar of 12,200. Standing-room only. Since Katie Koob had been an Iranian hostage for thirteen months, her mother and father were supposedly here as guests of Governor Ray. An Episcopalian pastor delivered a benediction. Orange and brown streamers were let loose. A pilgrim waving a bazooka chased a kid in a turkey outfit around the court, and the Stallion borrowed the pilgrim's bazooka as a megaphone to whip up the crowd. I felt like the only traitor under the big top, not singing the national anthem, not even pretending to sing, but standing in the eclipsed corridor, devouring the cheerleaders, who were perched on tiptoes with one hand holding their pom-poms and the other touching their breasts, their skirts hiked high to mid-thigh, their roan

17

braids holding their permed hair in place, the Stallion emblems on their cheeks gleaming under the glare.

While I was making my way through the crowd in the foyer, a great roar went up, not so much in appreciation of a good tenor, which I wouldn't know if it bit me, as in anticipation of the game. I heard the thump of the houselights going off before both teams were introduced. I was suddenly covered in blackout and tripping up the stairs. I paused at the first landing to catch my breath and peer through the shadows. I saw Menkus standing at mid-court in a circle of hot light. He was announced as the Stallions' starting guard. I heard the fans' clapping hands, which sounded like maybe a million horses trodding down a hard dirt path. And they were all for him.

Returning to press row, I was surprised to find Deborah sitting in my seat two chairs to the left of the last pole. She's not exactly what I'd call a basketball groupie, but she's open to almost everything and a great one for finding some zany meaning in it. She'd moved my coat and typewriter down a space and was drinking a Tab. On the table in front of her she had several student papers, the last draft of the last chapter of her book on autobiography, and a program to help her follow along. No one's got more going in the idea department than Deborah. All her verbal activity is just her brain doing double-time, pushing through the surface to assert itself. Even her elbows are sharp.

"Hello, hello," I said, kissing her and smelling all that delicious turkey and dressing as Omaha's starting five was introduced. "What are you doing here, hon?"

She cupped her hand over her ear like she was deaf, as a loud round of boos for the visiting Bluejays drowned out my question. I couldn't get over the fact that it was Thanksgiving and it didn't look like there were going to be any no-shows.

"Hi, sweetheart, I love you," I shouted just when the boos died down. Scattered chuckles from my colleagues. Tee-hee.

Albert plus Deborah. "I'm sorry I didn't make it. How was dinner?"

"Wonderful until everybody from American Studies started talking about your pieces on Belvyn and asking me how he was doing in class. Richard ended up rushing us through and insisting we all drive over to see what the fuss is about. I mean, is he actually that much better than the other boys?"

"Where are Richard and those guys sitting?"

"Behind one of the baskets," she said, pointing at the court with her straw.

"Where's Barry?" Our son, who is infatuated with farming equipment and so far doesn't feel he's being challenged by the second grade.

"I stopped by the house on the way over and dropped him off at Laurel's." His tomboy baby-sitter who lives down the block.

I was battering my wife with questions, curious how she got past the guard into the press section. She flapped an orange tag that she'd pinned to the bottom of her blouse and that said *A. Biederman, Sports, River City Register.* The picture on the tag looked nothing like me and even less like Deborah, who has willed herself into having almost classic Jewish features despite being raised Quaker. She has a full head of kinky dark hair and big eyebrows and brown eyes, a jutting nose and chin and wonderful lips and cheeks to chew on, but all of this softened somehow and curbed by her going to Society of Friends meetings in Rhinelander, Wisconsin, until she was seventeen. The balcony guard is an old gaffer named "Bat" Farrell.

"You didn't steal me any cornbread, did you?" I asked, hoping against hope.

She shook her head and offered me a sip of Tab.

When the referees walked onto the court, the Stallion and the pompom girls led the crowd in chanting what the *Register* always has to refer to as "barnyard epithets." These refs were the two guys, a greaseball Marine and a blond beanpole, who two years ago made a call against River State with no time remaining in the last game of the season which kept them out

19

of the NCAA's. It was a beautiful sight to see—young men rolling their wheelchairs onto the concrete apron, farmers in overalls, housewives trying to look like their daughters and their daughters trying to look like their mothers, students and the professors who would soon flunk them, fat-cat alumni, the obsequiously polite River State secretaries and janitors, all joined together in a spirit of hatred. Stallion fever runs hot. It's not uncommon for divorce settlements to pivot on who gets season tickets.

Menkus jumped center against Omaha's seven-footer. With his body turned sideways, leading with his left hand and his head pulled into his chest, Menkus looked like he was holding onto a parachute. For all I know, he might have been. Either that, or he tucked afterburners into his Nikes. At the top of his jump he did what only real skywalkers can do: contradicting all laws of gravity, he seemed to gather himself and jump again. The Bluejays got the tap, but you couldn't have asked for a more impressive debut.

In the first five minutes of the game, though, Menkus threw the ball out of bounds twice, missed three shots from the field including an uncontested lay-up, and was beaten back-door by the University of Omaha's slowest, shortest man. Maybe it was a case of trying too hard to meet outlandish expectations. The first time he touched the ball, he received a standing ovation from the Stallion Battalion and proceeded to double dribble. The second time, the field house roared encouragement, and he was called for charging. The third time, a smattering of boos originated in the northeast bleachers. Hinselwood chewed on a towel for nourishment.

Menkus' main impulse was to set up other players and organize the court, but the rest of the team was completely out of sync with him or he with them. He threw a lead pass that hit Cliffie Davis, a guard from Detroit who adopted the nickname "Black Stallion" the moment the movie came out, in the head. Menkus lobbed a lead pass that fell half a step out of Dwayne Gault's reach; Gault, a superserious forward from Chicago, stood arms akimbo for ten seconds in disgust. Menkus beat his man to the basket only to get hung up in midair when Norm Durland, a local moose with white man's disease, neglected to roll to the hoop. Gary Tomlinson, a good-hit, no-field small forward from Des Moines, was wide open off a Gault steal, and Menkus whipped a behind-the-back pass halfway to the Quad Cities. Menkus' teammates didn't understand how he could know they were open before they knew they were open.

So far it looked like he was just trying to show off a lot for any pro scouts who happened to wander into the stadium for his first non-conference game. If he was, it wasn't working. He was too unselfish, too unpredictable, too fast, and no one knew what to do with him yet. Least of all the good cop–bad cop referees, who whistled him for traveling when he beat his man so bad on a rock-and-pump fake that they either had to call steps or alter their understanding of how the game operated.

I must admit I felt an odd sense of relief that Menkus was having his first game jitters. He was a junior transfer from Sioux City Trade and Extension. He wasn't an archangel. Deborah tells me a lot of people like to think William Shakespeare didn't actually write all those dramas. They were written by a committee of clergymen who liked bacon. I forget how the theory goes. Sheer genius is a scary thing. Menkus dealt the middle of a three-on-two break and threw the ball into the box seats.

Behind 14–9, River State called time-out. The cheerleaders, who are semiofficially called the Mares, spelled out *Stallions* a few times too many. Omaha is from the lowly Heartland conference; the fans, expecting a rout, were restless with River State's slow start and didn't cooperate very much with the Mares' enthusiasm. The Stallion, knowing when not to force the issue, cooled his heels and bullshitted with little kids. One huge whale of a guy stood up and yelled at the bench, "Put in Malakovich," Malakovich being the last man on the team. You can tell when Hinselwood is mad because he pretends to consult with Ott and Nagel before talking to the players, but what he is doing is simmering down. The Omaha coach, a health nut, swigged Perrier.

I turned to Deb and asked, "Can you follow the game at all? Do you know what's happening?"

"It's kind of interesting, but I'm not really paying attention," she said, fluttering loose sheets from chapter nine. Peter Keil, a solid, smart scrapper, checked in for Cliffie Davis, which struck me as a good move: Menkus would become the only ball handler and might relax a little. "Why do they clap, though, whenever Belvyn has the ball, because he did something good?"

"No." I whapped the program against her leg, loving her for how little she knew about anything except the outer realms of literature. She looks so sexy, so slinkily professional in slacks. "They're hoping he'll do something good. They're trying to encourage him." I lowered my voice. "But what no one seems to appreciate is that he's already doing some pretty amazing things. They're cheering him on like he's trying to come out of a slump. It's not all his fault."

"Well, maybe they should stop trying to encourage him so much," she said, blinking her contacts into place. "He's a nervous wreck out there. I can tell. You'd think I was about to ask him for a definition of the perfect participle or something." Deb is Menkus' teacher for Rhetoric and reading lab, and has been working with a specialist to see if he has dyslexia.

The strategy worked: River State scored off a set play to Gault after the time-out and the 1–2–2 offense made more things happen inside than the 2–1–2, but Omaha continued to play better than anyone had reason to suspect. They did a lot of zoning and pressing and just generally outhustling the Stallions. The Bluejays led by seven with four minutes left in the half. The basic problem, so far as I saw it, was that everyone in the arena was looking to Menkus to dazzle, and he was looking over his shoulder, making sure he didn't trip. Which was a problem I had definitely contributed to, with my weekly columns of pre-season promo beginning the end of October when the football team was already fading fast.

Menkus wasn't god-awful, not by a long shot or short jumper. It's just that he wasn't a consensus All-American from the first buzzer, and that was mainly because he was out of mesh with his teammates. No one is more dependent on timing and intuition than a good give-and-go man. He made some great plays and some not so great plays. Twelve thousand people came for the picture of divine perfection, and so far we'd seen the raw stuff of youth, unconnected to anything but its own energy.

Then something happened.

With two minutes left Omaha played keep-away, trying to take a six-point lead into the locker room by putting the ball into the deep freeze. At about the ten-second mark Lamont Knight, their lead guard, telegraphed a soft bounce pass to his weak-side forward, who did not go out to meet the ball. *Go out to meet the ball,* one of the trusty pieces of advice that followed me from coaching camp to coaching camp throughout my youth.

Menkus intercepted the ball with his left hand. In one motion, he slapped it through his legs into his right hand to keep from drifting out of bounds while establishing an angle aganist Knight, who rushed back on defense to atone for his mistake.

"Please let it develop," I said to myself, begging for just a little magic.

"Look at him go!" Deborah yelled. She waved her rolled-up program like she'd been doing this forever. Menkus had brought the game alive for Deb, bookworm of bookworms.

Black Stallion, who had come back in for Tomlinson, sprinted across mid-court to help Menkus, hoping to pick up a cheap bucket on the break by slipping into the far corner. I was positive Menkus didn't see him as he worked one-on-one down the left lane. He took a quick look at the clock and three hard dribbles to drive off Knight, then performed the single most beautiful feat I have ever seen on hardwood.

He brought the ball to his hip like he was going to throw a behind-the-back pass to some imaginary player standing along the left baseline. At the last instant, thirty-five feet from the hoop, he lofted a wraparound alley-oop to Cliffie, who crashed down the key without breaking stride and jammed it home with two hands, though it was such a perfect pass he could have touched it light as a feather with his pinkie and it would have cut the cords.

Throughout the first and second balconies, on the north and south sides, steel support beams have been restricting fans' vision for over fifty years. I could have sworn those beams were bouncing when the whole place went bonkers over Black Stallion's buzzer-beating slam. Everyone's Thanksgiving dinner settled, I guess, just about the same time. We turned the field house into a great noise corridor that just kept shaking. Menkus and Cliffie jabbed fingers in each other's faces, then high-fived, and Hinselwood clapped clipboards with Ott. The fat guy who earlier had been calling for Malakovich clenched his fists over his head and hugged his wife. An overexcited whippersnapper sailed his little stick-Stallion onto the floor. A grizzly old man in a wheelchair popped a wheelie. My favorite cheerleader, Liz Cheng, matched the Stallion cartwheel for cartwheel. A typhoon of roan pom-poms.

Deborah jumped up and down and clapped, which you're not supposed to do in the press box. "That was so glorious!" she positively screamed, losing the cap to her pen and spilling Tab all over her students' papers. I cheered, too.

"It was a great pass," I said because I didn't know what else to say. I didn't want to talk about it. I kept reliving it in my mind, getting shivers down my back.

"What Belvyn just created was an absolute work of art."

"Oh, for Chrissake," I said, looking around to see if anyone was listening. I didn't want to get caught in a conversation like this when my pals were milling about, studying halftime stats. "It was an incredible move. Menkus is a born point guard."

"Oh, Albert, don't you understand?" she said, feeling as sorry for me as I was for her. Both of us were only children and we live in our own heads; that's how we get along so well. She lit up, but you're not supposed to smoke in the press gallery, either, and I blew out her match. "It was pure autobiographical expression, the self writ large through another self."

"Please," I said, looking around again. Everyone was too

24

busy talking field-goal percentage and turnovers to pay any attention to the professor's lecture. "I'm glad you're enjoying yourself, honey, but don't analyze it quite so much, okay?"

"Belvyn's always bored in class," Deb said, plopping a piece of Care-Free into her mouth since she couldn't smoke. "Due, I'm absolutely certain, to dyslexia. He's uninterested in learning about anything except basketball, but at that moment, when he directed the ball over to that other boy closer to the goal, one person became another person, one soul. . . ."

However much I love Deborah, this speech would have driven me crazy if I had listened to it any longer, so I offered to get us some coffee downstairs. She nodded and began working out what looked like a formula on the back of her program while I wandered Murderers' Row, chatting with a few of the fellows from Cedar Rapids, Waterloo, Dubuque. The main topics of discussion were Black Stallion's slam dunk and Menkus' first-period mistakes. They all groused about "playground ball," and, when I heard some idiot from Davenport say he hoped Menkus would be able to adjust to River State's more disciplined style of play, I nearly swung. These encrusted eminences weren't open enough to the game to appreciate what made Menkus special.

I didn't have any change for coffee and headed for Letterman Lounge, a VIP rumpus room tucked away in the basement. Bigwigs and press leeches congregate here at halftime. Standing in the outer lobby because she didn't have full credentials was Vicki Lynch, who's on the sports staff of the *Stallion* and works for us as a stringer. She's more or less my gofer, since Marty still hasn't forgiven the Baltimore Orioles for hiring batgirls and would sooner stop taking his nitro pills than let a coed run around the locker room, doing his legwork for him. With her Adidas and frayed jeans and short hair, her baby-blue headlights and pug nose, Vicki doesn't look just young. She looks like she couldn't possibly have passed the ninth grade. She usually acts nervous around me, tugging at her clothes and fixing her face, but she was worse now than I'd ever seen her and her twitch was going mad, like a bee caught in the corner of her eye, trying to get out.

"Boy, am I glad to see you," she said. "I've been looking everywhere. I went over to your seat, but some lady was sitting there, looking incredibly serious."

"What's up?" I said, walking into the lounge.

"I can't go in there." She hooked onto my arm.

"Sure, you can. Just don't act like you don't belong."

She scooted around the chunky dignitaries, who wore roan-colored suits and haircuts from the fifties and smiles tight as their belts. Beefcake bodies supplied with cupcake brains. Vicki piled her plate with cold cuts, potato chips, and carrots, and we sat in a darkish corner where she simply attacked her dinner. Gold cups sat behind glass, and championship pennants were the wallpaper. Inhaling the food seemed to calm her down somewhat, and when she finished her bug juice she said, "Thanks a million, Albert, really. I was famished." She swayed back and forth on a cushion and put her plate down, staring at the roan shag carpet.

"So why were you looking for me?" I asked.

"You're not going to believe this."

"Try me," I said, taking the few potato chips she'd left and getting my hand slapped.

"Fifteen minutes before game time I was standing in line for a Coke. This very slutty-looking girl, who was wearing a lot of burnt-red rouge and red-black lipstick and—"

A bell gonged, meaning the second half was starting soon. "Never mind her lipstick. What did she do?"

"She said she wanted to sell me 'the inside scoop' on Belvyn."

"How did she know who you were?"

"I figure she noticed my press tag. She threw me out of line and then kept squeezing my wrist. Strongest girl I've ever seen. She was wearing these very weird, tight—"

"What else did she say?"

"That was really it. That she knew Belvyn and wanted to

talk about him. I didn't exactly have an extra fifty floating around, so I told her to get in touch with you."

"Wonderful," I said. Some drunk booster nearly tripped over us and apologized.

"I'm sorry. Was that really stupid?"

"No, no, you did the right thing. I'm sure her inside scoop isn't a bag of beans. Friends of the family always show up once the season starts."

The bell rang again, meaning get to your seats. Vicki was twitching, so she went over to the buffet to get more punch and another sandwich before the grub got cleared away. When she came back she said, "What are you going to do, Albert? I mean, you're not going to pay her or anything, are you?"

"I don't know," I said. "If she gets in touch, I'll see what she has. I assume it's nothing."

Vicki suddenly looked mopey. She is one of this new breed of female that lives for sports talk. The only way I could lift her spirits was to ask, "What did you think of the first half?"

"Menkus is an incredibly brilliant playmaker. He could have had ten assists if they hadn't blown most of them."

"Good for you," I said and put my arm around her. I was relieved to hear someone agree with me in words I understood. She followed along back toward the balcony, trying to convince me to bring her to the post-game press conference, but stringers aren't allowed in the sports information office. That's a pretty strict rule, which made me curious where Wonder Woman might be hiding out.

Two posters painted roan-and-gray and hanging from the north balcony: B. B. THE BLUEJAYS and BLACK STALLION—BEST MOVER OF THE YEAR. When I sat down with the coffees, Deborah flashed a scary smile and said, "Who was that pretty young thing pawing you on the way up the stairs?"

"Just some kid who works for us. She was giving me bits and pieces of her research on Menkus. She says he loves electric trains."

"Huh, that's interesting, because it fits in perfectly with dyslexia. Trains stay on track, which is what dyslexics have trouble doing: their eyes jump all over the page."

Right then and there I suppose I decided I wasn't going to tell Deborah everything I discovered. Menkus was the first player to stir my imagination in eighteen years of covering River State basketball. I didn't want to hear nasty rumors about him and I didn't want to share him with anybody, which was odd, since he wasn't mine.

Deb took a couple sips of coffee, pronounced it tepid, and waved for the soda kid's attention while the teams took the floor for the second half. Happy shook every Stallion's hand and smiled and took pictures of their backs. Deb showed me the diagram she had drawn during halftime. Your ordinary person's halftime diagram will be a plan for, say, a 3–2 trap press off a made free throw. But Deborah's an English teacher and the only genius I've ever known. There were squiggles and arrows and boxes and algebraic notes and counter-arrows and boxes within boxes. It looked like a map of River City's Downtown Refurbishment Project.

"I'm symbolizing the game," she said.

"That's great," I said. "That's great, honey."

The second half was pretty much the same story. The Bluejays did even more pressing than they did in the first half, taking the Stallions totally out of its game. River State didn't look like it was in shape yet to handle such a quick pace. They just hadn't jelled. Menkus broke Omaha's press with a dribbling exhibition, then he and Cliffie squabbled over who was play-maker. Menkus leaped above the Bluejays' seven-footer for a board and tip-tapped the ball out to Tomlinson on the wing to begin a break, a blind lead pass that brought Deb, cheering and waving, to her feet. The only trouble was that Tomlinson wasn't on the wing, and Hinselwood brought Tomlinson and Menkus over for a quick consultation to avoid such shenanigans in the future.

I was certain Menkus could have taken the contest into his own hands and thrown up twenty-footers, but it was equally obvious he wasn't going to do that. The fans wanted a side-show, with him in the spotlight, and he attempted to produce just the opposite: a three-ring circus with Tomlinson, Davis, and Gault as star attractions. This was only the first game, after all, of a long winter, and he wanted to set the tone for the rest of the season. It seemed to me he was trying to teach the golden rules of basketball. Go and I shall give. Pick and thou shalt roll. When he gave, Tomlinson didn't go anywhere. And when he rolled, Gault didn't flash behind the pick.

Everyone ran around in circles like chickens with their heads cut off, trying to carry out Hinselwood's hallowed motion offense, which mainly consists of bodies running around in circles like chickens with their heads cut off. Menkus made Omaha's zone slide and slide and slide. Then, through the space that only he had created and only he had seen, he whipped the ball into Norm Durland who, unable to understand why a second ago he was surrounded by defenders and now was holding the ball, kicked the thing out of bounds.

In the second half, there weren't any spectacular alley-oop slam dunks to bring the crowd together and turn things around. The old guy in the wheelchair fell asleep. The Mares flirted. I finally located Deb's teacher contingent, and they seemed barely to register the fact that a game was going on as background to their colloquium. River State fell farther behind. It became increasingly apparent that it wasn't going to happen, not tonight, anyway. Menkus was trying to play chess in sneakers, and everyone else was still piddling around with Chinese checkers. The game plan wasn't working. Something had to change. Hinselwood, sucking on a water bottle, sent in Monroe Terry, a stumblebum sophomore with size 15-D shoes.

"Bat" Farrell, the balcony guard, brought me a note that said:

> Mr. Beaterman—
> Your assistant said maybe you'd like to
> talk to me about Belvyn. Give me a call,
> okay? I'll be here all weekend.
>
> Rita M.
331-0598

"What did you get?" Deborah asked.

"Oh, nothing, just a note from Marty about paste-up. He didn't leave me much room."

"Well, concision—isn't that what journalism's all about?'"

The Stallion Battalion chanted and stomped, trying to get a rally going, but with three minutes left the Stallions were down fourteen. When Hinselwood took Menkus out, he got a polite ovation that was a sad, low answer to the insanity he inspired at the end of the first half. They didn't know who they were cheering for, and neither did Deb, really, when she stood and applauded while Menkus wrapped a towel over his head on the bench. I was glad for an ally and happy for love, though there was no way she could gather how rare a thing Menkus had tried to pull off, and for some reason I couldn't or didn't want to explain it to her. This Rita girl was starting to emerge as a serious shakedown artist. Tell me her last name wasn't Menkus. The last thing I needed to explore was a paternity suit.

Deb's car was parked on the far side of the ramp, and she wanted to vamoose before getting caught in traffic. With reserves filling the floor, she was bored and made ready to leave at the two-minute mark. A lot of fair-weather friends joined her.

"I'll see you later," she said, stuffing student papers, diagram, chapter nine, program, notes into her blue backpack. "Have a good press conference."

"Don't ask for the impossible. I just hope maybe Menkus'll be there. I should be back by eleven."

"You may beat me home. I'm going to my office to do a little work on my last chapter. I just find the whole game and Belvyn's performance really provocative in terms of the self."

"Okay," I said. "Bye. Watch the ice on Melrose."

Menkus didn't show up for the press conference. Neither did any other players. They were too depressed. Hinselwood stood over us with his tie undone and a piece of chalk in his right hand, which he crushed every now and then to make sure we got certain sophisticated points of strategy. I've had trouble with this guy since he came here in '74. He was hired to return River State to its glory years of the mid-fifties, when they finished second and third in the NCAA's and won a conference crown or two. Shortly after that, their first two blue-chippers from Chicago got caught in a point-shaving scam, and the program floundered through the sixties and seventies. Dick Hinselwood was given ten years to turn it around, and he'd already blown the first six. The faculty despised him because, with his summer coaching camp, TV and radio shows, and endorsements on top of his base pay of $55G, he could buy and sell any four of them, though he smoothed over yelps of protest by paying constant lip service to "grades coming before games."

After coaching in Arizona high schools, northern California junior colleges, and at the University of Idaho, he developed a rep as a program saver, a motivator who could nudge a team out of the doldrums into high mediocrity. So far River State had moved from ninth to seventh in the Mississippi Valley Conference. Wherever Hinselwood went he took his Complete Achievement Chart, which awards pluses and minuses for every action a player performs. You can easily score fourteen points and grab half a dozen rebounds, but wind up in the red because you threw the ball away twice and hogged the water bottle during a timeout. The chart is based totally on fear, encouraging players to avoid errors rather than attempt miracles. The miracles are always what I've been most interested in.

More than any other sport, basketball is based on freedom. Only by letting out all the stops can you play the game right; only when you're completely out of control do you find a deeper kind of control. When it gets going good, it takes you out of regular time altogether. Onto this ad-lib ballet Hinselwood wanted to graft the virtues of predictability and safety. Some people feel he's just too well manicured and handsome to coach basketball, and I'm afraid I have to agree with them, as

I'm the one who started the rumor. He's 6'2", 185, Romeo-lipped and Valentino-eyed, and he has the perfect rugged jaw of all Viking hucksters. He should be out selling life insurance.

Now he was talking about "sloppy schoolyard ball and lack of mental composure," which meant Menkus shouldn't have been having such a good time out there on the court, and "the media putting too much pressure on the rookie," which meant I shouldn't have based my articles on athletic department press releases. If anyone was to blame for the loss, it was Hollywood himself, who should have handed the game ball to Menkus and let the other planets revolve around the sun. Francis Drexler, the best play-by-play man in the history of Iowa TV and radio, sat in the middle of the back row, monkeying with his cassettes while asking too many questions and smoking his life away. Two seats over, my editor, Marty Reeves, tied flies and took notes. What was he doing here? I was perfectly capable of covering the event which, even for a Hinselwood press conference, was Sominex city.

"What are you doing here?" I asked Marty.

"Tying flies," he said.

"Yeah, Albert, what are you doing here?" Francis said.

"Oh, just the usual—pursuing the truth wherever it leads me."

"You let me know," Francis said, "when it starts pursuing you."

Marty and Francis, Francis and Marty, my two best friends; Laurel and Hardy, and me smack-dab between them. Marty's a little hiccup of a guy who wears gigantic sweaters he's always tugging at and black glasses he pokes into his nose. The perpetually startled face of the runner-up in the junior high science fair. During the Civil War, when Marty was a teenager, maybe he threw a few rocks at apple trees or tackled his cousins in an open field, but he never played sports seriously. He's an old-style outdoorsman who tolerates organized athletics to the degree it frees him up to go beaver trapping. Francis is a little taller than Hinselwood, has the legs of a stork, the gut of a penguin, the shoulders of a little old lady, and a dark, chiseled Indian chief's head that bobs when he walks like he's lost at sea. He set the Des Moines prep scoring records I broke fifteen years later.

"So what did you think of the game?" I asked him.

"I thought it was one more game," he said.

"Hey, quiet back there," some out-of-town schmuck hissed at us, though we were whispering and Hinselwood was still just finding his stride.

"You didn't think Menkus was exciting in spurts?"

"In spurts I'm sure he'd be exciting." Francis is of the gay persuasion, though how many other people know this I've never been entirely clear on, because he always sends these gross jokes my way, confident no one else is going to catch his drift. "No," he said, "I don't think he has it. He's showy, erratic, impatient, and too clever by half."

"You don't think he has the promise to really—"

"Whom the gods wish to destroy they first call promising," Francis said, which to my ears sounded like a quote and also sounded like bullshit.

Some granddad from Des Moines cranked up an amazingly long-winded question, exploring all the ramifications of match-up zones.

When Hinselhound got through skirting that one, I stood up and asked him how Menkus did on the Complete Achievement Chart.

"Next question," he said. He knows in what low esteem I hold his numerology graphs.

"No, really, Coach. How did he grade out? I'm sincerely curious."

Painstakingly, he took an envelope from his inside coat pocket and said, "With all the passes he threw away and all the shots he missed, he's lucky he finished no worse than minus seven. Behind-the-back dribbling isn't on the list, Biederman, in case you forgot."

Everyone laughed except Francis, who was having trouble lighting his cigarette, and Marty, who wasn't listening.

"That's sort of what I wanted to get at. I know it's too early to tell and, sure, he looked jittery at times and threw some stupid passes, but it seems to me he has a deeper feel for the game of basketball than anybody River State has seen in a helluva long time."

"Deeper feel?" Francis said under his breath.

"Belvyn has all the tools, no doubt about that," Hinselwood said. He's Joe Family Man, and whenever he damns a player with faint praise he sounds like he's giving halting approval for one of his kids to use the car.

"Does he got a wrench?" Francis wanted to know. "My kitchen faucet's leaking." Tool: wrench. Francis lives in a fancy glass house overlooking the river and his kitchen faucet doesn't leak.

"What's your question?" Hinselwood said. He was running out of patience.

"A lot of people are already grumbling about Menkus fitting into the system. But it's not like he's a gunner. He's a playmaker who's still getting to know his teammates, and I just hope the system can bend a little to take advantage of his special talents."

"Who's coaching this team?" he said, which answered nothing.

"You are, m'lord," I said to pull him down a rung from the pedestal, but when he stiffened the other reporters went silent in his support. I couldn't help lashing back by asking, "There's no truth, is there, to this week's rumor about Menkus?"

"Next question."

"I don't know, I got this crazy note from—"

"Next," he said and was all ears for a veteran sycophant from the *Cedar Rapids Gazette*.

I got my coat, stepped outside, and shut the door. Francis gave me a sitting ovation. I walked halfway around the arena and sat in the lower deck, which was totally empty now except for a Boy Scout troop picking up garbage. Ed, who's been here forever, was folding and stacking metal chairs. He waved. I felt

34

like I was trespassing his territory by hanging around so late after the game. All the lights were down or dimmed and the air was gray, like a fog got trapped in the field house. I already wanted to be back in the sports information office, listening to Tinselteeth drone on and Francis make bad jokes. The scoreboard hadn't gone down to zero yet, and I kept replaying that miraculous pass Menkus made, the wraparound alley-oop; then I saw myself standing again on the blackened stairwell while Menkus was introduced. The loud thump, the crowd pushing past me on the way to their seats, Menkus shadow dancing: there has always been some strange connection for me between basketball and the dark.

I started shooting hoops after school in the third grade, and I remember dusk and macadam combining into the sensation that the world was dying but I was indestructible. I played all the time, in all seasons, instead of other sports, played until my sad, mousy, immaculate mother stopped long enough from showing houses to take me home. In fifth grade I developed a double pump jump shot, which in the fifth grade is almost unheard of.

Rather than shooting on the way up, as everyone else did, I tucked my knees, hung in the air a second, pinwheeled the ball, then shot on the way down. My friends hated my new move. It seemed tough, mannered, teenage, vaguely Negro. I don't know how or why I started shooting different. I must have grown weary sometimes waiting for Mom to drive by, or Dad to return from his unsuccessful tennis road trips, or maybe it was my attempt to copy the Drake players I watched at Veterans Auditorium. The more I shot like this the more my friends disliked me, and the more they disliked me the more I shot like this. It was the only thing about me that was at all unusual, and it came to be my trademark, even my nickname. Double Bubble Biederman.

One afternoon, when I was playing Horse with Beth Norton, she threw the ball over the fence and said, "I don't want to play with you anymore, Albert. You're too good. I'll bet one day you're going to start for Drake."

Beth had by far the prettiest eyes at Valley Elementary and a grin so infectious it made me grin whenever she looked at me in math. She had a way of moving her body like a boy but still like a girl, too, and that game of Horse is one of the happiest memories of my childhood: dribbling around in the dark but knowing by instinct where the basket was; not being able to see Beth but smelling her deodorant mixed with dirt; keeping close to her voice, in which I could hear her love for me and my career as a Drake Bulldog opening up into the night. I remember the sloped half-court at the far end of the playground, its orange pole, orange rim, and wooden green backboard, the chain net clanging in the wind; the sand and dirt on the court; the overhanging elm trees, the fence the ball bounced over into the street; and the bench the girls sat on, watching, trying to look bored.

The first two weeks of summer Beth and I went steady, but we broke up when I didn't risk rescuing her in a game of Capture the Flag, so she wasn't around for my tenth birthday party when I begged my parents to let Ethan Saunders, Jim Morrow, Bradley Gamble, and me shoot baskets in City Park until sunrise. Having been eliminated early from some class-B tournament somewhere, Dad was home for once, and he swung by every few hours to make sure we were safe and bring more Coke, more birthday cake, more candy. There is no safer place in the continental United States than City Park Playground in West Des Moines. Dad's occasional high beams were the only intrusion into the all-dark court we ruled this one night.

For short periods that night two or even three of us slept on benches like baby bums, and we had the usual disagreements about the last piece of cake and someone's dishonest count in Twenty-one, but all of us stayed till dawn. Around five in the morning Bradley and I were playing two-on-two against Jim and Ethan. The moon was falling. We had a lot of sugar in our blood, and all of us were totally zonked and totally wired. With the score tied at eighteen in a game to twenty, I took a very long shot from the deepest corner. Before the ball left my hand Bradley said, "Way to hit, Al."

36

I was a good shooter because it was the only thing I ever did and I did it all the time, but even for me such a shot was doubtful. Still, Bradley knew and I knew and Jim and Davey knew, too, and we knew the way we knew our own names or the batting averages of the Cubs' infield or the lifelines in our palms. I felt it in my legs and up my spine, which arched as I fell back. My fingers tingled and my hand squeezed the night in joyful follow-through. We knew the shot was perfect, and when we heard the ball, a George Mikan special, a birthday gift from my sweet mom, whip the net we heard it as something we had already known for at least a second. What happened in that second during which we knew? Did the world stop? Did my soul ascend a couple of notches? What happens to ESP, to such keen eyesight? What did we have then, anyway, radar? When did we have to start working so hard to hear our own hearts?

I heard a lot of commotion now at the other end of the stands, which probably meant the press conference was over.

"Yip, yip. Okay, Albie, let's go," Ed said. "I'm closing up shop."

TWO

IN the middle of breakfast Sunday morning Barry stopped stirring his oatmeal, put down the comics, and said, "We're gonna get a pig tomorrow."

I don't think Deb heard him or, if she did, she didn't say anything. She was reading a long article about Katie Koob's parents, who weren't at the game Thursday night, after all. They were at a church supper in honor of Katie. She'd been gone 395 days now, and they thought the two things she probably missed most were Vinton sausage and buttered popcorn.

"A pig?" I said. "What are you talking about, Bare? You mean a real pig?"

"Yeah, a course, Daddy. Oink, oink." He hunched his shoulders and wrinkled his nose. He has a chubby face, a chubby body, chubby hands, and his buttons are always bursting. Although it was a good imitation, it depressed me. "We'll put him in the backyard. Laurel said her uncle could deliver one."

Barry's baby-sitter, Laurel, has an uncle who owns a lot of land near Mason City. She reads Barry to sleep with ads from the *Farm Bureau Spokesman*.

"Our backyard?" I said. "You've got to be kidding. It's a bunch of dirt and gravel."

If Barry gets good enough at fertilizing, he can take charge of the lawn when spring breaks through around August, but why did we ever move into this tiny mock-Tudor travesty in the McBride tract? Deborah's idea was to put some distance between ourselves and midtown sprawl, so we traded the sound of sandblasting and our musty old house on the east side for this half-wood, half-brick place that's painted the colors of a melting Butterfinger bar. We can't afford the mortgage. The garage is too small by half. And the den is still uninsulated.

"Pigs are huge," Deborah chimed in. "They're not just like big dogs."

"But Laurel says they're practically the cleanest animal there is. Really, really smart, too. Can't we get one, huh, Daddy, can't we?"

"Pigs are clean—since when?" I said.

"They are," Barry said. "You can even ask Marty."

"Yes, they are," Deborah said, "but it would be illegal." She has such a good grasp of so many subjects that she can't help it if she comes across occasionally as an encyclopedia.

"What do you mean, Mommy?" I could listen to the sound of his voice, all high and hopeful, until the Second Coming.

"You can't have a pig on Westgate Court."

"That's true," I said.

"Why not?" Barry said.

"You just can't," Deborah said. "It's a residential area. This isn't the sticks."

"The sticks?" Leaning over close to me, he smelled like a rotting apple, which he does sometimes before his insulin peaks.

"How about an ant colony?" Deb said, pouring herself more coffee and dividing the last orange roll.

"It's called an ant farm, and you guys've already promised me that for Christmas. I want a pig," he said. He was getting sloppy with his oatmeal spoon until Deborah shot over the top of the *Register* a glance that told him he better not cry or he'd be looking at a very long day from his bedroom window. Only Deborah can zing Barry like that. I wouldn't know even where to begin.

"We could get maybe a real small baby pig. I'd take care of him and pay for his food and everything. I promise I would."

"No," I said. His pudgy little arm felt like dough in my hand. "Look, you thank Laurel, but tell her it just wouldn't work out."

"Do I still get to go rowing before the river freezes?"

Now he was really turning in the screws. I'd been putting it off for weeks, and there's no such thing as rowing after the river freezes.

"Sure. We'll go soon."

"Today?"

"You know I've got all those football stories to write." Today was my last day to get in touch with Rita, and if I was going to call her I figured I should do it within the next few hours.

"Ykkch."

"But soon, Bare, I promise. Okay?"

"You promised before, Dad." Calling me *Dad* meant he was mad at me.

"Come on now, honey," Deb said. "Don't get all worked up when you're digesting your breakfast. Daddy promised, and I'm sure he'll keep his promise. Next weekend you guys can go off and do men things while I get together with my TA."

I nodded. Barry and I shook on it.

He stared for a while into his bowl of oatmeal, then came out with: "Do you die when you fall in the river?"

"No, you don't die, because you don't fall in," Deborah said.

"Isn't the river fast?" I could almost see his blood sugar going berserk.

"Yes," I said.

"Isn't it cold?"

"Yes."

"You don't die?"

"No, you sit in the center of the rowboat with a life jacket on and paddle your oar."

Barry made a really weak pun on "oar," which Deborah and I laughed at to beat the band.

"Oooh, Albert, you're going to catch hell for this, I bet," Deborah said.

"For what?" I knew she meant my commentary on Menkus.

"You're liable to get a lot of flak from people who are fans but not necessarily aficionados like you are. It's so rigorously analytical."

She quoted part of it back to me. It sounded decent, though it was all pretty much the same point: shooters walk onto the court every day of the week, but a true passer is as rare as heat lightning. The Stallions should gather around him, rather than force the system. Give the poor kid a chance. The last paragraph went:

After the game a lot of people in the field house seemed ready to chalk up Menkus as another recruiting disappointment. Me? I wanted to anoint him king.

The only reason the phone hadn't rung off the hook is our number's unlisted.

Barry informed us he had a headache.

"Then eat your toast and grapefruit," his mother said. That took care of that, though he still hadn't made a lot of progress with his oatmeal, which was beginning to resemble the primordial soup. "I love how your essay tugs at certain questions of autobiography," she said to me.

"Honey, please, it's early."

Which cracked Barry up.

"Hear me out, Albino Man." Two Christmas vacations ago, I had wanted to go to California to see my father, who was still alive then, and the Rose Bowl and the Rose Parade. Deborah wanted to go to Miami in connection with a Modern Language Association conference; as a sort of protest, my legs didn't exactly turn cocoa brown in the Florida sunshine, so now she calls me Albino Man when she wants a favor. "You said that when Belvyn passes the ball to his teammates he's being generous, he's sharing himself with them."

"Yeah, okay."

"That's just what's happening in autobiography, and the

41

only difference is that on the basketball court the other players are in fact other players while in, say, Boswell's journals the other characters seem to be disguised versions of Boswell himself. That's what my book's about, and that's what Adrienne and I are trying to get into in our First Person course. Whether the true self is the self that has lived or the self that is writing, well, that's another . . ."

She lost me in the upper stratosphere. Before breakfast, Barry had pricked his finger and squeezed a couple drops of Type A on the little squares, clapped when the squares turned light blue and light green, and given himself an injection. Now he was putting his ChemStrips back in the cupboard, proud as a point guard because he's just started to learn the entire operation and he messes up as often as not. He's so impressive, he really is, the way he wants to take care of himself. Occasionally he OD's on sugar, but how many other seven-year-olds would even try to shoot their own insulin and draw their own blood? He's my hypoglycemic hero.

I tried to adjust the topic of conversation by saying, "I mean, as a student, Belvyn isn't interested in any of this stuff, is he?"

Deborah laughed, flashing her slightly crooked teeth and kissy tongue. She has the delicious full lips of someone who talks too much. "Of course not. He's a terrible student, you know that. And I'm afraid he probably would be even without dyslexia. In Rhetoric you're just trying to get the kids to read and write at a vaguely literate level. Belvyn doesn't show up that often, and when he does he isn't prepared. He's painfully shy and speaks in a low, whispery, half-black kind of voice that's hard for the other kids to understand. My theory is that he uses it to hide anxieties about speech because, as I'm finding out, dyslexia isn't just backwards spelling and reading. It's a jamming up of the verbal process at every level. The class is supposed to function very much as a unit, and Belvyn creates a problem by being so aloof," she said, then went into the living room for cigarettes.

Barry applauded something he read in the paper.

"Cheering for Menkus?" I asked him, a dumb joke I wanted to take back the moment I said it.

"Who's he?"

"The boy I wrote the article about. He's a wonderful basketball player. We should go together to one of his games."

"I hate basketball."

"Come on, Bare. He's a rare breed, like a prize Arabian."

"He's just another airhead. I'd rather have a pig," he said, really exploding on *pig* to provide the impetus to hop up and waddle down the block to Laurel's house, where a fifty-foot TV aerial dominates their rummage sale of a backyard. One of the key pieces is an Adam-and-Eve birdbath made out of limestone.

I was going to call Rita, but Deb came back with her cigarettes and a stack of papers, leafing through them till she came across one that looked like it had been scratched in charcoal on the back of a napkin. Her students were supposed to have written a short essay on what they were doing Thanksgiving vacation. Menkus didn't have a lot of plans, so his assignment was to the point:

> These are my Thanksgiving plans. Don't tɛke Grayhounb home. Do get keys to gym from Caoch and play ball. Maybe shoot some qool or snap a few qitures. These are my Thanksgiving plans. P.S. I like class alot.

"Jesus," I said.

"I know what you mean," Deb said, breathing smoke.

"He's not just a bad speller. He really seems to have a screw loose."

"It's not a disease, honey, it's a kind of mind."

"You can say that again. It looks like pig Latin."

"Dyslexics don't think linearly. They think spatially, in 3-D. Which is why shooting pool and snapping pictures are so interesting. They're both visual activities. Composition, but nonverbal."

"It really makes you wonder," I said.

43

"About what?"

"I don't know," I said because I didn't. "About everything."

The Bears game was on TV at noon. If anything requires more endurance than being a Stallions fan, it's being a Bears fan. Wearing a sweater and hat and trying to get the space heater to work, I sat at my desk in the freezing den, typed up copy, and watched the Bears roar back to only two touch- downs behind. I hated living in a house where all the wires weren't connected yet. The fact that it was raining in Chicago offered the consolation that at least I was high and dry while big brutes slogged their way through the slush. The football was slippery and took crazy bounces against the Bears. Which is why I'm a basketball nut. The ball is round. It bounces true. You can perform magic with it, but not by force. By touch.

I put off calling Rita by writing a wrap-up on high school football and finishing my profile of Jack Cannon, the new Rec Center supervisor, who wants us to cover adult league volley- ball and racquetball more closely. A table tennis team from Taiwan was coming to Cedar Rapids on Thursday, and I had a publicity kit on them to turn into a story, along with some photos of their aces to size and crop. Pieces on the River State wrestling team, swimming, intramurals, girls' b-ball. All the extracurricular clubs: the cross-country ski club, the hot-air balloon club, the women's rugby club, the ice-hockey club, the chess club, the water-polo club, the Akido club. It doesn't end. The Stallion Battalion can never get enough of itself. Ground down with play-by-play copy, I realized how bad I wanted the job at the *Milwaukee Journal.* My article would be in the mail to them tomorrow morning. Beating everyone on Menkus would have to boost my application. Being right about him wouldn't hurt, either. The advancement of my career depended upon being able to go one on one with Joe Enigma.

When Deborah finished with her fun call (Adrienne) and her duty call (her folks in Wisconsin), I phoned Sportsline to get area scores and checked in with our stringers in Kalona,

Lone Tree, Tiffin, North Liberty, West Branch for high school games, then started thinking again about Menkus, hoping like hell he was as good as I said he was. I gave him a buzz and got one of those recordings. First, for about fifteen seconds, a saxophone slid around in the background. Then, just when you thought you must have dialed a wrong number, a very loud lady sang, "I'm ahammerin', oh yeah, I'm just ahammerin'," or something like that. I couldn't really make it out. There was silence. Then Menkus, so low you could hardly hear him, said, "Hey, what's happenin'? I'm out shilly-shallyin'. Leave it, Jim, when you hear bells." The lady sang again, the sax rose, and a tone beeped. I hung up.

Why was Menkus so generous on the court and such a distant asshole off it? Dyslexia city, according to Deb, who was gathering papers and books, getting ready to go to the library. I was just procrastinating about Rita, hoping she'd be gone by the time I called her. This is silly, I said to myself, and dialed 331–0598.

"Hello, Rita?"

"Just a sec," a high-pitched girl said, and Rita got on the horn with "Yeah."

"Albert Biederman here."

"Well, hi. It took you long enough to call."

"I've been busy."

"I left a million messages for you at your paper 'cause you're unlisted." She had a strong Chicago accent, all brassy squawkiness. I could hear the assumed bustle in her voice, the sound of pans banging—a quality that made me want to stay right where I was, watching the Bears and typing puff, at the same time that it drew me on.

"So," I said, "you're a friend of Belvyn's?"

"Hey, hold on there, Mr. Biederman. Not so fast. We've got a few matters to work out first, don't we?"

We quarreled about the arrangement and for a while it looked like the deal was off, but I agreed to meet her and pay her forty dollars straight off and more money as her story merited it. Strip Wallet. I was pissed at Menkus for no one appreciating him, if that makes any sense, and now I wanted to figure out who the hell he was. I agreed to meet her at three under the main scoreboard of the field house.

"How will I recognize you?" I asked.

"I like to dress up," she said. "See you at three."

Barry was still at Laurel's, flipping through seed catalogs. Deborah was doing research at the library. I called Vicki. She wasn't home, of course. She's never home. I paced around a bit, watched the Bears cut the gap to seven, and asked Information for her parents' number in Des Moines. Her folks own an equipment rental store, which are very big in Iowa but which don't seem to have caught on too strong anywhere else. The year Vicki graduated high school, her father's blood pressure zoomed to 190/120, forcing him to semi-retire and the rest of the family to pick up the slack. Her mom keeps the books, her three brothers take business classes at night and run the store, and until she went away to college Vicki worked the cash register on weekends. She has an endless reservoir of stories whose moral is the lengths to which grown men will go to avoid admitting they don't know how to handle power tools.

"Vicki's back in River City now, but she talked about you all weekend," her mother said.

"Don't believe a word of it."

She managed a mild chuckle and said, "I don't know how to put this any more delicately than to say I think Mr. Lynch would sleep a lot more comfortable at night if he knew you were pretty strictly her mentor there at the paper rather than anything—"

"Mr. Lynch has nothing to worry about," I said.

"Thank you, Albert, I knew you'd say that. Vicki's learning more from you than from all her professors combined. You think she can go on, don't you? I mean, get a real job at a real paper?"

What was the *Register*, kitty litter? "Sure, she can. She's

46

very talented and determined and really knows sports. Everyone wants to hire a woman sportswriter these days."

"Well, she grew up with ball games. Her brothers hogged the TV set, and she either had to figure out what they were talking about or go be bored by herself in her bedroom."

"How's the store treating you?" I asked, and for some reason I finally saw it the way Vicki always described it—impeccably neat and clean, with cardboard boxes folded in a bin, the gassed trucks lined up out back, hand tools all facing the same way on the shelves, and the chain saws and sanders and other larger pieces in the display window, waiting like groomed beasts to be fed.

"The store's okay. Chas keeps talkin' about expanding, but I honestly don't think so. Consolidate is what we have to do. It's not a bad time for saws and vacuum cleaners, etcetera, but the real money is always in construction, and, what with the weather and the economy and all, not a lot of buildings are springing up around town."

"How's Mr. Lynch?"

"He's doing fine. He spends the whole day jogging around the store and taking his blood pressure. He gets to order us around without us being able to shoot back lest he get worked up. Oh, he's having the time of his life, coastin' to Easy Street."

Well, at least he has his own tractor mower to coast there in, I thought, and we talked a little more about the weather and the Stallions before she said she had to finish the laundry and then get to the books, even on a Sunday.

I watched light rain become snow, the wind blow the snow in circles, then I asked for Vicki at the *Stallion*.

"Yeah, Lynch," she said when she came on, which sounded like she was giving commands to a vigilante squad.

"Hello, Lynch. This is Biederman."

"Oh, hi, Albert, how's it going? Can I call you back? We're getting out a huge Monday supplement and I'm writing about a zillion articles. You don't happen to remember when Black Stallion fouled out, do you?"

47

I had it in my notes and flipped through them quickly. "With 2:41 to go."

"You're kidding. You remember that?"

"Mind like a zone trap."

"You're amazing. Hey, what happened with that girl—you didn't fuck her or anything, did you?"

"Christ."

"No one wears clothes that tight unless they're selling something. What did she say about Belvyn?"

"Actually, that's why I'm calling. I'm supposed to meet her in forty-five minutes, and I'm already such a Menkus fan I almost hate to hear what she has to say. Isn't that idiotic?"

"Yes. I mean, like you said, it probably isn't going to be a major revelation or anything."

"That's true."

"I got that Turkey Trot story done."

"Good. Drop it off."

"I already did."

"Have you seen my Menkus piece?"

"Your story on the game?"

"No, a piece that came out today. You haven't read it?" I could hear the Bears game in the background on her phone. They'd intercepted and were piecing together a drive.

"I haven't even had breakfast yet," she said. "I've been here since six this morning."

"How was home?"

"Oh, home was a thrill a minute, as always. My brothers played catch with me."

"That sounds like fun."

"No, I mean with me as the ball."

"I just called your parents' place when you weren't in at your apartment, and I talked to your mother for a while. She's great."

"She's a great salesman."

"What's so terrible about that?"

"Nothing, except the mounds of guilt she heaps on me for not rushing home every weekend to punch the cash register.

48

Anyway, Albert, I don't want to go into it. I have to get back to work here. As far as Belvyn goes, I think you really gotta pursue it. I love the way he plays as much as you do, but you're the one who's always talking about journalistic integrity. Here's a golden opportunity for journalistic integrity. Go for it, man."

Vicki Lynch is what used to be called a whirling dervish and now is probably known as a rotating energy field. I worry things, weigh each side, chew my cud, and she comes cutting through the bullshit with a machete. She always acts on raw instincts and is always right.

The Bears scored to tie Seattle but lost on a last-second field goal. I gathered together all the pieces I'd written and then pulled out of the garage, which is so unbroken-in it doesn't even have grease stains. Behind our house, down County Road West, bean fields and farmlands are getting gobbled up by more and more tracts as wonderful as McBride. On Westgate Court we're perched at the edge of River City: look one way and it's Finkbine golf course and the River State athletic club, look the other way and it's horses galloping through tall grass. It's difficult to understand why everyone's in such a hurry to send the horses packing—the Stallions but no stallions. The land breathes and the town council votes to pour cement over it.

As I drove down Melrose toward the field house, every hundred yards or so were long ice slicks like skating rinks for storks. My rusty wipers couldn't do a whole lot with the snow the wind whipped into the windshield, and I damn near drove into a kid on a motor scooter slicing onto Grand Avenue. KHAK said a cold snap was starting soon. I guess what we'd experienced so far had been a heat wave. Then they played a song by Crystal Gayle that made you so happy about your sweetheart you promised never to do anything dumb or dangerous again.

When I walked in the door of the field house, my skin

tingled a little. The building doesn't separate itself into neat little partitions; everything was getting in the way of everything else. Soccer players who are illegal aliens, wrestlers wrapped in rubber, ROTC cadets, fencers, med-school hoopsters, Deborah's grad students showing each other what animals they were at the volleyball net, cheerleaders dancing to disco and drinking Tab, Neanderthals on Nautilus—all humanity was here, all of youth's shenanigans and the first gasp of middle age, all of Iowa democracy.

I bumped into Karl, the trainer, and asked him the only question I ever ask him—if there were any injuries. He's a polar bear who wears tight white shirts and horn-rimmed glasses and the worried expression of someone waiting for accidents to happen.

"Just a few bruised egos," he said and kept walking.

River State's team had always been called the Indians. In 1972 all twenty-two American-Indian students, backed by the ACLU and the Anti-Defamation League, held weekly candlelight vigils until red-and-white-with-a-tomahawk became roan-and-gray-with-a-horse. But the football pennants from the Ice Age and the basketball pennants of the fifties and the wrestling pennants throughout have never been removed from the steel rafters. They hang here, red-and-white Indians banners, relics of a vanished past—when I would have given my gonads to be recruited by River State. But as RSU sports fortunes floundered during the seventies, the athletic department kept changing the Stallion symbol, searching for the perfectly inspirational stud. On a huge carpet covering the west wall a heavy horse faced right; then a light horse looked left; a roan horse on gray background bucked and pawed the air; a gray horse on roan background chomped at the bit menacingly; and now a roan horse on gray background neighed, teeth bared, full-face, giving a cheer. They'd find the right emblem yet.

A girl stood under the scoreboard, looking pretty much how Vicki had described our source. Her lips and cheeks were smeared with stuff the color of bruised fruit. She had crazy black hair and wore leather boots, white pants painted to her

50

legs, and a velvet blouse open to a dangling gold cross. She carried a tiny purse that looked like it could hold maybe a butane lighter.

"Lost?" I said. On the off chance she wasn't the Menkus connection, I didn't want to overcommit myself. I was afraid of being arrested for propositioning a minor.

"Hello, Mr. Biederman." Cool, tough city kid smoking a cigarette, blowing and popping bubblegum.

"How did you know who I was?"

"Your girl friend said you sorta limp sometimes."

"Vicki Lynch isn't my girl friend."

"Whoever she is, she digs you the most."

She squeezed my arm and beckoned toward the first balcony. Ed, the janitor, was patiently weaving around the Sunday athletes as he swept the floor. A volleyball bounced over toward him, and he whacked it back to Deb's grad students.

"Let's get to the point, man."

"And what is that?"

"I have some information, you want some information, and I need some bucks."

"Yes," I said, "yes, of course," nodding like a broken Kewpie doll. I was just so much putty in this girl's hands.

She stared at the bridge of my nose for the longest time, not saying anything. She wore a lot of perfume and smelled plenty sexy, but I couldn't get past associating her face with bruised fruit.

"Well, come on," she finally said, "come with me."

She had a great walk, all ass, like a horse going downhill. We went and sat in the northwest bleachers, where a few people were doing their homework, waiting for a racquetball court to open up.

"So what's your name?" I said.

"Rita," she said slowly, like she wasn't exactly sure.

"Rita what?"

She shook her head. Maybe she was a well-dressed orphan. I felt out of my element talking to this difficult girl and would have preferred to get my sneakers out of the trunk and go play

51

a little pickup three-on-three, but something held me right where I was. Probably just the way her blouse opened a button too low. What was the big mystery over her last name?

"You've got some sort of scoop?" I said.

She tapped her ashes into a coffee cup and said, "I need to see your money up front first."

I had a checkbook with me and was in a wasteful mood, so I gave her forty dollars straight out and said I'd give her another twenty when her story heated up. I even agreed to write the check to "Rita," surely one of the stupidest things I've ever done.

She exhaled twin tusks of smoke through her nose and, calm as a team captain, said, "I went steady with Belvyn all through tenth and eleventh grade."

"You did? Are you serious?"

"We got engaged beginning of senior year. We were king and queen of the Franklin homecoming."

"What was he like then?"

"Ben Franklin? Real old dude, wore granny glasses, flew a kite."

"No, I mean Menkus."

"I know, silly," she said, rotating my kneecap. "Just a joke. You seem tense."

"What was it like being sixteen and in the Windy City and in love with Belvyn Menkus?"

I knew that sounded naive, but I couldn't help it. To me it was romantic: getting engaged and being royalty with someone who was such a giver, on the basketball court, anyway. I thought the world of him already, and I'd seen him play for all of thirty-seven minutes.

"First thing," Rita said, "I've lived in Chicago my whole life. That ain't no big deal. Maybe it is to you guys in Iowa, but, hey, to me it's a street number. Second thing, don't make it sound like it was an eternity ago. I just turned nineteen, and we were still going together when I was seventeen. Third thing, it was like heaven, if you really want to know the truth." She brought the cross out of her blouse and played with it for a

52

few seconds. "Heaven, that's all. Everything else went bullshit, and me and him were on top of Old Smokey."

"Old Smokey?"

"That's from a song."

"I've heard of it."

She looked like she was about to cry, so I gave her my hanky and a cherry Lifesaver, but I also pushed her to keep talking. "So what happened?"

"That's the twenty-dollar question."

"How do you mean?"

"I need another twenty, man," she said, whispering. Maybe she thought Ed was just pretending to sweep and his broom was a boom mike. I tried not to watch the gravity-bound, every-man-for-himself basketball the med students played at center court because it would only depress me.

"How do I know the answer is worth it?"

"You don't. Take your coat, call a taxi, and guess the rest. What the fuck do I care?"

I gave her twenty in cash to make her feel better. Fencers' swords clashed like movie music before the big confession.

"We got engaged in October of '79, and the wedding was set for June. Everything was perfect until the end of basketball season. It was spring and everyone else was, you know, gettin' it on, and myself and him were having shouting matches during lunch."

The cheerleaders' disco tape died. Liz Cheng, my favorite, kept dancing, anyway.

"He had a fantastic season," Rita went on, "averaging, I don't know, thirty points and twenty assists." She was exaggerating. "We went to the state semis and every college in the Midwest was after my man's ass, though he knew he wanted to play in the Mississippi Valley Conference and he thought Mr. Ott was pretty cool." Bruce Ott, the River State recruiter and assistant coach, who is to smooth what Bo Derek is to well-built. "But suddenly Belvyn pulled away from me, backing off, making excuses not to go out, so I said fine, fuck it. I dated someone else, a second-string center, just to make Belvyn

53

jealous. Then one week the end of April he just stopped showing up at school."

"He just stopped showing up?"

"That's what I said."

"You mean he didn't ever really graduate?"

"Uh-uh."

"Jesus," I said. Silence. "Have you ever heard anything
about Belvyn being dyslexic?"

"No, he was always healthy as orange juice. I just think
everything kinda got too heavy for him, and he couldn't handle
it. He wouldn't see me anymore. It was his mother who kept
me away."

"So what are you doing here?"

"Visiting my girl friend."

"You're not trying to see Menkus?"

"Sure I am, but he won't return my calls. You don't have a
special number for him, do you?"

"No."

"Well, that pretty much brings us up to date, then."

"That's all you've got?"

"That's it. I've told you everything."

Now I was hooked. I offered her fifty bucks for more gossip,
but she insisted she'd told me all she knew, and I believed her
when she turned down sixty. I asked her why she was doing
this to someone she loved. She said she'd seen an article in
Wednesday's *Sun-Times* and realized she wanted revenge.

"For what?" I asked.

"For everything."

All that was left was saying good-bye, which she was cute
about, shaking hands very formally, then brushing her thumb
across her bruised fruit.

I drove from the field house to the *Register* to log my pieces
on the computer and dummy up Monday's page. Traffic was
congested with a lot of Ford wagons full of families taking
Junior back to the dormitory after the short vacation. "If you

don't like the weather, stick around a few minutes. It'll change." People around here say this so often only because it's true. The rain, which had turned to snow, was now hail battering my none too sturdy windows and giving my bald tires a real run for their money. I felt like the Bug was getting dragged the wrong way through an infuriated car wash. And everywhere I looked, building demolition was paving the way for fast-food joints and fake-fashionable shops to move in. River City was finishing its transformation from a cozy college town into a suburb without a center.

"A Place to Grow" is Iowa's PR slogan, but grow what— parking ramps like steps to the stars? On Dubuque Street a six-story hotel with 150 rooms and a 450-space garage is supposed to go up, which figures out to three cars per guest registration. Plaza Center One has reflecting glass windows with the capacity to blind. At the corner of Clinton and Washington, the heart of downtown, a two-story, two-block enclosed mall has been in the works since summer, and so far all they have to show for it is a stack of bricks, concrete cylinders, bundles of fence, steel rods, rails, pieces of pipe, and a bare skeleton slumping in the gummy foundation like the bones of a brontosaurus sinking for the last time into tar. And they still haven't finished the "outdoor greenway," which, according to bimonthly press releases we get from city hall, "covers four large intersecting blocks; is landscaped with bushes, benches, and kiosks; and is highlighted by a multipurpose fountain that doubles as a unique water feature and a stage for special events." Sooner or later every town in America will look like every other town in America, but River City should stay corn and soybeans, second-floor dentists' offices with dusty waiting rooms, the sticky sweet smell of pig dung. The light here has shades of color not yet found in paint cans. Why are we letting ourselves get taken on a detour by dump trucks dumping debris?

The *Register* building resembles a jail. It's got giant stone steps, windows so thickly ribbed you can't see through them, and, above the front door, in thirties art deco bas-relief, the scales of justice and a globe. Sometimes after sixteen hours of AP wire clacking away in my head, I'll look up at that globe and swear it was spinning. The key to the *Register* is that, after working your way through the weirdly angled door, the first thing you come to is the sparkling new bank of terminals for Classifieds. On a quiet Sunday afternoon, the terminals were by far the busiest thing in the shop. The efficient ladies who run them love the stuff—it's all one big never-ending garage sale to them.

"Hello, Albert," they all three said together. "Did you have a nice Thanksgiving?" Gerry asked.

"Hi, Mary; hi, Alice; hi, Gerry." Mary's old and white and pert; Alice is postcollegiate and pert; Gerry has five kids and is an earth mother and pert. "Well, no, not really. I had deadlines. I grabbed a burger, fries, and a shake at Arby's."

"That's terrible," Gerry said. "Deborah's not treating you right. Come have some of the leftover stuffing we're nibbling at."

It was crystal-cold and dry, and I was just starting to tell the Three Graces how delicious it was when the phones rang and new data came in on their printouts and they all ran, not walked, back to their terminals. They waved me upstairs, and up I went.

The *Register* was owned for generations by a farm family out in Solon, but sold in '73 to a few captains of industry—the local presidents of Procter and Gamble, K-Mart, Montgomery Ward. On Saturday half the paper is Classifieds; on Sunday the ads and inserts completely overwhelm the copy. River City is one of the only towns with 50,000 population to have its own Sunday paper, and though we claim to do it because "kids love the comics" there are other, less hilarious reasons. The Three Graces print money. The *Register* has come to be less and less a watchdog of the community and more and more a house organ of the Rotary Club.

It's a good place for someone on the way up, like Vicki, or on the way down, like Ira Barker, who once wanted to be

Will and Ariel Durant and has settled for squeezing weekly history lessons out of a turnip. He can worry 4,000 words out of a change in the timing mechanism of stoplights. It's the whacky ones here who are all right; the rest of us are just slaves of mediocrity. There's a River State junior who calls in humor pieces from his basement apartment, and half the time I can't make heads or tails out of his stuff, though it sounds funny. The whackiest of the whacky: upstairs in Features, "Sabrina," aka Susie Smyth, was doing her nails and listening to church music. On weekends she takes her show-stopping vamp-stripper parody to motel lounges and bars around town. What she really wants is to get her own talk show on Iowa cable. She has a chitchat column and does the Arts page.

"Hi, sweetie," she said, grabbing my arm.

She's very large but wears it so well I could imagine her weighing 275 in a football jersey and still being voluptuous.

"Nice nail polish." It was green.

"Listen, love, the Drama Department's doing a Shaw anachronism next week. Deb's a big Shaw person, isn't she? Any chance she'll review it for me?"

"I don't think you'd want her writing reviews. At the end of the thing you wouldn't have the faintest idea if the play was any good, but you'd get a thorough psychological profile of whoever happened to be her usher."

Sabrina blew on her nails and changed stations to bubble-gum rock, turning it down.

I avoided the deadheads over at Cityside and Editorial and walked around in back toward Marty, who was tucked away in the Sports cubbyhole, watching the pre-game bullshit on the Chiefs-Chargers game, which was a surprise because as a rule Marty tends to watch only what he gets paid to watch.

"You're actually watching a pro football game for the hell of it," I said.

"Here he is," Francis said, standing up from behind the open refrigerator door and greeting me with a Bud. "Husband, father, onetime great at this game, imminent journalist—I

57

mean eminent journalist—author of a very dubious opinion piece in this morning's *Reg*, and for at least a little while the most unpopular man in town."

"What are you doing here?" I said, taking off my coat.

"On my way over to the station, Marty was behind me and kept honking until I pulled over. I thought he was making a citizen's arrest because I was weaving in traffic. On the contrary. All he wanted to do was invite me over for an afternoon schnapps."

"What were you just babbling about?"

Marty handed me Rita's messages to call her back and at least a dozen telephone complaints that my Menkus story denigrated the River State program. The consecrated program. Hinselwood's almighty motion offense, match-up defense, and ten-year improvement plan. What else is there to do in River City anymore but wipe the dirt out of your eyes and get four-square behind the home team? Stallion fans are basically good, gracious people and loyal as the day is long, but the majority of them don't know basketball from lacrosse.

"Love letters from your fans?" Francis asked.

When I tossed them in the air, some landed in Francis' lap and one wound up near Marty's hunting rifle, which he was cleaning on top of his desk.

"I should never, ever have let that piece get by," Marty said. "Do you remember me reading it?"

"You took enough pills last night to be able to listen to Francis' old call-in show." Out of WHO in Des Moines, "Dutch" Reagan's old station, Francis used to have a talk show that was so boring and predictable that, during breaks, Francis would beg me to phone in hostile questions just to liven things up.

"That's real witty of you, Albert," Francis said, taking a silver flask out of his coat pocket and assimilating more than I drink during a leisurely dinner. He's so tall and small-boned that it doesn't show, but one of these days Francis is just going to float away.

"These people were pissed off," Marty said, trying to sound

really agitated. He sifted through the blue slips like he was looking for an answer to something. "They seriously wanted to hurt you." He pointed his rifle at me and made clicking noises with his tongue. The rifle was nearly as big as he was.

"Put that down," I said.

"Can't you see anything? The barrel's empty." He put the gun down and dipped his rag in some gunk. "I don't know how I ever let your piece through."

I took another bite on the Bud and sat at the terminal to punch in my headlines. SCROLL UP: SEND NEW STORY.

Francis announced, "Your column's total horseshit, Albert. A catalyst Menkus ain't—not yet, anyway. Not for at least another year, my friend. And to my mind his pro potential is next to nil. I thought I explained all this to you Thursday. A point guard's got to be able to step into the gap for the open eighteen-footer, and that he didn't do. Who cares about a few playground passes? Off the break he threw the ball on one bounce into the cheap seats." Though I didn't agree with him, Francis knows basketball. I never saw him play in his prime, but at gag games and charity events he pulls more than his share of rabbits out of the hat. "However, he does have gorgeous pecs and great legs. I'd happily forfeit a month's salary at KRCX to find out he switch-hits."

Marty laughed, either because he thought Francis was kidding or because he didn't get it and thought he should cover.

"Okay, he had some problems. But in a few weeks Tomlinson, Davis, Gault, and maybe even Durland will grasp what he's trying to do. He'll make them better. They'll come up to his level. He's a once-in-a-lifetime player, I promise. You'll see. You never played college ball, you don't know." Francis apparently had all the skills but couldn't take the battering underneath.

"Here it comes, rambling through the glories of yesteryear with the Drake bench-warmer of '61."

"Fuck you, Francis."

"Hey, hey, hey," Marty said, playing peacemaker as usual, slapping his empty rifle between us. I'm always afraid his beloved Browning automatic is going to explode, and his box of nitro tabs and the *Register* building will be history.

The Chiefs were playing scoreless snowball in Kansas City on the set, and Bill and Bob came over from Cityside to watch. Bill looks like an exhausted hamster. Bob is a Mason. They were putting off working on a piece about a jackhammer breaking a water main. They had a real story on their hands and wanted no part of it.

"Who do you like, gentlemen?" Bob asked, and this was Bob's attempt to sound locker-room.

Francis said, "Yes, I do."

"I'm sorry?" Bob said, applying Chap-Stick.

Bill said he was looking for the Chiefs to score an upset on the basis of the improved play of a wide receiver who'd been traded from Detroit a couple years ago, and we all had to nod and listen to this nonsense and watch a series of punts until a commercial came on and Bill and Bob went back to sidestepping the broken water main.

Once Marty's gun was back on the table getting oiled, Francis said, "I'll bet Hinselwood has your hero sitting on the bench before Christmas."

"That's ridiculous."

Marty, meaning well, said, "Albert, don't bet. Francis has his ways." Was Marty born apprehensive? No, he was born and grew up on a farm in What Cheer, which he should never have left for the thriving metropolis of River City. He would never have developed heart problems from the stress of waiting for me to do all his work for him.

"He's very quick and dribbles well, but he's never going to be much of a shooter. I say he'll be watching on the sidelines before the conference starts."

"First it was Christmas. Now it's the—"

"A case of Johnnie Walker Black," Francis said. These bets mean nothing to him because, between Channel 5 and KRCX, plus speaking engagements, he reels in sixty to seventy a year.

"I'm just grateful you have that kind of money to give away."

We shook on Christmas, and the three of us toasted one another. For a while we just sat there, me tapping away on the terminal, Francis draining his flask and getting pretty flushed in the face, and Bill and Bob looking over our way from the desert of Cityside, hoping to get invited back for the second half.

I had to shout over a whining vacuum cleaner to get the teenage janitor's attention: "Would you mind taking that somewhere else? We're working here."

"Yeah, you're working and I'm pushing a silver-dollar detector." Snot-nosed delinquent.

"Albert, that stringer of yours dropped off her story on the Turkey Trot," Marty said. "It's on my desk somewheres."

"Buried under copies of *Field and Stream*," Francis said.

"Not bad," Marty said, meaning Vicki can write.

"Not a bad story, either," Francis said, meaning, as always, the obvious.

"She constantly asks about you."

"She likes hearing battle tales from the noble ex-warrior," Francis said.

"Why don't you either lay off or check into a drunk tank?"

That was low and it hurt, so I apologized. Even Marty, who doesn't catch a lot of the complexities, could tell something went wrong. We watched the game like robots until Francis hoisted what little was left in his flask and passed it around. Marty took just a sip, on account of his angina, then picked up his gun and rearranged his hat. He was going out to bag some quail.

"Back in an hour or two," he said.

The time to catch Marty is when he's inching out the door to go quail hunting, since he'll agree to almost anything. I let him get halfway out of Sports before I said, "I want to write another article on Menkus."

He thought I was kidding and pointed the barrel at my head, making clicking noises with his tongue.

"No, really," I said, "I want to write a longer piece, maybe for the magazine section, and I need some elbow room to do it.

I've got a lead to track down in Chicago and Wednesday's my day off, so I thought—"

"Whatever you do on your day off is entirely your business."

Francis, who had been making a big show out of trying not to laugh, asked, "What's your scoop?"

"That," I said, "is entirely my business."

"For all I care, go to Alaska on Wednesday," Marty said. "Write a book on Menkus if you want. Just don't make the same mistake again, Albert. You're part of this community—don't antagonize it. Don't build up Menkus by knocking River State. It won't work. You can't do that here. You know that. Will you promise me that much?"

"Yes," I said.

"Good," he said and was gone.

True, I was enamored with Menkus, but all I had to do was draw the curtain to know I wanted to exit this rat's maze of roadblocks, and he was my ticket to Lake Michigan. Watching soot settle in the late afternoon gloom, I figured I either had to kiss Milwaukee good-bye or take it right at him. Do what I'd never done as a player: go to the hoop. No braking for the medium-range jumper. In your face, my main man. When I was a kid, my father used to walk around the house, swatting imaginary tennis balls and singing a nursery rhyme that went:

> *Chicken in a car,*
> *Car must go.*
> *That's the way*
> *You spell:*
> *Chi-ca-go.*

This was before he stopped getting invited to bush-league tournaments and before my mother started serious drinking. At her peak she was petite and pretty in a brunette bun, an attractively tight package. He had killingly good looks, and I think a good part of the reason he lasted as long on the tour as he did was that he was everybody's image of Jack Armstrong: big and broad and tall and dirty blond and blue-eyed and hope-inspiring, like a sailor in his first fifteen minutes of shore leave, before the debauch began. I have essentially the same features, though they don't come together to any particular dramatic effect. Francis had finished off the fifth, so he said he'd buy the first round at Phil's, and I thought: I am the chicken, the car is my broken-down Bug, and it is going to Chicago on Wednesday.

THREE

FROM here to the John Hancock Building is a four-hour drive if you leave at dawn and step on the gas. For me it's a trip all the way from God's country to an inferno. The light colors of the corn belt fade. The flatness of the fields turns hilly. The smell of cows and cereal gets choked in exhaust. The people harden and space shortens up. The soil loses its richness. I cross the Mississippi from Davenport into Peru, and factory fumes scar the sky. Towns become suburbs become the outskirts of Cook County, where people are automobiles. The dominant shade passes from yellow to gray. Go back, the road signs tell me, go back before it is too late because you are not a city boy and are coming into corruption. Go back. But I do not go back. I go on.

I made sure my favorite sea lions at Lincoln Park were still flapping their fins, then sat on a bench in the zoo and took out the River State student directory, which lists everyone's parents' addresses. If I was reading my map right, Menkus' parents lived in a fairly odd part of town. Directly under the Dan Ryan Expressway and hard by a tangle of train tracks. Eighty-seventh and Wabash, with Franklin Vocational at Eighty-third.

On the north side, everybody I asked for directions laughed at my green Iowa plates and said, "You're better off not going in there." Once on the south side, I saw what they meant. I couldn't believe it wasn't one project or one block but whole neighborhoods, gutted and burnt to a crisp. The wind was awful, and most of the people I saw on the street looked terribly cold and lonesome. Still, they were friendly enough to me. I got guided over to Eighty-seventh and Wabash lickety-split.

A hundred feet overhead cars tooled around the expressway, and a few blocks behind me a train clanked through, stinking up the joint. At eleven in the freezing morning kids bopped about, teenagers mainly, meddling with their radios and each other, all races, all pretty tough-looking, wearing leather and metal in threatening colors. Loose bricks and broken bottles lay in the gutter, waiting to help people get in trouble. I locked the car and put my camera in the trunk, hating myself for doing that, hating how easily paranoia happens to me in a poor area.

Menkus' home wasn't exactly the Herbert Hoover Memorial in West Branch. A trailer hitch, a mattress, some tires, and a tarp sat in snowdrifts on the front lawn. The house was a square shanty that had a window or two boarded up and needed a paint job. When I stepped on the front porch I felt like I was going to go right through the floorboards to the cellar. I opened the screen, which was off its hinges, and punched the door bell. No dingdong. I wished I had called ahead or at least wasn't wearing a coat and tie and carrying my cassette.

I knocked. A cat whined. Then a woman's gravelly voice hollered out at me: "We paid that already. We already paid you this month."

"I'm not a bill collector," I shouted back. "My name's Albert Biederman. I'm a sports reporter for the *River City Register*, in Iowa, and I was wondering if I could talk to you for maybe a few minutes."

"Albert Biederman, who wrote that story about Belvyn?"

"Yes, ma'am," I answered.

Abracadabra, the door opened. A woman wearing a nightgown and man's jacket hugged me and kissed me on both

cheeks while the cat clawed at my ankles. Mrs. Menkus was a
lot older than I expected her to be, but with none of the hard-
ness in her eyes that Menkus gets when he's on the court and,
instead, a semi-dazed quality that must have been the result of
spending her whole life genuflecting. The room was loaded
with Catholic knickknacks: crosses, rosary beads, Bibles, pictures and statues of Christ. A regular little cathedral. Her face
was lined, her hair looked dyed, and there was something
bleached about the overall impression she made, similar to
Shelley Winters.

"Oh, thank you," she said. "Thank you so much. That was
such a nice article. We don't like to let Belvyn make long-
distance calls, but he read the whole thing to us over the
phone. It sure meant a lot to him, and it touched me and Louie,
also."

"You're welcome," I said, "though I wasn't doing anyone a
favor. I honestly love the way your son plays basketball, and I
just hope other people give him a solid chance. I've been
watching him practice this week, and he reminds me of how I
finally learned to play the game." She gave me a funny look,
and I felt ridiculous. "Not, of course, with one-tenth his talent
but with the same goal, the same outlook about getting everyone to play together."

"Now don't you go talking basketball gibberish on me, like
Belvyn's always doing. To write that article after the team lost
was a manly act. Our family appreciates it." Another half-hug.
The cat looked for milk in my pants pockets. "I don't guess I've
properly introduced myself. Evelyn Marie Menkus. Won't you
please take your coat off and have some coffee, Mr. Biederman?" she said, showing me to a seat on the purple couch,
where I was boxed in by the cat and a set of square pillows
with religious sayings on them.

The living room furniture was just the couch, a couple of
gray chairs, a chest of china, her Catholic doodads, and Stallion coasters, mugs, lamp shades. In the corner gleamed a
brand-new Betamax with last night's network news on and the
sound off. Where did they ever get a Betamax?

"What's the cat's name?" I said. I'm allergic to cat hair, so I pretended to pet it, hoping it would spring off my lap.

Mrs. Menkus was in the kitchen, heating coffee. "Matthew," she said. "Come here, Mattie. Come to Momma." Mattie went over to her when she came back with Sanka in a Stallion cup and interesting-tasting crackers.

"Belvyn had trouble with a few of the words in your story and neither me or Louie got everything, but—"

"As you probably know, my wife's his English teacher, and she thinks he probably has dyslexia, that his eye flips words and letters around. Have you ever heard anything about that?"

"Belvyn's always telling me how much he likes Mrs. Biederman. I'm sure she means well. I think Belvyn just isn't the brainiest book person in the world, and they have a lot of ten-dollar terms now to let you down easy."

"I'm sorry," I said because I could feel her back off a bit. "I shouldn't have brought it up. It's really none of my business."

"Well, anyway," she said, recovering nicely, "I could tell it was a good article, Mr. Biederman. You were really saying something there."

"Thank you, that's very nice. It's really nothing I did. It's what your son is trying to do. Call me Albert, okay?"

"Okay, Albert," she said cheerfully, giving me another cracker. "That's important to Belvyn, what you wrote in the paper. He says how he likes to set up the other fellas, help them score buckets."

"That's great," I said, sliding the cassette into my coat pocket. She was talking naturally now, and I didn't want a mike to distract her. "Because that's really why I came here. There used to be a lot more teamwork, but now it's all grab the ball off the board and fire thirty-footers. Belvyn's different. He could do anything he wants on the floor, and he runs plays that were diagramed eighty years ago. You have no idea how happy that makes me."

"I'm afraid I don't follow you, Mr. Biederman."

"Albert," I said again. "All I mean is, Belvyn's a very unselfish athlete and I'd love to know how he got that way."

For quite a while she said nothing, then looked up at the ceiling. I looked where she looked and saw there was a tapestry of Mother Mary hanging from a chandelier whose lights were blown out. "Well, I'd like to think it's the influence of Jesus Christ, but he'd more likely say his basketball coach at Franklin." She said this regretfully, though not bitterly, and with a small smile. "He loves that man. You should go over later and talk to him."

"I'm planning to," I said, trying to get all this down as fast as I could without breaking my pencil.

She didn't know what to say next, and I didn't, either. The room hung on us heavy. You felt the wind on the windows and the cold coming in. I realized why she wore a man's overcoat: they couldn't afford to have heat. Mattie nibbled away at a cracker. Mrs. Menkus sat quiet, looking around at her religious tokens and counting her blessings, while virtually on her doorstep kids' radios sang craziness. You had to admire her concentration.

"Louie?" I finally said. "That's your husband? He's at work, I suppose?"

She came over to join me on the couch and whispered, "No, he's sleeping in Belvyn's room. He got laid off a couple weeks ago and is taking it pretty hard so far. Last night he stayed up until the wee hours, watching TV and . . ." She made a drinking gesture with her thumb.

The network news was no longer on. The screen was a blank. Betamax probably does everything for you but make breakfast.

"Where does he work?"

"Greyhound, the Randolph Street station. Ticket taker."

"This might sound pretty silly, Mrs. Menkus, and you throw me out if I'm being a pain in the side, but journalists are by nature busybodies. We like to see everything, try to know what makes people tick." I was really laying it on. "Sometimes you can get a strong sense of someone by where he lives. Would there be any chance we could peek at Belvyn's old bedroom?"

She thought about it for a second, shrugged, and said, "Sure, why not? So long as we're quiet."

She took off her shoes and had me take off mine. Holding my arm, Mrs. M. led me through the kitchen, which looked pretty bare, and past their closed bedroom into Belvyn's ex-quarters.

His father was fast asleep, turned away from us, and wearing his Greyhound uniform. He must have really loved the Randolph Street station. Most bus drivers I've met have a military bearing, and, from what I could see of him, Louie had the same manner. He was a big broad guy who looked like he might once have been an offensive tackle or dockworker. There was nothing of Belvyn in him except the nose. He had Belvyn's perfect Irish nose. On the far wall were taped a Stallion pennant and color posters of Earvin Johnson and Oscar Robertson and a black-and-white one of Bob Cousy—the three greatest passers in basketball history.

"All right," I said, still nine years old. "Magic, Big O, and the Cooz."

"Shhh." She shut the door, tiptoeing back into the living room.

"I'm sorry, I'm really sorry."

"That's okay. Louie's a sound sleeper."

"Did Mr. Menkus ever play any sports?"

"No, the only exercise he gets is leaping to conclusions, which is a little joke he heard at work. My gosh, does he miss the guys at Greyhound."

"If Mr. Menkus didn't teach him, how did Belvyn ever get to be so good? I mean, where did he learn how to play?"

"Well, Eighty-seventh Street was never exactly Lake Shore Drive, Albert. Still and all, in the early fifties, when we were first married, it was a mixed bag. Not rich, not poor. Now, of course, it's mostly black families, and Belvyn's friends growing up were black kids. Some got trouble in them, but they have deep souls. Belvyn used to come home howling, because they'd let him keep playing only if he passed them the ball."

It was hard to write everything down while standing, so I

sat, sipped the cold coffee, and took a different type of cracker to see if it tasted any better, which it didn't. The room was so cold I put my shoes back on and pumped my legs in place.

"I appreciate you being open with me, Mrs. Menkus. I want to write a real thorough profile of Belvyn for the magazine section of my paper, but every time I call him I get that darn tape he's got. When I tried to talk to him Tuesday after practice, he avoided me. You'd think he'd be more tactful, if for no other reason than to get in good with Deborah."

"Who's Deborah?"

"My wife. Belvyn has her for both Rhetoric and reading lab."

"He thinks the world of her," she said again.

"I understand his need for privacy and all that—"

"No, Albert, don't apologize. I agree with you a hundred and ten percent." She poured milk into a saucer and let Mattie slurp it up. "Me and Louie, me in particular, have been after Belvyn since junior high to be more open to good people such as yourself or your wife, but he doesn't completely trust no one, never has. He's like that old TV show, 'The Untouchables.' He just doesn't let people get close. The one person he let in hurt him real bad."

"Rita?" I said. What an idiot. The room froze. I stirred my Sanka with a cracker, gulped, looked down at my notes. I was far too eager to share in his past.

"How do you know Rita Manfredi, Mr. Biederman?"

I was Mr. Biederman again. I wrote *Manfredi* in my mind but didn't want to risk a roundabout answer to Mrs. Menkus, who seemed to have a built-in bullshit detector. "She was at the Omaha game. You weren't there, were you?"

"No, we haven't been able to afford—"

I cut her off, hoping to sneak in an explanation before she told me to leave. "She came up to me after the Omaha game, and I gathered she's still pretty bitter, you know. She—"

"*She's* still bitter? That little hussy. 'Judge not lest ye be judged.' With Rita Manfredi, I'll take my chances." She

70

chuckled. She had a sense of humor. I liked that about her. "Making like she was religious to win me over, then pretending to be pregnant to get Belvyn to marry her. A professional athlete's pampered wife—that was her goal, and she made no bones about admitting it. I'm sorry, Mr. Biederman, I don't go in for that kind of thing. I just hope she finds her way before it's too late."

"Rita said Belvyn missed the last couple months of senior year."

"Well, why do you think he had to do that?" she asked me. "I don't know."

"All the recruitment pressures from a zillion colleges were driving him nuts. And on top of that he had Rita haranguing him to 'make a commitment.' He needed some time to be by himself, so he went to live with relatives in Springfield until summer. Springfield is Abraham Lincoln's birthplace, did you know that?"

"How did Belvyn finish high school, then, if you don't mind me asking?"

She got off the couch, stepped over the cat, and tinkered with the little Jesus figures and pictures on the mantelpiece. There must have been at least a dozen of them. I haven't the foggiest what she was doing other than maybe saying a few Hail Marys for a fallen numbskull like me. I don't know that much about the Catholic religion.

"He took all kinds of special tests and things to prove he was ready to go on."

"Like the GED's?" The General Educational Development tests, to see if you read at a sixth-grade level along with all the other high school graduates. Student-athletes have been slipping through this loophole for years.

"My gosh, Albert, you seem to know everything. Belvyn passed, and of course the GED's as good as a diploma."

The Betamax has a soap opera going now without sound, and both our glances fell on it. I said, "The one luxury in the house, huh?"

71

"Yes, Louie's aunt died last year, the same one Belvyn stayed with senior year, and left us a little money, and we decided to spend it on one fun thing." She sounded like she hardly believed the explanation herself, but what was I going to do—demand to see Louie's aunt's will? Embarrassment was in Mrs. Menkus' eyes and a quaver was in her voice, and I couldn't stand either of them terribly much longer. It was too painful. I figured neither Mrs. Menkus, living in her own convent, nor Louie, hibernating in his Greyhound uniform, was exactly up-to-date on NCAA recruiting regulations. Even if the Betamax was a bribe from Bruce Ott or if Tomlinson had taken Menkus' GED's for him, I didn't have the heart to press her any harder than I had. I possessed no proof of anything, only leads leading nowhere. I thought about the *Milwaukee Journal* and Menkus' alley-oop to Black Stallion and River City's Downtown Refurbishment Project. I couldn't make sense of anything. Surrounded by all these religious gizmos, I felt like a shitheel for not trying harder to believe her.

She probably would have talked to me until winter was over, but I didn't want to hear anymore. I didn't need to know everything now, since it would all come out in the wash soon enough. I chugalugged the coffee, got my coat off the couch, and shuffled toward the door, putting my notepad and pencil in my pocket.

"You're a good man, Mr. Biederman," she promised.

"I hope so," I said.

Then she gave me her third hug of the day and a handful of crackers. I said good-bye and went out in the wind with Mattie meowing at my heels.

A bronze statue of Benjamin Franklin stood on the front steps. Across his stomach someone had spray-painted HONKY MOTHERFUCKER. Three stories of faded brick were bordered by a fence and not much of a playground. A lot of unemployed people wandered the chilly streets. It wasn't the ideal place to set up a school, and I assumed the stereotypical worst:

hallways awash in pints of Ripple, water fountains thick with roaches. The inside of the building was a nice surprise.

The first floor was, in any case: clean and quiet, tomblike at quarter of twelve. Everywhere you looked were bulletin boards jammed with events, walls lined with pretty good paintings of city scenes, and posters getting people psyched up for a big game Friday against Dunbar. You could tell it was really a school and not a reformatory in disguise. The spirit of the place reached out and grabbed you. Sports can do that if you're ready. It can tie everyone together.

Though here and there I heard a door slam or a shout echo from some distant room, I didn't directly encounter a single soul until a very short, very skinny black girl came prancing around the corner. Either she had copied Rita's walk or Rita had copied her walk or maybe all the girls at Franklin walked like they were trying to wiggle out of wet cement.

I stood in front of her and said, "Excuse me, miss, could you please tell me where the principal's office is?"

"Third floor, 308, top of those stairs, but you'd best steer clear of Braithwaite," she said. She was hot to trot. I asked if I could get in two more questions.

"Quick as quick. I gotta get to work."

"Did you ever know a girl named Rita Manfredi? A white girl," I said, as if the whole race were something of an enigma to me as well. "As pretty as you are."

"I never know no white chick named Rita."

"Have you ever heard of Belvyn Menkus?"

"Now I know who you mean. Rita hung around Belvyn. Shit, yes, that boy could play ball. Rita was a slut," she said, then lit a cigarette and skedaddled.

As I made my way toward Braithwaite's office, a bunch of kids streamed down the steps. I figured they were shop class let out early, since most of them were carrying a wood carving, a metal file, or a block of something.

"You a new sub?" a Spanish kid asked. They all thought that was a riot. Dressed up and holding my notebook, I guess I looked like an algebra teacher, but him calling me a sub made me remember sitting on the sidelines my sophomore year at Drake, benched by a broken femur, trying to watch, knowing I'd never play.

I didn't have that much time before everyone left for lunch, so I went right into 308, a gray little cubicle with the blinds drawn and one-way mirrors looking out. A secretary was talking on the telephone while running sheets through a Xerox machine. Her black hair was wrapped in a beehive, her mascara was caked on too heavy, and flesh spilled from her pant suit.

When she was through on the phone I said hello.

"Are you a new sub?"

I had to laugh and loosen my tie a bit. "No," I said. "My name's Albert Biederman. I'm a sports reporter for the *River City Register*. In Iowa." I heard a big voice booming from the principal's office next door.

"I'm writing an article about Belvyn Menkus, who—"

"What a dreamboat," she said, turning off the copier and stepping out from behind the counter. "Every girl and her mother had goo-goo eyes for him the whole time he was here."

"That's fascinating. I keep hearing about his love life or whatever, but actually I'm more interested in what he was like as a student, and I thought I'd ask Mr. Braithwaite if I could maybe take a look at his transcripts."

"My pleasure, Mr. Biederman," she said and buzzed Braithwaite. She talked me up to the principal, so he agreed to see me for a few minutes before lunch. The secretary showed me in.

All the money earmarked for Franklin must have been funneled into furnishing Braithwaite's office and feeding Braithwaite. His private retreat was as plush as could be— Persian rug, framed prints on the wall, a couple of complicated lamps. And he was a whopper, with a walrus face and droopy mustache to match. When he raised up out of the chair to shake hands, I noticed that he wore suspenders over a white shirt broad as a bed sheet and an empty holster at the end of the long journey of his gut.

"Why the gun?" I asked.

"Where do you see a gun?" he barked back at me.

"I don't. Just the holster."

"Where are you from?" he asked, fiddling with the picture frames of his family.

"River City, Iowa."

"Well, I don't know about Ioway. Maybe where the tall corn grows people are better behaved, but this is the south side. This is Franklin Vocational." He got physical with his knuckles on the desk top. "Seventy-five percent black. Poor black, Mr. Biederman. Most of these kids carry some kind of piece, and we have at least one major disturbance a month. I wear the gun only to establish order," he said. He felt around with his fist for open leather.

The school he described wasn't the school I'd seen so far. Maybe I was naive. "Listen, I'm not a sociologist, I'm a sportswriter," I said to get us back on the track if he was going to lunch in a few minutes.

"Well, we've graduated probably as many pro players as River State, as I'm sure you're aware. Is that Stallion Battalion as rabid as they say?"

"None crazier."

"So who are you snooping around on?"

"I'm not snooping around on anybody," I said. "I just want to get some background on Belvyn Menkus."

Braithwaite didn't blink, didn't reach in the top right drawer for his gun. He stared straight through me to the pictures on the wall and said, "What do you want to know?"

"The *Register* likes to emphasize the student-athlete angle, and I was kind of hoping to get a glance at his dossier."

He seemed to think the request was ludicrous and smiled into the little mirror on the wall. "No way in hell, Mr. Biederman, I can show you those files. Students' records are strictly confidential. Athletes especially, because they're in the news. The Buckley amendment and all, you should know that. My first and only priority is to protect my kids' privacy, but, if I remember correctly, Menkus was an adequate student and active in student government, and you can quote me."

"Do you remember anything about how River State recruited him?"

"That falls entirely within the PE department's purview, not mine. Now, if you have no further questions, I'm already late for a luncheon appointment with some people from the district office."

He didn't appear to be the kind of guy who was late for luncheon appointments too often. I tried to get in a question that would hold him. "I understand Belvyn didn't ever really graduate from Franklin."

"That's right. He passed the GED's. That's a matter of public record," he said and, leaning back in his chair, squeezed the handle of a file cabinet drawer. That was his only mistake.

"Can I see it?"

"No. He did well enough to just graduate, but not well enough to go to a four-year, which is why he went to Sioux City. Beyond that, I can't tell you anything, and I have got to be going now, Biederman. You'll excuse me."

He huffed and puffed and rolled his red eyes, then stood, ushering me out of the office. He sprained a few tendons in my hand shaking it. I pretended to thank him, and I'm sure he thought he'd put one over on the rube from pig country. The secretary was already out to lunch, so while Braithwaite was getting his coat off the rack in his room and pouring his massive arms into his sleeves I punched the button on the exit door, hoping that would release the lock. The oldest trick in the book, but it worked because he shut the door to his room and I stood against the exit door, holding it open for him, then walked down the corridor, thanked him again, nodded, talked about other athletes who had gone here, and told him, yes, I'd look up those GED's at the district office when I had a chance.

"Okay, Biederman, good-bye, I'm out of here," he said and lumbered down the stairs. I spent the next few minutes trying to calm my nerves passing as a substitute algebra teacher, wandering around on guard duty after a tough morning at the blackboard. I lost myself in the lunch crowd: kids screaming from all directions and out of every open door, goosing each other, gossiping, smoking, eating, necking, scuffling; but no real violence, none that I could tell.

I walked back to 308 and tried to peek in. The blinds were still drawn, and I couldn't see diddlysquat through the one-way mirrors. I rubbed a locker for luck and made to admire the architecture of some steel beams, took one last look around, and when the coast was clear I rushed into the room. Paranoia of a reporter: it seemed too easy, I suspected a trap. Francis, were you hiding behind a bookcase? No, you weren't. I checked.

The moment I was in 308 I was seized with the worst case of rookie jitters. The place was insanely silent. Clock ticks were like buckshots. My whole body shook, my knees knocked, and my pulse was as bad as Barry's. Every car horn in the parking lot was the police. I heard creaks and cracks from the floor below, but those were only the death rattles of a decaying tower and I felt alone.

Braithwaite's door had been shut but not locked, and the other good thing about his office was that it had no windows, so I couldn't be detected. Such nice kids he had on his desk, such a nice family, such good taste in artistic reproductions on the wall that you had to wonder why he became such a bully. There were three filing cabinets along the wall. I pulled out door after heavy door and didn't find anything even vaguely relevant until, in the middle drawer of the last cabinet, I came across a fat folder marked *Athletics*.

The front of the file had a lot of nothing. Scholarship applications. SAT and ACT info. Signed and unsigned letters of intent. Financial-aid requests. Loan info. Work-study regulations. Big Eight, Mississippi Valley, ACC recruiting pamphlets. Various expressions of gratitude and decisions not to attend. An amazing number of letters and honors bestowed upon Franklin alumni. Toward the back of the folder was a manila envelope labeled *Menkus*. Though it wasn't sealed, I couldn't open it for maybe a minute because my hands had suddenly become clumsy, trembling mitts, and I was further distracted by some rattling pipes on the second floor and the sensation of sitting in Braithwaite's chair, which was designed for a man with a hippo's girth.

The first sheet was a computer printout of Menkus' mid-40s scores on the math, reading, writing, science, and social studies tests. Good as gold, that thing, since it made him a high school graduate. After that were four transcripts and nothing else. I copied all four on the Xerox machine, and the first one looked like this:

Student's Name: Menkus, Belvyn	**Fall-9th**		**Spring-9th**	
Nathaniel	Geography	B	Spanish 1	A
Address: 8758 South Wabash Avenue	Math 1	Drop	Math 1	Drop
Telephone: 534-6877	English 1	C	English 2	C
GPA: 2.77	Typing 1	B	Typing 2	B
Rank: 89/174	Phys. Ed.	A	Phys. Ed.	A
Comments: Excellent college prospect	Am. History 1	C	Am. History 2	C

Fall-10th		**Spring-10th**		**Fall-11th**		**Spring-11th**	
Public		Journalism	A	Spanish 6	C	Spanish 7	C
Speaking	A	English 1	B	Composition	C	Biology 3	B
Math 1	Drop	Math 2	B	Chemistry 1	B	English 2	C
Basic Writing	C	Spanish 3	C	Am. History 3	C	Chemistry 2	C
Spanish 2	C	Phys. Ed.	A	Phys. Ed.	A	Phys. Ed.	A
Phys. Ed.	A	Biology 2	C	Math 3	C	Math 4	C
Biology 1	C						

Extracurricular activities:
Catholic Youth Organization

Fall-12th		**Spring-12th**		
Astronomy	C	Math 3	B	Photo Club
Typing 3	B	Biology 1	B	Car Club
Am. History 4	C	English 3	C	Jazz Band
Math 5	C	Spanish 8	C	Student Government
Phys. Ed.	A	Phys. Ed.	A	Varsity Basketball
Spanish 4	B	Chemistry 3	C	

It had smudge marks and what looked like scrapings off the carbons. Eight A's in PE were counted in his grade point, which is against NCAA rules. The shyest kid in the Midwest got an A in Public Speaking. He got a B in Typing 3 two and a half years after taking Typing 2. Menkus active in CYO and student government—tell me about it, Braithwaite. These were borderline. Then there were the out-and-out impossibilities. A solid B in Math 2 after dropping Math 1 three straight times.

Taking Spanish 7 as a junior and not getting around to Spanish 4 until senior year. A simple repeat of Biology 1, going from a C to a B.

This transcript was the most obvious fraud, but the next two exhibited the same kind of shenanigans: revisions, suspiciously steady grades, inverted and repeated courses. The first three transcripts, though, were nothing compared to the final fourth, the only page with the official school seal:

Student's Name: Menkus, Belvyn Nathaniel		**Fall-9th**		**Spring-9th**	
		Phys. Ed.	A	Phys. Ed.	A
Address: 8758 South Wabash Avenue		Woodshop 1	C	Engineering	C
Telephone: 534-6877		Auto 1	D	Electronics	D
GPA: 1.31		Math 1	F	Spanish 1	Drop
Rank: 172/174		Am. History	Drop	Reading	D
Comments: See GED		Reading	F	Woodshop 2	F

Fall-10th		**Spring-10th**		**Fall-11th**		**Spring-11th**	
Phys. Ed.	A	Phys. Ed.	A	Phys. Ed.	A	Phys. Ed.	A
Photo Lab	C	Math 1	D	Jazz Studio	D	Woodshop 4	D
Electronics	D	Am. History	F	Auto 2	C	Auto 3	D
Spanish 1	Drop	Typing	Drop	Reading	F	Reading	D
Reading	D	Engineering	F	Spanish 1	F	Am. History	Drop
Woodshop 3	F	Reading	F	Speech	Drop	Spanish 1	F

Fall-12th		**Spring-12th**	Extracurricular activities:
Phys. Ed.	A	NO COURSES	Varsity basketball
Woodshop 5	D	COMPLETED—	
Auto 4	D	STUDENT	
Reading	D	LEFT SCHOOL—	
Am. History	Drop	DID NOT	
Spanish 1	F	GRADUATE	

Menkus' real grades wouldn't have got him into braille school for the blind. Who had jerry-built this blunder and what was I supposed to do about it? I tried to laugh, which echoed weirdly in the silent office before I heard some footsteps a couple doors down. I put the papers back in the envelope and the envelope in the file and the file back in the drawer. I closed the drawer and got the hell out of there as quick as I could.

✿   ✿   ✿

In the hallway I felt numb and crazy as I kept bumping into people, apologizing. One little guy I nearly decapitated said, "Watch your 'bows, you ugly asshole." Lunch hour wound down. Nobody wanted to return to class. I felt like I had algebra to teach. I walked down two flights of stairs to the cafeteria, which was deserted except for a group of pale geniuses playing with their calculators at a far table. Apparently, it was still uncool to get caught inside during noon. Ordering everything on the menu, I shoveled in the mush. I had guilt pangs about sneaking into the office and kept expecting Braithwaite to tap me on the shoulder and say, "Okay, pal, the jig's up."

On the first floor I ran into a janitor, a nice fellow wearing a Sox cap who pointed me toward the gym, which was in the farthest, wettest section of the basement and next door to the band room. Down the corridor, the overhead light was out and you felt its absence, you craved its heat. A girls' volleyball class was in session while I climbed into the balcony.

It was what is called a crackerbox gymnasium. Fan backboards with black rims were attached to the walls, and on the other side of one wall you could hear people in the band room playing trumpet. There was no space along either sideline. Rusty pipes ran all the way around. The floor was tile, which is hard on the ankles, and about a hundred blue pennants hung from the low ceiling. An open door let in a little air.

Lying back on the benches, I zoomed back to the day Deborah spent searching Del's Used Books for some tome she needed. Deborah is barely civil to Del because ten years ago he dropped out of the English program just before getting his Ph.D. While Deborah foraged, Del dug out of the bargain bin a little number called *Great American Baskets* and handed it to me. This tattered paperback had no text other than place names, no listing of players, just pictures of the hoops. In Bridgeport, Connecticut, a metal ring looked like what you dangled your worst enemy from. In Madisonville, Kentucky, a huge washtub was nailed to a tree at the edge of a farm. Rims without nets, without backboards, without courts, with just gravel and grass underfoot. One basket in Shaker Heights,

Ohio, featured a white net blowing in the breeze and an orange shooter's square on the half-moon board. The game of basketball has not been exactly flooded with great point guards from Shaker Heights, Ohio.

Deborah was exasperated since she was unable to find the first edition original-hardcover blah-blah-blah while Del and I were on another planet, rapturously turning pages. The backboards were made from every possible material and tacked to anything that stood still in a storm. The rims were set at every height, at the most cockeyed angles, and draped with nets woven out of everything from coat hangers to ladies' lingerie. All types and shapes of posts, courts, boards, rings, but what you realized after a while was that it was finally the same damn thing, the same view over and over: from Wheeling, West Virginia, to Medford, Oregon, the same wells to throw your deepest dreams down.

Most men talk about cars. What the fuck do I care about cars? I care about basketball. Deborah should have been grateful Del and I weren't discussing overhead cam engines, whatever they are. I like to roam new neighborhoods, tugging on twine, checking out the give. I like jumping up and down on hardwood floors. I like measuring foul line to foul line, comparing basket supports. An eight-foot hoop for Laurel's younger brother is tacked to a telephone pole in the street, and I like standing in the cold, watching snow drip off the rusty rim.

And now, here in front of me in the Franklin gym, were long white nets Menkus had helped so many people make dance. The girls trotted off, I took a snooze, and half an hour later I awoke to my favorite sound in the world—the patta-patta-patta of basketballs being dribbled. One of the players turned up his combination radio/suitcase to drown out the band next door, and the kids jumped all over each other, hugging, inventing new handshakes. It was a bath of love in the unlikeliest of places, and standing in the middle of the commotion was a man so fat he looked like he'd never shot a ball in his life but who obviously knew a thing or two about lighting fires in young men's minds.

81

They warmed up with ball-handling drills, and they all had very quick hands, even the two white kids. Then they got in line for lay-ins, and everyone dunked. Everyone. One-hand slams. Two-hand slams. Jumping off the wall and jamming. Tip-bangs against the boards. Reverse tomahawks. Rockabye babies. A final 360 from a kid who couldn't have been any bigger than six-four. So this was where Menkus learned to leap.

Even more, it must have been where he learned to pass. Once scrimmage started, I went completely bananas when I saw that *as a rule* they refused open shots from the foul line to hit someone else standing free from nine. They rebounded and found the outlet man before touching the floor, dribbled through their legs, always led the cutter, broke full court presses easily with no-look lobs. One boy swished a beautiful jumper from top of the key and got chewed out for cherry picking.

The coach stood on the sideline, stomping his feet, clapping his hands to some crazy rhythm that only he heard, and said, "Jumpin' *bean,* jumpin' *bean,* move that mother like a *jumpin'* bean." The way these kids moved the ball, it might have been a heat-seeking missile. I worked myself into a tizzy just trying to follow it.

The last thing I wanted to do was wreck the mood, but I was dying to discuss Menkus with the coach. During a water break, I went to compliment him and plead for an interview. Before I got to the bottom of the stairs he filled the doorway with his immensity and said, "You a spyin' piece of shit from Dunbar. Out."

"No, no, I'm not," I stammered and tried to maneuver, but he pinned my shoulder blades with the strongest hands I've ever encountered. He was at least as big around as Braithwaite. Everything about Jumpin' Bean was gigantic. He had huge eyes and teeth like talons.

I took out ID and convinced him I wasn't a spy from Dunbar.

"Then what the hell are you hunkerin' around here for?" he wanted to know.

"I'm writing a story on Menkus for a paper in Iowa and wanted to see his old gym, maybe talk with you a while."

The kids went back to shooting free throws when they saw he believed me. He took a deep breath. When a man that big sighs you want to give him all the room he needs to exhale, but he didn't let me budge an inch.

"That's long gone. That's booshit. I'm livin' in now."

"Watching your scrimmage, I can see how much Menkus learned from you. Just ten minutes after practice, a few anecdotes, what do you say? Braithwaite said I should speak with you, and Belvyn's mother told me—"

"You don't hear me, mister," he said, pulling me to him and then pushing me away one last time. "We don't talk about booshit here. We play basketball. I got nothin' more to say to you, little man. Out." And with that Jumpin' Bean rejoined his troops, who were all ears.

I admired him more for not talking to me than if he had sat down with a quart of vodka and told stories all night. He and Menkus and his kids were out on the court, taking it to the hoop, and I was dallying around the water fountain, cheering them on. What did they have to say to me?

"Okay, then, fine, I'm going," I said to no one in particular and walked out the door into the thin rain on Eighty-third Street.

FOUR

WHY *do you have such a funny name? Did you really score 45 on all the GED's? Did you really take the GED's? What's the story with you and Rita? Why did you drop out of Franklin? Why did you go to Sioux City Trade and Extension? Were you aware what was being done with your transcripts? Do you take after Jumpin' Bean and have no intention of ever talking to me about any of this? And why do I care? Why do I get lost so easily in these details? Why do you haunt me? What am I looking for when I watch you play? Could you throw a pass so perfect it would set me free?*

Coming home in the drizzle, I compiled a lot of questions to ask Menkus if I ever caught up with him. I took 90/94 out of the Chicago suburbs toward 80 west and Joliet. The only country song on the radio was a weepy thing by Conway Twitty, and there was no four o'clock news, so I kept talking to myself about Menkus to keep from feeling guilty about busting into Braithwaite's office. Take away twenty years, give me a quicker first step, and no pin in my left leg—maybe I'd have been as good as Menkus? No way. He was my last chance to be serious about the idea of basketball.

What threw a monkey wrench into this type of thinking was the *Milwaukee Journal.* If I wrote a tribute to Menkus and sent it to them, I might get called for an interview, but if I uncovered a recruiting scandal they'd probably hand me the job on a paper plate. Although Deborah was up for tenure in a year, she wanted Barry to see the city lights before he turned into a combine, so maybe Milwaukee was the place. For all I knew, Marquette had a great Autobiography department where Deb would fit right in.

The sky got dark. I sailed through Ottawa and La Salle, near the Illinois River toward Princeton, Sheffield, and Geneseo, such exotic-sounding names of absolute shit towns. The rain let up in the Quad Cities at six. It was a pure and empty night as I crossed the bridge over the Mississippi.

I didn't know much yet about River State wrongdoing, but I'd read enough about other colleges to make me ill. The NCAA's Intercept program shadowed the best fifty high school athletes and leaked reports that turned recruiting corruption into a hot topic. The president of the University of Oklahoma said he wanted a university his football team could be proud of. A basketball squad in New England supposedly had ties to Mafia gambling. At Wichita State a power forward's mother suddenly moved out of the low-rent district, while an off-guard's girl friend, a cheerleader, got her abortion paid for by the athletic department.

A real estate tycoon urged kids to come to UCLA by giving them the keys to new Camaros, and at USC track stars got credit for a speech class none of them ever attended because it didn't exist. The Arizona State football coach punched players whose performance disappointed him. Two basketball coaches at New Mexico State forged ticket stubs and collected thousands of dollars in reimbursement for trips they never took. A Big Eight school's athletic counselor announced that 95 percent of his counselees were reading below a tenth-grade level, and he seriously doubted whether scores at other powerhouses were significantly higher. Blue-chip recruits were offered everything from once-a-week girl friends to Samsonite sets lined with unmarked bills, and when the season ended jock after jock was arrested for assault or rape, then released when their victims were persuaded not to press charges. Did Menkus' case pale by comparison? Probably, but it was the one I was working on. I kept trying to push down my burglary, and it kept popping back up.

Whatever happened to a pounding heart and sweat in your ears? College football and basketball had been turned into a televised farm system for the NBA and NFL, and the athletes were coddled through school and paid megabucks in the pros, and everyone put up with it because they were the only American heroes left. Something good would be made better by making it bigger and taking away what was special in the first place. The Downtown Refurbishment mentality: gut the best bar in Johnston County to install a new Hardee's. The colleges were being offered a king's ransom if they were good enough to appear on the tube, and they were selling their grandmother to get there. The kids were meaty entertainment.

The faces of *Street and Smith's* '80–'81 high school All-American basketball players are goofy and barren; they have those hard eyes Menkus has. Flipping pages, I sometimes find it difficult to remember whether I'm looking at well-rounded student-athletes or Wanted posters at the post office. I start wondering what I'm doing in the PR business, writing hype for this racket.

But Menkus the passer had to be different than these gunners. I crossed the Iowa border into Bettendorf, heading toward West Branch. The land opened up for me, the sky got deeper. I didn't see how really foul breeze could blow through our fields. It didn't seem possible. It didn't seem right. And I held on to that hope.

Twenty years ago a point-shaving scandal surfaced at River State, and the guilty parties were expelled. Francis likes to harp on a rumor that whenever the basketball team wins the starters find a roll of twenties in their sneakers, courtesy of Calvin Raeburn, who's made millions manufacturing pearl buttons, lead and zinc, dairy supplies. Francis and Raeburn go way back to Francis' days as sports director of radio station WHO–Des Moines, where during the Depression "Dutch" Reagan turned teletype summaries into color commentary.

Raeburn bought a lot of air time for his pearl buttons, got Francis in on the ground floor of a chain of shoe stores and a take-out fish-food joint, and a beautiful friendship developed. The *Register* calls Raeburn a patron, which means he buys what he wants. But those were the only whispers of impropriety I'd ever heard about River State. After a while there is only so much niggling I can heed, because what I come back to is the game. They can't take the game away. The game doesn't ever really change, and it is still good.

When you're standing knee-deep in horse shit, you get bored talking about the smell. Sooner or later you want to get back to the horses galloping. Jumpin' Bean bringing those kids together in the darkest corner of the darkest school on the darkest side of Chicago. Once a week during winter, 12,200 people in the field house creating community for a couple hours. Menkus' blind alley-oop to Black Stallion.

The game will survive Dick Hinselwood and TV timeouts, and I knew that for a fact because I saw myself as a seventh-grader in Des Moines, and I saw us, the Windsor Bobcats, working out in a tiny gym with loose buckets and slippery linoleum and butcher-paper posters exhorting us on. I remembered late practices full of wind sprints and tipping drills. One night the coach said, "Okay, gang. Let me show you how we're gonna run picks for Biederman."

My old friends, Ethan Saunders, Jim Morrow, Bradley Gamble, and a new guy named Dean ran around the court, passing, cutting, and screening for me. All for me. Set-plays for me to shoot from top of the circle or the left corner, two spots I couldn't miss from if I tried. At home nothing I did was good enough for my father, who was bitter about becoming a tennis coach, or my mother, who was hitting the hard stuff harder and harder, whereas on the linoleum floor of the Windsor Junior High gym I felt like the whole world was weaving to protect me, then release me, and all I had to do was pop my double pump jumper. After practice we would go to a little market down the street. Sometimes I bought paper bags of penny candy for everybody to make sure they didn't think I was getting conceited. Wanting never to eat with my gloomy parents, wanting never to open my books, I walked slowly home in the crusty snow. Still hungry after eating my candy, still wanting something, I was trying to figure out how to live in the gym forever.

I love the cornfields and alfalfa between West Branch and River City, but as I entered town I ran smack into a roadblock on Dubuque. I went east on Jefferson, looking for Gilbert, and wound up on a dirt pavement that culminated in a ditch. Circling back toward the Iowa River, thinking I'd outfox Downtown Refurbishment, I reached a dead end surrounded by jackhammers. What a joke River City has become in the last ten years. What a fucking labyrinth.

We've got a fake old-fashioned ice cream parlor, a special T-shirt joint, a dirty bookstore. Xerox your tax forms at twelve cents a page, muss up your hair for thirty bucks. Tickytack crap. Imported coffee shops. Stallion Medallion booths in every five-and-dime. Designer-jeans places. Designer-sunglasses boutiques. Sunglasses? I can hardly believe it. None of this junk used to be even a possibility.

One mall parking lot looks like a bad imitation of topsoil, and the other looks like stacked caskets. First, Financial Investors, Inc., brought Procter and Gamble into the industrial park at the edge of town. Then K-Mart and Montgomery Ward threw up shopping centers to give Procter and Gamble employees something to do on Sunday. Then the Save Downtown group started paying art students to paint murals on buildings that the Save Downtown people proceeded to raze so they could turn them into travel agencies. Most of the poems Deborah reads me leave the same ear they go in, but I'll always remember this line: "What is beautiful alters." I forget the name of the poet or the poem.

What was beautiful were the Zesto custard stand on Highway 218 and the Quonset huts the college used as dormitories and the gold hot-water tap in the Iowa Memorial Union and the Me Too grocery store on Davenport and the apothecary on

Linn, but what remains are the Dutch white porches of east-side houses with their pyramid supports and square, curtained windows giving onto perfectly perpendicular streets.

On KHAK Johnny Cash's daughter sang about wildlife, making the trashing of River City seem even more offensive. I worked myself up into such a tizzy about it that I drove onto the lot where the mall was going up. At night, with the wind blowing and my high beams on the shell of the Old Capitol Center, the unfinished mall looked not so much anymore like a brontosaurus sinking into tar but exactly like a beached whale sporting dozens of harpoons. Steel jutted out everywhere from the massive shape buried at the bottom of a messy concrete canyon. Johnny Cash's daughter kept singing about the bluebirds in Kentucky or wherever. I darted in and out of the whale's bulging belly in my Bug, dodging huge beams, bouncing over nails and boards, whipping the wheel tighter, getting crazier, blasting the music. I spun out into the cyclone fence, and an amazingly young cop sirened over to me to say, "Excuse me, sir, do we maybe want to be heading home about now?"

No thank you, officer, we don't. We've got business to tend to first. I had to talk to someone other than a twenty-year-old cop wearing a roan-and-gray scarf. It depressed me that I didn't want to be with Deborah. She gives all the Tender Loving Care you could ask for, but she's too calm in a crisis.

I wanted to stay out in the cold night awhile longer and catch pneumonia, do something even if it was wrong. Vicki wasn't at the *Stallion* or in the magazine room of the library, so I drove over to her place on Van Buren and have never been as happy to see her Raleigh five-speed chained to the stairs. It's a black clunker with baskets and a horn. When I see Vicki riding it with her coat flapping in the wind, she reminds me of the wicked witch of the west, only much nicer.

She must have heard the engine clatter to a halt, since she

was standing at the top of the steps. She wagged her pen and said, "Jesus, Albert, what happened?"

"How do you mean?"

"I mean you should see yourself in the mirror. You look like shit."

"Thanks."

"Your forehead's bleeding," she said, leading me down the hall to the bathroom she shares with eight other girls. She was right: my forehead was bleeding and I looked like shit, but I pressed a hot rag to my face and Vicki lent me her brush and put a Band-Aid on the cut, then took me back to her little alcove. What a sweet girl—one earring, a sweat shirt, her hair in her eyes. Who made it so easy for her to be pretty? I love how she doesn't even seem to try.

"So what happened?" she said again when I sat down with her on the floor, which was thick with a million pieces of binder paper scattered between a bowl of popcorn and a pitcher of lemonade. Her place is always a mess—revenge on her parents' too-neat store—but this was awesome.

"I must have hit my head on the dash when I banged into the fence."

"Good, Albert."

"I got so pissed about everything I went driving around the mall like a madman."

"Everything being what?"

"I don't know. A lot of stuff. Downtown. Transcript tampering. Menkus' mother."

Vicki perked up when I mentioned Menkus' mother. She stopped poring over her papers and said, "You went to Chicago and didn't tell me? You knew I wanted to go."

Once you get used to pink lemonade it's pretty good, especially with buttered popcorn.

"The Menkuses live in a very poor section on the south side. All of Belvyn's friends growing up were black, and he became such a good passer because they wouldn't let him play unless he set them up for easy baskets. Isn't that great?"

"It's perfect," she said. Vicki knows a good basketball anec-
dote when she hears one. "But—"

"I'm getting to it. Mrs. Menkus is very, very Catholic. The
whole house is full of Jesuses and crosses and things, then right
in the living room was this huge Betamax."

"If they're so poor, how could they afford a Betamax?"

"Well, that's pretty much what I asked Mrs. Menkus, and
she said her husband's aunt had left them a little money."

"Did you believe her?"

"I don't know. I wanted to."

"Why?"

"I don't think she was totally honest with me, but she was
very sweet. I liked her a lot." Vicki looked almost let down.
"She's proud of her son and loved my piece about him. I mean,
I wasn't totally honest with her, either."

"You didn't lie to her. What else did she say?"

"That was about it. After a while I couldn't bear to listen to
her anymore. I had to get out of there."

Sharing all this innuendo in Vicki's attic suddenly got depressing. Her mattress was thrown against a corner. Not much
heat or any furniture, only Vicki's papers spread out all over
hell. Why did I tell her everything? Because I had to tell
somebody, and she couldn't wait to hear about it.

"So you didn't scope out Rita's lead?"

"No, I did. I went over to Franklin. From the outside it
looked like a detention center. Inside was all right, though.
There was kind of a spirit to the place. The kids didn't seem
defeated yet."

"What did you find?"

"An envelope of fudged transcripts. I snuck into the principal's office during lunch."

"God, you can really hustle when you have to," Vicki said
while stacking a handful of papers and putting them in a green
binder. I assumed they were notes for stories she was working
on. "Who do you think fudged them?"

"I don't know; it could have been anyone. Along with the

91

fake grades were Menkus' GED scores, which clear him of any problems since they make him a high school graduate. To be honest, that was sort of a relief."

"Why?"

"I sat through RSU's whole practice Monday and Tuesday just to watch him throw bounce passes. I'm not sure I want to find out he's a criminal."

"I told you I thought Belvyn was great Thursday night, but my first loyalty sure as hell isn't to protect some—"

"Maybe mine is."

"Then," she said, "you're in the wrong profession."

I didn't like my stringer telling me I should quit work. "Listen, young lady, I was sitting in the Franklin gym and the coach, this great big guy, had those kids—" I made a violent gesture with my hand and tore a couple pages of her notes.

"Goddamnit, Albert."

"I'm sorry." I tried to piece the pages together. "What are you working on, anyway?"

She was writing a paper on Watergate for her journalism class and had taken so many notes from so many different sources, had made so many false starts that she could practically cry or shit. Or both, as she said. She was fifteen when Nixon resigned.

"I can't always keep the names and dates straight," she said, "but I love these two divorced guys not being able to sleep, so they spent nights waking everyone else up. They met that Deep Throat guy in an underground parking lot. I love that. It sounds so perfect, like a movie."

"It was a movie."

"You gotta feel whatever Woodward and Bernstein did was okay because of what they uncovered."

"So the end justifies the means?"

"Oh, right. I forgot. You're Mr. Purity. I'm just saying I want to get at the truth even if the truth is, you know, negative."

"You've taken too many journalism classes. You should be hanging out more at the gym."

"I'm there every day, playing racquetball."

"Not the same," I said and was launching into a tirade against the pseudo-sport of racquetball when Vicki tromped across her papers on the floor, leaned up, and kissed me.

"Albert Biederman," she said.

"Vicki Lynch," I said. I didn't know what else to say. I already felt guilty.

She kissed me again. This time I kissed back. She said, "Albert Biederman, why do you have to make everything, even racquetball, into such a heavy moral issue?"

She smelled like lemonade. Kissing her reminded me of necking in junior high. Her face was as fresh and undefined as an eighth-grader's.

"I don't know," I said, "I don't think I make everything—"

"Everything," she said, pronouncing it slowly so she could kiss me between each syllable.

I was holding her. We hugged, swaying in her cold efficiency. I saw Barry trying to take his urine test and Deborah applying Ko-Rec-Type to page 367 of chapter 9. It was great to touch someone so excited she shuddered. Her lips were thin and had a lot of little cuts in them but were soft as melting candy. I loved kissing her. It was pretty easy just to let it all happen.

"You're wonderful," I said.

"You're so old-fashioned, Albert. I adore that about you. But you're wrong about Menkus."

"Fine," I said, "we'll go to Sioux City, check out his records, dig up what we can, and you'll want to go double by-line with me so you'll land that internship on the *Globe-Democrat*." She couldn't help but laugh since I'd hit it on the button. I didn't mention my own high hopes for Milwaukee. "And if you drop so much as a hint of this in that fucking student rag, I swear to God I'll—"

"Deal," she said, kissing deeper in my mouth.

Vicki tumbled toward the floor, taking me with her. We squeezed each other, talked about going to Sioux City, picked up pieces of her Watergate notes, and laughed at her unreadable handwriting. She was right. I did make a heavy moral issue of everything. I felt guilty enough with her bandage on my forehead and her popcorn in my mouth. I said, "I should go." She slid over on the soft mattress.

I nearly bought out the entire dairy section of Quik-Trip, planning to be a big hit when I walked into the kitchen, but Barry was dead to the world and Deb was driving herself so hard on the end of her book that she'd actually hung up one of those PLEASE DO NOT DISTURB signs. I didn't disturb her.

Thursday morning I worked like a maniac on high school football all-star lists so that I could grab Barry on his way home from school and take him rowing two days earlier than promised. He was walking with a friend who wanted him to come look at pictures of RKS gleaners. It was a tough choice for Bare, and I made it tougher by saying his friend was more than welcome to tag along, but Rich didn't want to, so Barry climbed in with me. Off we headed for the river. A perfect fall day, windy and clear.

As we drove over to the boathouse he acted pretty glum, fiddling with the latch on his lunch pail, giving me one-word answers to how classes went, even letting me play KHAK, which he usually shuts off immediately.

"What's the matter, champ?" I asked.

"Don't call me champ."

"Why not?"

" 'Cause I'm not a champ," he said. "This whole week I got picked last during recess, and today I got hit in the head with the kickball during PE."

"That's okay."

"No, it isn't. I have a headache." He rolled down the window and looked out at all the healthy collegians walking around the river.

"I just meant it doesn't make one bit of difference to me whether you want to be a farmer or an astronaut or whatever. I

94

hope you know Daddy loves you like crazy, no matter what you do."

"Yes, I know Daddy loves me like crazy no matter what I do," he said, mocking the cutesy voice I'd used, which cracked me up but didn't break the mad he had on.

A special report cut in on Merle Haggard's "The Way I Am." Three American nuns were killed in El Salvador.

"That's terrible," I said, "don't you think?"

Barry usually sends out his heart airmail to every victim in the news, but he just shrugged and said he guessed so.

"You're sure you're up for this?" I said, pointing to the rental dock down the way. "Because, I mean, if you'd rather—"

"No, I am." He tugged on my jacket. "I am, Dad. Really. Let's get our paddles." He gave me a big smile that was supposed to show he couldn't wait to be on the water.

The other boaters were a lot better than we were, but we tried to keep rowing and not let that bother us. We drifted past the footbridge, which had an old Indians sticker stuck on its underside, and toward the rickety tracks that carry the Rock Island Railroad. Ducks floated by, looking for handouts, and Barry obliged since he had with him his usual bag of graham crackers and Pepsi. His pants were rolled up to his knees, an orange life preserver was tight around his waist, and the guy at the dock had given him a skipper's cap: he looked serious. Hard by the west bank an elderberry bush snagged us. Barry thought this was so funny he stopped frowning.

"Your side's caught in the tree," he said, munching a graham cracker.

"I know we're caught. Just relax, okay? Don't panic."

He didn't. He no longer seemed to be in a sulk. Sometimes a little exercise and Dad fucking up can work wonders. He slurped his Pepsi and studied the pussy willow along the shore. Then he said, "All you gotta do is lean over and push us away without falling in. You're not afraid, are you, Daddy?"

He was definitely over his depression.

"That's what I was going to do," I said. "The boat might rock a little, but just sit still and you'll be fine."

"Full speed ahead." He saluted.

I stood shakily and the boat rocked. I got us disentangled and at last we were out of shallow water, sailing smoothly downstream.

"Keep paddling now," I said. "It's easy. Right, left. Right, left. All strong strokes. Good."

"Steady as she goes."

Barry didn't come even close to following directions. He had a lazy paddle and he looked at people and bikes on the path, the endless line of emptying elms, the building where the orchestra plays. He thought he saw a professor guy named Harris who'd talked tillage with him at the last Labor Day picnic. It wasn't Harris.

The current was so quiet I was able to spin us about before scudding into the bank. Student boaters seemed to have an eye out for us. I felt happy as a lark, and Barry wasn't far behind.

"This is the life, isn't it, Bare?"

"Yep," he said with his back to me, eating a cracker.

"Beautiful scenery, huh? All the trees and ducks and everything."

"Yep. Too bad you couldn'ta got Marty to come."

"Maybe no corn fields or tractors. It's a different kind of—"

"Look, Daddy, a swan!"

I was sure there weren't any swans in the Iowa River, but what was that thing with white feathers and an orange bill if not a swan? Maybe it was a fraternity prank or someone's pet bird out on a stroll. It circled our boat and barked like a puppy dog, not exactly what I was hoping for. The base of its bill was black and it had a knob on its forehead. I thought about Vicki putting that Band-Aid on my bump.

"Don't, Barry. Don't. Keep your hands to yourself."

He didn't listen. He knew I was too far away to spank him.

"Please, honey, don't feed the swan. He may look nice." I didn't think it even looked all that nice. "But he can get nasty. His mouth has little ridges and he'll bite."

Barry unwrapped a package of graham crackers and threw

the crumbs in the water, which drew the swan with its feathers flapping.

"Okay, fine, you fed him. He's nibbling the crumbs. Now don't stand up."

He stood and rained more crumbs on the swan's neck, then tried to stroke the bird. It arched its feathers over its back and beat its wings, making a weird noise like a broken tennis racquet. Barry squealed, dropped his crackers, and plopped into the cold river. The swan swam away.

Thank God for Red Cross swimming lessons. That was the first thing that came to mind when Barry bobbed to the surface and kicked over to the boat. I hoisted him up. He'd saved himself, and I was proud as a peacock. But now came the crying. His clothes were rags, his shoes were leaky buckets, his tears were just more water dripping out of a drenched body. He shook his shoulders and chattered his teeth. He was really on a jag. Kids are like that when they're seven. All day long is one big roller-coaster ride. It's a miracle they ever make it to eight.

I wrapped him in my jacket and turned the boat around under the railroad tracks to head home. The last thing you want diabetics to do is catch cold. It can become pneumonia in nothing flat.

The current was against us going north and I had to steer away from that moody swan, but I was bent on getting Barry under the electric blanket with hot milk in his hand as soon as possible. I paddled from the stern like a mad Indian, and we made good progress. Barry's paddle was silent. He sat in the middle seat, quivering, crying, staring grimly through the river that had come up to greet him. His snack bag was soaked.

"Hey, Bare, get your goddamn head off your chest and check out the view," I said, trying to bring him back from the dead. We could see the east bank in a way we couldn't coming downstream because of the elms. That didn't do anything to perk up my melancholy baby. As we passed the footbridge and neared the dock, we saw a lot of River Statesmen pretending to study along the grass. All their backpacks, Frisbees, and ten-speed bikes, their books and blankets, all the delicious things they were eating that Barry would never be able to eat, all their colors, all their life pulled Gloomy Gus out of the dumps.

He swung around and said, "Bring us closer to the bank, Daddy," so I did. Feathering the oar to let the boat drift into shallow water, I saw a couple that from afar looked for all the world like Deborah and Menkus. It was around quarter of five. I figured Menkus was at practice and Deb was chained to her carrel in the library. I was imagining things, allowing my guilt to get the best of me. But the current guided the boat, and I paddled closer to the bank to sneak a second look.

"What are we doing, Daddy?"

"We just got caught in a little eddy. We're going to be fine."

Deborah and Menkus were sitting together on a blanket toward the top of the hill. They were so deeply involved in their reading lesson they didn't notice us. Deborah was wearing that camel coat of hers and gray slacks. Menkus was wearing sweats. They were sharing my thermos. I half expected the river to flood or lightning to strike Barry while he was still wet, but nothing like that happened.

"Hey, isn't that Mommy with someone?" Barry shouted. "Hi, Mommy!"

When Deborah waved at us to come over and join them, I felt guiltier than ever for kissing Vicki last night. I smelled her lemonade on me. I let the current carry us and then helped Barry out of the boat onto the bank.

Standing on the grass, wearing a Stallions baseball cap backwards and scratching a week's growth with his outsize claws, Menkus could have been Captain Hook's grandson.

"Hello," I said, getting jerked around in a black shake, all wrist and thumb. Basketball leather had made his hands as rough as tree bark. "I'm the guy who leaves messages on your phone machine, asking you to call back. I don't think we've ever actually met. I'm Albert Biederman, and this is my son—"

"Barry, sweetheart, are you all right?" Deborah asked, getting up from her blanket and wrapping it around him. Deb and Barry cuddled.

"He tried to feed a swan, but it snapped at him and he fell in," I said.

"You shittin' me?" Menkus said. "A fuckin' swan? In this mudbath?"

"It sort of surprised me, too, but there it was, circling our boat, flapping its feathers." I pointed toward the train tracks.

Barry got everyone's sympathy by shaking and shivering. Now that I'd finally met up with Menkus, though, I wanted to stay and talk. Deborah gave Barry some coffee from the thermos.

"Didn't you have practice today?" I asked Menkus.

"The Man cut it short when we hit the skids."

"What's your sense of Hinselwood so far?"

"My sense is he's the Man."

"I bumped into Belvyn running around campus half an hour ago and talked him into getting his reading lab done today so he won't have to come in tomorrow."

"That's nice," I said. I didn't want to hear about reading lab. I wanted to get the scoop on Raeburn and Jumpin' Bean.

"We found out this morning from Martha that Belvyn definitely has dyslexia."

"Huh," I said.

Menkus snorted and pawed the ground, obviously embarrassed.

"Albert, we really should get Barry home," Deb said.

Barry sneezed. I gave him my handkerchief and patted him on the back.

"Now," she said.

"Okay, okay. Two minutes." I turned to Menkus and said, "I'm the guy who wrote that piece about you last Sunday."

"You workin' on another one now, huh?"

"What do you mean?"

"My mom says you were snoopin' around the home front yesterday."

"Hey, I didn't—"

"What's going on here?" Deb said, folding the reading lesson into her satchel.

"I went to Chicago yesterday, you know that," I said to her. "I interviewed Belvyn's mother about his growing up, that's all." I turned to Menkus. Just sitting here, he gave off a certain heat and energy that to me was the sum total of every play still in him waiting to be made. "In order to write a longer story on you I have to do research. Your mom gave me some wonderful stuff. But so far you haven't exactly been bending over backwards to—"

"Look, man," he said, popping to his feet in one move like he was a cat. "Don't crowd extra-close. I got to have room to do my shit. You can't be breathin' down my neck like no fuckin' Columbo."

"Everybody needs their privacy, but, I mean, how about just shootin' the shit over dinner after the game Saturday night? I've never seen a college player set up the court the way you do."

"I can't be rappin' too much with you. I just got to do it."

"That's exactly what your coach at Franklin said."

"Mr. Hoover."

"You really are his prodigy, aren't you?"

"What's that mean, progidy?"

"A prodigy," Deborah said, "is an unusually talented or gifted child. For instance, when Mozart was six—"

"I ain't no child," Menkus said. A lower-class Catholic kid speaking pidgin black to screen out the non-basketball-playing world.

"After the Omaha game, I really went to bat for you with Hinselwood at the press conference. I was trying to explain what you were laying the foundation for, how even if things weren't—"

"I gotta go," he said.

"Okay, Belvyn," Deb said. "I guess we had a pretty good session, then. Bring your paper in Monday, and we'll go over it before class. Good luck against the Jayhawks. Do try to get in some oral reading and spelling practice off the word lists."

"Later, Professor B.," he said, then sprinted off down the path.

"What a strange human being," I said.

"I hate that guy," Barry said.

"Well, that, my two loves," Deborah said, "is why he's so fascinating. He's not a conventionally 'nice' person. He doesn't make small talk. I doubt he would even know how to."

I looked for his shadow in the woods.

"I find it so silly that you went chasing around Chicago for tidbits of information about his past. Who cares about *data*?" She pronounced this last word like it was a social disease contracted abroad.

"I do," I said. "I want to understand who he is."

"He is who he is," Deb said, which was a great deal of help.

"Let's forget about that kid," Barry suggested, sniffling and starting to cough. "He's not even from Iowa."

"The autobiographer becomes every other self except his own living, sleeping, waking self. It's paradoxical, sure, but it's the buried substructure of my book, and working with Belvyn helped me see it."

While she discoursed, the three of us were moving toward her car in the faculty parking lot. I still had to get back to the boat and row it over to the dock. Barry was between us, holding our hands, swinging up in the air on every third or fourth step. We passed Gail Lewis, a frumpish member of the French department, who waved and looked at us with utter envy, thinking we were One Big Happy Family. The blanket was wrapped around Barry's whole body twice and made him appear to be a midget wearing a green coat twelve sizes too big. We kept walking along until we got to the footbridge, where I stopped and tugged on him to come back with me and finish the last leg of our journey. Deb tugged him the other way toward her car.

"Honey, please," she said. "That's crazy. Let me get him home into a hot shower."

She was right, but I wanted him to finish what we'd started, to go the last couple hundred yards so he wouldn't be scared of the Iowa River the rest of his life. He wasn't going to drop dead from a few sneezes.

I tugged and Deborah tugged. At first Barry thought this was really fun, getting stretched out like a scarecrow, but then the ribbon of the blanket unraveled. His arm socket was going to be next. I let go just when Deb gave a yank. Barry went sprawling in the cold grass. We all sat there for a minute, watching the day grow darker, laughing our heads off, not knowing what else to do.

I returned the boat and drove home alone. Barry's lunch pail smelled like sour fruit. KHAK ran a capsule biography of Katie Koob. The information wasn't beside the point, not to me. Far from it. All the facts were like notches connecting us together. We loved who she was and needed to know more. Born and raised in Jessup, she graduated Radcliffe College in Massachusetts, rose through the State Department and Foreign Service with a record shiny and clean as a baby's bottom, and now was surrounded by armed guard in a cell on Death to Carter Avenue.

FIVE

BARRY didn't catch pneumonia. He didn't even take a hot shower or drink hot milk, with honey, or get directly to bed under an electric blanket. By the time I got home he was happily ensconced in the bathtub, and when the phone rang Deborah was happy to hand him over to me since drawing the water and soaping him down had pretty much exhausted her maternal instincts. Adrienne, her pal in American Studies, was coming over in half an hour for dinner and a high-minded huddle about the meaning of life, and Deb had to try reaching Godfather's Pizza before their line became unbreakably busy.

"Shampoo his hair twice and really rinse the soap off, and get him nice and dry with one of those big towels from the hall closet, okay, honey?"

"Extra cheese and pepperoni and sausage," Barry said, which sounded a bit on the salty side, but Barry was calling all the shots tonight.

The water was lukewarm, so I hit the hot knob and the pipes made spitting, coughing sounds like downtown construction on low. It's ridiculous: the bathroom is all marble and tile, all white and ultra-modern and motel-impersonal, but the plumbing in Westgate Court is so new they're still working the kinks out: either it drips bronze guck or knocks back air. Barry sat in the middle of the white bathtub in the white bathroom, playing with his plastic white duck decoys, which were birthday presents last year from Marty. All soaped-up white, he was the Pillsbury Doughboy.

"You really think Marty's great, don't you?" I said.

"Sure, don't you?" He sent the ducks, which had necks disconcertingly like swans', out on a search-and-destroy mission to the far wall of the tub.

"Of course. I think he's God's gift to the human race. It pisses me off, though, whenever you quote him as the ultimate authority on Mother Nature."

"When did I do that?"

"This afternoon on the river. We were having the time of our lives, and then you said it was too bad Marty hadn't come along."

"I'm sorry, Daddy," Barry said, offering me a soapy paw. "It's just that he's into a lot of the outdoor stuff I am and you're not. I think he's neat, but I think you're neat, too. Even neater."

Grudging approval from the butterball. Rinsing the soap off his body, I scrubbed hard. I got the rag good and hot and, wrapping it around my fist, washed under his armpits and behind his ears and in his pale little crotch and between his toes; really gave him a workout. I was goosing him and he giggled, but it also burned and he knew what I was telling him. The ducks came floating back and surrounded him now with their long necks, like a covy waiting for Marty to blast them out of the water. But these weren't swans. This wasn't the Iowa River. Marty wasn't lurking behind a duck blind. This was a warm bath.

"It's funny, isn't it," I said, "how this water's safe and warm and you're happy, and the water you were in an hour ago was totally spooky and mucky and—"

"Yeah, Dad, that's so funny I forgot to laugh."

"No, I just mean you came out of it all really nicely, you swam some good strokes. It was fun rowing. Too bad Rich didn't come along."

"Too bad Marty didn't come along," he said and broke into

104

a big laugh that I wanted a life-size photograph of to keep forever.

"God, I'm hungry, aren't you, Bare?"

"Daddy, what do you call sudsy water with these decoys in it?"

"What do you mean what do you call it?"

"You call it 'duck soap.' "

For the last year Barry's been laboring under the belief that puns are the calling cards of genius whereas I've always looked at them as conversation masturbation, but I laughed and whipped up waves in the bath and congratulated him on being so brilliant. Although it would have been a lot easier for him to stand and turn on the shower nozzle, he insisted on sitting among his ducks while I massaged his scalp with Prell and poured plastic buckets of water over his head. Sitting on the edge of the tub and working up another lather, all I could think about was Deborah and me renting a third-floor walk-up our first year of marriage, having a TV set, a German short-haired pointer named Pete, a fireplace, and a record player, but sensing something missing. Deborah was only a half-time instructor and kept saying she wanted to wait until she got at least a lectureship, and I kept saying we'd be able to afford it easier if Marty ever stepped down and I became editor. Adrienne was still married then, and one night her ten-year-old daughter had a slumber party. For some reason, Deborah and I were over there early the next morning, and we gazed upon a row of beautiful blond girls sleeping in rabbit-feet pajamas with "Satisfaction" playing softly over and over again on the stereo. Absolutely, positively I wanted a kid. I would die if we didn't have a kid. We went home, and the only protection we had was ourselves and each other. Rinsing Barry's head, rubbing his skull, I remembered Deborah trying to read in the hospital the day after Barry was born and, for probably the only time in her life, being totally unable to concentrate, beaming cheek-to-cheek, happy as light, postponing the major existential questions until tomorrow.

On our bedroom phone we have a ridiculously long extension cord because Deb needs to pace while pontificating to her minions. She opened the bathroom door, dragging the phone in, and raised the lines in her forehead while arching her eyebrows, which could mean only one thing: her folks were on the other end. I didn't want to talk to them any more than she did and put the phone down, lifted Barry out of the tub onto the rug, started drying him with a towel Deborah had brought in from the closet, and put the receiver to his ear. He must have sounded like he was talking out of the middle of a Mix-Master.

"Hi," Barry said, giving me a fake smile to show he was hip—he didn't like them, either. "Hello, Grandpap, how are you?" You would think he'd adore his only living grandparents, but Errol Rasnick is an all-business botanist at a leaf lab in Rhinelander, Wisconsin, and Louise is a retired registered nurse who plies Barry with wonderful food, then, worrying about his weight, sends him dietetic fodder I wouldn't visit on Laurel's uncle's pigs. They have formal feelings, these people; they're north-country igloo dwellers and beneath their cool exterior beats the brute heart of a block of ice.

"No, no, I'm okay, really. I just fell in for a second," Barry said. Louise was quizzing him about the rowing accident and telling him he should take a few lessons this spring on the lake behind their house, that he could get in tip-top shape that way, slim down nice and svelte.

"Daddy's a good teacher," he said.

Suddenly I was Joe River Guide. Our shared impatience with them brought us together, and I dried all up and down his plump stumps and flabby chest and mussed up his hair, looking at the needle marks across his ass and arms and thighs and in his stomach, like a map of a million roads never taken because they went nowhere promising. Now that he was learning to do it himself by making a lot of mistakes, there were cross-hatchings and slight puncture wounds and a mutilated battlefield in his upper left arm, where he'd poked so many times there wasn't any space left to grab new skin.

Errol asked him what he wanted for Christmas, and he said a horse. No, really, Errol said, and Barry said a horse.

"It's such a shame we didn't get together for Thanksgiving," Louise said.

"We'll see you at Christmas," Barry said, unconvincingly, and it was almost eerie how easily he imitated our distance toward her parents.

Louise asked him how his friend Laurel was doing, and he used it as another opportunity to say her uncle could get him a horse. It was like Errol and Louise had a list in front of them, and they each had four questions to ask and would check off the covered topics as they went.

Barry said good-bye to them, and the first question Errol asked me was: "So how's the weather in Iowa?"

"Cold," I said.

"But Barry's okay?"

"It's cold generally, but today was mild. Barry's doing great. He's the original comeback kid." I dried him off, wrapped him in a towel, and started combing out his curls, which he resisted, but his hair got full and fluffy and smelled good and it was fun to push it up into a pompadour.

Errol said: "Deborah told us you were applying for a job at the *Journal*. Is that a solid possibility? It would be so great to have you all that close."

"Yes," I said. "I'm one among many right now, but, sure, there's an outside chance. What's your sense of it as a paper?"

"Albert," Louise said, "you know Errol doesn't really read newspapers."

I forgot that the *Journal* had drastically cut back on its chlorophyll coverage.

How's your health? How's your job? How's the weather? How's Barry? How are you treating our baby? How much snow are you getting up there in Wisconsin? With me, too, it's as if twice a month we have half a dozen assigned subjects to touch on, and if one of us ever broke out and started talking about a movie deep inner revelations might blot the horizon. Leaf-formation monographs, nitrogen-exchange experiments, who needs them? Old Man Rasnick studied the soil, Barry revered it.

Deborah, Barry, and I were on the phone so long that Deborah was just calling Godfather's when Adrienne showed up carrying a six-pack of Coke and an extra-large green-pepper pizza. Deborah hadn't told Adrienne, and Adrienne hadn't told Deborah. This kind of thing happens all the time between the two of them, and by now they have come to take it totally for granted. They'll go out and buy the same blouse or be at school and have the same insight. They've convinced me there's nothing bizarre about it; they're just best friends who're on the same wavelength.

"Hi, Barry, hi, Albert," Adrienne said as we came down the stairs. "Wow, Barry, you look squeaky clean. Do I get a hug? No more swan dives into Swan Lake for you, huh, kiddo?"

Swan jokes were wearing real thin with him real fast, so he passed on the hug and went right to work on a can of Coke and the biggest slice of pizza with the heaviest topping.

We sat on the floor against the living room couch, getting involved in serious eating, not talking too much, but vaguely watching the news, which Adrienne insisted on. She feels it's her duty as professor of American Studies to keep up with "popular culture" practically minute by minute. She was at least as interested in the Excedrin commercials as she was in the reports from El Salvador. She takes a tax deduction on her subscription to *People* and quotes from it the way Laurel does from the *Farm Bureau Spokesman,* as wisdom. Her favorite phrase is, "What thou lovest well remains American," and I'm with her all the way: it rings the deep bells in your belly.

"Do you see how they're skirting the possibility that the nuns were CIA operatives?" Adrienne said, pointing at the TV with her Coke. "There was recently an article in *Mother Jones* about Central America, and you wouldn't believe the kind of stuff those goons are up to."

"Ade, that's ridiculous."

"Yeah," Barry said, putting his crust back in the cardboard box, "that's really loony tunes."

"Fine, you guys, ignore reality. Wake up one day with a gun to your head."

Adrienne is from the sixties school of everything-including-the-kitchen-sink conspiracy, although she's an All-American blonde who looks like she once rowed for Ohio State, which she did. She was raised in Columbus, which is apparently a demographer's dream: if the cross section that is Columbus likes a product, it gets sent on to Peoria. She grew up wanting to know what that meant.

Deborah and Adrienne team-teach a course called American Autobiography, and when the news was over they started arguing about what direction they wanted the class to go in.

"I think it should be more about the American mythos."

"I think it should be more about the individual in search of him/herself."

Etc. Terribly fascinating, surprising stuff.

Adrienne was working on an oral history, with photographs, of the transformation of the Coralville Strip from an oasis of family-owned diners into a mile-long line of fast-food ticky-tacks for I-80 truckers. Deborah had finished a rough draft of the last chapter of her book on autobiography. They had exchanged chapters, and this was supposed to be a work session. While Barry and I killed the pizza and looked at the paper and made funny faces, the two of them dug in.

"This section here, Deb—on iconography? Why not include stuff from pop autobiographies: Dick Cavett, Lauren Bacall, Muhammad Ali? They're icons. Open it up a little bit."

"I think the oral history sections would be so much stronger not just as snippets but as real narratives."

They were under the impression they were critiquing each other's work, but it was pretty clear they were telling each other what their own books were about, what they wanted from themselves.

Barry was fading and, before taking him up to bed, I said, "Adrienne, give us a riff on pizza."

"Jesus, Albert, don't interrupt. I was thinking."

Adrienne can take anything you eat or drink or watch or ride or wear or want and tell you how it fits in with the mood of the nation, and it always comes down to the basic fact that what you love well remains American, especially if it's over-priced schlock.

Deborah didn't want Adrienne to lose the thread of their conversation, so Adrienne just said, "I know a man who went to Naples, where the stuff *originated,* and came back saying it couldn't touch Pizza Hut. I think that's really all I need to say."

Barry kissed his mother and Aunt Adrienne good night and thanked Adrienne for the pizza, then trudged upstairs. He freaked out when his Clinitest tab turned orange, making tractor noises and banging corncob magnets against the wall until I showed him how to do it and he took the test over again. It came out beautiful, normal blue-green. After that, he fell asleep.

I lay on the bed and turned pages of the *Register* sports section, looking for something that wasn't an Associated Press wire, a Gannett release, a box score, or a sports information office handout, for something that was ours, that was mine, that had some meat on its bones. The only thing I could think to do was take out my Gousha map of the United States. I didn't like the fact that Deborah's parents would be within easy striking distance, but I loved the wintergreen sound of "Wisconsin" and the way all the roads led down to the yellow light of Milwaukee, like a magnet illustrating the principle of attraction. Milwaukee had its own map, and I got almost turned on by how Lake Michigan cut into the city to make it look like the purple-yellow-and-white dress of a large though lovely woman, as seen from profile. I wanted her with her dress on and dress off. I wanted to lick her all over. Milwaukee is probably not too many people's dream metropolis, but compared to River City right now it was Elysium itself. The bratwurst and the brandy and the famous parks and zoo and the Milwaukee River winding through downtown; home of Golda Meir's high school and college and the country's first kindergarten; the long history of Socialist mayors and all-night bars and worker-owned *Journal. Community,* my Milwaukee brochures shouted out at me, *community.* I desperately wanted to live here and ghostwrite Quinn Buckner's autobiography.

110

Being around Adrienne always makes Deborah horny because she sees herself ten years down the road and doesn't want to be twice divorced, a little heavy, book-obsessed, and chaste not by choice. She recoils, finally, from that closeness with Adrienne and likes to make sure I know she's tighter with me than she is with her. She came to bed hungry as a wolf. She went straight to the bathroom, put in her diaphragm, then crawled on top of me, rubbing my hands over her breasts. I was a horse and she was its rider, posting up and down, whipping her head around, grabbing her stomach as it tightened, growling. Sexy. But, shutting my eyes, I didn't see her. I saw Menkus throw a perfect pass between his legs through heavy traffic.

For the first time since our anniversary I said, "I love you."

"What does that mean?" she said. She was licking her lips, about to come, and wanted a gloss on my statement. Fifty years from now Deb'll be on her deathbed and quibbling about the typeface of her obit headline.

"It means what I said."

"You had a sudden access of feeling because you had a sudden access of blood."

"That's true, but it's not quite as romantic."

"You're sweet, Albert. I love you, too."

She kept posting and I held her high wide hips, bouncing slowly until we were locked in beautiful solid serious rhythm.

Reversal of form: Deborah conked out immediately after coming and I was restless. Even after all the pizza I ate, I was still hungry and wandered around the breakfast room in my bathrobe and slippers. The toaster-oven not only burnt my bagel but also short-circuited a better part of the kitchen due to electronic wizardry performed by our contractors. Goddamn papier-mâché house, goddamn home appliances. I shoveled in some stale doughnuts. It was below freezing out, but I walked onto the porch and looked up at the moon, round and gray as an old dime, then looked down the block to where Laurel's father was adding ten, twenty more feet to his TV aerial and the guy across the street was repaving his driveway. We were all going to get our lives in order by putting in a new sprinkler system.

As a slowly lit Saturday morning rose off the Finkbine golf course, I drove over potholes and around detour signs to the House of Pancakes, where Hinselwood was holding a pre-game press conference during the team breakfast. He did this before all Saturday night home games, and it was not really a press conference so much as a fireside chat with the great man, only no fireside, just Stallion place mats and coffee mugs and that unbeatable IHOP coffee. Hinselwood was named Father of the Year two out of the last three years by the Iowa Jaycees: his perfect, pixie, bejeweled wife ("my number-one assistant"), Elaine, and his Brady Bunch sons, Kurt and Doug, sat at the lead table with him, smiling for the cameras, while he received powderpuff questions from the press corps at the adjacent table and fans at the tables behind us. The fans, most of whom were wearing gray pants and roan shirts and all of whom had paid twenty-five bucks for the privilege of being here, tried to impress him with moderately technical questions about strategy, which rolled off him like water off a duck. The only time I've ever liked him was once on a call-in show when a little girl from Garden Grove wanted to know what his favorite food was, and he got absolutely ga-ga over Breyer's ice cream. He just kept describing how much he anticipated eating it, how happy it made him, how he couldn't get enough of the stuff, and I saw him in the brilliant kitchen of his California-style ranch house at three in the morning in pajamas and robe, hacking away at a box of butter brickle, wrapped securely in sugar shock against the evils of the night. He didn't go off on too many tangents like that, though. His off-the-cuff remarks were about as off-the-cuff as cuff links, and we were supposed to cover this fatuous fund raiser as a news event.

Bruce Ott and Gary Nagel, Hinselwood's assistant coaches, entertained a handsome, dignified-looking, black recruit and his mother at a far booth. The Stallion players sat at three tables, clearly divided into first string, second string, and scrubs. Menkus, Davis, Tomlinson, Gault, and Durland were at a big round table with lots of water pitchers and extra honey and syrup and waitresses buzzing around in orange costumes like bees. At the next table were Rod Williams, a black guard and Norm Nixon look-alike from Washington, D.C., who was a real disappointment; the Kendall twins from Bettendorf, nice guys, big hulking forwards, not great ballplayers; Peter Keil, the make-it-happen sixth man, ugly as sin, a major-league prospect as a second baseman, from Fargo, North Dakota; and Monroe Terry, a talented stick who just hadn't developed yet. Greg Milakovich and Christopher Jenks were all alone at the last table, just trying to get served. Nobody else was talking. They were mainlining carbohydrates.

Hinselwood's major revelation was: "Kansas College has an outstanding lead guard in Tiny Murphy and a front line that really pounds the offensive boards. There is already enough grumbling about our loss to Omaha without self-appointed prophets adding fuel to the fire or us going 0–2, even if this is non-conference. I'll do what I can to avoid the latter if the people in the media"—he stopped dramatically and wagged his ice cream spoon at us—"will try not to fall prey to the former."

Hearty laughs, thanks and good lucks, requests for more hot coffee. He works this crowd like a vaudeville act. Fans brought him caps, hats, buttons, shirts for him to sign. There's not much else to do in River City on winter evenings, and he fills the vacuum nicely because he's such a personable son-ofabitch.

When he was through signing the last wave of autographs, I grabbed him by his four-hundred-dollar lapels and said, "Coach." Publicly, everybody has to call Twinkletoes Coach. His wife and kids surrounded him like the entourage of the Pope, buffering him from the peasants below. "Listen, I'm backgrounding a piece on Menkus, and I was wondering if you could tell me why he went from Franklin to SCTE."

I didn't seriously expect him to answer, but I couldn't resist firing the first shot, letting him know I'd started the hunt.

113

"Oh, for Chrissake," he said, signing a few more autographs on place mats for the IHOP staff. "Are you still on that high horse of yours, Biederman? Looking for every little infraction of the rules? I'll tell you what I've always told you. I'm a basketball coach." Not a den mother. "Not a den mother. We're the last cowboys left, college coaches, out there on the prairie all alone with the unbearable pressure, struggling to survive on guts, luck, and sheer determination, and you want to arrest us for being litterbugs."

He thought this was the wild west and he was wearing a white hat and I was wearing a black hat. Trouble in River City. But I don't wear hats. They make me look twelve years old. "That's a lovely speech," I said. "The only reason I'm not teary-eyed is I'm still hoping to hear an answer to my question."

"If it's really bothering you so much, go get on the next bus to Sioux City and scour around. Sorry, pal, Menkus is clean."

We were standing next to the exit, and his family was already outside in the cold, waiting for him. He left me standing on the welcome mat, chewing my pencil, looking around for Francis, who for the first time in his life had passed up a free meal.

Like conquering heroes through a ravaged village, the Stallions navigated the rubble of downtown toward the field house, which was open until noon for them to shoot free throws and find their range. People honked, waved, yelled, "Kill Kansas." In damp weather the rod in my left hip pinches and I limp a little, so I lagged a block behind their giant strides. I couldn't even stay up with Menkus, who dawdled, truly oblivious to everything including oncoming cars. He was shielded by his weirdness: dangling legs and shoulders like a snapped-stringed marionette, hopping half-steps off the back foot, floating in space, gliding over crumbled concrete in padded Nikes, untouchable, unknowable, seeming never to graze ground, unaware he was wearing skin.

In the locker room I asked Keil what he thought about today's game, and he said, "We'll try hard and hope we win."

I wanted out of River City. I wanted the *Journal* job bad. I went into the weight room and popped right out when a gang of wrestlers, whose combined record was 23–0–2, threatened to beat me up. Karl, the trainer, whapped me in the ass with a towel that had a Stallion monogram and he said, "Come on, Albie, no reporters in here until later tonight, you know that."

I asked Rod Williams what he thought about today's game, and he said, "We'll try hard and hope we win."

Hinselwood had these guys on a six-inch leash. I wanted the *Journal* job bad.

After playing racquetball, some alumni wanted to talk to me about Kansas, but I couldn't think of anything to say because I was sent for a loop by the stink of their bodies and how happy they were, getting rid of their work weeks. The student managers were putting balls on the ball racks and the coaches were behind closed doors, talking X's and O's. I finally found Menkus standing at a urinal. Although he's only an inch and a half taller than I am, I felt like he was looking down at me from a great distance. I had a strong urge to cut open his body and exchange blood cells. For a second our streams criss-crossed. As I faced him to apologize for barging in on his reading lesson the other day, I lost control and had to turn back to the urinal before wetting my pants. He knotted his sweats and flew upstairs to the gym.

Two players each were at four of the baskets, and Menkus was by himself at the far one. The Kendalls. Keil and Tomlinson. Davis-Williams. Terry-Gault. Durland must have gotten lost on the way over, and Malakovich and Jenks were probably still buttering their blueberry pancakes. Nagel, Karl, and the managers fed passes to everyone except Menkus, who was shooting up the net like Bob Pettit's ghost. I was surprised that he wasn't doing any dribbling drills, and I sat in the shadow of a support beam, close enough to the court that I could watch but with my collar pulled up and my hat pulled down so he wouldn't recognize me. Taking notes, my hand got cramps.

On dribble drives from top of the key, every time Menkus fakes left I could swear he's going left, even after faking left and going right ten times in a row. A solid fake is the body lying. Menkus is such a good liar he believes the lie. For a split second he becomes the player doing what is faked, then snaps back.

He is definitely Jumpin' Bean's baby. The brushoff Thursday, now every dunk in the book. It looks like he's going to bang his head against the board, but he slams and just gets out of the way. When you learn how to dunk you're up so high the hardest thing is supposed to be knowing how to land. I would love to feel nothing between myself and the rim. I once jammed a tennis ball on a 9′6″ hoop. Doesn't count.

After shooting, he spreads his fingers in follow-through for the longest time like he's still gripping the ball, holding the whole gym in his mitts. Then he blows on his balled-up fist. He must think "having a hot hand" means your hand is actually hot and he's trying to cool off.

He's hitting at least 80 percent on line-drive jumpers all around the circle. He doesn't waste any time between the front of his hand and the back of the rim. He just drills it dead on. His shot doesn't sound pretty by rippling the net. It takes paint off the hoop. Ka-choong. Ka-choong.

His body is a single motion from his knees to his wrist. He gets a great leap off the floor. Relaxed hips, arched back, squared shoulders, effortless release over his head. He puts so much reverse spin on the ball it returns to his hand. His hand to the hoop through the net to the floor to his hand to the hoop, etc. . . .

When Kansas came onto the court for their warm-ups, most of the River State players left. Menkus and Black Stallion took a breather on the bench, going over the game plan together, and I hurried downstairs to join them.

"So you're not just a sissy playmaker," I said to Menkus. "You can really fill it up."

Menkus liked that, me jiving him. He laughed a little and sucked on a water bottle while BS stared at the rafters. "Hey, man, we're reviewin' strategy. Could you, like—"

"I was just surprised to see Menkus working so hard on his jumper," I said.

"You know Murphy?" Menkus said.

"Tiny Murphy?"

"Charley Murphy," Black Stallion said. Players don't call each other by their nicknames. It's a point of pride. The game's interesting enough without turning the protagonists into cartoon characters.

Menkus said: "Charley hits town last night and *pronto* gives me all kindsa grief how he's gonna deny me the ball, cut off my lanes, clog the middle. He's gone and told—"

"When Murphy sags you'll pop your jumper to bring him out and open up the court."

Cliffie Davis looked at Menkus. Menkus looked at Cliffie Davis. Both of them looked at me.

"All right, man, you hip, you hip," Cliffie said. All three of us tried to high-five, and our hands didn't really connect and there was a self-conscious silence after whooshing.

"You ain't gonna blab this now to nobody," Menkus said.

"No, sir," I said, saluting, and he laughed again that bizarre laugh of his, which sounded like he was clearing his sinuses. Black Stallion didn't like Menkus laughing at my jokes and got up and left without saying good-bye. Never looking down or coming close to losing control, Menkus dribbled the ball in and out of his legs with his left hand. There are at most half a dozen people in the world who can do the same thing, and he made it look about as difficult as rolling dice.

"How do you know Murphy?" I said. He was a black gamma ray who'd been the Jayhawk point guard the last three years and was presently turning handsprings at half-court to get loose.

"Me and Murph been goin' at it since junior high. He can really play some D."

"So you're just gonna stand back and gun?"

"No, man. If I got to pop to open up the lanes, okay, I pop. If the lane opens up, okay, I take it uptown and dish off. You take what's given."

He sat on the bench, dribbling, humming the "I'm just ahammerin'" tune I get whenever I try to phone him. The Stallion student managers were putting the balls on the rack.

"Look, Belvyn, I don't mean to keep hounding you. All you gotta do is clear up a few questions and I'll leave you alone."

"What do you wanna know?"

I seemed to have gotten him at a good time, tired, happy, and maybe two-fifths honest.

"Well, mainly, why you ever went from Chicago to Sioux City."

"'Cause T & E's the easiest fucking school there is."

"Who arranged it for you?"

"Nobody arranged it. I just decided to get go there 'cause I heard it was easy." He was lying.

"Did you actually take the GED's?" I asked.

"Fuck, man, you probably know my social security number, too." He stood, looked at the court and over at me, then stopped dribbling to pick up his sweats, waving off Charles, the woman-breasted manager, who wanted to collect the ball. "How are you ever gonna prove I did one ways or another?"

He laughed his sinuses laugh once more, dribbling away from me toward the steps to the locker room. At the door he pivoted and threw a perfect pass off Murphy's heel so it bounced right back to him, to Menkus. They stared at each other for a long second, pointing spindly fingers.

I hung around for a while, lashing myself for blowing it again by pushing Menkus too far. I figured maybe I should talk to Murphy, but he didn't look like he wanted to talk to anyone about anything, least of all to me about what Menkus was like growing up in the ghetto.

I went back to the office, where the Three Graces were now offering perfectly round and perfectly tasteless oatmeal cookies to anyone quick enough to say hi, bye, thanks, and yum during the half-minute while the Classified terminals kept shorting out. On my way up the stairs, Sabrina, wearing a baseball cap, boots, a leather skirt, and a windbreaker, stood in front of me and said, "Well, what did she say?"

"Who?"

"Deborah." Sabrina has thighs like tree trunks. I read an article once about how rabbits' eyes are poked out in order to get the right tint for makeup. Sabrina looked like, just today, she'd blinded most of the bunnies in Johnston County.

"About what?"

"About reviewing the Shaw."

"The Shah of Iran? I can tell you right now she thinks he's no better than Khomeini, maybe worse."

"Don't be witty, Albert. G. B. Shaw. *Man and Superman.*" She had now helped me off with my sweater and was buttoning my shirt sleeves for me.

"I don't know. I forgot to ask her." I forgot to ask her because I didn't want to hear Deborah draw for the hundredth time her distinction between scholarship and journalism along the lines of which one she thought would last.

"Well, you ask her, my dearest, because it opens Thursday, and I'll be goddamned if I intend to sit through two hours of student actors mouthing platitudes."

Sabrina floated away, and the only other people in on Saturday afternoon were two guys in Editorial still working on what they should say about the water main being fixed. They felt they should say something, but just what they weren't sure. Gratitude? Civic pride? Gratitude and civic pride mixed with a tough note of irritability? These guys weren't members of the Fourth Estate. They were Chamber of Commerce emissaries in disguise, hankering after a good credit rating. All the other departments had broken typewriters, weak light, ratty carpet, used paper cups, tables with two legs. Editorial had a glass partition dividing the Coke machine from the water fountain, famous newspapers and decent terminals sitting on immense oak desks, and in that rarefied atmosphere it was all but impossible to get too terribly excited over the little inconveniences of progress.

Marty had dummied Sunday's paper and left me a piece on wrestling and my usual pro football preview to wrap up. All in all a pretty slow afternoon at the office, and I wasted it, tinkering with Marty's layout, thinking about the game tonight, trying to get in touch with Vicki, then grabbing a bite of artery trouble at Arby's and staring at the stacked caskets of the unfinished parking lot, which helped make downtown look like war-torn France. Where was the war, though? Who were we supposed to be fighting?

I went over to the arena an hour before tip-off. Scalpers were already working the corridors, vultures in raincoats waving blue tickets in your face and shrieking, "I got two for you and your sweetheart." They ought to hang these guys at dawn in front of the trophy case. The ushers adjusted their roan coats and caps, shooing sneaks out of the loges. The vendors greased their grills. Ed unfolded the lower stands. Film crews took turns getting light readings and doing promos. Francis was the only person already ensconced in the TV-radio side of the press balcony, and he sat beneath the KRCX banner, munching a hamburger and malt. I love how all these things happen before every game. None of it changes. Basketball is always played with ten players, two hoops, a round ball, and a clock ticking off time that doesn't exist.

I lifted the headset over Francis' ears and slurped his malt. His engineer wasn't in the building and the pre-game show didn't start for another twenty minutes, so I sat in his color man's seat.

"Francis, in five hundred words or less tell me everything you know about Sioux City Trade and Extension."

"That's where Menkus went to junior college," he said.

"Thanks for the scoop."

"I don't know," he said. "Raeburn probably owns it along with everything else in the state." To Francis, Raeburn is the dark shadow behind every Iowa mystery. Raeburn, who lives twenty miles from River City in Oxford and gets hospital wings named after him. Raeburn, who began his button factory with a three-hundred-dollar investment in 1946 and now owns the soil-transport industry and many of the most lucrative malls in the Midwest. Raeburn, who once wanted to be Yogi Berra. What I didn't understand was why there was always a nearer-to-God-than-thee tone in Francis' voice whenever he mentioned Raeburn.

"I mean, it's practically like you're bragging every time you mention his name. 'I know Raeburn, Raeburn runs the state, therefore I'm Lieutenant Governor.'"

"It's just that, when he and I were living in Des Moines in the sixties, it was phenomenal what he could get his hands on like that." Francis snapped his small, smooth fingers. "It was phenomenal the range of action he controlled, and that was fifteen years ago. Since then it's probably multiplied fifty-fold."

"So you're saying you think he runs SCTE?"

"Not at all. I'm saying he's a genius at making his influence felt without being directly involved."

"So you don't really have anything very specific on—"

"What's the big deal about Sioux City all of a sudden?"

He took his flask out of his pocket and drank a quart or two of the stuff. Puffing out his cheeks and squeezing his Visine eyes, he had never looked so much like a bloated fish. The only way to get any information out of Francis is to be direct, so I told him about the transcripts and the GED's and the Betamax.

"Jesus, Albert, I go on live with this gossip and I win our Johnnie Walker bet before the night's over. Menkus won't be benched. He'll be thrown on his ass out of school."

"But you wouldn't do that because you're such a compassionate fellow, and you know how disappointed you'd be if John Capella ever talked." Francis seduced Capella in a Des Moines hotel room when he was supposed to be running the

121

steeplechase at the 1972 Drake Relays. Capella quit the track team, entered River State business school, and now owns what must be the only gay bar in Iowa. Every year or two he calls me up to work on a who-drops-the-soap-in-the-RSU-shower exposé, then calls the next day to back out. I've never understood this aspect of Francis. It's always just been sort of a locked diary. Sometimes he'll kid me about coming out of the closet and put his hand on my shoulder, but other than that it's his hidden life. I once tried to half ask him why, and he said, "Jesus, Albert, nothing *happened*, nothing went wrong. It's just my sexuality. Why are you heterosexual? No explanations, okay? Accept me or don't accept me." I'd go nuts in River City without Francis, so I accept him. I think it's weird, but I accept him.

"Righto," Francis said, clinking his flask against the back of my chair, then doing something technical with two discs. Even between old friends, especially if one of them is Francis, there are your little trade-offs. "All I know is what you know, and that's how many kids have made the trek from Chicago to Sioux City to River State."

"Yeah," I said. Though it was a migration I'd been dimly aware of for a while, I'd never really pursued it—out of laziness, I guess.

Ed finished dusting the floor and pulling out the stands. A full house was expected and a lot more people were now in their seats, getting greeted by the Stallion. Francis' sound man and color man were making their way toward us.

"SCTE's a two-year rinky-dink at the Nebraska border where inner-city jocks have been going for years to predict out 2.0 GPA's for state colleges. It's a diploma factory. So what? The kids do the work. Maybe Raeburn foots bus fare for some of them so they'll come to River State. That's not against the law."

"Maybe he pays their tuition all the way through."

"Maybe he holds their hand and pats their pillow when they're lonely at night. Albert, I don't know the whole story. I don't care to know the whole story. That well I understand

Raeburn. But if you think you have such a hot lead, run your balls off chasing down transfer credits. I guarantee you no one's going to be interested."

The sound man and color man came up the spiral of stairs to the second-floor platform. I thanked Francis, rearranged his tie, and asked around press row until a guy from Oskaloosa had an all-sports roster I could borrow.

On the football, basketball, baseball, and track teams at State, twenty-nine kids were from Chicago or the Chicago area, which struck me as a lot, but only twelve of them went to Sioux City, and only seven of them, counting Menkus, were stars or even starters. I planned to contact them as soon as possible, especially a junior named Larry Hutchins, who quit the basketball team in October and now was supposedly wandering the stadium, peddling bags of peanuts. Surely he had something to get off his chest.

I should have found the peanut vendor and wrung a confession out of him. Once the game began, though, I forgot about everything except the Murphy-Menkus duel. Murphy never let Menkus get more than one step on him, never came out of the lineup, never even took a deep breath. He stayed down in his crouch and stared at Menkus' stomach. He was at least as quick as Menkus, and the two of them knew each other's moves so completely it was a stalemate, which hurt the Stallions a hell of a lot more than it did Kansas, since River State looked to Menkus as a scorer while Murphy was mainly a defensive whiz. All over the court flew a bat after a body, locked into an angry chase you couldn't have broken up if you'd tried.

The refs were two young scrawny guys, agile and hard-working, who didn't know how to let the players play. The lead official made a call midway through the first half that put Kansas in position to go up by eleven. Hinselwood threw his program to the floor, nearly getting a technical, and called time-out before the free throw. Ott looked worried and explained what was going wrong to Rod Williams, who didn't care, and Nagel shouted at Ben, the unflabby student manager, to provide water bottles as if the stuff came directly from the fountain of youth. Karl, the trainer, helped Peter Keil and Monroe Terry off with their sweats. Stick Keil on Murphy and hope that took away some of his energy at the other end. Get Terry in for Durland and let him take that nice little turnaround from ten to open things up.

Good ideas, but they didn't work because, though Menkus scored garbage points and a few baskets off the break, Murphy definitely shut him off, which controlled the flow. What was even more surprising was that Menkus refused to take the long shots Murphy gave him and instead forced passes into the middle that just weren't there. The margin at the half was still eleven.

The Donna Summer record for the Mares' dance routine kept skipping. The Stallion stood to greet the president of RSU, smarmy elegance personified, and tripped over his own tail. A poster urging the Stallions to trounce the Jayhawks was misspelled and another one was torn. The roan and gray threads worn by the capacity crowd, which usually look like battle flags, conveyed dried blood and ancient oatmeal. The only happy people were the hundred visitors from Lawrence toasting one another and Happy, who walked around taking pictures of unhappy faces.

With eight minutes left in the game River State still hadn't gotten it below ten, the magic number for a run, and Murphy, feeling cocky, started harassing his old pal. In his heart of hearts, Menkus is a gentle soul who a long time ago got things confused and so takes the slightest touch as a shove. *I'm dry ice*, should read a sign taped across his forehead, *but feel the fire*. Or, as Menkus would spell it, *I'm bry ice, dut feel the firs*. "Don't mess with *me*, motherfucker" is the way they put it at Franklin Vocational.

Murphy messed with him. He came in too tight, breathed on his neck before a free throw, followed him halfway into the huddle of a twenty-second injury timeout Hinselwood called to give Terry a chance to catch his wind. Jabbing his finger at him, taunting him, Tiny probably called Menkus a candy-assed showdog who hadn't shown Mr. Murphy shit. And that was about all she wrote for Mr. Murphy, because no one in his right mind should tell that to Belvyn Menkus. The late-night announcer on KHAK likes to say there's a part in every country song where the train arrives, and I know what he means. Mr. Murphy's train just arrived at gate six.

Menkus stopped trying to force the ball into the middle and took Tiny to the hole. Menkus didn't even pretend to show any interest in working the weave with Cliffie or running Teakwood's offense or getting the ball into Durland or Gault to see what they could do against Kansas' smaller front line. Cliffie called for the ball, clapping, and Gault whapped Menkus upside the head when he was wide open in the corner off a setplay, and Menkus didn't give it up. For once and once only Menkus went all out for himself, and I got goosebumps watching the team game of all team games get back to basics, the team player of all team players go one-on-five.

The fans, who had been sitting on their hands all afternoon, responded with passion. The English department secretary let loose with a wild warbling noise, and the woman next to her, who had incredible breasts, bounced up and down with a banner. The Battalion sounded their kazoo charge and got VIP's boogying with dirt farmers, local yokels high-fiving physics profs. Menkus went down deep, faking until Murphy either had to foul or concede the bucket. He made Murphy guard him twenty-seven feet away, because Menkus wasn't even nicking iron, and when Murphy came outside Menkus took power to the hoop, freeing the key, as he had predicted, for Gault, Tomlinson, Durland, Davis.

With two minutes left and the score tied, Menkus was the lone defender against a break. He feinted left, sprang right, intercepted the pass, went once between his legs, reverse spun to avoid Murphy, and lobbed the ball the length of the floor, blind and behind his back, to Tomlinson, who no one but Menkus could possibly have known was standing alone at the other end. Tomlinson blew the one-footer, and the Jayhawk small forward was going lackadaisically to the glass when Menkus jumped over him and jammed the rebound with his left hand. He landed in the lap of a paraplegic who, so far from being frightened, applauded with delight. The only thing left for Menkus to do was drag cripples out of their wheelchairs and have them do a jig.

Murphy fouled out with eighteen seconds left and the Stallions ahead by six. The Stallion Battalion, ever courteous, booed him off the floor for having tried so hard, but he didn't mind the multitude and strode straight to center court, where he wrapped his wiry, chocolate arms around Menkus, mussing up the white boy's fake Afro. He gave Menkus a bear hug. The Stallion Battalion, raining pom-poms, thought it was an empty gesture offered too late. I didn't. I liked seeing Menkus and Murphy together as the house lights came up and people were starting to leave. Going at it for two hours through each other, utterly in love with the game of basketball, they were more closely connected than anyone else in the building. You could just feel all the games they'd been in together before. Menkus' moves were old skin to Murphy, they were part of him. I was so happy for Menkus I shouted his name louder and louder, over and over again, and a fat farmer in overalls yelled down to me, "Yeah, yeah, we know that's Menkus. Take a seat, you idiot."

I was too excited to sit. While Menkus played keep-away with Black Stallion and ran circles around the Kansas press, calling out directions, pointing, permitting himself a half-smile, I walked across the balcony to go rub it in to Marty while the rubbing was good.

He was whistling, waving his hunting hat, clutching his heart through his Pendleton shirt, and I thought: this is it. The excitement finally got to him, the myocardial infarction's burning his right arm, he should never have left What Cheer, he should have been a fur trapper. He'd seen me coming, though, and was putting me on because he thinks I worry about him too much. A laugh a minute, that Marty.

He shot me in the stomach with his finger and said, "You

were right about this kid all along. How did you know? That's got to be the best seven minutes I've ever seen out of a River State guard."

"That one move," I said, "where he had Murphy pinned to him and used Murphy's own body against—"

"That fadeaway from the far left corner! Faking to Black Stallion on top, going up, turning his body all at once. Shades of Biederman's high school days at West Des Moines, huh?"

"Marty, please," I said, but it was good to hear him expressing the kind of enthusiasm for basketball he usually reserved for dead deer. The crowd, led by the Battalion, gleefully counted off the clock while Menkus dribbled around and finally got fouled with a few seconds left. "How about that blind pass to Tomlinson and then racing all the way down to dunk?"

"You rascal, you," he said, popping a pill. "I bet you wrote that piece on his passing just to get him to limber up his shooting arm."

"He was great against Murphy but, when he has his whole game together and everyone else is plugged into it, I promise you tonight'll look like an off night."

"That I doubt," he said, receiving congratulations from sloppy drunks and Kansas reporters for the win. "But you're the basketball analyst. You can get the story in by eleven, can't you?"

"Sure," I said. "I just have to hit the locker room, then I'll type it up and take it over. Who's working the desk?"

"That Vicki girl of yours. She's a good little stringer. She's patching together some late scores and leaving you fourteen inches on the front page."

I chuckled, thinking Marty was making a joke, but he wasn't. He didn't get it, I stopped chuckling, and we stared at each other for an endless moment, smiling like baboons.

"What's the first thing you think of when I mention Sioux City?" I asked him.

Menkus made his free throws. The game was over. The roan-and-gray fans filed out, exhilarated and exhausted. The band played the Stallion song:

RSU
For me and you—
Can do, can do!
Be true for you!
Whoo, whoo, whoo!

It's an old song they've never updated. A high school kid with terrible acne asked Menkus for an autograph and, when he shook him off, I thought maybe the standard one-liner was literally true for Menkus: he could do everything with a basketball except autograph it. He ducked into the locker room, and I wanted to catch him before he gave me the slip again.

"I think of quail," Marty said, shooting an old Indians pennant with his hand.

"Quail?"

"Sioux City quail are one of the most difficult birds to bag in North America. Barry and I should go on a hunt together sometime; I think he'd love it."

"That's all that comes to mind?"

He studied his hiking boots for inspiration and said, "I'm afraid so. Why?"

"I asked Francis the same question, and he said Raeburn."

"Raeburn?"

"That SCTE had probably felt the force of Raeburn's muscle like every other institution of higher education in the state."

"I'm sure it has, but do you really care? The less I know about all that claptrap and chicanery, the happier I am."

"Ignorance is bliss?"

"Never mind ignorance. Bliss is quail season."

I couldn't say I didn't wish I agreed with him. I envied him his wide world of wilderness, against which everything else measured up short. He unleashed a long lecture on how strangely I'd been acting since I began researching the Menkus piece, warning me to make my game story not just about Menkus but about the rest of the fellas, too, who scored a combined total of twenty points. He also said the article should be upbeat and have lots of positive observations concerning Hinselwood. However, as I tried to explain, Hinselhide's strategy had got thrown out with the bathwater. Menkus completely ignored the game plan, and Hinselwood appeared to let him: for the first time, Coach sacrificed symmetry in exchange for the excitement, not to mention the triumph of one boy, all alone, juking the opposition.

I told Marty toodaloo. I had to get into the locker room before it emptied and went pushing through other reporters, photographers, friends and family of the players, through singed rubber, sweat, steam clouds from the shower, soaked wool and, above all, the sweet smell of bodies used to their limit. I slapped Black Stallion five, Gault ten, and the Kendall twins a total of twenty. I sensed the tentative happiness of a promising pre-conference win. I couldn't find Menkus anywhere. Finally I opened the door to the laundry room, where he sat on top of a towel bin with his head in his hands.

"Tough night, I know. Only thirty-eight points. It's all part of the pain of growing up."

"Fuck you, you wise-ass motherfucker. I thought you dug my activity. That wasn't ball. That was bullshit. If that's all it was, I could beat off by myself. No one knows what my shit's about."

Then he shut the door on me and locked it. No matter what he thought, I did know what his shit was about. I once had the same dream—creating forty minutes of basketball so electric the court exploded. I believed in this kid. But on Monday I planned to go Sioux City quail hunting.

SIX

I TYPED up the story, took it over to the office, and gave it to Vicki, who set it on the computer without saying a word. There were only a couple lights on and absolutely no one else around except the kid janitor, who was making as much noise as he could emptying baskets at the far end of the office and playing the radio. You couldn't see the other desks and general dinginess very well, and you could pretend your co-workers were brave souls blowing the clear clarion of truth. I love the *Register* late at night, when it feels like a real newspaper.

Vicki and I had no idea how to act around each other. She didn't want to talk about why she wasn't talking. I thought maybe she was trying to demonstrate how businesslike she could be, since I was supposed to write a recommendation for her to get into journalism school in case she didn't get the job at the *St. Louis Globe-Democrat*.

"Are you pissed about pulling desk duty alone Saturday night?" I asked.

No answer.

"Are you pissed about something I did Wednesday?"

Ditto.

The kid janitor, pouring the garbage into a larger bin, dropped a wastebasket, and, when I looked over, he said,

"Fuck you, you asshole, mind your own beeswax," turning up his radio just a tad so we could get all of Genesis.

"Do you want to go have a drink or a burger at Phil's?"

"No. I've got a date with a boy my own age who rings the phone off the fucking hook, but thank you, anyway, Mr. Biederman."

"The last three days you've been unreachable."

She preferred to pout, and, frankly, I was too tired to get into it. I wanted to go home and watch Barry's stomach rise and fall, listen to Deborah talk about books until I was dreaming. I helped Vicki on with her coat and scarf and walked her to her bike, which was chained to the handrail.

"See you later," I said in a voice cold as the night. Two can play the distance game.

Both Deborah and Barry were asleep. Freezing rain fell all night and into mid-morning. Written to deadline, my game story was pretty uninspired. Plus, I was trying to save up my Menkus impressions for the longer article. The only thing worth reading in the Sunday paper was a piece on Katie Koob's religious conversion. Her father said she was born again during college and he felt she'd have broken down in the first couple months without Christ. Her mother imagined her really boosting everyone's spirits by reading Acts of the Apostles to the other hostages. Laurel came over to discuss a new horse-buying scheme with Barry while Deborah curled up with one of those TV shows I've never been able to watch, where a gang of reporters bushwhack a public official and ask him why he's botched his job so bad.

"Verbal crises are always so revealing," Deb said.

Tell that to the poor schnook who's fielding questions.

With the space heater on the blink, the den was even colder than usual, but I needed privacy to talk to Vicki, so I put on a sweater and shut the door. She wasn't in at the *Stallion* or at her place. I called Celia, her best friend, who gave her to me.

131

"Hey," I said. "The Sunday page looks great. You did a good job."

"Gee, thanks, boss."

"What's the matter with you? What's going on?"

"I can't talk now, Albert."

"Tell Celia to leave the room for five minutes."

Even before Vicki asked her, Celia was gone and took her screaming radio with her. I liked that girl.

"So what do you want to talk about?" Vicki asked.

"I want to know what was going on last night and why you're acting so nasty now."

"You honestly don't know?"

Upstairs, it sounded like Laurel was riding Barry around the room to show him how much fun it would be to have your own Apaloosa.

"No."

"Well, how would you like it if someone dumped on you practically in the middle of making out? What would you think?"

"I couldn't go through with it Wednesday night. I'm sorry. I wasn't ready. I thought that was obvious."

"Why didn't you at least call to explain?"

"I did call, but you were never there. You could have called me."

"Yeah, and have your wife answer."

I walked over to the door to make sure the *Issues and Answers* idiocy was still going on in the living room. "Listen," I said, "what do you know about Sioux City?"

"It's a fucking junkyard," she said like a no-nonsense cashier, which made me want her again.

"No, I mean Sioux City T and E, where Menkus went to school."

"I don't know," she said. "It's a little cow college in the middle of nowhere. You're just trying to change the topic."

I told her what Francis said and what I suspected about SCTE and my plans to go check it out.

"I knew Sioux City wasn't exactly Harvard, but I never heard it was a diploma factory," she said.

I suggested we divide my list of Chicago natives and give them a ring. She had to finish her Watergate paper and get some swimming copy into the *Stallion* by tonight, she was still sore at me for slinking away, but she was a sucker for a scoop and said, "Okay, let's do it."

We each made our calls. The only one who was at all receptive was Larry Hutchins, the peanut vendor and ex-basketball player, who agreed to meet Vicki for lunch on Friday.

"He had the deepest, calmest, sexiest voice I've ever heard in my life," she said, seeing if she could get a rise out of me. I didn't say anything. I heard Deborah curse whatever politician had made the mistake of showing up for *Issues and Answers,* and I heard Laurel whinny. "So, anyway, in the meantime, let's go to SCTE and case the joint," she added, whispering, like she assumed Deborah was tugging on the telephone.

On such late notice it was hard to convince Marty to let me go tomorrow, especially after he'd just bawled me out for letting my work slide, but he loved my story on the Kansas game and felt he owed me a few for all the times I'd covered for him when he goes hunting or into the hospital for tests. He warned me I wouldn't have another full day off nearly until Christmas. Then, too, Vicki hated to cut Poli Sci, Lit, and History. I really had to twist her arm to get her to come. Sioux City's three hundred miles away and we wanted to leave around dawn. Sunday night I went to bed early.

It's not that much farther from River City to Sioux City than it is to Chicago. But at five in the morning, with nothing between you and the open road, it feels like forever. Moving east into urban blight, your pulse picks up and your field of vision just naturally narrows, whereas when you head toward Sioux City the sunshine is rising in your rearview mirror. All you really need is automatic pilot and a snooze alarm. Vicki was sound asleep, snoring softly, snapping her head up and back in my heavy parka.

Skate west on 80. Everything feels larger and open-skied. You smell pigs stinking up the joint. In New York and Virginia, Brooklyn and Williamsburg may be famous historical cities, but between the Amana Colonies and Newton we passed a Brooklyn and a Williamsburg that are prosperous little farm towns in their own right. Going on, getting deeper into the fertile land, I felt like I was coming to the edge of the map; at some point the highway was going to drop off into horizon. I looked out in the blueing morning at stalks of corn sticking up like a million busted pencils, billboards advertising milling equipment and fertilizer, farmhouses and cottonwoods and sheep in the semidarkness. All along the road I saw Menkus reaching out that cleaver of his to stop a three-on-one break and go the other way with a blind pass, sprint downcourt, and dunk.

Acres and acres stretched out in front of my headlights. Vicki's mouth pressed against the window. We passed Altoona, population 4,141, and the Training School for Girls, whose training for what I didn't want to even think about. At six I was hungry but wanted to get to Sioux City, so we sailed by a very good twenty-four-hour dive I know in West Des Moines, my old stomping grounds.

River City is street repair and parking ramps. This was the land. It was part of me and part of Vicki, too. Her face on the glass in the cold sun was more than just sharp and pretty. It was absolutely natural, like the side view of a deer. Vicki's not a morning person, but I couldn't help it: I woke her up.

"What?" she said, groaning. "Are we there?"

"No, still quite a ways to go, but I was just thinking—"

"I was having the most delicious dream about Jeb Magruder, that really handsome Watergate guy."

"I was thinking about how you and I are both from Des Moines."

"Death Moans."

"I mean, this is our earth, this is our soil."

"This is a crock of shit." She smiled and tried to bat her eyes alive. "You're romantic about farm stuff because your father was a tennis player and your mother sold tract houses. My parents actually have to deal with it all. To them it's just agribusiness, okay?"

"Okay," I said.

"Good night, Albert, I'm going back to bed."

She played with the heater and shuddered. I made my coat into a better blanket for her. Turned toward the sun, she was asleep again before we reached Ankeny. For some people the ping of a VW motor is like counting sheep.

Going north on 35. The National Animal Disease Center, which smelled like it was trying to go worldwide. Driving across Iowa is a lot more fun than driving to Chicago. You're out here with livestock and manure, and your nose can't help get involved. At the 35/20 junction near Webster, I pulled over to consult my AAA guide, where I discovered Fort Dodge is a world leader in gypsum. More fields, more farms, more equipment and animals as the sun came up and stayed up in the clear sky covering the country. Barry would have been in seventh heaven. There were a few more cars on the road now to keep us company, and I rattled on at fifty-eight mph. The Bug can't go any faster.

As we approached Sioux City, signs gathered: eighty-five thousand people, point of convergence for the Big Sioux and Missouri Rivers, tons of trade, the place Vicki Lynch called a fucking junkyard, etc., etc. The grave of Indian chief War Eagle was on West Fourth Street. The Floyd Monument, marking the burial place of the only member of the Lewis and Clark Expedition to lose his life during the journey, was at the top of Floyd's Bluff. I wrote things down in my notepad to add a touch of local color when I discussed Menkus' junior college days, but I didn't come here to grave-rob or statue-hop. Besides, the sign that nearly took the wheel out of my hands and sent the car careening into a gulley came just a few miles outside city limits.

SIOUX CITY TRADE AND EXTENSION
NEXT EXIT
HOME OF THE BRAVES

Well, okay, some honest-to-goodness sports enthusiasm, and they hadn't changed their nickname to the Nags. Maybe people here had appreciated what Menkus' shit was about better than RSU boosters did. I saw signs similar to the first one, and they were such a shock to my system that the heater suddenly exploded on.

"What was that?" Vicki said, popping awake.

"The heater working now that we're here. Don't go back to sleep. We've already had signs welcoming us to the home of the SCTE Braves."

"Tell me you're kidding."

"No," I said. "Keep your eyes peeled. There's probably a Menkus statue coming up on the left next to the grave of Indian chief War Eagle."

Vicki probably thought she was still dreaming. I took the turn and got off the ramp, but we weren't a mile up the road, heading for Sioux City, when a rash of new signs ushered us into a side path toward the college. We'd made good time. It was quarter of twelve. I drove down the narrow street, which was lined by huge cedars, into an area that promised to open up into an academic retreat. When we got to the end of the road we were disappointed. Stunned is more like it. There was no college.

"What the fuck is this?" Vicki asked.

My sentiments exactly.

No campus, save one building. No student union. And almost all the people walking around looked older than college students. With some exceptions, they could clearly be divided into businessmen or carpenters. I couldn't imagine Menkus as either.

136

"Well, it is Trade and Extension," Vicki said, snapping pictures of the parking lot with her Instamatic. "Half these guys must be taking biz courses from Adult extension, and the other half are learning how to build stuff."

The parking lot was ringed by a barbed-wire fence, beyond which were bare radials, garbage cans, chunks of glass. The cars tended to divide along the same lines as the people, beaten-up trucks with tools in the back or '78 Buicks. The one building was four floors, a square monstrosity that looked like someone's lost wedding cake set down among the weeds, as white as snow. No windows to the thing and no doors, either, that we could find.

Vicki had an idea. "Maybe this is like the registrar's office or something."

I gave her a funny look.

"Where they add up everyone's GPA and send out U-bills," she said. "Maybe the real action's closer to town."

I hoped so, since this was such a sorry excuse for a university. A drab building, a parking lot, and a flag whipping in the wind. We wandered around, trying to figure the place out.

"If Menkus actually went to school here, he probably felt right at home," I said.

"What's that supposed to mean?" Vicki took a picture of litter on the gravel.

"Well, it's just like Franklin. No-frills education. A vertical building and a lot of broken glass."

"Desolation city."

I wondered where the gym was. All the way around back, we finally discovered a door and decided we better go in. I expected bats to fly out and maybe a dead body to land on my shoes. But the inside of the wedding cake resembled nothing so much as a medical complex for dentists.

A linoleum floor stretched down the hall. Fake-brass knobs were set on fake-oak doors that stood one after another, all very close, not like classes but offices. Twenty feet to our left hung a bulletin board directory.

FIRST FLOOR—EXTENSION DIVISION
SECOND FLOOR—BUSINESS OFFICE
THIRD FLOOR—TRADE DIVISION
FOURTH FLOOR—NIGHT SCHOOL

"What do you think?" I said.

Vicki shrugged and took a picture of it.

Looking for stairs or an elevator, we heard a lot of pounding away at typewriters, adding machines, copiers, terminals. The first floor must have been owned by IBM. At the other end of the hall we found cement steps spaced widely apart, daring us to tumble into oblivion.

"Oh, Albert," Vicki said, holding onto my arm, "this is so weird. It really is."

I figured the second floor was a good place to start because it was a business office and a lot of secretaries were running around, but Vicki said she had a hunch about the night school and I don't monkey with her hunches, so we kept climbing stairs. She very nearly slipped going from the second to the third floor, where the trade school was producing a real racket. Metal and wood got hammered, glass got blown, lathes were spinning. If you hung around long enough, you'd pick up everything you ever wanted in the way of totally useless objects.

On the fourth floor the walls were cracked, the tile was gummy, every door we tried was locked shut, and the only light came from a room at the far end of the hall.

"Do you think—" Vicki started to say.

"I think you should put that camera in your purse and we should see what's going on in that room."

"This is spooky."

"There's nothing spooky about it," I said. "This is a night school and it's daytime. The ghosts don't come out until much later."

"Very funny," she said and attempted a laugh.

The door swung open. Behind it, smiling, Midwestern-pretty, stood a woman wearing a red dress and high heels and brunette hair in a bun. To me she looked a little like Jane Pauley without the intelligence. Her neck was the swanny kind grown men kill for. Boxes were stacked in a twelve-foot-by-twelve-foot space that made the other rooms we'd seen seem like bridal suites at the Ritz. Cabinet drawers and loose papers covered the floor, and in the middle of the mess was a frail little fellow crawling on hands and knees, wearing wire-rim glasses, smoking a Camel Light, and carrying a calculator in his coat pocket. He had a rabbit's eyes and ears.

"Hello, is there something we can do for you?" the woman in the red dress asked with a Nebraska accent.

"We're looking for the night school," I said.

"Well, this is it."

"This is it?" Vicki said.

"This is the office," she said. "Kind of makeshift, huh? My husband and I are leaving next week. We were just packing up."

A green binder slipped through the frail fellow's hands. It flapped its wings, landed on its metal folders, and papers splattered up like feathers. My strong first impression was that he was at the very least overworked and probably delirious. "I'm Jeffrey Fischer and this is my wife, Jo," he said.

"Hi," I said. "My name's Albert Biederman and this is Vicki Lynch, who works with me."

"Hi," Vicki said as we inched into the room.

"Hi," Jo said.

"Hello," Fischer said, being dignified. Handshakes and happy faces. What was this, couples meeting at a picnic? I figured the Fischers were stalling.

"Have a seat, you two," Jo said.

Vicki and I sat on a box that looked sturdy and immediately sank under our weight.

"So what can I do for you guys? Did you want to sign up for next semester's night school?" Jo asked.

"No, we were just looking for some information."

"What kind of business are you in, Mr. Biederman?"

"The newspaper business."

No response from them one way or another, no nothing.

"You realize," Fischer said, "what SCTE night school is, don't you?"

"No, not really."

Fischer looked at Jo, then said, "For the last five years we've been in charge of it. It's an outreach program for local tradesmen and businessmen, as an adjunct of T and E. Learn a trade, learn a little more about the business world. Adult education. That kind of thing." He was throwing up smoke screens as transparent as glass.

Vicki and I just sat there, sinking deeper into the collapsing box.

"On Friday we're leaving for Bellingham, Washington," Jo said. "I got a deanship at a girls' boarding school, and it sounds like something might open up for Jeffrey, too."

"God, way to go," Vicki said, fingering the camera in her purse. "I hear it's so hard to get any sort of teaching job these days."

"What is all this stuff?" I asked.

"Well, like Jo said, we were just packing up our boxes and papers. The semester, such as it is, finished Friday. Your timing is uncanny."

"What do you have to do to graduate around here?" Vicki asked, subtle as a train wreck as always.

"Well, the kids in night school take classes downstairs either in the Trade division or the Extension division, which is mainly business. Some of the trade courses are admittedly pretty easy, and if you can handle power tools you can usually do all right. Some of the extension classes are fairly challenging, though. Would you like to take a prospectus?"

"No, not really. You see, we're reporters for the *River City Register*, and we're backgrounding some information on Belvyn Menkus, who was enrolled here '78–'80. We were curious what kind of student he was and hoping we could take a look at his records. Was Menkus enrolled in the night school?"

"I guess so."

"It was only last year, wasn't it?"

"Yes, I suppose he was enrolled here last year. I really can't know every student as well as I'd like." I didn't believe a word he said, but he had down a certain gobbledygook style.

He climbed across the floor to the other side of the room, where we were sitting, then walked into the hallway. The three of us followed him and watched him stare out the window. He jabbed his finger against the pane and, surveying the parking lot four floors down, said, "That was supposed to grow into a real campus. A community college that could burgeon. New buildings, new departments, dormitories. But none of it ever happened. The money wasn't there, and Jo and I got buried in the night school."

It was a sob story, and Vicki wasn't moved. The room was cold. I put my sweater back on. Fischer kept talking: "We hoped things would get better, but they never did, did they, honey?"

"No, they didn't," Jo said, looking with him out the window at the weeds and cars.

"I don't know. Maybe we were naive. Maybe we should never have expected money to get pumped into the Extension division."

"Who did you expect to be the major pumper?" I said.

"I'm sorry?" Fischer said.

"Who did you think would pour money into the Extension division?"

"Oh, you know, various sources—government grants, state and local things, foundations, private donors."

"Like Raeburn?"

"Calvin Raeburn?"

"Yes, where do you know him from?"

"He's on the SCTE board of directors."

"Is he also a big contributor?" Vicki asked.

"That we wouldn't know," Jo said.

She was lying. I nodded and made a million mental notes with my mental pencil. All of us walked back slowly to the papers and boxes in the one-room night school. The Fischers didn't say anything for a while. They had a regular Abbott and Costello act going here.

I threw out: "What you said earlier might explain why Menkus was such a gunner here."

"Jeffrey mentioned nothing about crime," Jo said.

Vicki cringed.

"No, I mean gunner on the basketball court. Why he shot the ball so much the two years he played for SCTE."

"I don't think I follow you," Fischer said.

"He couldn't have had too many very good players to pass to, with a bunch of house painters and insurance salesmen making up the student body."

"I'm starting to catch a sarcastic tint to your comments, Albert."

"Well, you've got to admit there have been a lot of kids here from Chicago, athletes who use this place to go on to four-year schools."

"There are always a dozen or so jocks getting credit from Extension, which has been weakening somewhat and which, frankly, is part of why we're leaving. Standards have really eroded here, but everybody pays tuition. Everybody does the required work even if the requirements have become less than stringent."

He was about nine yards ahead of me, issuing denials for accusations I hadn't formulated yet in my own mind. If he was in a talkative mood, I had more questions to ask him. "Two things I've been curious about for a long time is why SCTE isn't in a league and why it plays so many night games. There's obviously no gym here, right?"

"Occasionally they play at Sioux City Convention Center," Fischer said.

"That's true," Vicki said and got a look from Fischer because he didn't think he needed confirmation. He didn't frighten her off. She came right back with our final question. "There isn't any chance, is there, we could take a look at Belvyn's transcripts?"

The Fischers glanced at each other again, then Jeffrey

142

spread his arms and knocked the back of his hand into an adding machine that was sitting on top of a drawer of desk supplies.

"The papers from the past three years are on the floor and Menkus' grades should be here somewhere, but I can assure you his transcripts are completely unremarkable—passing grades, no great ups or downs—and would take at least forty-eight hours to find."

"Did anyone here even know he has dyslexia?" I asked.

"He does?" Vicki said.

"Yes, and no one gave him any remedial help with it at T and E, did they?"

"This isn't that kind of school," Fischer said, "and, as I told you, I never had the kind of one-to-one contact with the students I would have liked."

"Listen, if we come across something we'll send it to you, okay?" Jo said.

"Hey, excellent," Vicki said.

By now we both knew we were being had, and so we told them how much we appreciated their time. I shook his hand, pumped it, gave him my card, and encouraged him to call if he remembered any Menkus anecdotes he wanted to share with the public. I shook Jo's pretty little hand. Vicki hugged Jo and congratulated her again about the Bellingham deanship, then held Fischer's hand.

They invited us to have lunch with them in town and I was tempted on account of starvation, but Vicki was visibly disgusted and said we had to get back for a game at six, which was untrue.

I turned on the heater and radio, both of which come in better close to big cities, and Vicki and I sat in the car for a while, writing down to ourselves everything we could think of that the Fischers had said. We pretty much agreed on what we'd heard, with Vicki emphasizing a little more than I did the depravity of the place.

"I'm really proud of you," I said. "You handled yourself well with them. You asked most of the questions that got us anywhere. You're becoming quite the journalist." And I tried to put my arm around her.

"Fuck you, Albert," she said, not mad or kidding but flatly, like the voice of truth. "Patronizing compliments I don't need. I thought we worked together. I'm younger than you, I've learned a lot from you, and you know how much I like your work, but, Jesus, don't make such a big deal out of your infinite experience as Ace Reporter."

"Okay," I said. "I'm sorry. I had no idea." I changed the station from her punk-rock crap to Waylon Jennings, jacking up the volume.

Vicki got me so rattled I took 129 south rather than 20 east and didn't realize we were going the wrong way until we passed Browns Lake and tiny towns like Salix and Sergeant Bluff. A few miles outside Sloan, we stopped at a roadhouse and scarfed chicken and hash browns. To break the ice Vicki said, "You look almost relieved."

"What do you mean?" I said. I knew what she meant.

"You don't seem too upset about getting stonewalled."

"I don't trust them. I don't believe much of what they said. But I didn't expect them to come clean just because we were carrying notepads, did you?"

"No, of course not. Pass the ketchup, okay? They're leaving, and they want to bury the facts before they leave. That makes sense. What I don't understand is why you can't bear to see Belvyn implicated."

"That's not true. The only rule I'm following is that nothing sees the ink of day until all the pieces fit. And they don't yet."

"Does Belvyn really have dyslexia or did you just make that up?"

"No, he does. Deborah has him working overtime with a reading teacher."

We walked out of the greasy spoon for less than eight dollars. Across the highway was a theme motel neither of us had noticed earlier. Knights' Inn had a moat and carriage out front, a wooden drawbridge, and a lot of castle stuff. We shivered in the cold, contemplating clouds, because we were thinking the same thing and embarrassed about it.

Vicki nodded and said, "Let's. Let's do it. I'll split the cost with you."

"Right," I said, like all we were doing was going off to get an Orange Fanta. We walked across the road to the motel office, where an old man dressed as a courtier took us over a drawbridge to room 9, which had unreadable scrolls tacked up and ram's horns shooting out of the walls. At heart, though, it was your Motel 6 special: single bed, color TV, pitcher of water, and Gideon Bible. It occurred to me that if Deborah saw us she would be angry and upset but also appalled at the tackiness of the setting. The medieval touches gave the effect of a kinky whorehouse, and I had to fight off that idea, especially when Vicki plopped down on the bed and whispered, "Come here, my prince Albert. Stop worrying about everything and just come kiss me."

Our petty arguments finally came to a physical act, the only way of resolving anything.

We both had a lot of clothes on, and it took a long time to get undressed, kissing all over, tasting the kiss, then taking off each other's heavy socks. Vicki smelled like lunch, warm and greasy, anchoring us to Sioux City. I had no idea how much I wanted her until she started kissing my ears, which have too much hair, and my chest, which doesn't have hardly enough.

"You have such nice fingers," she said. "I love the way they feel."

I was behind her, kissing her shoulders, licking her legs, piling up her hair and letting it fall back down. I talked about how straight and firm and perfect her back was, about her body seen from behind being beyond improvement, until she said, "Don't romanticize me so much, okay, Albert? Let's just make love."

"Okay," I said, "but first let me tell you that I adore your feet. Their miniatureness. Like you've bathed them so many times they've shrunk."

Corny thing to say, I suppose. Too Hallmark for the 1980s. But it cracked Vicki up, which helped me relax a little. The TV hung overhead like a dead turtle, and the Bible sat on the edge of the table to make sure I continued feeling guilty. I thought about how much fun Barry would have had on this trip and how little Deb and I put into making love anymore, just because we've grown bored. We weren't always bored: her parents paid for the honeymoon suite at the Sandburg, overlooking Lincoln Park and Lake Michigan. Next door a man beat his wife, cops patrolled the hallways, skin magazines dominated the downstairs drugstore rack, pimps and prostitutes roamed the cafeteria—against all that, our room was a haven in the Christmas vacation cold while the local color made sex raunchy and deadly serious for us. We took cabs to jazz clubs and blues clubs and German and Greek restaurants and B-minus movies and A-plus plays and Bulls and Black Hawk games, and we gave off so much afterglow strangers asked if we were sick. We both were only children finally finding a playmate, and that was our high haven, that was our best nest that came unraveled strand by strand as we retreated deeper and deeper over the long haul back into ourselves.

How good this felt with Vicki now, how good I felt, how young I felt again, how alive.

We lay side by side, squeezing hands, looking up at the speckled ceiling, waiting till we were both ready. After Vicki got Koromexed, her right eye went into a twitch. I stroked her hair and rubbed her stomach, trying to calm her down, but her blood was pumping and so was mine.

"Are you okay?"

"Sure."

"You're twitching," I said.

"I know that, Albert. It's no big deal. I'm just excited."

"There's no reason to be nervous."

"Can we please stop talking about it?"

When her twitch got bad it was difficult not to fall in love with her, since it made her appear to have figured out the universe but to be in too much pain to tell you about it. Her

146

tender voice tested my heart. I blew into her ears and spelled her name with my fingernails, drawing needles down her spine, cupping her cuppable butt, then massaged her meaty thighs and made circles with my index finger. She was so strong that hugging her was similar to wrestling and, even though it was freezing outside, we sweated as we pawed at each other. We went real slow and gentle. Inside her body I was cool, then Vicki wrapped her legs around my back, tugging, and I was warm. She bounced all over the squeaky bed, though I could tell not too much was happening for her. A gold goblet peered down at us from the desk. We never established any rhythm, nothing ever got going, and I came just as she felt a little flutter. It was bad sex, but it felt nice to lie here, just holding each other.

"We'll get better," I said.

"You're such a sweet lover, Albert."

"So are you," I said. "You're so physical."

She laughed and I did, too, because it was such a dumb thing to say. We drank the pitcher of water. After more rubbing and kissing, Vicki said, "Let's not have sex again right now, okay? Let's make sure we remember this." She was head over heels, and I wasn't exactly levelheaded, either.

"Fine by me. It usually takes me a while, anyway, to recharge my batteries."

We showered together and ended up on the bathroom floor.

She insisted on driving home. In the passenger seat, with the sun dropping into the soybean fields behind us, I kept falling asleep and waking up and drifting off again. The 80/35/20 path from River City to Sioux City hardly qualifies as a scenic cruise, but matched up with the 129/141/30 route we were on now, it was a tour through Disneyland. Very little traffic the whole way back on 30 and nothing to look at save the blackest, richest soil in North America and the tarmac ahead of us and wooden fences and grazing cattle.

"This is going to work out great," Vicki said, "so long as in

147

between getting scoops and being famous we can French kiss."

We kissed and I smiled, but I felt I had to say again, "We don't really have anything yet. We still have a lot of legwork to do."

Though she pouted for a second, she was too excited to let it last and squeezed my thigh to make a pun on legwork.

I slept happily with my head on her shoulder, mixing daydreams of me and Vicki in the motel with plays Menkus made: his wraparound pass to Black Stallion and Vicki's legs wrapped around me; Vicki kissing my ear, me sucking her slender breasts, the slam tap with his left hand. And the referee above the action, calling the personal foul on me, was Deborah with a whistle between her lips, putting Barry on the free throw line. I couldn't get Menkus' moves out of my head. As a reporter I worked like a beaver to chop away at him. As a fan I wanted to stomp and whistle until he turned cartwheels. Which was the real Biederman? The fan, I hoped. Which was Menkus—victim, delinquent, point guard? All three.

We stopped at a drive-in place around Arcadia and held hands and fed each other french fries. The Bug squirted past Carroll and Grand Junction and Colo, then near something called the Mesquakie Indian Settlement in Montour, and the Iowa Juvenile Home, which is on the Milwaukee Railroad to make it easy for the boys to jump a boxcar one-way to Lake Michigan. Vicki station-hopped, getting static and weather reports. I thought we should have more to talk about, there ought to be some way to bridge the gap our intimacy caused, but we were exhausted and neither of us could bring the other closer. At eight, when the sky was black on an empty stretch of 380 between the Cedar Rapids Airport and River City, I was wondering only one thing: what am I going to tell Deborah?

Vicki pulled into the parking lot across the street from the *Stallion* office. Her friends were walking in and out of the building and waving to her, so she gave me a quick peck on the cheek and said, "Bye, hon, see you later."

Driving over the bridge, I planned what to say to Deborah, but the moment I got home she flashed a check in my face and said, "Albert, sweetheart, you better have a good explanation who Rita Menfrodi is."

"Manfredi," I said.

"Who is she?"

When Deborah went through our November bank statement, "Rita" in my handwriting and "Manfredi" in Rita's purple ink must have looked pretty suspicious. The check had been cashed at First National Trust of Chicago the day after I gave it to her.

"The date on it is Thanksgiving weekend," I said, "which proves she wasn't south-side chippie I—"

"I never suggested any such thing."

"She's Menkus' ex-girl friend. She called me up the day of his first game and sold me a tip about his past." My guilt was getting the better of me, and I needed to confess at least part of the story.

"People do that? How ugly."

"She was still mad at him. She wanted a little revenge."

"Well, I guess I'm relieved," she said and kissed me.

"Don't you want to hear what she said or about my trip to Sioux City?"

"No, I don't. I'm trying to conceptualize Belvyn as a metaphor of the autobiographer's art as a revenge upon the indignities of his life, so please don't tell me any gossipy tidbits. They'll ruin it. Only his performance on the court should matter, to you as well as me: dyslexics apparently adopt incredibly complicated strategies of coping, and I think his inventiveness as an athlete has evolved out of that."

"Interesting."

"You see a thing clearest when you can't touch it. That's paradoxical, sure, but my whole book is based upon that principle, Albino Man."

She stood in the kitchen, orating, getting farther and farther from the world as we know it, and I didn't have the patience to bring her back. We both blew our chance right then and there. I honestly believe I would have told her everything if only she wanted to hear about it. But she didn't. She wanted to keep working on chapter nine. I trudged upstairs to our bedroom, where Barry had left a note on my nightstand:

Dad—Ed Wolf called
Guy from Milwalky
Call back

The phone number Barry scribbled had a 3 that looked like a 5 and a 7 that had an outside shot of being a 1, so I tiptoed into his room to see if he could help. His yellow night-light and blue night-light crisscrossed his face like he was a new department store getting christened. One foot was on top of the sheets, dangling over the edge. Laurel's farm toys were scattered everywhere.

"I'm sorry," I felt like telling him, "I'll never do it again," but that rang like a lie in my ears. He was sound asleep. I covered his foot, kissed his neck, and fed his fish with a tap-tap of the smelly box, then walked back to the bedroom to get the Milwaukee area code from the operator. I chalked up a couple wrong numbers until I finally got Ed Woolf, sports editor of the *Journal*, who said, "Oh, hell, yes, hello, Biederman. How are you doing?" He had the slightest trace of a stutter, which made him sound excessively intelligent.

"I'm doing okay," I said.

"Listen, I called to tell you there's real interest in your work here. We got the commentary thing you sent us a few days ago. We liked it. We like your stuff generally, but we're waiting to see a longer piece with some real meat o-on it, do you know what I mean?"

"I do indeed." I never say *indeed*. The piece they were looking for sounded like Menkus city.

"Listen, there are only eight or nine people left in this horse race, and you're very much one of them," he said. "You have a good eye, Biederman, and a nice light style. You're funny. We like that."

"I've got a real meaty piece under way, sort of an investigation thing."

"Sounds solid. You gonna give us the inside dope on how River State's pulling itself up by the bootstraps and money-belt?"

"What?"

"What's the focus—alumni, recruiters, coaches, players? Send us the works."

"I really don't have anything solid yet."

"I'm just teasing you, Bieds. I'd love to see U. Madison crawl out of the cellar over River State's back, but when push comes to shove we're both journalists, am I right? You think you can send it to us by Christmas?"

"Righto," I said. I never say *righto*. My palms were flooding. We talked awhile more and agreed that Bart Starr was the a-a-apotheosis of an asshole. Then I said, "Thanks for everything, Mr. Woolf, thanks a lot."

"Thank you. Listen, good night now."

What was I, a candidate for a job or a stool pigeon at the right price? Still, I liked him and was flattered that he seemed to like me. What a great place that would be to work—a lot of funny guys running around writing in-depth sports pieces in nice light styles for a paper they all owned a piece of.

I dialed Menkus' number. I didn't know what I'd say if he answered, but of course I got a tape. No "just ahammerin'" or loud drums. This was new, a man with a very high voice singing scat, which I actually kind of liked. Something in me wanted to call Menkus' mother to warn her or at least get her side of Sioux City before I launched a full-scale investigation to wow the *Journal*. It was late. I felt confused about a lot of issues.

Mr. Menkus answered and said, "Yuh? Yuh? Yello." Louie was drunk.

"Hello. Is this Mr. Menkus?"

"This isn't the repo man, is it?"

"It's Albert Biederman. I'm a sports reporter for the *River*

City Register, in Iowa. I was over at your place last week, talking to your wife about Belvyn."

"Belvyn?"

"Your son Belvyn."

"Beerman? Got some beer, Beerman? I'm a whiskey and wine man myself." Apparently. He was stoned to the bone.

"No good news from Randolph Street, huh?"

"Randolph Street says hello."

"Listen, good luck on getting the job back."

"Oh yeah, oh yeah."

I could hear music downstairs at my house and the Betamax from his end.

"Hey, what's the matter with the Black Hawks these days?"

"Huh?"

"You don't follow hockey?"

"The wife didn't understand," he said.

"Hockey?"

"I paid him back."

"You paid who back?"

"Raeburn," he said.

"Raeburn, for what?"

I knew that if I just paced this right he'd spill everything. I felt awful pickpocketing a drunk, but here was my speedboat to the shores of Lake Michigan.

"I paid him back for everything."

"I'm sure you did. What do you mean, like the Betamax?"

"The Betamax, Sioux City College, everything. Ellen didn't understand that I paid him back." Louie talked some more about the bus station and whiskey and wine and Evelyn and Belvyn and Raeburn, making less and less sense.

"Well, look, thanks for clearing things up," I said. "I appreciate it."

"She didn't understand. I paid him back."

"I know you did, Louie, but I gotta go now. You get some rest."

I'd just been handed, as Vicki would say, the smoking pistol. Excited, ashamed, weirdly depressed, I hung up the phone and couldn't sit still in the bedroom. I went downstairs to tell Deborah at least the good news from Woolf. "Guess what?" I said.

She took her face out of her hands and said, "I already know." She was crying herself blind.

Had she been listening in on the other phone? Did she somehow already know about me and Vicki? I was terrified as I asked, "Know what?"

She pointed at the radio, which she'd been listening to as she did her work. K101 was playing "Imagine."

"John Lennon's dead."

"What?"

"Some kid carrying a copy of *Catcher in the Rye* asked Lennon for his autograph, then shot him. *Catcher in the Rye!*"

She sank her face in her hands again. I comforted her but was aghast. Even someone's death she wanted to blame on a book not being read the right way. I was tired of her turning everything into an interpretation. I was tired of the Downtown Refurbishment Project. I hated our cookie-cutter house and wanted to make the move to Milwaukee. I wanted Katie Koob to come back to Jessup. I wished John Lennon weren't dead. I wished Steve McQueen and Mae West and the nuns in El Salvador hadn't died, either. I wished people didn't just keep dying on us. I wished my parents were still alive. I turned up the radio all the way and stomped around the floor, feeling drunk, dragging Deborah out of her doldrums until Barry appeared at the top of the steps. His tiny mushroom of a penis hung out of his pj's.

"Hey, you guys," he said. "I'm trying to sleep."

Deb and I both broke down. Barry toddled over to join us.

SEVEN

THE next morning was real hard on most people. Walking across town, I passed groups of girls splashing through the rain with red eyes, singing Beatles songs. I saw in these student faces their anger at what I had done to Deborah and my guilt, like when I was in college, no longer in love with my girl friend, and dreamt I was dying. Rain flooded tarps covering two-by-fours in the construction lot. In a month Ronald Reagan would be President. Francis kept reminding me that "Dutch" once held the job that, more than a quarter century later, Francis held—until he was fired for busting the balls of a monstrously uninformed Cubs fan at the tail end of a call-in show. "Dutch" hitchhiked to Hollywood while Francis moved to River City. Who knows to what heights Drex might have soared if only I had rescued him with a phony phone call before the Cubs fan got to him? While at WHO at least he had met and befriended Raeburn, whom I now had to confront before too terribly much more happened.

After work I tried to reach Vicki, but everywhere I called said she'd just left for somewhere else. When I finally caught up with her at the *Stallion* she was up to her neck in backlog with a 9:00 P.M. deadline and couldn't talk, so she threw me a kiss through the mouthpiece. I was calling from a public phone and had to hang up because an old lady was waiting in the cold.

Tuesday night one good thing and one bad thing happened in our family. The good thing was a very good thing, and the bad thing wasn't a total disaster. The good thing happened first. For some reason dinner was a little later than usual, and Barry was sitting at the table, killing his appetite with disarmingly small spoonfuls of ice cream. Deborah banged a knife against a glass and said, "Hear ye, hear ye, I have a major proclamation to make."

I thought maybe she was going to announce she was flying east to be closer to Lennon's body for the funeral, and I guess my anxiety showed.

"Don't look so gloomy, Albert. It's wonderful news."

"We're not pregnant, are we?"

"No, we aren't," she said, reaching under the table to pat my spare tire.

Ordinarily by this time Barry would have asked if the big news was that we were buying an RKS Gleaner, but he was immersing himself in vanilla ice cream.

"What is it, then?" I asked Deborah.

"Duly note that on December ninth, nineteen hundred and eighty, Deborah Rasnick Biederman completed *Metaphors of the Self* and dedicated it to her patient husband and doting son."

I wished she'd have knocked off this archaic bullshit, because it reminded me of Knights' Inn and made it hard to celebrate.

"Really?" I said. "It's actually finished?" I got up and hugged her. I was so happy for her. I'd been hearing about the book on and off since '75. "Why didn't you tell us earlier?"

"While turning the pork chops, I finally realized everyone's an autobiographer. That's my conclusion, opening up autobiography as an ongoing process we're all engaged in every second of every day, creating our lives. Do you understand what Mommy's saying?" Deb asked Barry, whose skin glistened a little, which worried me. "Mommy finished her book today. Five years of work, three hundred and eighty-eight pages."

"You don't have anything in there about insecticides, do you, Mom? 'Cause Laurel was saying—"

"No, it's about why our minds are the way they are."

"Why's that?" I asked, not expecting an answer, but I'd sold Deborah short.

"When we look out a window at a garden we see a pane of glass. There's no direct access to the garden."

That left Barry and me lost in the ether, and once Deborah gets on one of these rolls you'd have better luck trying to stop Amtrak. I brought the pork chops and potatoes and salad to the table before kissing and squeezing her, lifting her up in the air. She was talking of breaking out some cheap champagne when the bad thing happened.

Barry stood in the chair for a while, rolling his eyes, then sat on the table, spinning around with his arms out and making crop duster noises, saying, "Mommy saw the garden, Mommy saw the garden, Mommy saw the garden." It finally dawned on me he was trying to get back to talking about insecticides. He climbed off the table and sat in the chair, squinting hard. Suddenly he slid off the edge of the seat and was lying down on the linoleum, saying, "I'm sick, you guys. I feel sick to my stomach." His hands were sweaty.

Deborah knelt on the floor like she was praying for recovery and said, "Barry, sweetie pie, are you okay?"

Barry wasn't in as much trouble as she thought he was. He was just nauseous from too much ice cream and needed a little insulin to counteract the sugar.

"Earth to Bare, Earth to Bare," I said, trying to lighten him up, which is the best thing to do in the situation: make the muscles relax.

"For God's sake, Albert, don't be playing games. Barry's lying here—"

"Come in, Earth, what is your message?" Barry said. The little bugger has the only quality that really matters, what my high school coach used to call "bouncebackability."

"My message is that you ate way too much ice cream and probably need a hit or two of regular insulin, huh, Bare?"

He had an idiotic grin pasted across his face that scared me half to death. Deborah felt his forehead and stomach, his heart, looked into his eyes, took his pulse, unbuttoned his shirt, did everything except administer CPR, à la her retired registered-nurse mother. If she tends to overreact, that's only because she cares so much.

I got some insulin from upstairs and shot him in the keister. You can wait the better part of an evening for the dope to start working, but it almost always has an immediate placebo effect, and he ate his dinner nice and easy and he had already quieted down a lot when I carried him to bed.

Deb stayed in the kitchen, washing dishes, while I sat in a mini-chair, reading to Barry from the *Farm Bureau Spokesman*, watching him fall in and out of sleep. I took his urine sample with Acetest and the tablet didn't turn lavender, so the acidosis worries were over.

Barry is now seven. When Barry was five, my father was living in Los Angeles, where in exchange for free rent and a piddling salary he was the tennis pro at Lakewood, a condo sports complex for senior citizens. The president of the Lakewood tennis club called me one afternoon at work to say my father had just had a heart attack and I should get out there immediately. I had planned to go the year before and opted for Florida. I asked: "Is he going to die?" The club president said: "It's going to be a tough five-set match, but all my money's on Mike; he's a gamer." Deborah, Barry, and I flew to L.A. and took a cab to Lakewood. Ducks quacked across an artificial pond. Obscenely well-preserved and sunbaked septuagenerians strolled the putting green. Grandmas in string bikinis strode from the swimming pool. Dad's disciples ran around the courts, wearing tennis whites and floppy hats and state-of-the-art shoes and movie-star sunglasses, wielding their oversized rackets like canes and butterfly nets. There was a jacuzzi, sauna, racquetball court, weight room, bingo parlor, and dance hall as long as love. In thirty years Hinselwood could happily retire here. Jet-black parking lot, jet-propelled automobiles, white stucco apartments, ice plant growing everywhere. This was a place tough old birds came to die, and they thought it was an Olympic training camp. Mineral water and Frisbees. Dad's studio was remarkable only for the sheer number of rackets, racket presses, tins of balls, shirts, shorts, sweatbands, warm-up suits, sweat socks, shoes, jocks, glasses straps tossed about. It wasn't an apartment, filled with my father, whoever he was. It was a pro shop, filled with the sport of tennis.

We drove Dad's car to Cedars-Sinai Hospital, and by the time we got there he was already under an oxygen tent, making futile gestures. Mr. Tennis Club President, this wasn't a five-set match gamers pulled out. Sports clichés about getting tough were of no use to anyone now. The Japanese doctor said an angiogram had shown most of Dad's main arteries were completely closed. Though the chances were twenty-to-one Dad would die on the operating table, the doctor recommended bypass surgery, because without it Dad would die any day. Nurses hovered around his bed like angels, ministering to his every need, while we stood in the far corner of the room, next to the TV set, overdressed foreigners from Iowa. I wished we hadn't gone to Florida the year before.

His hair, combed by the nurses, was still straw-blond and he was still big and hard and handsome, but he was wearing a bib and his handshake, which had always been a bone-cracking attack, was a wet noodle, and his face and blue eyes had a ghoulish gray pallor, like they'd been injected with the stuff of smog. Deb and I scribbled him notes and tried to make out his murmurings, and the nurse-angels kept telling me to tell him whatever I had wanted to tell him, but what was that supposed to be? He never pretended to be a tremendously understanding or affectionate person. He was a distant he-man who didn't get what he had wanted but came close enough to be bitter about it. I saw a tapered elegant figure waltzing across clay courts, and I saw this mummy in front of me and I didn't know how to explain what had happened to him. His breath breathed six inches away from me, and there were no bridges built to travel such short distances. I could have told him I thought he was Pancho Gonzales, whom he once took to five sets in an exhibition match, and he wouldn't have heard me. Too little too late. I kept hearing the sound of good wood on public courts' asphalt—he would throw his racket at me for bailing away from cannonballs he hit at my midriff when teaching me to play the net. He always saw me as something of a failure for not blossoming into a professional athlete and even more of a flop for not pushing Barry into sports. Barry had worse relations with him than with Deborah's parents, and watching my old man die made Barry skittish and perpetually pouty and thirsty, because in his heart of hearts he dreaded Papa.

The bypass was scheduled for the end of the week, so we would spend all day at the hospital with Dad, watching TV, trying to rave about the hospital food, cheering if he had a little flush in his cheeks, talking to the technicians performing a million tests on him, but being able to say almost nothing to Dad, having nothing to tell him except good-bye, good-bye, I never knew you. Although it was the beginning of December, it was eighty-five degrees out, and at night Deborah and I would swim in the heated, well-lit pool with the old people who, with their caps and goggles and fins, looked like so many floating turtles. Another major activity was trying to avoid the tennis club president, who desperately wanted to "defeat the sportswriter love-love so you'll write me up." Deborah, for once, was the all-supportive wife and upbeat daughter-in-law and obsessive lap swimmer, but Barry's lips got sweatier and sweatier and, unable to sleep, he stayed up watching movies and boosting Coke stock. We figured the combination of the travel and the trauma were enough to explain his jumpiness until one of the angel-nurses said, seeing as we were already here, we might as well check out his heavy-perspiring mouth. While Dad was getting hooked up for an ECG, Barry and Deborah went off with a nurse to Internal Medicine and came back just before dinner in the company of a plump doctor, who said, "Your son has diabetes."

In Lotus Land, everything was white and blue and blond and yellow and pink, like a color TV that got only pastels, and you wanted to shoot a hole in the screen. Partially because of Dad's condition and partially because we were in southern California, whatever they told us about Barry's diabetes seemed weirdly irrelevant or trivial. I couldn't get over the feeling that we'd get it all straightened out and back to normal once we were back at River State Clinics. Deborah was at her best. She demolished the diabetes section at the UCLA library and developed meal plans for three square a day and made up charts and ran around shopping for dietetic snacks and blood-test kits and urine-test kits and insulin bottles and syringes. It struck me as totally unfair to be poking Barry's bouncy thighs with a needle, turning his body into a battlefield, before Dad even had time to punch out.

Dad died on the operating table, and at the funeral there were just the three of us and a hack minister Lakewood dug up somewhere and a few of Dad's tennis cronies, wearing Adidas and sunglasses, in case a decent Sunday afternoon doubles match materialized. In my coat pocket, like a bet against the future, I fondled Barry's new syringes, the miniature insulin bottles, half a pack of graham crackers.

For the next year and a half Barry was content to let Deborah do the meal planning and food fixing and me do the testing and insulin shooting. Until last summer, when he and Laurel started palling around more and more, and suddenly he wanted to plow his own body, even in drought. He was six and a half years old, and he looked at himself as a farm he wanted sole ownership of. He wanted to be the one poking and picking and testing and breaking skin. He wanted to be in control. So one brilliant Saturday morning in August which reminded me of L.A., I set out for him on the breakfast table all the different kinds of insulin bottles and swabs and packets and pamphlets and needles and food-combination charts and syringes and tablets, and I felt at the end of it like an exhausted road-circus medicine man selling his wares to the lowest bidder. With

Laurel helping him, Barry quickly progressed from shooting insulin into oranges to shooting himself in the stomach and shoulder and ass, and now he has his whole body needle-tracked like a drug addict's nightmare. Though Deborah was so great about everything when the diabetes first developed, the major burden of Bare-Care ever since has fallen upon me. She says she can't stand causing pain or the sight of blood. I supervise the urine and blood tests and insulin shots. Barry keeps saying, "I've got to grow up sometime," but he still fucks up the operation often enough to need a pretty constant coach, and he knows it.

Deb came upstairs around eight to peek in and asked all cheerful, "Feeling better, sweetness?"

"I'm sorry," he said. "I'm really sorry, Mom."

"Sorry—for what?"

"I wrecked our celebrating your garden book."

"What matters is that you're feeling better," she said.

"Getting tired?" I asked.

"Sorta."

"Your test came out fine." He'd drifted off just after I'd taken the sample. I grabbed ahold of his leg through the blanket and squeezed till he giggled.

Deborah said: "How about the three of us doing something special tomorrow to celebrate my book and Daddy's call from Milwaukee and your coming through this so strong? A party in honor of promise."

"Great," Barry said.

"Where should we go?" Deb asked.

"A farm," he said. "Definitely a farm."

That made Deborah squirm. She had more in mind a movie or dinner out and is terrified of snakes, but I nudged her and said, "I know the perfect place, too, I think. There's a man I want to visit who has a lot of land. I'll call him and see if we can go."

"Yahoo. Thanks." Barry flipped and flopped on the pillow before we pinned him to the sheets, giving him quick good night kisses. What he needed to do was rest and let the insulin interact with his food.

"Are we actually going to someone's farm tomorrow?" Deborah asked as we walked down the hall toward her study. "It would be such a nice contrast to all these books and papers."

"Why not? You're free, right? I'll get free. Barry wants to."

"Where are we going, though? You've got to tell me. You know how I hate surprises."

"I can't. You'll see tomorrow," I said, jabbing her, fake-fighting, loving how happy she was about her book, not ten pages of which I could understand.

Deborah practically read my mind when she asked, "What happens, honey, if the *Journal* hires you and I get tenure? What then? They're good news separately but bad news together."

"You could teach at Marquette," I said, leaning against the door frame.

"Oh, so you have my whole career figured out for me. Marquette's quite Catholic. I don't want to teach Jesuits. Besides, you know as well as I do tenure doesn't transfer. If I get it, I stay here."

"I looked at a map. Guess what town is exactly between River City and Milwaukee?"

"My parents."

"Hardly."

"Honolulu."

"Dixon, Illinois."

"Uh-huh."

"Reagan's birthplace. We can move there and moonlight in Dixon's booming touring industry. In the morning we'll each drive one hundred and fifty miles in opposite directions."

"We are not amused," she said.

"Look, let's not worry it. Let's wait till you get tenure and I get the job. Then we'll worry it plenty. They're both a ways away."

Deb couldn't celebrate just yet, though she did suggest a champagne toast at midnight. First she had to talk through a critical transition with Adrienne. She really couldn't let that book go. I tried to imagine her not pounding on her typewriter and couldn't. Her study is like the dentist's X-ray closet used to be for me as a kid, a cramped room where specialized, incomprehensible things got done. There were changes in the conclusion she needed to smooth over.

So who was this old fart sitting on a farm in Oxford with most of Iowa wrapped around his tallywhacker? Watching the ten o'clock news, I called Francis to get Raeburn's number. Unlike most people, Francis is a puppydog when drunk. He gave me the number, saying that there were places only fools would tread, then sighed and half-snored, half-whistled until he became a dial tone. I lay on the couch for a while, thinking I'll call Raeburn, no, maybe I won't, maybe I'll wait until tomorrow morning, maybe I'll call, maybe I'll let Francis make introductions first, until my right hand involuntarily punched buttons.

Mrs. Raeburn answered. She reminded me of the really chipper receptionists you get when you call Northwestern Bell to complain about rate hikes. I went into a whole spiel—who I was and how much I'd admired her husband and that I had a six-year-old diabetic boy whose birthday was tomorrow and who lived and breathed farming equipment. All of this meant nothing. Mrs. Raeburn didn't budge. But when I mentioned how highly Francis thought of Mr. Raeburn and that Francis and I were like this, crossing my fingers, the pitch of her voice literally changed, went high and breathless, and she said she'd go get Cal, who was out doing something or other to the horses. She used a technical term that I didn't quite catch. Francis must have got in on a lot of fish-food ground floors; Raeburn must have bought a heck of a lot of air time.

A couple minutes later Raeburn got on the horn, puffing from branding horses' behinds or whatever.

"Yep," he said in a birdier voice than I expected.

"Hello, Mr. Raeburn. I was just telling your lovely wife

how much my little boy, Barry, who has diabetes and whose birthday is tomorrow, wants to meet you and see your farm. Plus, my wife just finished a book she was writing and wanted to unwind by spending a day in the country."

"You're pals with Drexler?"

"That I am," I said.

"Then why hasn't he told you to call off the dogs yet?"

There was silence on the line, then static, then more silence, and I didn't know what to do. What he said didn't seem like a joke, but the way he said it sounded like he was kidding. Finally he laughed, letting me off the hook.

"Come to the farm tomorrow afternoon, and 2-to-1 I'll have you straightened out by suppertime."

"What's that supposed to mean?"

"Tomorrow at four. Bring the kids. You know how to get here."

"Kid. Only one kid."

"Bring him, too. He'll ride the pony. And bring Mrs. Biederman, one of the best teachers we've got."

"Thank you, thank you very—"

He hung up in mid-sentence. He was old enough that he didn't bother to chitchat on the phone. It was just there to carry hard information. I already enjoyed him more than I thought I should.

After pulling some file pieces and writing a preview for the Saturday away game, I let Sabrina give me shit for not asking Deborah if she wanted to review *Man and Superman,* which meant Sabrina was going to have to suffer through the anachronism herself. Then I called Francis to get directions to Raeburn's house.

"Let me come along," Francis said.

"No way."

"Why not?"

"It's a family thing. Deborah finished her book and Barry—"

"I'll protect you. I know how to deal with him."

164

"Come on, Francis. He's a wheeler-dealer with his fingers in a lot of pies. He's not the Wizard of Oz."

"If I can't come, I won't give you directions."

Francis is capable at times of being a world-class asshole. I got directions from Marty, who had once been to a coon chase near there and wanted me to report back with a picture of the Oxford pheasant-hunting situation.

As we drove through Coralville onto 80 west, Barry's nose was pressed to the back window of the Bug and he identified for Deborah pieces of trailer equipment as they passed by, but other than that he was incommunicado, in love with the beasts of the land. It was one of those electric-blue December days when it's probably a lot colder than it feels, since you're bundled up and the colors are so warm—gold farms, silver silos, muddy horses, pink cattle. I switched on the radio, which had news of Blue Cross rates going up, and switched it off. I turned back to Barry and said, "What's the first thing you want to do when we get to the farm?"

"Ride his deer."

"You don't ride deer."

Barry snickered, couldn't believe I didn't know the lingo at least a little bit. "His John Deere tractor," he explained, exasperated. "Mr. Raeburn practically invented the engine for 'em."

Deborah laughed, pretending she'd known my mistake all along, then asked, "We're not staying late, are we? I mean, we're not going to be invited for dinner or anything, I hope, because I've got a night of calls to make to set up thesis committees."

"Jesus, Deb, we haven't even got there yet and you're already working out the return flight. I thought—"

"Are we almost there?" Barry asked.

"Almost," I said. "Just a few more miles."

"Barry, what kind of horse is that?" Deb asked, pointing south.

"Just a quarter."

"Huh?"

"Quarter horse."

"What kind of tractor is that?"

"It's not a tractor, Mom. It's a harvester."

He knows the names of these things better than he knows the letters of the alphabet. Farms are all he cares about. Deborah kept asking him questions, and he kept answering them for miles. It was awesome, and it helped pull Deborah out of the dumps.

Most of Iowa is nowhere near as flat as some people would have you believe, but an air bubble in a pancake is Pike's Peak compared to the land bordering 80 west as you come into Oxford. Grain elevators like giant dominoes. No markets anymore and, instead, fields where the food is grown to put into markets. When you've been living too long in River City, sometimes you forget, unless you're Barry, that fruit doesn't grow in Produce.

We took a left over a feeble bridge and down a badly rutted path, then around a pond and past mailboxes and trees. With Barry going bonkers and Deborah trying to remain indifferent to nature by smoking a cigarette, we came to a sign that said:

RAEBURN FARM
PRIVATE PROPERTY
PROCEED AT OWN RISK

There didn't seem to be too terribly much risk involved, so I proceeded at ten miles an hour over the bumpy road. Raeburn's farm was probably the one spot in all of Oxford above sea level. The real estate sprang at you like a big gift: hundreds of acres of bean stalks on one side and pumpkins on the other as far as you could see. White-hatted workmen's heads popped up here and there among the stalks like rabbit tails. A whole pack of gorgeous Labrador retrievers came barking down the hill at my tires. Sheep or what I thought were sheep foraged the back of the hill, nearly out of view. Pastoral city. The farm was a postcard of heaven, and Deb was so taken by it all she put out her True.

"Sheep, right, Bare?" I said. "Pretty neat, huh?"

"Uh-huh." He was drinking in the animals and machinery.

A pony and two saddle horses ran around a fenced-in yard out front, nuzzling each other, stepping over three-foot jumps. Clouds hung on the edge of the property like Mrs. Raeburn's wash. It didn't seem like the kind of place real problems entered, and I already felt how hesitant I was going to be about bringing up some of the issues I needed to discuss. I mainly just wanted to fall asleep sucking on milkweed.

The house was chocolate brown, its white shutters going to yellow in the four o'clock sun. Mrs. Raeburn raked the riding ring, and, although he could have hired the local Boys Club to go cutting through the grass with scythes, Raeburn sat atop a tractor mower, turning the immense lawn into a putting green one last time before the freeze set in for good.

All ga-ga, Barry ran over to Raeburn and shouted to him. Raeburn cupped his ear and slowed down but didn't come to a complete stop, going up and back over a rough patch of grass. His wife waved at us from the other side of the parking lot. A snowplow and snowmobile were already out, ready for winter, along with a spanking new jeep, a station wagon, a blue Caddy, and a BMW lined up across the circular parking lot. Just in case the missus had trouble turning over the motor in the morning. They all had roan-and-gray Stallion bumper strips.

Both of the Raeburns appeared to be in their mid-seventies. She was a big, high, handsome woman with leathery skin and a mane of white hair. You couldn't get past the fact that she resembled nothing so much as one of her own horses. Raeburn was built along the lines of a leaf. I knew why he might worship athletes: two of him could fit into Mean Joe Greene. He was short and slight, and was wearing an FS feed cap with work clothes. He had the soft, buttery face of someone who could hardly conceive of inner turmoil. I got the feeling the Raeburns had forgotten about our appointment and didn't know who we were, really, or what the hell we were doing here.

"Hello, sir, I'm Albert Biederman, and this is my wife and my boy. You and I spoke yesterday about the visit. You were expecting us?"

Raeburn nodded a Buddha nod.

"Well, I'm very pleased to meet you," I said and made more specific introductions while continuing to shake his hand.

Just when I thought maybe he'd been left outside too long, he showed he was still with it by turning off the mower the moment Barry started crawling up the backside of the thing. We all just stood in the cold, digging at the hard ground with our feet, slipping our hands in and out of our pockets, squinting—and the sun was hidden behind clouds.

"Hey, there, little fella, watch your fingers," Raeburn said to Barry.

"Yes, sir," said Barry, who says "sir" to nobody and was awestruck in a way I've always wished he'd be around Bill Buckner or Reggie Theus.

"Would anyone like to ride?" Mrs. Raeburn asked, motioning toward the horses.

"Actually, as a child I took quite a spill once," Deborah said, "and since then—"

"I'll bet I can show you what you were doing wrong. Come on." And off to the stable Deborah got dragged by the horse lady.

"Happy birthday to you, young man," Raeburn said to Barry. "How many candles on the cake?"

His birthday wasn't until August. I'd lied to get invited out here, so now I had to give Barry a hard, fast look that indicated: the old man's crazy, humor him, tell him it's your birthday.

"I'm seven," he said.

Raeburn smashed down his feed cap over Barry's head so he couldn't see, which made him lose his footing and fall off the running board of the mower onto the grass. Raeburn wore a scuffed-up old pair of white country-club shoes, of which he must have had twelve more pairs inside. Barry rolled around, happy as a pig in mud.

"What do you say, Barry?"

"I'm all right. I didn't hurt nothin'."

"No, I mean don't you want to thank Mr. Raeburn for the cap?"

"Thank you very much, sir. I like it plenty. Do you think maybe we could take a ride on your Deere?"

Barry was totally in love with him. Raeburn had a stick-figure body and a creampuff face and a bird's chirp for a voice, and Barry thought he was Superman. Raeburn didn't seem just comfortable out here. It was more like he'd grown straight out of the earth like a plant and these machines were his stems.

Raeburn pointed toward Deborah and Mrs. R. in the riding ring and said, "Absolutely first-rate gal you've got. Quite the teacher, is what I hear. One of the hardest-working profs we've ever had."

"She just finished her magnum opus."

Barry was bored and climbed off the mower, wandering down the road to look for Raeburn's Deere. Mrs. Raeburn was sitting on a black horse and instructing Deborah, who held tight to a pony as it clopped around the ring. This I had to get a picture of.

"She's up for tenure soon, isn't that right?" he said.

"Next fall. Menkus is taking a class and getting reading help from her. Deborah's working with him, trying to correct his dyslexia, did you know that?" I said, trying to shunt the conversation over to where it might do me some good, but Raeburn had been around way too long to get thrown off by such a simple maneuver.

"I do indeed," he said. "And I'm proud of him for staying with it. I keep up on all my boys." He baited me with a grin, daring me to go after him, but I backed off. He did some more squinting and I did some more pawing of the ground and staring into space and he finally contributed: "So you know Drexler pretty well?"

"Oh, yeah, we've been working the same beat for more than a decade. Plus, when he was in Des Moines—"

"What's your opinion of him?"

"I think he's the best college announcer in the Midwest, TV or radio, color or play-by-play."

"No, no, I mean personally." I could tell he meant: do you know our friend fucks fellows? Somewhere along the line Raeburn must have caught Francis with his pants down and extracted a heavy debt of loyalty.

"Well, maybe he could get a better handle on the booze. I don't know."

I pretended I couldn't figure out what he was trying to get at and stood with one foot on the damp ground of the front lawn and the other on the running board of the tractor, getting blitzed by a master bullshit artist. He sat in the driver's seat with his hand on the ignition and charmed the socks off you with that lopsided grin of his. He turned the key, started the motor, and I had to jump out of the way as he rode down the hill toward the barn.

I ran after him, thinking this wasn't an interview, it was a game of dodgeball. The Labs came yelping toward me like they'd just heard a secret bell or something. Mrs. Raeburn and Deborah called to me from the riding ring. With the mower on, I couldn't hear them and skirted around all the metal in the driveway to see what they were making such a fuss about.

"Barry," Deborah said, almost out of breath, though she was only holding the reins of a nearly static pony.

"What's the matter?"

"He's fine, he's fine," Mrs. Raeburn said, putting her ancient, muscular hand on my arm. "He's in the barn on top of a haystack. He wants you to take a picture of him and help him down."

"You really should join us," Deborah said. "Riding's so much fun." Just when Deborah seemed to have gotten comfortable, her pony wouldn't go the way she wanted it to and Mrs. Raeburn had to whap it on the butt with her crop until it turned around. The first time I saw a horse schlong I thought it was a fungo bat.

I took the Instamatic out of the glove compartment, but by the time I got inside the barn door Raeburn had already caught Barry's jump. Barry looked at Raeburn like he was the grandfather Barry always wanted, and Raeburn was pleased as pie having someone around who worshipped every tool on the lot. He walked around back and showed us a huge grain combine behind the stables.

"Holy Toledo," Barry said. "A Massey-Ferguson."

"This boy you've got is one in a million."

"Don't you think I know that?" I said.

"You could take a few pointers from him."

"Oh yeah, like what?"

"Like how to respect your elders," he said, laughing, taunting me again, gripping my arm in the same death-lock his wife had just used.

Barry stood in front of the contraption, ogling the machinery, and said, "We can take a spin on it for a sec, can't we?"

"Now isn't exactly optimum time to thresh. You realize that, don't you, little fella?"

"But we could go out for just a few secs, don't you think, with the mixers off?"

Properly impressed with the pipsqueak's farm knowledge, Raeburn said he was dog-tired from mowing all day but would get Mrs. R. to ride with Barry for a while. She left Deborah to fend for herself with the pony and removed the blades in a minute flat, then climbed into the cab and called, "All aboard."

"Come on, Dad," Barry said, getting a boost up from Mrs. Raeburn. "Come on the ride with us. You can sit in the middle."

"Yes, come on, Albert, let Calvin rest his heels and have a glass of wine with your thoroughly lovely wife. She is one sharp lady. During the Depression, before I met Calvin, I was also a schoolteacher. Fourth through sixth grade in Lone Tree. When it snowed I would have to . . ."

She talked on about 1934. I haven't the foggiest idea what she said. The day ended about as perfectly as a day can end, with the sun burning the pumpkin patch. The air, as they say on the six o'clock report, was unseasonably warm for December 10. As we took a tour of the crops back of the barn, the machine galumping along without its mixing blades, I strained to get a look at the screen porch, where Raeburn and Deborah were now talking keenly while the housekeeper poured more wine and left the bottle. What the hell were they talking about? They weren't discussing only the bouquet. I wanted one solid shot at the old man.

I tried to feel everything I knew Barry was feeling, but I got antsy after a while with a six-mph combine, no matter what the view, and when Mrs. Raeburn stopped to turn around and head out for another loop around the south forty I said, "You two bring 'er in." I got out of the cab, slid off the machine, and crossed the lawn.

Opening the door to the porch, I said, "This has been one spectacular day."

"Yes," Raeburn said, banging his wineglass.

"I just wanted to come over and thank you. Barry's had such a good time here. I've never seen him so happy. He's really on cloud nine."

"Well, I've enjoyed him a lot, too," Raeburn said. "He's welcome to come back anytime and talk shop."

"You must have the most beautiful farm in Iowa. It's really such a gorgeous place. And we even had pretty nice weather today."

"Honey, please," Deborah said. "Mr. Raeburn and I were having a very interesting conversation."

"This spread must be great for entertaining," I said.

"We do some," he said.

"Ever have the team out here, banquets before the season starts or anything like that?"

"What are you trying to get at, Biederman?"

"Yeah, Albert, really."

"Oh, I don't know, I'm just thinking aloud."

"Drexler warned me about you."

"Drexler?"

"He said you'd been nosing around."

"Francis told you that?"

"We were battin' the breeze, and we both feel you're goin'

172

after the wrong bananas. Forget the witch-hunt, Albert. Forget about the goddamn witch-hunt entirely."

"Hear, hear," said Deborah, blotto on excellent white wine.

"I've talked to Menkus' parents, Mr. Raeburn. I've been to Franklin. I checked out Sioux City Parking Lot, where you're on the board. I know how Menkus got here from Chicago."

"And how is that?"

"On wings of flattery."

"Albert," Deborah said.

"Please," Raeburn said to her. He wasn't going to apologize for anything.

"Then you don't deny it?" I said.

"I'm prouder than a peacock of that kid."

"That's not the way pride was expressed in my day."

"That's because you weren't a blue-chip baby," Raeburn said, almost laughing and apparently without spite.

"Touché," I said. He had me there.

He wasn't a mean man. This was all one big hobby to him, and nothing really ever went wrong. His white shoes gleamed in the setting sun. He poured more wine.

"You want to tell me it's a crime to give a kid with dyslexia a shove in the right direction? Do you honestly want to tell me that?"

He had me confused, and he knew it.

"Look, there's a game coming up Saturday at Dayton," he went on. "Build up the whole team for that. Dick Hinselwood's doing a good job, and you can help him do a better one. Belvyn's a special kid, but you're up to no good when you harp only on him. If you think he's Mr. Basketball, why are you so busy digging up dirt on technicalities no one gives two hoots about, anyway?"

"Because that's my job," I said.

"Albert, Mr. Raeburn is a truly concerned philanthropist who's gone to pretty extraordinary lengths to insure Belvyn's progress. I mean, I think he's rather—"

Raeburn broke back in: "No one here has a lock on sainthood. I'm not going to tell you you can't uncover peccadilloes

173

in anyone's closet, but I am going to tell you no one cares about the piddly-ass bullshit you're in such a dither about. And I'm also going to tell you—"

"I'm going to tell you you've been instrumental in turning a great game into an industry that—"

"Well, look then, Biederman, if that's the way you feel about it, I wish you'd get the hell off my property and head back into town with your precious little conscience intact."

I stood on the edge of the porch. Raeburn and Deborah sat in front of me in wicker chairs, finishing their wine. The porch door was behind me. Barry and Mrs. Raeburn were pulling into the barn. What the hell, I thought, I'll go out in a big way. I tried to make a full reverse spin down the stairs and damn near threw out my hip. As I turned, my bad leg tightened up on me and I had to make my exit half hobbling, holding on to the rail with the Labs loping over to smell my shoes. The pain eased up once I was walking on level ground, but it hurt horrors just popping in the clutch when I drove the VW into the middle of the driveway. Raeburn's cars surrounded mine like Bug-hungry dragons. I sat in the car, trembling, and honked the horn every ten seconds until Deborah realized she had better shake hands and say good-bye and get Barry. The two of them piled into the backseat.

The Raeburns didn't seem to be overly ceremonial people, so I didn't worry too much about not taking my proper leave. Going back over the bridge onto the highway, Deborah and Barry discussed how wonderful the Raeburns were and what an ass I'd made of myself—how embarrassing that was of Daddy. I reminded them who had arranged the expedition in the first place, which sent my wife into a giggling and tickling fit with my son. The whole point was to make me insanely jealous. It did.

They talked about the combine and the tractor and the mower and the pumpkins and the soybean stalks and the Labs and horses and generous Mr. and Mrs. R. I flipped on KHAK and turned up the volume even when the song was the theme from a new Burt Reynolds movie.

"Thanks, Albert. I mean, thanks a million for ruining what could have been a perfect day in the country."

I turned up the Burt Reynolds movie to drown them out as they discussed what a fun day they'd had.

Clouds spun north to south, 80 thickened with dinner traffic. The rest of the way home no one except the radio said anything I paid attention to.

Immediately after getting home, Barry had to eat. He was a little jangled, so he sat in the kitchen, dipping graham crackers in milk while Deb warmed up leftovers. I drew a bath for my aching leg. Listening to the water, to the sound of Deborah's and Barry's voices, then hearing the vague murmur of phone calls she made, my mind got on a roll about being fifteen and frightened of everything I bumped into except basketball: the junior varsity played immediately after the varsity, and at the end of the third quarter of the varsity game all of us on the JV, wearing our good sweaters, good shoes, and only ties, would leave the gym to go change for our game. I loved leaving right when the varsity game was getting interesting. I loved everyone seeing us as a group, me belonging to that group, and everyone wishing us luck. I loved being a part of the crowd and then breaking away to go play. And then, when I was playing, I knew the crowd was there, but they slid into the distance like the overhead lights, all except Dad who, unlike my friends' fathers, did not have a nine-to-five and so was free to attend games on Wednesday afternoon as well as Friday night. It embarrassed me to know he was always there, and I had a sixth sense of his presence—sitting in the last row against the far wall, squeezing a black plastic hand grip to improve his finger strength, wearing a tennis sweater to remind everyone who he was. In our relatively new but crummy gym, Dad was remote and regal, like an F. Scott Fitzgerald hero who had wandered off into the wrong book.

Stroking his golden locks, Dad would pipe out whenever I had the ball, "Take it to the hoop, Albert. Beat somebody." He always wanted me to beat somebody. Anybody but him because, having been retired from the circuit, he had no more sojourns to the West Coast or South for warm-weather racket play. Even when he did, though, he never had the foot speed to quite cut it in singles, and he played doubles with limited success because he didn't have the teamwork temperament. He'd been an All-American at Purdue, where he met my mother, who was a Boilermaker cheerleader and little-girl cute, and he turned pro with great fanfare; but after fifteen years of clutching to the outer fringe of the tour and crossing the country to get bumped in the first or second round and losing money for the year as often as he made any and gaining little solace from the knowledge that he was one of the best two hundred players in the United States, he finally put himself to pasture at thirty-six, coaching tennis at Iowa State in Ames and chastising me for missing the cut-off man.

The bath was hot now and nearly full. Barry and Deborah were yakking away during dinner over the TV news. Barry was still high as a kite over the visit to Oxford. The phone rang and Deborah answered it. From Deb's tone, I could tell it was Adrienne. I went back to my youth.

Even in high school I was never as dominant as Menkus. I couldn't create my spots or see openings, but oh how I could shoot! Give me a step, some space, and a screen, then watch the ball tuck into twine. I was at least a half-step slow, couldn't pass or dribble very well, and what saved me was a point guard named Dicky Schroeder, who would have arm-wrestled mountain lions to get me the ball. I palled around a lot with him to get out of the house and because a great passer is Santa Claus. Every Wednesday and Friday Dicky gave me the best part of himself, and I felt I should do something to reciprocate. I took to buying him dinner, since he was even poorer than I was and good meals weren't cooked at my house. Mom studied the market listings and called clients and showed houses, selling people the dream of a house as a home while ours was strictly a hotel. She also wrapped herself around a fifth of gin every night, and the sharp, animated, perky quality of her face degenerated into prematurely shriveled meanness. When I took up smoking, both Mom and Dad said they thought Dicky was a bad influence on me.

Downstairs, dinner sounded like it was over. Deb and Barry went into the living room. Washing my legs, I smelled Vicki, thought about us clawing at each other in the motel room, thought about the summer between my sophomore and junior year, during which I played basketball. I don't mean I got in some games now and then when I wasn't taking Driver's Ed or working at A&W, or that I tried to play a couple hours every afternoon. I mean the summer between sophomore and junior year I played basketball. Period. Nothing else. Nothing else even close to something else. All day long that summer, all summer, all night until ten.

My mother was moving houses, so I didn't have to get a summer job, and Dad put the fear of God into me by telling me that, when I wasn't practicing, someone else was and that boy would get the bacon. I wanted to get the bacon. The West Des Moines court was protected by oak trees and ivy and the back of the school. Orange rims with chain nets were attached to half-moon boards that were kind only to real shooters. The court was on a grassy hill overlooking the street, and when I envision Eden I think of that court during the summer—shirts against skins, five-on-five, running the break till we keeled over. Alone, or with Dad retrieving the ball for me and keeping count, I did drills Bob Pettit outlined in *How I Did It: Basketball Tips for Boys*. A certain number of free throws and lay-ups from both sides and with each hand, bank shots, scoop shots, set shots from all over, sweep hooks (which were still big then), turnaround jumpers, jumpers off the move and off the pass, tip-ins. Everything endlessly repeated and, when Dad was there, endlessly scrutinized. I wanted my shoulders to become as high-hung as Pettit's, my wrists as taut, my glare as merciless. After a while I'd feel like I was becoming the ball and the rim; my head was the rim and my body was the ball. I was trying to put my head totally inside my body. The basketball was being shot by itself. At that point I'd call it quits, keeping the feeling until I returned home to Mom's stinko breath and Dad's bellyaching about TV coverage of Forest Hills.

Barry came upstairs into the bathroom but didn't say anything, not even when I squirted water at him. He got something out of the medicine chest and padded downstairs to watch TV. Deborah's typewriter began its drumroll, but she got interrupted by another call, and when she hung up on that one she made several more calls herself—thesis-committee bullshit. The acoustics in this house make the field house sound like Carnegie Hall. I lollygagged in the bath, reminiscing about a fat older guy named Doug Beacham, who came to the court every afternoon that summer starting in July. My mother and father thought he was a bad influence. He drove a red truck, fondled his beard, and told dirty jokes none of us were sure we completely understood—not even Jim Morrow, whose older brother owned every *Playboy* ever published. Beacham would tell me, "Basketball isn't just shooting, Al. You've got to learn the rest of the game." He could barely bend over to tie his shoes, but he had the sweetest corner shot you'd ever want to see. Not even I could stay with him in Horse. In real games, though, he didn't do very well because he needed about an hour and a half to launch his jumper. He set up garbage cans around the court that I had to shuffle-step through, then dribble through with my right hand, left hand, between my legs, behind my back. On the dead run I had to bounce the ball off a banked gutter so it ricocheted as a perfect pass to myself for a lay-up. He was teaching me the rest of the game.

Beach was sort of an unofficial Midwest scout and had a lot of basketball contacts, and that summer and the next two summers he got me in free to the Bob Pettit coaching camp in St. Louis. Every summer was the same steaming cement, the same sweaty boys, the same second-rate coaches, and I would always be the best player in my age group, but I wouldn't connect with any of the other campers or learn anything from any of the coaches. I was so grimly serious about earning people's admiration for my one talent, so isolated, so afraid, so driven that I wouldn't work on the hard parts which would have made me a great guard. So I would return essentially the same player I was when I arrived and would look forward to the beginning of the season, when the cheerleaders would come to all the players' houses to give us cupcakes for good luck. Their uniforms made them look like nurses who had come to comfort and rescue me from the horrible dungeon of my own house. I would always be torn between wanting them to stay and begging them to leave before they saw my mother careen between the white walls of the den, quoting sales figures, crying for her bottle like a baby before brandishing it like a gun.

Dad liked the varsity coach because he had played his college ball at San Jose State in California, the site of Dad's only semifinal pro finish, and Dad waxed nostalgic with him about the Golden State every chance he got. Mr. Ruiz was one of the very few Mexican fellows living in Des Moines at the time. He was wiry and quick, and most of us believed him when he mentioned his days as an all-conference floor-leader. He never said much: he showed a tight smile, but every now and then he'd grab you by the jersey and stand you up against a locker. Then he'd go back to smiling again.

Though we barely broke even junior year, Mr. Ruiz let us play how our bodies wanted. Eric Keyes, a tall black guy, cleared the boards. Dicky Schroeder handled the ball. The forwards played D, sweating. Eric, Dicky, and I specialized in the enforced timeout on the road. Eric would whip an outlet to Dicky and fill a lane, Dicky would deal the middle, and I'd fill the other lane, calling for the ball. Pressing full-court, we might run off ten or twelve points in under two minutes, and the opposing coach would call timeout. The noise in the gym would go whoosh. You heard the absence of noise, not silence. There would be a humming buzz, but you'd hear the noise you had been hearing that was no more. It was like pulling the plug on someone's oxygen tank and suddenly hearing

179

the noise the tank had been making. Afterward, I'd have trouble getting revved up to play. Only the sound of Dad's popgun clapping would keep me going.

Shampooing my hair, flexing my legs, running all this back in my brain, I returned to the Iowa State Fair in Des Moines, summer of '57. Beth Norton, who had broken up with me over a Capture-the-Flag dispute when we were ten, was friendly again because her family knew my family and she admired me for "bucking up so well." She didn't know anything about basketball, but she knew she wanted a pink panda hanging by the scruff near the basketball toss at the fair. The free throw line was eighteen rather than fifteen feet away, and the ball must have been pumped to double its pressure, hard as a rock. Your shot had to be dead on or it bounced way off. You weren't going to get any soft rolls out of this carnival. The rim was rickety, bent upward, and was probably closer to ten and a half than ten feet. A canopy overhung both sides of the rim so that you couldn't put an arc on your shot. With people elbowing you in back, you could hardly take a dribble to get in rhythm. The deck was stacked ever so slightly against you. I won around twenty-five pandas. I got into a groove, and sometimes when you get into a groove from eighteen feet straightaway you can't come out of it. As I held the ball in my hands before each shot, I saw exactly how the net would look when it lifted. Standing among spilled paper cups and September heat and ice and screaming barkers and glass bottles and darts and crash cars, we handed out panda bears to every little kid who walked by.

Doing good deeds was very high on Beth's list, and passing out pandas was probably about as simple and good a deed as she'd contributed to in a long time. She ended up going to Carleton College and becoming a labor lawyer in Minneapolis. When I bumped into her parents recently at a game, they said she'd gone on to meet a lot of terribly important politicians up there, but I couldn't help secretly wondering whether she looks at them with as much admiration as she looked at me while giving away stuffed animals. Her hand fell into mine when we were watching a sulky race. At the agricultural show she leaned up and kissed me. She still had that infectious grin and come-hither eyes, but she didn't move like a tomboy anymore, and she had beautiful full breasts and nice hips and eager hands. In the middle of the night we wound up in some alfalfa fields at the far end of the fairgrounds.

My mother thought she was a bad influence.

Beth and I went unsteadily steady again senior year, and our basketball team won the first six games, and Mr. Ruiz smiled happily, clapping sometimes. While we were dressing for our first league game, he stood at the blackboard in the locker room, shaking and crumbling chalk. At first we thought he was just trying to get us psyched up. He mumbled Mexican phrases and stubbed his toe on the bench. We got on our road uniforms and tube socks and assumed maybe he'd had a taste or two too many. Then he burst out with it.

"Deeky Schroeder," he said. And we all realized where the hell was Dicky, home with a head cold when we had Lincoln at Lincoln? Give him a couple aspirin and send him over there in a cab *muy pronto,* right, Mr. Ruiz?

"Deeky Schroeder has bad accident last night at sausage-pack plant. Forkleeft crush Deeky. *Lo siento, lo siento, o mi Dios.* Deeky dead."

We closed our lockers. It took us a while to grasp what Mr. Ruiz said, and it took us the rest of the year for it to sink in. When I told my parents, my mother wailed and drowned her sadness in drink and Dad called Mr. Schroeder with a pep talk. Dicky Schroeder smoked Raleighs and drove a souped-up Chevy he bought from working at the sausage-packing plant since junior high. He was always buying new clothes and car accessories and bullshitting you about getting laid. He was too busy to be dead.

Around a week later the school paper ran an obituary, quoting people saying what a solid student he'd been, which was an insult to everyone's intelligence because he was a tough kid from the wrong side of the station and about as solid a student as I was. Solid C-minus. The article finished up with a quote from Ralph Waldo Emerson saying, "Death isn't an ending, it's only a transition," which did everyone a lot of good, knowing Dicky wasn't gone forever: he was just running the transition game.

Immediately after Mr. Ruiz told us Deeky was dead, no one did anything. No one talked on the bus to Lincoln and no one took any warm-ups. Once the game started we all tried to play like Dicky, looking to pass, working the give-and-go. All of us, even Eric—hell, even me. Everyone was looking for the open man, and the open man was Dicky. We were all hoping to wake up and find out he was only kidding. If we all tried to play like him, maybe he'd pop out from under that forklift and show us how to run the break.

The play I'll remember until I'm ninety was Eric all alone on a breakaway dunk, me trailing. He stopped and set the ball like a wreath on the grave of the key, for me to pick up. I looked for someone to follow after me; I kept waiting, but no one came. I banked it off the board, and we won in a romp.

The water was freezing. Barry went to bed with farm reports on the radio. Deborah drilled a storm of footnotes. I shivered once for Deeky as the tub drained hairs from my balding head. Lights out.

EIGHT

THURSDAY night Deborah and I lay on the couch, flipping through magazines and eating Rice Krispies treats. She pointed out how Ted Koppel's new haircut made his head look like a mango. Deb should let herself unwind more often, I thought. This is even more fun than arguing.

"I'm having lunch tomorrow with Larry Hutchins. Vicki—" I stopped, started again when I realized I had nothing to hide. "Vicki, my stringer, says he's sharp and sounds cooperative. Black kid from Chicago."

"Great," she said, not really listening, watching the tube, though there wasn't any hostage news, and the show divided into one segment on Afghanistan and one on seat belts.

"Hutchins was cut from the basketball team in October and now works as a vendor at the games. Maybe he'll be all I need."

"Need for what?" she asked, taking the last Rice Krispies treat.

"He could give me the dope on how River State recruits. The sense I'm getting is Raeburn runs a travel service: signed, sealed, delivered."

"Stop using so many clichés, okay, honey?" she said, pronouncing *clichés* like it was French perfume, like she was trying to wow Ted Koppel, who droned on about product safety.

We were sitting a ways away from each other, but our wool socks touched.

"I just want to find out what Raeburn's role is in all of this."

"I thought you two settled that yesterday. He's done a lot of good for RSU. He seems to like athletes especially but helps everyone out. Why don't you leave the poor guy alone?"

"You mean you really did fall for the crusty old codger act? He's worth only nine or ten million. He bought off Menkus' parents and in all likelihood his high school principal, railroaded Menkus through a joke of a JC, and now he's probably picking up the tab here."

"I doubt that, but, even if it were true, so what? A kid's in school who'd never be here in the first place if it weren't for Cal Raeburn. And where else would he have gotten help with dyslexia or even known he had it? He would have been swimming in alphabet soup the rest of his life. His handwriting is still incredibly cramped and his sequencing and scrambling are atrocious, he's not exactly acing Rhetoric and reading lab, but he's learning a heck of a lot more from me and Martha than he would hanging around the south side." Martha's the reading teacher.

"That's not the issue," I said.

"Of course that's the issue. Look, Albert," Deb said, and I felt like we were debating both sides of the question for the benefit of the *Nightline* audience, "I teach Belvyn four days a week. I don't just watch him perform miracles in screaming gymnasiums on Saturday nights. I'm not Hinselwood amassing a personal fortune off the dubious skills of illiterates. Despite the fact that Belvyn has absolutely no business being in a college classroom, he has a way of walking, of carrying his body totally within himself, that's quite beautiful. You have it, honey, or you did when you were in condition. It's an athlete's grace."

"That's all very pretty," I said, "but where does that leave my article? What am I going to do, have the whole thing a description of Menkus walking down the street?"

"If you had the nerve to do it, it would be the best sports story ever written."

"Uh-huh. Tell that to—"

"I'm serious. If you could just capture the aura."

"Ed Woolf likes my features and opinion pieces, but he wants something more substantial than aura. The only way I have a real shot at the job is to come up with something solid, which is why I can't wait to see Hutchins tomorrow."

"Do we really want to live four hours from my folks? That's a real consideration. Plus, what about *my* job?" Deb whined. "I have a responsibility to stay here."

"I realize. I mean, I'm sure I won't get the Milwaukee job, anyway. Your book'll be published and you'll get tenure and we'll die in River City, so just try to relax and take this thing one step at a time, all right, sweetheart?"

She cooled out when I put my pillow on her lap, then flipped the channel to a less factual program. Tom Snyder interviewed a singer we'd never heard of who was now making a comeback.

Up this one-way street, across that dead-end avenue. Roadblocks and jackhammers taking downtown out of commission. West, east, south, and west again, away from the action. Park, walk, drive, park some more, drive some more, deal with meter maids. Who brought this litter here? I was a good half-hour late for lunch and hoped Vicki and Hutchins were still at Cats, a student hangout on Gilbert.

Cats had photographs of cats all over, couches with cat hair, cats crawling around outside, benches with paw prints in the wood, and cartoons about cats taped to the windows. Every sandwich was called by a different breed of cat or a nickname for cats or the name of a famous cat. The waitresses wore high heels and leotards, and their eyebrows jutted out like whiskers.

When I ordered a Reuben I should have been able to just order a Reuben. A grown man shouldn't have to say "Burmese on pumpernickel, and a beer—hold the Tender Vittles." I stood in one of Cats' many cubicles, looking for my lunch partners. Everything was wood and set close together. Chairs, tables, and walls bumped into each other at crazy angles, and if you took three steps in the wrong direction you wound up in the kitchen. I weaved from room to room until I turned a corner and heard Vicki talking a mile a minute, then saw the two of them sitting together, hunched over their trays. The college girl with her down jacket and backpack and three-ring binder. Hutchins looking spiffy enough to hit the road selling *Watchtower*. His hair was cropped close, and he had a high forehead and such a small nose you wondered how he got enough air to breathe. He was wearing a blue suit and nicely blocked tie. His skin was the color of Baskin-Robbins' coffee ice cream, what used to be called high yaller. I didn't join them immediately. I decided to fence-post for a moment.

"Oh God, do you guys have Logan as a TA?" Vicki said.

"Yeah."

"You know what we used to do? No one paid attention to what she was saying 'cause everyone was too busy betting how many cigarettes she'd line up on the chalk tray. Sometimes she came damn close to going through a whole pack in an hour."

"The lady's high-strung," Hutchins said, "but she knows her stuff on muni bonds, mutual funds, tax defer—"

"You sound like you're not bullshitting. I wish I sat behind you last year instead of my friend Celia, who's a moron, though, Jesus, Larry, you're so tall you woulda had to scrunch all the way down for me to copy anything."

Hutchins stirred his Lipton's, acting stiff and dignified, while Vicki reached across the table to touch his shoulders and show him how tall and wide he was. He seemed to be one of these black guys who think the only way to make it is to act really white. Before Vicki could finish demolishing Hutchins' lunch for him, I broke up their little love feast. Vicki tried to make introductions, but the conversation came to a dead halt.

"Gee, I'm sorry—did I bust in on a crucial revelation or something?"

No answer from either of them. They acted bashful. Hutchins sweated while eating delicately. His knees banged up against the table like he was visiting kindergarten.

Vicki finally said, "We were talking about classes. Larry has the same Econ TA I had."

I hadn't had the same Econ TA and didn't want to talk about her, even if she was a chain smoker, but I figured I should confab for a while, so I said, "Vicki, why don't you loan Larry your exam questions?"

Hutchins looked at me, appalled, and said, "Hey, man, I don't do that kind of thing. I don't have to. I have a 3.4."

"Calm down, okay? I was just kidding. You look to me like you could sell surfing gear to an Eskimo."

"I'm going into business management, not sales."

"So River State must have a pretty good Econ department, huh?" I was trying to keep things going but not doing too well.

"It's okay," Vicki said, getting up to go find the waitress and bring my order back, because she needed some new food to munch on.

"You don't take any history or science or anything like that?" I asked Hutchins.

"Oh, sure, what I have to," he said, "but I'm mainly interested in how money works."

"Listen, you should do a cost-benefit analysis of the Downtown Refurbishment Project. You'd make a mint. The reason I'm so late was I got held up in all this mess. Did you know the detours now have detours?"

He laughed. "The investors overcommitted their capital in the wrong sectors and didn't factor in rising building costs."

"Right," I said. He sounded like he actually knew what he was talking about, but I didn't want to get into a big discussion on the price of concrete. I was grateful when Vicki came back with my sandwich and put it down in the middle of the table for everyone to share.

"What did you have?" I asked Hutchins.

"The Persian," he said.

"What's that?"

"Nice fat slab of salami on a French roll."

He picked at his salad, which Vicki helped him with since this was as close as she could get for the time being.

"Researching this piece on Menkus, I was looking through some SCTE tapes, and I was struck by two things," I said to him. "First, Menkus was nowhere near the gunner his highlight film made him out to be and, second, you can really play ball: you go strong to the glass, have a nice soft fadeaway from the left side, and play tough D when you want to."

"You mean that?" he said.

"Of course he means it," Vicki said.

"Don't you miss playing?" I asked.

"I don't know," he said. "Nah."

I looked at him.

"Well, maybe that much," he said, splaying two fingers an inch apart. "I still play a little pickup ball now and then."

I ate my sandwich and he ate his chips and salad and Vicki helped both of us. The waitress refilled Vicki's coffee and took her order for cheesecake but didn't say boo to Hutchins or me. I told her I didn't care what Cats called their pastrami and Muenster on rye; it was by far the best sandwich in town.

Then I swallowed and said, "I guess what I'm really curious about is how you got recruited by River State, how they manage to recruit so many players from the south side."

"The *ghet*-to," he said like he'd just heard of it recently. "Look, I agreed to talk to you guys and I'm here to deliver the goods, but Larry Hutchins ain't nobody's Saint Sister of the Poor. I need to see some talent."

"Fifty bucks," I said, winning Vicki's awe at my "ruthlessness."

"Seventy-five."

"Sixty," I said. "I'm buying lunch."

He turned his thumb and forefinger into a gun and shot me, which meant okey-dokey. Sugar Ray Leonard's 7-Up commercials have ruined black athletes. They all want to be smooth millionaires. The last Basketball Jones left will be Belvyn Menkus.

"So, anyway," Vicki said, "when did you meet Raeburn?"

I cringed, but Hutchins said, "He has a rep. Him and his people were always just sort of around."

"Who are his people?" I asked.

"Ott, mainly. He's the recruiter." Bruce Ott, the ex-player and current assistant coach. "A lot of dudes wouldn't truck with Raeburn because they didn't want to leave the city, but if you were willing to travel he was the Man. You had to impress him. You can't snow Raeburn, and he liked my game fine. He'd lend Ott spending money to help me with my car."

Deborah should have been listening to this. The simple Oxford farmer buying fifteen-year-olds for market.

"What do you mean—help you with your car?" I said.

"This is all anonymous, right?"

"We'll do everything we can to protect you," Vicki said, which was the best answer to give. Your whole article can't be based on confidential sources. Hutchins wasn't as smart as he thought he was, because Vicki's answer was good enough for him and it shouldn't have been. The prospect of sixty dollars in cash made him mellow. The atmosphere put him at ease. Usually I wouldn't be talking about recruitment violations in a restaurant, but people were crowded so close together everyone tuned everyone else out. In its own way, it was like meeting in a phone booth.

"I already had the car. An old Duster that was constantly biting the dust. Sometimes Ott'd pocket the repair bills. Sometimes he wouldn't. It was all just month by month. Raeburn dug my hustle. That was my dream then: pro ball. We all wanted a piece of that pie, Belvyn more than anybody. I wasn't too involved in the academic side of life, if you know what I mean. My tendency was to goof off and just glide through. Me and school didn't see eye to eye."

"Did you go the GED route?"

"Ott was always telling us about that, but any idiot can get through Westinghouse High, and that's all I was then. I graduated okay, and after that came what we called the corn-field express, out to Sioux City, then back to River City for big-time ball."

The waitresses took our trays without asking whether we were done, so Vicki had to lunge to get what was left of Hutchins' salad before it was gone. That was the appeal of Cats: you got treated like a dung beetle. Apple crisp all around, with coffees. Most of the clientele was part of a new look involving black jeans, shades, and Mohawk haircuts. Theater types acting like death itself.

Hutchins kept talking: "If you didn't want to, you didn't have to move to Sioux City. You could just show up now and then for certain tests and roll calls and things, and be guaranteed C's if you were one of Raeburn's boys."

"And that was true of everyone?" I said.

"Everyone I hung out with."

"To be honest, that's sort of what we suspected, but Jeffrey Fischer tried to convince us things were legit."

"Fischer's a bootlick from the word go."

"You think he's one of Raeburn's people?" Vicki asked.

"Nah. He's just a T and E stooge."

"He and his wife were packing up to leave when we arrived," I said.

"Maybe they finally had enough. But I took a class with a very good guy in the business school, Mr. Horner, and I got so heavy into that, Accounting and Investment and Econ, that Donley and Raeburn both—"

"Who's Donley?" Vicki asked.

"B-ball coach at SCTE," I said.

"Right," he said. "Donley was against my taking any classes for real. He thought it would *di*-ffuse my concentration, which it did ultimately, in a big way. We played other independent JC's, and I doubt anyone ever came within ten points of us because Belvyn was unstoppable. You're right about him: he was just as much a playmaker there as he is here. I swear he's got two eyes in front, two in back, and one on each side." Dyslexics are 3-D; they seem distracted only because they're paying attention to too many things at once. "I'd get open down the lane for a split second, and the ball would be in my hands. He breathes the game. He feels the flow like no one I've ever seen."

"Has he always tried to act black?" I asked.

"Ever since I've known him. He grew up with the brothers around Franklin and wanted to pass." Hutchins didn't catch his own pun. "The way he talks sounds jive to me."

"Me, too," I said. He and I laughed.

"How'd you get to River City?" Vicki asked.

"Well, I can't draw a map for you, little girl," he said. "Rae-burn bankrolls you at T and E, and he does the same thing here if you make the team, especially if you're a starter. It's not all laid out. You just sort of know where your next meal's coming from, if you hear my meaning. While I was growing up, Rae-burn was someone you knew about, and that just continued, him giving what you could call guidance. He wants to do good, he really does. He gives kids opportunity. He loves being pals with athletes. I was best of the bunch until Belvyn emerged. It was discouraging to see a white boy that good and know even he has no lock on making the NBA, though he thinks he does. Maybe I should have given it one more year. I mean, in JC ball, I think I averaged around sixteen or eighteen—"

"Fourteen-seven," Vicki said, who'd done the same research I had and was getting tired of Hutchins' act.

He smiled. He had the confidence that comes to people who leave one field to go into another and stay successful. He bordered on being an Oreo, and I wondered how much bitterness he'd tucked away into that leather briefcase of his. But he'd made a totally corrupt system work for him, and you couldn't take that away. Any inner-city mother would kill for a son like Hutchins.

"By the time I got here, my education was more important to me than running around in my underwear." I got the strong impression he'd rehearsed that line. "I didn't play any hoops this past summer 'cause I was working for a commodities trader in Chicago. I didn't do good in fall practice, I wasn't putting out, so Hinselwood cut me. I can't say as I blame him."

"I figure Hinselwood's knee-deep in the cash flow," I said.

"He never sees any of it. They keep him real clean. It's mainly just Raeburn and that real estate agency he owns. They're the sugar daddies, with Ott as bag man."

"Has your aid already been cut off?"

"I don't get no more pin money, if that's what you're asking, but I still have my scholarship. I want to get my degree, then go to business school at Northwestern. An MBA'll be better than the NBA." He laughed again. He wanted to make sure we knew he was the jolliest guy in town.

"One last question," Vicki said, slurping the sherbet that had melted off my apple crisp. "If you've held onto your scholarship, how come you're working as a vendor?"

"You don't understand. People who haven't played never understand. I love basketball. I love watchin' what Belvyn and Cliffie are trying to do out there. I just don't want to be doin' it anymore. Plus, you'd be surprised what you can pull in hawkin' dogs. My contact person got me work-study."

"Your contact person?" Vicki said.

"Most of the starters on the football and basketball teams have someone, a dean or a teacher or whomever to go to when they might need help."

"Who's Menkus'?" I said.

"I don't know."

"Come on, Larry." Three-to-one it was Deborah.

"I don't," he said.

"I'll find out," Vicki promised.

When our check came Hutchins made a big deal of offering to pay, but I declined and gave him his money outside. The kid's certain to make a million or die trying.

I had to get back to work and they both had two o'clock classes. He offered to drive her back to campus in his Duster which, for all the trouble it was supposed to have caused him, didn't look in such bad shape. Vicki said okay, but not before talking to me for a minute about meeting in Dayton for the game Saturday night. I was taking the team plane later this evening, and she was driving Saturday morning with friends. She gave me an impish grin that said Hutchins hadn't succeeded in doing anything more than provide valuable information while coming off like an accountant. She kissed me quick on the cheek and I shook Hutchins' hand, regular style.

I drove to North Liberty for high school girls' basketball. Save me, Marty, from three-on-three half-court action performed in slow motion, from toes glued to the floor, butch haircuts attached to grim faces, swaggering girls with thundering thighs and knees with seventy-five-degree bend. Save me from girls wearing black knee pads and staring at the ball and dribbling with their right hand while shuffling left. Save me from two-hand push shots and crying on the court and passes rolled out of bounds and girls guarding each other with both arms stretched out like a stone wall. Save me from fifteen-year-olds twisting their limbs to play a game their perfect bodies were not meant to play, a game I love with all my heart and soul. Take me off this beat, Marty. Let your hair down, girls. Give basketball back to the boys.

Some people have been saying for years that college sports should go pro since it already is now, anyway. Bring these kids in as hired hands. Turn them into full-time pieces of meat. Cancel classes. Whenever I'm asked what I think of this plan, which has been bandied about seriously in recent years, I say the same thing: have you ever seen a Chicago Bulls-Washington Bullets game in the middle of March? Don't. The fans are drunk, the cheerleaders are on Quāāludes, and the players are snowheads. It's a big ugly circus, which Menkus, like every other red-blooded American boy, wants to run away to join for $1.4 million.

Do this, instead: allow colleges to recruit only as many players as graduated the previous year, which isn't a new idea and isn't going to revolutionize amateur athletics but at least would put pressure on schools to educate their heroes. Francis, reiterating his belief that basketball is just a business like everything else, thinks I'm hopelessly naive. However, he doesn't get shivers down his back when the ball catches in the net before bottoming out.

When I got home, Barry said, "Grandpap called and blabbered about the Hodag," a mythical beast that inhabits Thompson Lake in Rhinelander. "Mom's gonna be at the library all night. Laurel says there's a really great movie on cable called *Days of Heaven*, which has lots of fields in it. Can I go watch it at her house, then sleep over, can I, Daddy?" After the Raeburn excursion, Barry was more insatiable than ever for pictures of the great outdoors.

"You're sure you don't want to come with me to the game?" I asked, just teasing him.

"Ykkch, no."

I had to be at the Cedar Rapids Airport by seven to catch the team plane. I walked with Barry down the block to his baby-sitter's house. Laurel yanked him up the stairs and into the living room, since *Days of Heaven* was already starting and the beginning was really boss. Plump as a dumpling, she somehow managed to exude zesty health.

"Enjoy the movie."

" 'Night, Mr. Biederman," Laurel said. "Win the game."

I drove the Bug through a shower to Cedar Rapids, where on last call I hurried up the steps to the plane. It was a twin-engine chartered job put together with epoxy. The cabin wasn't pressurized and the seats smelled like they'd been vacuumed too many times. My ears popped and kept popping at a thousand feet and on up. Hinselwood, Ott, and Nagel sat in front. The row behind them sat Hinselwood's suited wife and kids; Ott and Nagel are still "baching it," as my long-ago landlord used to say. The players, divided to a depressing degree by race and status, sat in the middle section; their retinue consisted of Karl the trainer, playing with his first-aid kit, and the two student managers, flabby-chested Charles and Ben, who looks like an advertisement for Iowa. The press sat in the tail so we'd be first to feel it when the plane crashed. Most of the players were listening with earphones to their boxes or flipping through magazines. Only Tomlinson had to wreck the mood by pretending to study. Every time I caught Menkus' backward glance he looked away.

I heard Francis talking into his recorder a couple rows behind me, and, when I went to interrogate him, he said into the machine: "Ladies and germs, I have the distinct pleasure of introducing to you the redoubtable Albie Biederman, intrepid reporter excavating information no one in his right mind gives a flying fuck about. Albie, grab yourself a cushion."

"I tried to call you at the station all day yesterday. I wanted to congratulate you for being named Raeburn's number-one stoolie."

"Listeners, Albie is upset."

"Thanks a lot, pal."

"For what?"

"I'm surprised he hasn't told you already."

"Actually, he has," Francis said, fishing in his coat pocket for cigarettes. "He called me this morning and said you were a royal pain in the ass."

The plane lifted to go over clouds, and my ears just about exploded. We were past the Mississippi, the pilot said, angling for Peoria, then Terre Haute and Dayton. All the bright lights of the midland.

"What do you do, have a walkie-talkie to tell him when I'm digging up too much dirt close to his farm?"

"Relax, Albert, he calls me up from time to time to get the scuttlebutt. There's no great conspiracy going on. You make such a big deal out of everything. No one else cares."

"*He* seems to." I lowered my voice. "He asked what I thought of you, 'personally.' The way he said it, with that lop-sided grin of his, I think I knew what he meant, and I think you know what I think he meant."

"Run that through again for me," Francis said, bluffing.

"I told him I thought you were the best college announcer in the Midwest but should get a better grip on the bottle. Maybe I'm adding up two and two and getting four hundred, but I figure you owe him one."

"He lent me some money to get through a rough period in Des Moines," he said, and that was all he had to say and all I wanted to know.

"A little bit of the ole *quid pro quo*," I muttered.

Karl and the managers seemed to be picking up their ears, but Francis paid no notice. The rain beat on. The unpressurized plane got smaller. "Hey, who appointed you palace guard, Bieds? You've developed a moral streak a mile wide. It's unbecoming. I thought we were just supposed to talk about sports."

"Oh, and you don't have a stake in any of this, of course, like your reputation or our bet or your piece on Menkus."

"Sure I do," Francis said, accepting the assist nicely and pushing the ball upcourt out of trouble. "I still think he'll be benched by Christmas. He plays too weird a game. I talk to him when I can, trying to get a tape together, but this kid doesn't come together. He's off in his own space suit. I mean, way out there, moonwalking. That'll get hard for Hinselhorse to take, I guarantee you. Listen, Albert, I have to finish this pre-game crap and I'm not sure I can hold up anymore under your ruthless grilling, so run up front for me, will you, and tell Tinselheels to come to the back of the bus for our powwow, okay?"

Which gave me a good excuse to get up and go put the screws to Mistletoe. On a private charter there weren't any stewardesses to contend with, and the way the plane was dipping and diving you couldn't be dead certain there was a pilot, either. Francis was never going to do anybody any real harm. Tough guy with a heart of glass. Looking out the window at lovely downtown Peoria, I felt guilty but grateful.

Dead-serious earnest, Karl rerolled tape, and his manager, Ben, lightened things up by trying to trip me as I passed. Tomlinson, ever polite, said, "Hello, Mr. Biederman," as did Peter Keil, who was squeezing his pimples in the reflection of the window. The Kendall twins and Monroe Terry, the black seven-foot pencil, were still trying to figure out how to fold their legs. Malakovich and Jenks were now studying, because the third string didn't promise to see much playing time tomorrow. Rod Williams, the Chicago disappointment, sulked in his new threads, and Gault and Durland slept while Menkus and Black Stallion squabbled over what tape to put in the box.

Before I even opened my mouth, Tonsiltone said, "Listen, Biederman, come cool your heels in first class. I got a favor to ask you." He patted the window seat.

With Ott and Nagel sitting next to him, working on sets to run against Dayton's multiple defenses, I expected some simple gag at my expense—a plastic frog leaping out of the fold-down tray, whatever. Ott is the eternally youthful, pseudo-happy ex-jock, as good-looking and glib as Gifford. Nagel never played anything that I'm aware of but is a good organization man and scout and stats freak; he has the strapped, scrunched features of wimps who start pumping iron late in life. Nothing comical happened, perhaps because Hinselwood's wife and kids were sitting the next row back, discussing recipes for apple pie and Rover's backyard antics. Kurt and Doug agreed photogenically. Mrs. H. grasped her necklace to remind herself it was real.

"Big game tonight," I said to her husband.

"Yep. We win and we go 2–1, start building a winning. We lose and—"

"You go 1–2, start building a losing record."

"Good," he said. "You're quick, Biederman. You been at this long?"

"Forever."

"What's your instant expert analysis of tonight's game?"

"You want my advice? Give Menkus the ball and let him make you a genius."

"But in Sunday's *Reg* I don't want to read about one player, and I sure don't want to read about one play. I want to read about this team as a team. You're ruining our unity by building Menkus into a star. You have an obligation to me and the ball club to support us as a group."

"I have nothing of the kind. The only obligation I have is to write what I see."

"Then you're blind, because what we've seen so far from Mr. Menkus is showboat jungle ball the rest of these kids outgrew their first year of high school. Write about Tomlinson's percentage from the field or Cliffie Davis' steals. Talk them up, get them sky-high for next week. You could be a positive force."

"Does Calvin Raeburn tell everyone around here what to say?"

"Well, he has the right to. He does a great job for us."

"What's that supposed to mean?"

"Just that he's the most loyal supporter we've got."

"The day before yesterday I finally met Raeburn," I said. "Today I talked to Larry Hutchins." For December twelfth, Dick Hinselwood had to have the deepest, darkest tan of any man in the history of Iowa. He looked at me with those shit-brown eyes of his oozing out of his adobe skin.

"Larry's become quite the gentleman-scholar, hasn't he? But he could have been an outstanding player. He lost what he had in here," Hinselwood said, pounding his breastbone.

"He said Bruce Ott was a very effective recruiter."

"He certainly is. Tell him yourself—he'll field compliments directly."

"That Ott really got you where you wanted to go."

Ott looked up from his charts to say, "Larry Hutchins: consider the source. If you have something to offer other than innuendo, please pass it on."

I didn't, so I said, "We're passing the Windy City. One big breeding ground for you guys, huh?"

No response from Hinselwood or Ott or Nagel.

"Hutchins said they call it the corn-field express."

Ott went back to mapping strategy with Nagel, and Hinselwood giggled. For some reason he liked "the corn-field express." Now it was time to get palsy with me. "I'll level with you, Albert. These kids aren't Einstein." A major scoop. "SCTE isn't a first-rate JC." Hold the front page. "I know that. You know that. They learn a little. They play a lot. They get a chance. People applaud. No one gets hurt."

"That's where you're wrong," I said. "One in a hundred makes the pros, and the other ninety-nine go home to sell shoes. You've used them to make a quick buck."

Mrs. Hinselwood leaned over the seat and kissed Dick and said, "Kurt just had one of his visions—we're gonna win by twelve tonight. Isn't that beautiful?" She was beautiful. She was a year or two older than I was and looked thirty. In her elegant Chinesey pristineness she bore a real resemblance to my mother at her very peak.

"Where did you go to school?" Hinselwood asked me.

"You know I went to Drake."

"Drake, what's that, a mallard's dildo? You can poke fun at any college, see what I mean?" Ott and Nagel had the hopeless assignment of having to laugh at this, shaking their shoulders and knocking their clapboards against their knees. "No institution's completely clean. Injury or no injury, you weren't good enough, so you became a writer. Okay, I can accept that. But maybe now you're tryin' to get back at the game a little, huh, Albert? Is that my fault? Should I have to fend off your crazy questions week in and week out because you'd sell your left testicle to have had Black Stallion's first step to the hoop?"

I didn't know what else to say, so I said, "Francis needs you for a pre-game chat."

He hadn't said anything new. He really hadn't. I've always known I became a reporter when I realized I couldn't be a pro guard. Who wouldn't admit the obvious? I stood and walked back toward my seat.

All the players seemed to be suspended in a state of narcolepsy, all except Menkus, who grabbed my arm, guided me into the aisle, and said, "Al*bear*, my man, take a load off your lobes."

Menkus had the home entertainment system on his lap and earphones plugged in, but the volume was so loud you could tell he was playing the same tape that had been on his answering machine since Tuesday:

> *On and on and on and on and on*
> *The beat don't stop till the break of dawn*
> *I'm not as tall as the rest of the gang*
> *But I'm rappin to the beat just the same*
> *On and on and on and on and on . . .*

He sat in his seat in the clouds, tuning you in and tuning you out when he wanted and banging his big feet on the carpet. Cliffie had moved across the way to get some Z's. Menkus was the only player not wearing a tie, and he had on white boots, a white shirt, black slacks, a black hat. His fake Afro was puffed to the ceiling, and his eyes, as always, told you nothing other than that you felt uncomfortable.

"Al*bear*," he said again and gave me about thirty fingers of handshakes. "Your old lady gave me a cussin'-out in class this A.M."

"For what, not fondling enough letters?" We're talking elementary education here: Deb says Martha, the reading teacher, has Menkus run his hands over sandpaper cut-out letters to learn their shapes.

A low blow, but he didn't flinch. "No, no, we was yakkin' about you. I can't be seen rappin' with you no longer."

"What do you mean?"

"Every time I see you I got to slink away. Mrs. Bieds say you see a thing when you ain't touchin' it. Can you dig that? See here, I touch you." He squeezed my elbow. "But I'm too close to you. I can't really see you with my fat eyes." He shut his eyes. "She says only what ain't already in your head be real. Do you understand what I'm trying to tell you, man?"

"No," I said. This time Deborah had me completely stumped. It seemed to fly flat in the face of the dyslexia exercises.

"The lady says don't let you do no more talkin' to me 'cause it's the only way you can write good. Use your imagination a little, like the song says."

200

"What song?"

That was all the clue he needed to whip the volume up to ten and blast out the middle section of the airplane. Even Black Stallion told him to turn it off. He turned it down but not off, and you could still hear it fine. The plugs must've been no good. In everything Menkus was the exception that proved the rule: Deborah says dyslexics have huge trouble trying to listen to TV or radio while talking, writing, or reading. Menkus couldn't read or write to save his life, but he could fill your ears with smoke.

"You can drop your shit on my phone machine," he continued. "But I can't call you back, ain't that a panic? This way you got to make up all the facts."

"Right. Make up the facts."

"That's what she said, and the lady's my teacher. I ain't even supposed to have told you what she said. She says do not fill in my love on nothin'. I just got to explain it to you so you won't be holdin' no grudges. She says not to say nothin'. She don't want you to get snagged by the facts. Go off on your own. Free-lance, man. Mess with your mind."

"Yo, Menkus," Gault bellowed from a few rows back.

"Yo."

"Shut the fuck up." The player section of the plane applauded. "We're tryin' to get a little shut-eye."

It sounded like one of Professor Biederman's annual intellectual experiments—I was supposed to stay away from Menkus in order to understand him better. Get at him through guesswork and daydreams. Great stuff. Write a description of him walking from one end of the airplane to the other, write the autobiography of the end of my career.

"Stay away if you want to write the article good," he said, lowering his voice a little to discourage Gault from releasing the emergency exit. "So this is it, my man. It's been good knowing you."

"Hold on a minute, Menkus."

"She said for you to leave me alone, which you should, 'cause I'm goin' to sleep right about now like every other normal human being on this airplane," he said, and up went the volume again.

Kooky. Menkus finally talking to me in order to tell me he was never again going to be able to talk to me. Saying goodbye at the same time as hello. Discussing the end of the Relationship with your college crush before the Relationship ever got to first base.

Francis was still talking to Firewood. I went looking for liquor, but no one had any. Tomlinson discouraged me from indulging. Monroe Terry gave me religious information, near to Thee as we were. Rod Williams said to get back to him if I located any. When Dogwood left, I told Francis, and he thought it was so funny he almost broke the window. He also said he didn't think Menkus was bright enough to make up such a preposterous idea, and I had to agree.

The landing in Dayton was pretty rocky and my ears hurt. The rain had cleared. The minute I got to the motel I called home, to no answer. I called the RSU Library, and the desk girl said faculty in third-floor carrels don't get interrupted. I said this is kind of an emergency, and she said they don't get interrupted. Johnny Carson had on the same lady I hadn't heard of when she made a comeback last night on Tom Snyder. I drank gin and sucked lemons until I conked out, and by the time I woke up the next morning, Deborah had already returned to the library and Barry would only talk about *Days of Heaven*, which was the bossest movie he'd seen so far at age seven. He said he'd remember the wheat in the sunrise forever.

The rest of the day I walked in and out of college bars, getting into arguments with Dayton kids about whether their tow-headed Scotty Rollins was better than Menkus.

"Please," I said, "we might as well compare Red Auerbach and Dick Sandalwood."

At least that got them laughing. One fellow with a backpack and a beard, who suffered from the sort of skinniness I associate with disinterest in life, asked me if my wife happened to be Deborah Biederman, and when I said yes he said he thought no one wrote better, more empathetically about Maya Angelou than Deb did. I nodded and said I'd be sure to tell her and she'd be sure to tell Tolliver, her chairman; then I pretended to be a lot drunker than I was.

The Tigers, defending champions of their conference, were favored to repeat and had won their first three games, including an upset at Tulsa, a difficult place to get out of alive, let alone triumph. Just outside Dayton, surrounded by rubber plants and dairy cattle, stands a huge meditation center, apparently one of the major places in the country to get your consciousness checked. The Dayton coach believes meditation's a good way to concentrate while staying calm, so you get a funny mix sometimes at press conferences here. Kids being asked about a rebound and coming back with words of wisdom from the inscrutable East. Young men totally at peace with themselves and their mantra until they get yanked in the final minute of overtime.

Dayton State tends to be a solid, no-nonsense team that works its ass off every second of every game, every inch of the floor, but is dull. Patterned, white basketball, not all that different from what Lemonwood had up his sleeve until Menkus showed up. They never beat themselves, the Tigers, but they never shake you out of your winter coat, either.

Even in press row before the game, everyone wanted to compare Menkus' performance against Kansas to Rollins' act at Tulsa, which was absurd because that game was an aberration for Menkus whereas all Rollins ever did was put it up from around the perimeter. A deadeye, but slow as ice melting. A referee baiter who shook his fist at the crowd whenever he did something good, which was often, since he was a great scorer. Yet to me he couldn't carry Menkus' water bottle. To quote from my own column: "Someone put Ronee Blakely on earth to sing songs that tear your heart in half. The same person put Belvyn Menkus on 94' x 50' to show what the human body can do before it dies."

You could see the effect the meditation center had had on

the gym, as it was a relatively old place spruced up to look like a large church—everything touched up with a coat of white and nice, neat seats like pews. All the fans were terribly polite, and there was a poster that afforded a rare road greeting: WELCOME, STALLIONS. The fans might have been dressed in slippers and pajamas for all the energy and noise they conveyed, which had a subduing effect on the couple hundred Stallion fans who made the trip, as well as the cheerleaders, including the nearly irrepressible Liz Cheng. Both refs looked like they'd eaten too many bran muffins or refereed too many high school blow-outs. The players looked dead on their feet out there, Karl counted sweat tops, Ott and Nagel doodled, even Hinselwood had to suppress a yawn. I looked all over the balcony for Vicki but couldn't find her and hoped the rain hadn't sent her scurrying back home on Highway 70. The Tigers took the lead on four Rollins jumpers from downtown Dayton and, in keeping with the soporific mood of the place and the sound of people snoring, went directly into a slowdown to protect their advantage. Rollins ran in and out of the key, slipping behind pick after pick for perfect bombs from the circle. Shades of Biederman at sixteen.

Hinselwood put in Keil and, for a shock, Rod Williams to get things stirred up, but Keil was overeager and committed three fouls in as many minutes and Williams hadn't got in this early since high school and threw up a few bricks. The fans lulled themselves back to sleep with their mantras. Bortz, the Dayton coach, buttoned and unbuttoned his check coat and smiled beatifically. With nine minutes left in the first half, the Tigers were up by seven. Rollins had no personal fouls since he never plays any defense, so he guarded Menkus coming downcourt. Menkus slapped the ball behind his back, dribbling through his legs as he brought Rollins left to right. Rollins hand-checked him all the way, hounding him with angry hands cutting the air. Menkus passed to Tomlinson, and Tomlinson gave it right back. Ironwood had Menkus clear a side, and, even more surprisingly, Dayton didn't collapse into a box-and-one or even a three-two zone. The game, the season, and my heart pivoted on this play. Though I'm positive he could have eaten Rollins for lunch, Menkus refused to take him to the hoop and, instead, dribbled in place until Tomlinson broke free around the horn. Menkus fed him; Tomlinson fired and missed. A minor action to the denizens of the Dayton gym, where what few rowdies there were were treated like disturbers of the peace. To me, the pass was Menkus' signal to his teammates that he wasn't going to go playground every time they got eighteen points down. After dismantling Charley Murphy, he had said: "If that's all it was, I could beat off by myself."

I am not hallucinating when I say that during halftime Muzak came on and a slide show on the beauty of southwest Ohio was flashed on a big screen above the scoreboard. I walked around the squeaky-clean auditorium, gazing at the glee in people's faces.

During the second half, Menkus continued to refuse to go one-on-one. He didn't just give up the ball, however. He brought Norm Durland low and Dwayne Gault high and got them finally to start setting screens for each other. He fed BS off the break. He hit Tomlinson in his favorite spots. A Menkus press produced an interception for Keil and a dunk for Williams, who was showing glimmers of getting his game together. Whatever each player did best, Menkus made him do better.

River State may have looked like it was trying to beat Dayton at the shut-off, which is tantamount to trying to beat an Eskimo at a nose-rubbing competition: it isn't done. And that's not what was going on. It's hard to explain, but you can feel it. A team is either together or it's not. Subtly, undramatically, in the silence of the Dayton Anglican service, the Stallions came together. Gault expected and caught a blind pass from Menkus. Black Stallion finished off a zone trap by stepping into the gap for the interception. A Tomlinson fast break ended not in a jumper from the foul line but a three-point play for Terry down deep. For the first time in his conscious adult life, Norm Durland picked, then rolled *toward* the hoop.

No one in the stands really noticed, no one really cared. The referees barely had the breath to blow their whistles or last legs to wobble up and down the court. And the RSU contingent was sucked into a stupor because, although the Stallions were finally playing the game the way it was supposed to be played, still in some ways it was their worst performance of the year: they hadn't made all the adjustments yet. There were growing pains. Boxing out, helping on defense, trailers calling their position—all this you would have thought was brand-new to them. It was just Hinselwood's or even Dayton's basic offense, but with guts. They were hustling to make good plays rather than struggling to avoid boo-boos. What could Tinselteeth do but stand on the sidelines, tan hands behind his head, and finally admit the team belonged to Menkus?

With four minutes remaining and the Tigers stretching their lead to thirteen, the negligible raucous part of the crowd began the obligatory *Belvyn Who?* chant. The flip side of the sublime serenity of meditation consciousness. To them Menkus had dudded. Fine. Who cared about them? Menkus scored his points, trying to keep things close, but refused to engage in a trigger duel with Rollins. That wasn't what he brought to the sport. Before the game was over I'd already written my lead for the game piece and I had an angle on the Menkus article, which was due in Milwaukee in two weeks.

> The Stallions may have lost a basketball game last night before an SRO crowd in Dayton. But they found something far more important and of far greater value than a tally in the win column. They found each other.

NINE

I'D never much liked Jimmy Carter, but now I felt sorry for him. He lived all by himself in a big house with the Christmas tree lights turned off, the flag at half-mast, and no one wanting him around much longer, including his brother. A lame duck wearing cardigan sweaters, having to listen to Ghotbzadeh.

The prime rate was twenty-one, which didn't make a lot of difference to me, as I wasn't exactly Perpetual Savings' most preferred customer, anyway.

A year ago the actress Jean Seberg, who was born in Iowa, killed herself. On the anniversary of her death her husband, a movie director, joined her. Rita Jenrette, the wife of an Abscam congressman from South Carolina, called a press conference to discuss politicians screwing secretaries on the steps of the Lincoln Memorial, which would be "Dutch" Reagan's backyard any day now, right, Francis? No one was happy doing what they were doing. Everybody wanted to be somebody else. A lot of people from Iowa have gone on to make it, but they didn't make it by staying in Iowa.

A running back's mother told a grand jury she was offered an '81 Thunderbird loaded with extras. A coach was fired for acting as his player's agent. The first question one kid asked was who the boosters were. A quarter-mile relay team got credit for classes at a correspondence school they'd never heard of. Kids were given wads of tickets to scalp and lifelong health insurance. Altered transcripts. False vouchers. A district-court judge said colleges were maintaining professional squads under the guise of amateur rules. Another judge said the notion of the student-athlete was a charade. Menkus was maybe the least among many evils. Just reading the Sunday *Register* gave me a spleen full of righteous juice.

Governor Ray announced impossibly steep spending cuts, especially in education, especially to River State, which sent Deborah into a tailspin, since it meant tenure would be even less likely. My attempt during dinner to confront her about the Menkus Layaway Plan led without detour into an incredibly tedious debate on the nature of Understanding and sent Barry shuffling down the block to get a little bit of the genuine article.

On Monday rain turned to snow. I hate hearing about mild winters. You get to a point where you expect to be skinny-dipping by January, but the river has frozen over and you haven't seen your driveway for a month. It's winter, it's Iowa. It's miserable. Forget about mild.

River City was in hibernation. Final exams started Thursday, and now all the students had to do for real what they were supposed to have been doing since September. A lot of fraternity boys like to say they do nothing more strenuous than drink Bud and listen to REO Speedwagon, but most of the undergraduates seem to be busy little beavers, good Anglo-Saxon stock. Vicki hadn't come to Dayton Saturday because she'd panicked about not passing her Child Development test, and she was supposed to be in the library again Tuesday night. When I went looking for her, it was wall-to-wall with coats and gloves and books and yellow underliners and kids sick from pulling too many all-nighters, passing around their colds, sucking Halls Mentho-Lyptus.

She said she'd be in the third-floor stacks. The third floor was a big place and I couldn't find her anywhere. Polished glass divided the rooms, and you had to be careful not to break your beak in the process. I bumped into Adrienne, who looked great in a purple turtleneck and boots and jeans; she gave me a hug but couldn't stop to shoot the shit because the map room closed at eight and she needed to know the bevel of the bank of the exit ramp as I-80 cruised through Coralville. I saw Tolliver from afar, lecturing in his slouched scholar way to an underling and, though I knew I should have passed on the Dayton grad student's compliment about Deborah, I didn't. I couldn't. I was too pissed at her. A thousand minds motoring at once. I wondered what would happen if you had all this brain activity going at once on the same circuit.

I finally found Vicki sitting in a mess of gum wrappers, soda cans, and crumpled papers at a carrel pushed against the wall. Screeching a chair across the linoleum, I got greeted with "Shhh" and a pencil poked in my ribs. "My God, Albert, don't you realize people are studying for finals?"

I apologized, but the kids were happy for any excuse to take a timeout. I've always loved the sound of whispering in public places. Its dead seriousness dazzles me.

"Well, how's it going?" I asked. "When's the test?"

Vicki looked down at her book, across her notes, then at me. "Pretty good," she said. She looked down again, flipped some pages. "Pretty good." She played with her pencil, looking at me once more and braving a smile. Gathering all her pens and papers and underliners and loose papers, she threw them in the air and collapsed on the desk. I figured she'd been studying too hard. When I tried to lift up her shoulder, I saw she was crying.

There were a lot of fluorescent lights, desks, chairs, librarians walking around, and other serious people. It wasn't a very private place to console somebody, but I dug out my hanky, which she honked her nose with and rubbed her eyes.

"What's wrong, sweetheart?" I asked. Bad question. It opened the floodgates, and her pals along the west corridor of the third floor were making a field day out of the event. Up went her textbook and down went her head again onto her carrel. She was crying herself silly.

"Come on, Vicki, why don't we get some fresh air?"

She went to blow her nose in the ladies' room and wash her face, which struck me as a major move in the right direction. I sat on a blue couch in the lobby, looking around at kids who couldn't have been any older than eighteen, hoping that when Vicki returned her big explanation wasn't going to be that she was pregnant.

It wasn't. She came back cracking Dentyne and hugged me hard.

"I'm really sorry," she said.

"Are you okay now?"

"I don't know, I just—" She smiled and leaned against me on the blue couch. We got a number of looks over our way. I guess this wasn't usually done in the third-floor lobby. "I feel so stupid. I can't seem to get these ideas down. I know I'm gonna flunk and—"

She would have got going again if I'd given her half a chance, so I cut her off. "Give yourself some time," I said. "You hadn't even looked at the book before the weekend. When's the test?"

"Monday."

"You've got a whole week."

"I know I'm never gonna get it," she said and started in on stages this, psychosex that, hard concepts to get behind. Before Barry was born, Deborah and I read everything that was ever written about raising children, though it turns out in the case of juvenile diabetes you can pretty much throw those books out the window. Vicki and I sat on the couch, our legs touching, her head on my shoulder, and I told her whatever I could remember about Deborah nursing Barry; me teaching him how to use the toilet; when he became aware of, as he calls it, his fire hose. Funny stuff, which anyone would find interesting.

When he was four Barry got preoccupied with not transporting dirt on the soles of his shoes and would have to race back to the spot where he thought he'd first contacted the smudge. Vicki was able to tell me what stage that meant he was regressing to and why it was related to how insane her mother gets whenever packing boxes aren't broken down and stored properly. Suddenly it didn't seem only theoretical. It was about people, which is what I tell Deborah till I'm blue in the face: real life beats the hell out of books.

"See?" I said. "You understand this a lot better than you thought you did."

"You're a whiz."

"You're the whiz. You put it together. You'll do great on the test."

"I don't know. I can sort of explain it to you, but when I try to read that fucking book I can't concentrate. The words are like Jell-o."

"Maybe dyslexia's contagious and you picked it up from Menkus."

"Don't be funny. I need to get at least a B in Psych Thirty for my scholarship and for J-school."

"Journalism schools don't care about grades. All they're concerned with is your newspaper work. You'll probably get the job at the *Globe-Democrat*, anyway."

"What do you mean?" she said, squeezing my sweater. "Did you hear something?"

"Maybe next year we'll meet between Milwaukee and St. Louis in Chicago for DePaul games."

"What are you talking about?"

I hadn't told her about the *Journal* job so she wouldn't be jealous, but when I did she got so excited I had to remind her I was still only a candidate. "Let's get out of here," I said. "Come celebrate with me at the Coralville Reservoir."

"Celebrate what?"

"That I'll get the job and you'll pass your test."

"And . . ." She gave me her bee-sting pucker.

"And you'll get the St. Louis internship."

"Deal," she said. "But no celebration. I have to keep studying."

"It'll be beautiful along the dam."

"I really should stay here."

"Just an hour."

"Just an hour?"

"An hour and a half."

"An hour," she said and buttoned her coat, stuffing things into her purse. "Okay, lifesaver, let's go." Deborah says the cruelest thing a man can do to a woman is take her away from her work. Vicki may have felt the same way, but I didn't stop to ask. We took the steps two, then three at a time going down, holding hands.

Vicki called it the Blooper Beetle because there were so many things wrong with it. As I swung into the right lane of North Governor for Highway 1, she switched the radio from the Statler Brothers to Elvis Costello, a definite dip, and kept making digs about the broken gear knob and the glove compartment not staying shut.

"Vicki, please," I said. "There are limits. All dinner I argued with Deborah. I don't need more grief."

"I'm sorry," she said and to prove it switched the station from new wave back to country. "I'm just so hyper. I must be in an oral mood." I looked glum and she went on: "Jee-*sus*, I was just trying to make a joke." We smooched, but all I felt was the physical awkwardness. We'd known each other for two years, and now, after going to bed once, we were suddenly supposed to be intimate as hell. "Were you guys arguing about me?"

"No, she thinks we're friends."

"Well, we are, aren't we?"

"Yes, but, you know—"

"I know what?" She wanted to toy with me, and I let her.

"Something more's going on."

"More what?" she asked. We looked at each other for the longest time, then burst out laughing. I nearly lost control of the car, bumping down a dirt road toward the dam. "No, really, what were you guys arguing about?"

212

"On the plane to Dayton Friday night, Menkus said Deborah came up to him after class that morning and told him to keep his distance from me so I'd write a better article."

"What?"

"Making up the facts, Menkus called it, which is what it is. Deborah has this cockamamie theory that I should never interview him or do any research. Just kidding, I said what am I supposed to do, then, have the whole piece a description of Menkus walking across the street? She said that would be the best sports story ever written."

"Sounds nutsy."

"It is."

We were at the bottom of the road. It was dark and deserted, I was lost, and Vicki wasn't sure where we were, either. When I tried to turn around, my tires spun in the gravel and a jeep passed by out of nowhere, blowing his horn.

"Fuck you, you asshole," Vicki howled at the stranger to show her support.

A ways away tower lights overlooked the dam. The snow had stopped but was piled in drifts everywhere except the main road, which was a river of slush.

"In a weird way, though, I see what Deb means," I said. "My Dayton article had no interviews and almost no stats. I was pretty pleased with it, and Marty didn't seem to mind. What did you think?"

"Honestly?"

"No. Lie through your teeth."

"It seemed thinnish. The players and Hinselhorse always say the same things, but I missed reading them. And I don't know if I think Menkus really brought them together."

"Ah hah. So you weren't studying?"

"I took a break at nine to watch the end of it at the Union. If you agree with her, what's the argument?"

"She loved my piece on the game and that made everything easier, but during dinner tonight my anger boiled up again. I mean, it's outrageous when you think about it—her trying out these ideas on my life. She'll probably add an epilogue to her

213

book in which her dodo student and unsophisticated husband are examples of existentialism or something."

"How do things stand now?"

I realized we were within shouting distance of the reservoir. The tower lights lit the lake and there was a little stretch of fake beach, but everywhere we looked were other cars, which had roan-and-gray Stallion stickers in their rear windows.

"They stand the way they always stand. We yelled at each other, then kissed and made up. I'm tired of arguing with Deborah. I must like you too much."

Then I told her about the Raeburn visit and said the only reason I hadn't told her earlier was that she'd been pushing me so hard to publish I wanted to wait until I was confident it would gather into something. Looking hurt, she said she understood, and I had to say of course we were a team and would stay a team, of course she was going to pass her Psychology test and get the *Globe-Democrat* job. Of course.

No new topics of conversation bubbled up out of the dashboard, so there was nothing to do for a while other than stare at the windshield and listen to the radio, which was pumping hard rock to humor Vicki. My lights and everyone else's were off, but the moon was full and the tower threw its beam across the whole area. The dam wasn't nearly as secluded as I thought it would be. I had no idea it was such a popular place to take your date for an hour break from cramming. The parking lot, the other chairs, the fake beach, the reservoir, and the frozen swimming hole were all illuminated for us until Vicki suggested we spin away from lovers' lane into a wooded space surrounded by poplars.

I said, "You know, it's funny. When I walked in on you and Hutchins at Cats I was afraid the two of you were going to wind up out here together."

Vicki took my hand off her knee, put it on her mouth, and pretended to gag. "What, are you kidding?"

"Well, I stood behind the wall for a minute, eavesdropping, and you seemed to be going great guns there for a while. He liked you, you really had eyes for him and were touching him, eating his leftovers, flattering him—"

"Give me a break, Albert. It's the oldest trick in the book. It's called softening up your sources."

I said that wasn't all she was doing.

"He's a smart, handsome man, but not my type. Kind of a prig for a black guy, know what I mean?"

"It's hard to believe he was ever a basketball player."

"I mean, Jesus, what were you afraid Hutchins and I would be doing out here, discussing IRA's?"

You would have to be as skinny as Vicki even to think about what she did next. She pushed the front seat forward, slid around the gear shift, and climbed into the backseat, saying, "Come on, Hutchins, come on, kill me with your cash flow."

I tend not to waste a lot of time in this type of situation. I couldn't do what Vicki did, so I flopped over the driver's seat into her lap. Her twitch was like a wink that wouldn't stop and was saying: fix me. Change me, Larry Hutchins, slam dunk me into delight. I kissed all up and down her lanky left leg from her shins to her hips, all over those jeans, faded material that tasted like black licorice, and I love black licorice. Her legs were tight and muscular from too much racquetball.

"God, Albert, that feels so good. It really does. You have such a nice touch. So slow. That feels so wonderful. Even better than Hutchins."

"Enough about Hutchins, okay?"

"I was just kidding."

I kissed her right leg as thoroughly as I had the left and said, "Deborah hasn't had gams like these since Johnny Wooden retired." I was feeling old, and this put me in historical perspective. I wasn't archaic.

"I'll stop bringing up Hutchins if you stop with Deborah, okay?"

"Okay," I said.

We tugged each other's pants off.

"It's been so long."

"A week."

"It seems longer. You've been keeping a low profile."

"No, I haven't.

"Yes, you have."

"I kissed only one person in the last decade. I'm still getting used to this."

"I can't stand being away from you. I think I'm falling in love."

"You're infatuated," I said. "Maybe you like me."

"I like you very much," Vicki said.

"I like you very much, too. I think you're great. Your legs make me happy."

"Good. Then kiss me, Mr. Money Market."

It was dark. Eight at night in the middle of December. I couldn't see the other cars and kids or the tower, but I could sense them and felt trapped, especially when the wind scraped branches against the antenna and tossed snow across the hood and the radio played on and on, all that whining crap. I was caught between the stick shift and the floor, kneeling on the little bump where most people rest their feet when they're sitting in back.

We kissed on the cheeks to warm each other up, all around the neck and across the forehead. My God, what a perfect face she has, so pure and serious. I want her twitch to stop, I want to melt into snow.

I touched her lips with my fingers, then fully with my lips, and it damn near broke my breath. The booky smells of the library mingled with her own minty scent and, beneath that, the juiciness of her mouth ripened. Soft, melting, milky candy. I love kissing this girl.

She took off her sweater, blouse, and bra. Vicki's small breasts seemed meant for a lady tennis player or long-distance runner. Now I was lying on top of her, kissing her lips and lungs. The only clothes she had on were her untied Adidas.

But I went *pffft*. Puny limpness, no life to speak of, and I knew from previous battles with the dead dragon that it wasn't going to be brought back easily, not tonight.

Trees waved in the wind. The sky was black. The heater smoked, making the car hot, claustrophobic. As my body went cold I could feel my face on fire. We were sitting next to each other in the backseat, naked. I kept kissing her softly on the lips, little pecks like water drops, but I couldn't taste her breasts. I couldn't. While my masculinity played hooky, I didn't want her even to see me.

"It's okay," she said. "It's already in. I put it in when I went to the bathroom at the libe, just in case." She pinched my ass playfully, which didn't help matters any. "You don't have to hold back."

"I'm not," I said.

"Not what, not in?"

"No. Not holding back."

"You're not?" she said, feeling around for excitement.

"No."

"Then what's the matter?"

'I'm not sure," I said. I was still trying, still rubbing, squirming, heaving, imagining buckets of water tumbling from the tops of tall buildings. "I think everything from the past week finally wore me out."

Vicki persisted. She'd never heard of such a thing actually happening and couldn't accept it. I'd helped her with Psych 30. She thought she might love me. But I wasn't much help, try as I might, try as she might. She used her hands. She used her mouth until the nine o'clock news came on K101. She used her dinky breasts. At one point she tried her toes. I simply didn't have it in me. And the more she twisted and turned, from her back to her knees to her stomach to her side, the more obvious it became how little I had to give her.

I flashed to seeing Menkus at the field house urinal and how completely primitive he was about it. He just whipped out his dick and sprayed the floor, then ran upstairs without washing his hands. I thought about Barry calling his penis a fire hose, which was definitely the wrong thing to think about, because by now Barry's was probably bigger than mine.

Although at first Vicki said, "No, I don't like that," she let me lick her for a while, but I was too depressed to get very passionate about it, and she didn't appear to be having the time of her life, either. Soon both of us were cold and self-conscious.

"It's okay," she said. "It doesn't matter, honey. Tomorrow night, or whenever. It's just nice to be with you." The girl with the twenty-four-karat heart.

So we ended up just hugging in the backseat. I was too big for her to hold like that, and I was too old, I finally realized, to be spending Tuesday night at the Coralville Reservoir—too damn old.

Somewhere someone honked his horn. I heard a splash. The radio spun out sex music and the night widened, opening up into your capillaries, making your blood go dark. It scared the bejeezus out of me. This was a depressing place to hang around if you weren't necking, and I would like to have died if we weren't dressed and driving out of here in five minutes or less. Vicki agreed.

"Take me back to the library, okay?" she said with love and understanding and no twitch in her eyes.

It was a long return trip back to town. Sleet fell and I couldn't get the wipers to work. The wind wailed through the floorboards, the heater went on the fritz, and whenever I pushed the speedometer past fifty the backseat sounded like we'd broken the springs. Maybe we had. My snow tires weren't on yet. Traction was a joke.

Sitting in front and wearing clothes, we weren't doing a whole lot of hugging or handholding. I wasn't in the mood for music or late sports scores. I wanted to be left alone with my own mind and the general silence. Vicki sulked, gazing out the window at the farms along Highway 1, not talking. By the way we were acting, you would have thought we were total strangers, a man with a receding hairline giving a pretty girl a lift home in the dark.

I swung off North Dodge onto Burlington for Madison. As

we approached the library I made a feeble joke about how I'd made sure we hadn't contributed to child development.

Vicki riffled papers in her purse and said, "Thanks again for helping me so much on this." Then she scampered up the steps and joined the parade. Adrienne was probably ensconced now in the Engineering stacks, computing the possible degree of variance in exit ramp bevels.

It was ten, but I couldn't go home, couldn't face Deborah or Barry, not stone sober. I drove to Phil's Bar and Buffet, the only tavern on the east side where I've ever felt I belonged. The foggy glass dividing the booths makes you feel like you're swimming around in a carpeted aquarium. So does the Hamm's waterfall that constantly changes backgrounds.

Deborah thinks Phil's is called Phil's because the Philosophy department practically lives here. Every night Professors Neikrans, Billings, Feldman, Dobrinsky, Wistrich, and Middleton sit at tables in back, drawing circles and squares and arguing how you know for sure a chair is a chair. They all have hacking coughs from smoking a carton every third day and pregnant stomachs from believing truth is found at the bottom of bottles of Lowenbrau. Each philosopher has his little branch of the tree of knowledge—Logic, Metaphysics, Ethics, what have you—and they are fully capable of making Deborah appear by comparison to have both feet planted on the curb. They'll drag anyone into the discussion, if you let them, and they can be plenty entertaining, but sometimes I feel like butting in and saying, "Just try to sit down on it. If you fall on your ass, it isn't a chair."

They wouldn't listen to me, and there's no reason they should. They're not my crowd and I'm not theirs, though they always have great things to tell me about Deborah, what a brilliant analytic mind she has, etc. Phil's is what I call a combination bar because it solves the town/gown dilemma by letting the academicians have all the tables from the middle of the room on back, while people who work for a living take the counter.

219

When I walked in, Gregory was ringing the register, the mountain behind the lake was becoming a waterfall, and my bad leg was killing me from all the backseat acrobatics. Marty, who is not supposed to drink, was dead drunk at the window table by himself. Everyone else was gathered around the television, watching *Stallion Standouts*.

During the football and basketball seasons, Francis rolls highlight film of the past week's action and interviews players. No one pays attention during football season because there usually aren't any highlights and most of the athletes have a tough time articulating. The basketball show hasn't been all that popular, either, since the film tends to look like it was shot from the top of the Astrodome, but everyone's eyes were trained on Francis, who looked fatter than usual and frog-eyed as his hands roamed Menkus' legs and shoulders in a way that almost any viewer who wasn't asleep would find offensive.

"Did you see Biederman's piece on the Columbus game?" said someone who was wearing a fishing hat. "He's full of shit 'cause if that team's comin' together I'm—"

"Biederman's right here and I'm telling you just give them three weeks, pal, then tell me who's full of shit."

Earl and Danny, two young, decent, grungy *Register* guys, cheered me on, and most everyone turned around to say hello. A few who agreed with Fishing Hat thought I must have been paid off by Menkus or Hinselwood or the athletic department.

A guy named Bill, who dispatches ambulances for River State Hospital, said Menkus was the worst kind of punk ingrate, a white nigger, and lit into Francis: "I've heard that man's an alcoholic. He's fat and he can't hold his liquor. They should give him the boot."

From the other side of the bar at his lonely table, Marty shouted just one word: "Tests." Tests? He didn't like River City during exam week? I tried to figure out what he meant and told myself to go visit with him. Earl and Danny and I exchanged one of those concerned-but-don't-ask-me shrugs. Danny wrote the one semi-critical piece about a deal the council cut with an anonymous hotel chain which backed out of its commitment at the twelfth hour, leaving River City with one more underground garage it didn't really need and one less playground.

Gregory said, "Come on, Billy. We've all known Francis for twenty years. We all think he's great."

"We all think he's a great boozehound."

"Hey, pal, lighten up," Danny said, in his best City Hall reporter voice. "Drexler has more knowledge stored in his little pinkie than you do in your home library."

"Francis is going through rough times," Gregory said. "Weight trouble, drink trouble, age trouble. He doesn't know where—"

"He doesn't know where to pour his next drink," said Fishing Hat, whom I didn't know and was glad I didn't.

Everyone cracked up but the Citysiders and Gregory, who brought me my usual, a hot basket of popcorn and a draft in a Stallion mug, and said, "I saw what you saw Saturday, Bieds. I think they're gonna do it." Gregory has no fingers on his left hand and counts your change in the crook of his arm. I've never put much stock in his sports predictions, though, because for sheerly sentimental reasons he always supports the underdog.

"Tests," Marty hollered again, sounding totally iced. Get over there and talk to him, I told myself and the Citysiders told me, but I wanted to catch the clips.

"Lay, Lady, Lay" crooned out of the jukebox. Professor Dobrinsky shook a chair over his head to prove it didn't exist, and his philosopher-friends cowered in the darkness. I waited for film to roll, for Francis to stop prattling. Menkus stared into outer space. I was watching the lake behind the waterfall become a camping ground when Francis and Menkus vanished, the color went to black and white, and the highlights started.

Menkus commented upon the action in that squeaky but somehow still cocky voice of his. I couldn't hear what he was saying due to comments from the peanut gallery.

221

"Yeah, right, Albert," Billy said, "they're really coming together."

Fishing Hat: "Great moral victory—team ball, but they lose by twenty."

Earl wondered, "Why is this in black and white?"

What Francis had done, of course, was choose the sequences in which River State played sluggishly and Menkus in particular looked awful. On the moves Francis screened, Menkus was so tentative and confused he seemed to be almost afraid something would happen. By contrast, Dayton was daring and exciting and, the more Francis showed, the worse things got. It was an amazing editing job, done to discredit me and embarrass Menkus. I only hoped tomorrow's *Stallion* wouldn't have a sports editorial calling for Menkus to be benched, signed *VL*.

"You musta been really shit-faced, Albert," Ambulance Billy said. "That kid's terrible."

"What game were you watching, my friend? River State looks like the Girl Scouts," Fishing Hat contributed.

"If Menkus is pro material, I'm a shoo-in for secretary of state," said some satirist.

Real gamers in the clutch, Danny and Earl yukked it up along with the rest of them.

Bringing me another draft, Gregory was as solicitous as always, and we talked a little about the way Menkus saw the floor, his instincts, his ability to control the flow and move people around, his generosity with the ball. We simply believed in him, and no one else did.

"Well," Francis harrumphed, "what do you have to say for yourself, young man?"

Menkus shrugged.

"Nothing at all in defense of your offense?"

"Don't know, Mr. D. Just tell 'em I'm workin' it out."

"Scintillating investigative interview, huh, Albert?" Earl said, trying to win back points.

Was I seeing something in Menkus' game that wasn't really there? The outlines of a fat man and skinny boy swiveled in swivel chairs on a darkening set. Then a slow-motion isolation prolonged the agony of Menkus trying to work the ball into Durland, who was so out of sync that when Menkus tried to go against the grain Durland was also going against the grain and the ball flew out of bounds. The slow-mo dissolved to a freeze frame: in a rare display of on-court frustration, Menkus cringing and whapping his hands together.

The waterfall turned to mountain scenery. Professor Neikrans was pulling the plastic suction cups off the legs of a chair to demonstrate the concept of chemical dependency. Gregory tried to bring me my third beer in fifteen minutes.

"No, really, I can't. I have a huge batch of stories to write tomorrow."

"On the house," he insisted, though what I'd done to deserve a draft I didn't know. There aren't many free beers left in the world, and down the hatch went this one.

Some people hung around to watch the news or have another drink, others left or broke into card games, and Earl and Danny hit on two women staring into their glasses at the opposite end of the counter. My leg was hurting so much I had to hop over to Marty's table. He was sloshed. His glasses were off, his head was tilted back, his face was Stallion-roan, and his skinny arms dangled at his side. He didn't look unlike a dead chicken, hung up to dry.

"What's this with tests?" I said.

"Huh?"

"You've been blabbering about tests all night."

"Do you know how tired I am of taking tests and getting back the results and then taking more tests? Liver tests and ulcer tests and blood tests and kidney tests. Watching how much sex Carol and I have and how many cigars I smoke and counting out my nitro pills. And you know I'm not supposed to be here, potted. What kind of life is this, Albert? Tests. Their fucking tests. They can shove them up their stethoscopes."

"Just stop taking them," I said stupidly.

He nursed his beer for a while, not saying anything. A couple of songs later he said, "I'm afraid to stop, Albie baby.

There, I admitted it. I'm scared." Then he flipped channels. "Your work is getting sloppy, my friend. You're missing deadlines and turning in trash. You've gotta finish that Menkus story and get back on schedule."

"By Christmas."

"Before." Now that he was criticizing me, he cut through the smoke and the haze and the booze to my heart's desire.

"I just have to get a little better grasp on Menkus."

"Grasp, shmasp . . ." He completely lost his train of thought and went back to: "Albert, when are you gonna start taking my tests for me?"

"Tomorrow. Tonight I'm going to drive you home."

"Darn tootin' you are," he said.

We stopped first in the john, where he lost it all and freshened his breath, then we sailed out the door into the parking lot, singing like cowboys. The night didn't seem to work any miracles for Marty, who went for his own car, a red Toyota truck, and kept trying to open the door without his keys.

"Carol can bring you in tomorrow," I said. "I'm driving you home tonight."

"Good idea. Great idea. You're our idea man. I'm our dead man."

"Come on, Marty, stop talking like a sicko."

I threw my files and papers and some other junk in the backseat, which I hoped no longer smelled of human failure, and we got in the freezing Bug and chugged west. Grabbing the gear knob was like squeezing a snowball.

"Do you maybe want to stop by and say hi to Deb on your way home?" I asked my boss, who was slumped over with his hands clutching his stomach and his head resting against the dash. "You guys haven't seen each other in ages, and she has this secret potion she whips up that is dynamite hangover protection. I have no idea what's in it other than that it works."

I was just babbling to keep myself company. The reason we don't see them is that Carol sells Mary Kay cosmetics, and Deborah's interest in cosmetics starts and stops, as Deb says, with the interesting etymology of the word.

Marty didn't say anything. He lifted up his head off the dashboard, looked out at the cloudy night, and put his head back down.

"Why don't you come over?" I said. "You can protect me."

"Protect me from what?" he muttered.

"We can be two deadbeat drunks together and diffuse her anger."

"Tell Deb to bring her secret potion to our New Year's party. Tell her to bring a bowl of the stuff."

"You're having a New Year's party?"

He suddenly looked over, came to, and said, "We are now."

He had a sweet smile on his face, and I tried to take the stops and turns soft so his head didn't go banging against the headrest, which had the stuffing coming out of it. We whipped through a lot of stop signs that seemed to me to be spelled upside down and backwards—Menkus signs. As I drove over the bridge into the hills and onto the west side, the town was beautiful and dark in its silence; it could have been the way it used to be when I came here in '62; everything was as it once was, a little piece of paradise on the prairie, before it all got turned into a toy town.

Marty was in bad enough shape that it seemed best to take him right home, and I said I'd probably just drop him off and be on my way myself, no coffee or cookies with Carol, who is the great coffee and cookie maker of River City. She is the queen bee of hearth and home, and Deborah despises her. As Vicki would say, I think Carol threatens her.

Sometimes Marty and I will get on exactly the same wavelength. I mean exactly. He said, "Remember when you first came here?"

"I was just thinking that," I said.

"Hey, so was I. We were both strong young bucks back then, and our minds were sharp and we wrote our articles in about two hours flat and spent the rest of the time marching around town, being greeted by strangers. Don't you remember that, Albert?

This was maybe a mite exaggerated, but the thing of it is is that from afar it felt like that. It all seemed to be in such solid place back then.

"Remember your job interview?"

"Do I?"

"Do you?"

"How could I forget?"

"Where was it?" he asked.

"At Phil's."

"Okay—what did we talk about?"

"Just one subject."

"And what was that?" Marty was hepped up, emerging from one fog to enter another.

"The equestrian competition at the '60 Olympics. You did all the talking and I had to ask questions, pretending I had the slightest idea what you were jabbering about."

"Because I already knew you were my boy." Unless it was moonbeam, I could swear I saw a little tear at the edge of Marty's sore left eye, and I was glad he blinked it back because I don't think I could have dealt with another case of the boo-hoos. But then he skipped back a quarter century: "I was just a junior at River State, writing up reports for the *Register* on the archery team, one after another. I was good at it and I needed the money and I wrote reports on other clubs and on games because I actually liked sports then. Suddenly old Billy Tyler died—you didn't know him—and I'm filling in, and Ned Wall ups and leaves, and before you know it my feet are bronzed. Whatever happened to What Cheer? Where went the fields of my youth, where are the hunting seasons?"

It was all such sentimental slop, such easy gliding nostalgia, but every time Marty punches life history synopsis #249 he chokes me up because I'm right here with him in River City, and I was glad we were past the golf course and athletic club, past my house, going past the small farms off County Road West and up the drive to Marty's place, where we were greeted by Carol, who worships the ground he trudges across.

"Well, the two of you look pretty shit-faced," she said.

There's that side of her, too, which I sometimes forget about.

"Yes, I suppose we got a little tight talking about old times," I said, feeling like I had to apologize.

She stood on the front porch with the door open and light on. She's a big woman, not fat, but big like an opera singer, bigger than life to be equal to life, as Marty once said, quoting her, I assume. A nice head of graying hair, surprisingly soft blue eyes, and tits like major ski slopes. Marty walked right by her into the kitchen, where cocoa and brownies were awaiting him, and I felt like I'd just delivered a runaway kid to his momma, and in a way I had. She protects him and, though she didn't invite me in, she stood on the porch with the door open and said, "Thanks so much for dropping him off."

"Sure."

"We're going to have a New Year's party," Marty called from the kitchen.

"We are?" she said.

"We are," he said, "on April Fool's Day."

"His car's over at Phil's," I told her.

"No sweat," she said.

"Billy Tyler," Marty said, "Ned Wall, Marty Reeves. You're the best, Albert."

"So how are your wife and son?"

"Barry's breezing through second grade and Deborah just finished writing a book. I've got a couple whiz kids for room-mates."

"What kind of book?"

"It's about autobiography."

"Albert, come on in, really. These are great brownies, sweetest," Marty said. It was all dark down at the end of the block with no immediate neighbors and a wooden fence around the house, smoke coming out of the chimney, horses in the distance, Iowa tourist brochure.

"No," I said to Carol, "it's about other people's. Why they write them, what they mean. It's very complicated. I don't entirely understand it."

"It sounds fascinating," she said, which was my cue to lean in the door one last time and tell Marty I'd see him at work. He was safe; he was warm; he was home, eating and drinking chocolate. He might as well have been back in What Cheer.

"Well, good night, then, Albert," Carol said.

"Yes, good night."

"Who knows—maybe we can make something out of New Year's."

"Yes," I said, "who knows?"

I slipped on a slick part of the pavement, waving.

Guilt city the second I walked into our house with the whole first floor dark. I sat on a stool in the breakfast room, flexing my knee. Three beers and a few exercises gave back some bend to my joints. I tiptoed up the stairs as quietly as I could.

All the hall lights were off, and on the way out of the bathroom I crashed into the hamper. I heard the rat-a-tat-tat of Deborah's typewriter and thought I could hear in the background "Winter" from her *Four Seasons* tape, which she plays whenever she's on a roll.

I turned the knob, creaked the door, and for a second I stood feeling the flab beneath my shirt, watching my wife, who sat in the room's only light, a circle of yellow lamp glare, with her slacks and turtleneck sweater a perfect fit on her perfect figure, her hair pinned back in a bun, a cigarette sizzling on the edge of her desk, and that gray animal of her IBM Selectric purring away.

Into my mind squeezed the memory of our first meeting at a Hillel House cocktail party for graduate students and young professionals. A Jewish proofreader at the *Register* invited me on a horrendously cold night the beginning of December 1970. Deborah was in her first semester of teaching, and though she wasn't Jewish, either, everyone at Brandeis and all her friends at Northwestern had been. I was lonely as a fallen leaf and missed my mother, who had died ten years ago to the day.

The other people at the party were science professors, hospital interns, and physical-therapy majors who told jokes about youth camps while drinking plastic cups of white wine. It was nice, but Deborah and I felt left out, since neither of us had been to Jewish retreats as a kid or were much interested in science. She came over to me and said how grateful she was to find a "humanist" and started discussing all the books she was reading and how excellent the Linday collection was at the library and how there was a certain four-French-words-that-I-didn't-quite-catch about River City that she found extremely conducive to the purity of her thought process.

While listening to her for hours in that freezing room my ears buzzed, the walls receded, and my whole body felt warm. In a way it was like coming down with pneumonia. She was the only person in the whole group who had friendly eyes, the only one who seemed at all excited about anything. Never in my life had I met anyone who sounded half as smart. I pretended to have read a number of books whose dust jackets I'd glanced at, and we walked home in the snowy blackness. But no kisses. No possibility of kisses. No kissing for a month while we got to know each other.

At the time I could listen to Deborah Rasnick read the phone book and get shivers across my chest.

Instead of going back to Hillel House, we went to a lot of movies that were difficult for me to follow and lectures I thought might never end until one morning she read my yearly column about the first ice skating of winter, and suddenly all she could talk about was children. Throughout the sixties I'd been having romances with women at work, secretaries at River State, impressionable fans, stringers from what was then called *The Daily Indian*. And when push came to shove, when the idea inevitably came up of buying a car together or her moving in, when in other words things got *serious*, I would always back off, stalling till that season's girl friend would simply have to quit out of pride. I grew up in a house in which family meant failure, and I wanted no part of domesticville. So, too, had Deborah gone through any number of passionate young scholars without staying power, though her home life growing up was much more stable if not necessarily any happier than mine. To speak of our courtship is something of a misnomer. Rather, it was a recognition. We were both breathing heavily on the big 3-0, and from the very first, we knew this was it, do or die. Not now or never, not last chance, but first good shot at the real thing, and we didn't want to blow it. Sex was sexy but also weirdly solemn, laden with import and portent in a way it never had been for me before. You could blink, but you couldn't look away: our bodies were ready and were trying to tell us something. For once, we listened. School was out. In the Sycamore Mall jewelry store, surrounded by nagging salesgirls and teenagers eating ice cream, Deborah quoted from memory a poem about bells and elves while picking out an engagement ring.

The wedding couldn't occur until Christmas vacation. My mother was no longer alive, but Dad flew from seventy-five-degree California to ten-below Rhinelander, where the wedding was held in the Quaker church Deborah had rebelled against to go to Brandeis on the advice of a Jewish high school English teacher she idolized. I hadn't really known Francis that long, so he was an usher, and Marty was my best man. Dad kept talking about how much warmer it was in California and adding one tennis sweater on top of another and folding and unfolding his arms across his chest until he looked and sounded like an aging Laguna Beach lifeguard. That's what I remember, Dad in his tennis sweaters, accusing me of trying to marry into "intellectual society," and the Rasnicks being beautifully civil to me and Dad but privately confessing to Deb their concern she was marrying "patently beneath" her, that is, them. And the only thing that saved the afternoon reception at the Rasnicks' house, the only good moment before Deb and I bolted to our honeymoon suite in Chicago, was the two of us skating together on the white lake behind their house, to everyone's ovation. The relatively thin ice gave in places but didn't crack.

Now, in the vacuum of the present, Deb took another drag on her cigarette, adjusted her contacts, turned to look at me, smiled, and finished typing her paragraph. "Listen to this," she said, "and tell me what you think:

> 'Albert writing on Belvyn is a bird watching a butterfly, is the autobiographer searching his own life, seeking the consolation of beauty, an impenetrable realm of grace, a perfect box holding only the holy.' "

"That's not going into your book, is it?" I asked.

"No, of course not. It's just diary stuff, but I kind of like it."

"That's what you write in your diary?"

"Why, what's the matter with it?" Deborah said.

"I don't know. I thought most people wrote what the weather was like and what they had for lunch. When my mother died, I opened her diary and practically every page just said, 'Uneventful.' "

"I have two pieces of great news. I've definitely, positively finished the book and am sending it off to River State Press."

"Fantastic," I said, but my heart wasn't in it because we'd already celebrated. I pushed aside a file folder to sit on the edge of her desk.

"And the second piece of good news, which you'll probably be a little more genuinely excited about—"

"Honey, really, I'm so proud of you."

"—is that Barry wants to go with you to the game this weekend."

"What?"

"Laurel told Barry about the '81 Pork Queen getting crowned during halftime Saturday. He has a crush on one of the candidates, and Laurel's jealous. Isn't that funny?"

"I have something to tell you, Deb, and something else I want to ask you about."

"First I want to reshape this journal entry."

We had lapsed to flinging monologues at each other. I finally realized the reason "Winter" keeps playing over and over is the cassette's broken. While Deborah shook a bottle of correction fluid, I got down off her desk to go check on Barry, who'd already lost all his animals and sheets to various chairs and rugs on the floor. I didn't want to disturb his slumber. I made myself watch from a safe distance.

TEN

MY rebuilt Bug engine wouldn't turn over Wednesday morning in temperatures that, with the wind-chill factor, ranged from a low of six to a high of nine. Deborah had already left in her Honda Civic. Taking the bus into town, I listened to a pimply kid tell his roommate about the time he took his girl friend to Minneapolis and pigeon shit landed in the motel fan. The shit didn't just hit the fan. It stayed thick in the air and he could smell it on his clothes through three washings. I never before had grasped what the phrase meant. Wednesday, December seventeenth, the shit hit the fan. And it wasn't any old pigeon shit. It was more like dive bombings from a dodo bird.

Marty was so lubricated last night and so hung over this morning I don't think he would have remembered half of what he said if I hadn't taken his advice to heart. I was tired of chasing geese and wanted to get back to the routine of pounding out copy. My ode to Anthony Carter got blue-penciled from a Rose Bowl preview, but everything else went as is: junior varsity sports wrap-up, pro football, pro basketball, college wrestling. River City sports fans are agate gluttons. Marty wanted an article on the owner of a Coralville skating rink who was buying three ads a week that read, "The only proof God exists is ice." Another piece on the thirty-five-and-over coed volleyball league, since the new rec director thanked us with a note for our profile of him. A feature on the guy who made sure he came in last in the Turkey Trot by stopping to have beer and pastrami sandwiches with well-wishers along the way.

Downtown Refurbishment finally came to the *Register*, as the sidewalk in front of us got sandblasted for reasons no one on the crack City staff could quite fathom. All day long we heard that screeching beat, and it was extraordinary the way people responded. A film of dust drifted slowly into the office windows, so people just spoke three times as loudly and brushed soot out of their hair. Some of the women in Features didn't like what it was doing to their clothes, but Editorial spent most of the day commenting on the action and Sabrina ended up getting a lunch date with one of the hardhats. I suppose if we got sawdust poured down our ears we'd all learn to wiggle them in thanks.

Marty came over to me and said, "The Colonel died last night. So what's Kentucky Fried Chicken doing in the mall?"

"First, two questions: how are you feeling?"

"Still spinning a bit, but better, thanks. You're a pal."

"Doesn't all this bother you?"

"All what?"

I pointed outside. "The impermanence, boss. Billy Tyler, Ned Wall, Marty Reeves, Albert Biederman, Downtown Re-furbishment."

He thought about it a second and said, "No. No. You learn to adjust. Why, does it really bother you?"

"Nah. Okay, so is this a joke—what's Kentucky Fried Chicken doing in the mall?"

"Offering a Colonel memorial wings-and-legs sale."

I had to call to find out if he was making it up. He wasn't. Mall culture had come to this.

With today's paper already to bed I got bored writing one short piece after another. I went over and shot the shit with Danny and Earl, who were announcing to anyone who would listen the details of their conquest, and I asked if they were planning to run it as a banner headline.

"No," Earl said, "as the lead sports story. It was an athletic event. I mean, you're looking at a combined total of six hours' exertion."

They both went into hysterics. Fine—just don't run a sidebar on Albert-Vicki. I tried to work on my Menkus story but got stuck. I needed new information and, calling Menkus, got the usual business:

> *I'm not as tall as the rest of the gang*
> *But I'm rappin' to the beat just the same . . .*

Drums were followed by glass breaking, the volume sliding around, then Menkus clearing his throat and saying, "Hey, the Wind here. Catch me if you can, man."

Okay, I thought, I've finally had enough. I was still pissed at Deborah for pushing me off Menkus and I still hoped he was going to save me and the soul of River City, but why am I begging to talk to someone who knows twelve words in the English language, half of which are *man*? Deborah's harebrained idea was a good excuse to stop beating my head against his head. Time to bother his friends and enemies, especially his enemies.

Marty went to go check out new heat at the gun shop. Gerry, from Classifieds, brought up Kentucky Fried Chicken bargain boxes for lunch. Big bargain—you had to leave three bucks in a kitty downstairs on your way home. With teletype and computers and sandblasters thrumming in my ears, with dust and soot settling in solidly on my desk, I did nothing until three o'clock except dial numbers and take notes. I needed someone to confirm my suspicion that Deborah was Menkus' contact person so I'd stop feeling paranoid. The highlights of my phone campaign—

Mrs. Menkus: No, Albert, Mr. Raeburn hasn't called us. Why would he?

Me: I don't know. I had a big discussion with him. I said some things about recruiting I probably shouldn't have.

Mrs. Menkus: Well, he's always been a saint to us.

Me: You don't happen to know who Belvyn's contact person is at River State, do you?

Mrs. Menkus: I thought it'd be you.

Me: What do you mean?

Mrs. Menkus: You seem like the closest to him of anyone there.

Me: That's not true anymore, since he isn't supposed to talk to me. My wife convinced him to stay away from me so I could concentrate on how he plays.

Mrs. Menkus: I don't get it.

Me: Neither do I. I still want to write a really good profile, but I need to sit down with him at least once and just gab.

Mrs. Menkus: It's great that Mrs. Biederman's helping him along so much with his reading problem, dyslexics, what have you, but, like I told you when you visited, he's not a great one to open up, give his heart to Jesus. Albert, by the way, did you talk to Louie last week?

Me: Yes.

Mrs. Menkus: He wanted me to tell you he was quite drunk and half-asleep and that what he said was nothing but stuff and nonsense from a daydream-nightmare he was having just before you called.

Me: Okay, Mrs. Menkus, I believe you. I figured something like that must be the case.

Braithwaite: What the fuck do you want now, Biederman?

Me: One last question. Do you have any idea who Menkus' contact person at River State might be?

Braithwaite: If I knew what a contact person was, I'm not sure I'd tell you, and since I don't I won't tell you, anyway.

Me: Thanks a million. Send me over to the athletic department, will you? I need to get some high school stats on Menkus.

Athletic Department: Yo.

Me: I'd like to speak to the head basketball coach, Mr., uh—

Jumpin' Bean: You're talkin' at him.

Me: Oh, hi. This is Albert Biederman, sports reporter for the *River City Register*, in Iowa. You threw me out of the gym a couple weeks ago. I'm writing that story on Menkus.

Jumpin' Bean: I've seen some of those ignorant articles of yours lyin' around here. You keep talkin' up the team game, but your Stallions is losing their sweat shirts. You play the passin' game for real and there ain't no possi*bili*ty of your boys losin' nothing but their virginity to the adoration of pom-pom girls.

Me: Hello, is Francis Drexler around?

KRCX switchboard: He's taping a news spot right now. Would you like to leave a message?

Me: Tell him I saw the show and he has some explaining to do at my house tonight, over chess, if he wants to live to tape another news spot.

KRCX switchboard: This is Mr. Biederman?

Me: Who's this?

KRCX switchboard: Francis said to expect your call. I'll issue your challenge.

Deborah: Biederman, English.

Me: Hi, honey. I just wanted to tell you I was sitting here, calling all these people, and thinking how much I love you.

Deborah: Who *is* this?

Me: Herman Melville.

Deborah: I really gotta get back, sweetheart. I've got so much preparation to do for my seminar.

Me: Tell me you're not Menkus' contact person.

Deborah: I'm not Belvyn's contact person. What's a contact person, anyway? Oh, honey, wish me luck. I'm having dinner tonight with a guy from River State Press to talk about my book. You can heat up a TV dinner for Barry, can't you?

Me: Sure.

Deborah: I shouldn't be home any later than ten.

Rita: Huh, what?

Me: I'm sorry, were you sleeping?

Rita: What time is it?

Me: Two o'clock, Iowa time.

Rita: Chicago time, too. This must be . . .

Me: Albert Biederman.

Rita: Could you maybe like call back?

Me: One quickie. Do you have any idea who Belvyn's contact person is?

Rita: It used to be me. We used to be in constant contact. We used to be the only contact person in each other's lives.

Me: Sorry to wake you up. Go back to bed, okay?

Me: Hello, Mr. Woolf, this is Albert Biederman, from the *Register*, in Iowa? I just wanted to make sure you got the latest batch of stories I sent you.

Woolf: We certainly did and we like them enormously, but we're still looking for that investigation piece, am I right?

Me: I'm nearly finished with it.

Woolf: What kind of subject matter would you define it as?

Me: Well, if it all works out it will be sort of a recruiting exposé.

Woolf: Jesus, Albert, if it's big enough and ballsy enough I hope you'll want to send it straight to us, do you hear what I'm saying? It'll make ten times the splash it would in Iowa.

Me: I can't do that.

Woolf: Why not?

Me: I'd feel like Benedict Arnold.

Woolf: What are you talking about?

Me: I can see the headline already, LOCAL REPORTER SELLS SECRETS TO OPPOSITION.

Woolf: Secrets to the opposition? Come on, Albert, you and I are beyond that. The battle here is not River State versus U. Madison. It's Biederman versus Biederman—how well can he tell a story that has some meat on it and how much is he willing to invest in his future? Whenever you can I want you to come up here for an interview and bring the piece, whatever shape it's in. We'll see what we can do. No promises, of course, but you're one of four.

Me: I don't know, Mr. Woolf. I don't know whether the piece will be—

Woolf: What are you trying to tell me?

Me: I'm telling you that I'm still working on it, and when it's showable I'll bring it with me to the interview.

Woolf: Good. You have a great eye for details, Albert, a real nose for the beat and o-o-offbeat. You tell a certain kind of story as well as anyone I know. And we're eager to see what you've done with—

Me: Thank you.

Woolf: Don't thank me. Bring us the scoop.

Me: Hello, is Vicki Lynch there?

The *Stallion* sports desk: She's here, but she's very, very busy.

Me: Tell her it's Albert Biederman calling.

Vicki: Hi, Albert, what's up?

Me: Last night I forgot to ask whether you'd found out anything yet about Menkus' contact person. I've started assuming—

Vicki: Nope. Haven't had time to get to it. Albert?

Me: Yes.

Vicki: How's tricks?

Me: Tricks is fine.

Vicki: Good, because I think you really are the sweetest man, and I can't wait to see you once I get all this work out of the way.

Me: Well, I won't blow it all out of proportion so long as you don't.

Vicki: I'll blow something else.

Mark Twain Elementary School: Good afternoon. Twain.

Me: Would you please give a second-grader named Barry Biederman a message?

Mark Twain Elementary School: Is this an emergency?

Me: Yes. Please tell him his daddy is dying to go to the game with him Saturday.

Mark Twain Elementary School: And you're sure this is an emergency, Mr. Biederman?

Me: Yes. Yes, it is. It's an emergency of my heart.

Sioux City Trade and Extension Night School: This is a recording. Night school is closed for Christmas vacation and will be back in session January fifth. Please leave a message at the sound of the beep. Our new codirectors, Mr. and Mrs. Edward Bingham, will return your call at their earliest possible convenience. Merry Christmas.

Mrs. Raeburn: Hello-oh?

Me: Hello, Mrs. Raeburn, this is Albert Biederman. Please don't hang up.

Mrs. Raeburn: I'm surprised you have the temerity, Mr. Biederman, to—

Me: I'm calling to apologize for my behavior last week.

Mrs. Raeburn: That's quite big of you, I'm sure.

Me: I'm sorry. I really am sorry. I got frustrated. I was upset. Both of you're very good and generous people who have given a lot of time and money to the university, my wife and son and best friend all think you're the cat's pajamas, and I'm just an ink-stained wretch trying to make heads or tails out of my own confusion.

Mrs. Raeburn: That's laying it on a little thick, wouldn't you say, Albert?

Me: Okay, then. All I want to know is what a contact person does exactly. That's all I—

Mrs. Raeburn: Old dog, same bad manners. Good-bye, Mr. Biederman.

Hinselwood: No, I didn't think it was the kind of piece that brings a team together. I thought it was typical of the horse manure you've been depositing on my doorstep since the day I got here. It's one of the real reasons why we've never had the kind of program we could have. Clowns like you are content to praise mediocrity. You're soft on us when you should be tough, then you're tough on us when you need to be soft. Just once I wish you'd write about the game, Biederman: who won and who lost and who rebounded and how many points they scored. It's a pretty straightforward sport, after all. It's not the hostage negotiations. Belvyn Menkus isn't Warren Christopher.

There were only seven shopping days left until Christmas. Wreaths had been up for a while, I guess, but I'd never noticed them. Papier-mâché Clauses hung from lamp posts and stoplights, grinning reindeer gave the plaza a colorful feel while the bulldozers and drill presses competed in Demolition Derby. When I stopped in at the *Stallion* Vicki's editor said, "She just finished proofing and went over to the library, but please leave her alone, Mr. Biederman. She's got to pass Kiddie Growth, okay?"

Okay. I left her alone.

I walked across campus to Pell Hall, where most of the university offices are located. The transcripts department took up most of the basement, nice and isolated, getting dusty all by itself. For three o'clock on Wednesday, it wasn't as busy as I thought it would be. At first I did a lot of looking lost and walking around, taking drinks of water, getting a feel for the place, trying to think what to say, angling for an opening, waiting till it felt right. I side-glimpsed Gail Lewis, the French department spinster Deb, Barry, and I bumped into on our way to the parking lot after the skirmish with the swanny Iowa River.

The half-dozen middle-aged women behind the long counter looked like they weren't allowed to give Yes for an answer—big, stocky, booster wives who guarded the files. Toward one end was a young Oriental girl. Maybe a graduate student on work-study or married to someone in the Engineering department. Lots of Japanese at River State in the sciences. She smiled, a little too trusting. They were probably still breaking her in.

My chest was hiccuping and my hands were flying birds, but it was time to take it to the hoop.

"Hello," I said. Very deep voice. "Good afternoon."

"Hi, what can we do for you?" Her night-black hair; heavy makeup; soft features, promising help.

"My wife's Mrs. Biederman. She's in the English department."

"Assistant professor, right?"

"Right," I said. "She's incredibly busy, you know, writing a book, teaching a million classes." My voice went into a semi-whisper. I didn't want the battle-axes bullying in on what was going great so far. "One of her students is named, I think, Menkus. M-e-n-k-u-s? Something like that." I lucked out. She hadn't heard of him, the one person in River City who wasn't a fan. "He has Rhetoric with her as well as reading lab. She's worried about him and wanted to see what his past performance was like so she'll know what he's capable of. I was planning to be on campus, anyway, and she asked me to pick up his file for her."

"Isn't that just like Mrs. Biederman?" she asked. I thought sure she was on to me and was pulling my leg. Students crowded the counter to ask the militia for transcripts and registration forms. A lot of coughing action down here in the basement, kids catching their first real winter colds. "Everyone I talk to says Mrs. Biederman gives students all her time. She cares. She's really a teacher."

She put such strong emphasis on this last word that I seriously considered backing into the elevator when she left to find the folder. It took her a while and I was afraid she'd bumped into her supervisor, who was telling her to filibuster me until I could be arrested. But she returned cheerful as ever. I had to sign out for the transcripts and scribbled my name so no one could read it. Then the big fat file was all mine.

"Thanks," I said. "I hope this helps my life. I mean my wife. I'll return it for her tomorrow."

"Great," she said and was off to help the next person.

I walked down the hall, praying for once that I wouldn't bump into Menkus, and finally found a bathroom two flights up. A couple of kids were combing their hair at the sink and another was working on his cigarette stance, but a stall was open and I went in and sat down, locking the door.

At first came a lot of evaluations of his week-by-week performance, written by Deborah and his other teachers in Math, General Science, World Geography, Reading. He was skipping class; he was near flunking; he was up, he was down; he couldn't read, write, spell, or speak; he was a functional illiterate; he needed to work hard if he wanted a D. A copy of his General Education Development certificate. A signed letter of intent. Financial-aid forms, full scholarship. Work-study permits and loan applications, none signed.

His Sioux City grades were, like Hutchins said, straight C's for two solid years in the unlikeliest courses, with no rhyme or reason to any of the sequences. This copy of his Franklin transcript was even worse than the ones I'd seen at Franklin. It was actually torn in spots, and you could tell where the erasings had been done.

These things confirmed my worst suspicions. Then came the kicker, which I'd hoped against hope wouldn't come:

Student's Name: Belvyn Nathaniel Menkus
Address: 8758 S. Wabash Avenue, Chicago, IL
Phone: (319) 645-2902
Date of Birth: November 22, 1960
Height: 6'3"
Weight: 181
Disabilities: None
Parents' Names: Louis and Ellen
Father's Occupation: Busdriver
Mother's Occupation: Church volunteer
GPA: Transfer student
Rank: 137 of 212 at SCTE
Counselor: Biederman

His phone number wasn't his parents' in Chicago but Raeburn's in Oxford, his Sioux City GPA was a hoot, and Deborah
was in fact his contact person. She taught him all week, talked
about him almost as much as I did. She liked him and he liked
her. Publish or perish or agree to be a bodyguard, is that what
tenure-track meant? So that's what the little stay-away game
was about. All is fair in love and war and college athletics. To
avoid the charging foul, I decided to go back-door on her.

Francis can't resist a chess challenge any better than he can
stay away from Chivas Regal, Sony recorders, or well-built
boys, and he agreed to come over for dinner and a few games.
Barry's baby-sitter, Laurel, was supposed to stay until I got
home, but I found the Bare sound asleep in our room, flat on
his back with pillows all around him. A note from Laurel was
pinned to his shirt. She had to go home early to help her
mother. Mrs. Biederman would be home later, TV dinners
were in the freezer, Barry needed another shot around eight. I
owed her $3.75.

I was watching Barry sleep when Francis came in the front
door and started banging things around, looking for shot
glasses.

"Stop stalling," he said. "Come out here and play me, you

coward." He already sounded crocked. By the time I got down-stairs, he'd set up the pieces and was spilling whiskey on the board.

"You idiot," I said, mopping the table with the cover of some journal of Deborah's and giving him White because he looked like he needed it. "You gotta get a grip on—"

"Yeah, thanks a million for the advice, pal."

Francis' openings are incredibly predictable, so I held my own without too much trouble even though I wasn't concen-trating. I had both ears cocked for Barry to wake up or the phone to ring with an explanation from Deborah. Francis' at-tack shifted to the far two files and involved a lot of hocus-pocus with his queen and leaping knights.

After waiting awhile for me to move, he said, "Come on. You're not in that much danger yet."

"I wasn't thinking about this. I was thinking about what a fool you tried to make of me and Menkus on that goddamn show of yours last night."

"I didn't invent those clips. They happened. You wrote about a game that no one else saw."

"But you showed only the plays that made him look bad."

"They weren't too hard to find."

"There were moments when he had those guys on the verge of clicking," I said, castling one step before Francis would have put me in check. He groaned and pushed a pawn up on the opposite side.

"Look, Albert, I really couldn't care less about our bet, and I'm certainly not going to do any big feature on him if he keeps playing like this. No one'll care. I put together last night's show to make a single issue stand out: he's an overrated point guard. People will be hoping for too much if they listen to you. I've said it before and I'll say it again: he just doesn't take over enough for pro scouts, and I have that on—"

"Hello? Were you at the Minnesota game? You're probably just bitter because he hasn't come out of the closet for you."

"You're the one who's ga-ga for him."

"True. I could watch him shoot lay-ups all day."

"He's your problem, then, not mine."

After a messy trade-off in the center, Francis had me on the run deep in my own territory. He tried to press mate by bringing up the knights, who'd been cooling their heels after exhausting themselves in the opening. Then he committed his queen, and once he pulls her into the action it usually means curtains. It did. I tipped the king's head to the wood in defeat. Francis was gloating and analyzing the game, pointing out where my defense began to buckle, when the phone rang. He burped, collapsing on the couch, and I picked up the receiver to hear Deborah say, "Hi, honey, hold on to your hat. I've got some very big news."

I held. Here it came, the confession.

"Mr. Hemley, from the Press, has read the first three chapters of the book and says he likes it a lot. A lot, a lot."

"That's it?" I said. "That's the big news?"

"Well, yes. I would say that's quite enough, wouldn't you?"

"Yes, it is. That's great, Deb."

The crush of the restaurant clanked in the background, and I wrestled down a strong urge to drive to the Blue Room and confront her with Menkus' bio-card. I wanted to figure out what was going on, but I didn't want Deborah to be as guilty as she looked at the moment.

"I mean, what were you expecting?"

"I don't know," I said.

"How's Barry?"

"He's fine. He's sleeping. Work went late, and Laurel was gone by the time I got home. Francis just beat me at chess for the hundredth straight game, but other than that I've got everything under control. I'll give Barry his shot when he wakes up. You'll be back around—"

"Whenever."

"Right. Whenever."

"This is a work session-cum-celebration. Tolliver and Adrienne are both planning to show up later for Kahlúa toasts. You sure you don't want to join in the revel?"

She asked only as a formality. She knew I wouldn't come. I

checked on the TV dinners in the oven and rustled up some salad things, then went back to the living room.

"Hi, Dad," came a voice from somewhere. "Hi, Mr. Drexler. When did you guys get in?"

I knew I knew that voice, but while shell-shocked I couldn't place it for sure until I saw Barry standing in his pj's at the top of the stairs. He looked solemn, as he always does, and serious way beyond his years. He walked toward us like a cadet, and there was a perfection to how he held his back that awed me.

Francis jammed the bottle into a space between two cushions. The Chivas neck stuck out like a bronzed microphone. In one of the stories that's a staple of Deborah's Great Books class there is a character who has no nose. A block away, that character could have smelled the scotch on Francis' breath. Barry backed off. I went after him, holding him high in the air away from the odors, and asked, "When did you wake up, big guy?"

"I don't know," he said, rubbing his ear against my shoulder. He was shy around Francis. "When the phone rang, I guess. Who was it?"

"Mommy," I said, bouncing him, trying to shake all that sleep out of his head, loosen him up a little so he wasn't as afraid of the Whiskey Man. "I get to give you her kiss." A wet smooch atop his noggin. I'm not sure what dough right out of the oven feels like, but it can't have much of an edge in freshness over my baby's skin. "Did you get the message at school?"

"Yeah, Dad, that was really weird. Everyone looked at me all period like I was sick."

"We were trying to play chess here," Francis said, peeved. "It's similar to checkers, only with a few more moves. Wanna watch?"

"Sure," he said and went into the kitchen, walking like a cadet.

"Barry, don't eat anything now, okay? Dinner'll be ready in ten minutes."

He came back with his usual, three graham crackers and a glass of milk. Francis set up the board again while I went into the kitchen to slide things around in the oven, finish the salad, wash silverware. Francis was great at explaining how each piece worked, and Barry, with his mother's mind, grasped the rudiments awfully fast.

"If you move that guy with the conehead there, that Christmas-tree thing'll get him, won't he?"

"Good observation," Francis said, pumping Barry's hand. It was beautiful to see Barry's fear of Francis fading. And when Barry spilled a little milk on Francis' sock, Francis didn't even seem to notice. I assumed he'd take it easy on Barry, but every time I looked in on them Barry was in worse trouble.

"What should I do now, Dad?" he asked.

He was in check, facing mate.

"Tell your opponent some people never grow up."

"Huh?"

Francis Drexler, a sick man, chortled.

I sat down next to Barry and got him out of check. Francis played the obvious. I hid the king in a corner. Francis' queen, protected by her rook, swooped down for the capture.

"You just learned one of the key lessons of modern chess," I said. "Never underestimate the ruthlessness of Francis Drexler."

"What's ruthla-whatever?" Barry asked.

"The Yankees of 1949," Francis said.

"Hilarious," I said.

During dinner I kept trying to talk about the election of Miss Pork Queen of Iowa, but all Barry wanted to do was ask chess questions. After dessert he thanked Francis again for the game, shook his hand, and said good night. Taking him to bed and tucking him in, I said, "Aren't you really sort of mad at Francis?"

"Heck no, Dad. He showed me some really neat moves."

Maybe Barry could take defeat like a man. I couldn't. I slammed doors and marched into the living room. "You bastard," I said.

"What did I do now?" Francis wanted to know, looking for his glass.

"You dog. You come in here, drink my booze, eat my food,

248

then demolish my son on the chessboard. Do you have any idea how much that upset him, which, with his sugar imbalance being what it is—"

"You're lying, my friend. He's not upset. Any bimbo could see he went off to bed happy as a clam. You're the one whose feathers are ruffled. You just can't deal with losing."

"Maybe you're the best goddamn chess player in the Midwest," I said. "What do I care? I'm not talking about that. I'm talking about how demented you must be if you're unable to tone down your game for a seven-year-old kid." I still hadn't gotten over being angry at Francis for fitting so neatly into Raeburn's hip pocket.

"You're wrong if you think you're doing him a favor by letting him believe whatever he does is good enough. He's a bright, funny kid and I like him, but he can't beat me at chess and he might as well know it now."

"Let's go play some basketball."

"Lovely idea, Albert, only neither one of us can stand up."

I did jumping jacks to prove him wrong and said, "One-on-one to fifteen at the Rec Center. I'll give you ten points. Double or nothing on the original Menkus bet."

"Fine, you asshole. You're on. You never saw me play when I was in my prime. I swept the glass—"

"You swept the floor was what you did. You're a bright, funny kid and I like you, but you can't come close to beating me at basketball and you might as well know it now."

Francis laughed loud enough to wake Barry and chugged all but the last of the blended whiskey. I got my ball, sweats, and hightops out of the closet, and gave Francis some old Jack Purcells of Dad's I still had hanging around for some reason. I breathed in a trace of Dad's special sweaty smell, which brought back to me his beautiful hustle. He and Francis had small feet for their size. After writing a note to Deborah, I checked on Barry, who looked like he was counting pawns in his sleep. Then we were off, though not without one last argument about DWI. I didn't let Francis carry the bottle in the car, and I would have been an imbecile to let him drive. His breath was indictment enough.

Riding downtown, Francis had to shiver to show how cold he was—Francis, who would have turned into smoke if you'd dropped gas on his 86-proof tongue. Johnny Cash came on KHAK with that great old song about a boy named Sue, followed by news about no news out of Iran. Lows were in the teens with light snow expected, which sent Francis into a fit of more shivering.

The Rec Center is next to a desiccated creek and a series of busted railroad ties. The parking lot wasn't any busier than either of its neighbors. We tiptoed around puddles toward the back, and I was afraid Francis was right when he said, "It's not open. Let's hit Phil's."

Francis was wrong. The Rec Center was open, so we didn't hit Phil's. The girl behind the counter said, "What do you guys want to check out?" She wore a River State jersey and a sweatband.

"Only the ambience," FD said. A doltish thing to say, since it made him sound even fruitier than usual, and the girl snickered.

"We have our own basketball," I said, holding it up, spinning it on my finger to show I used to be a star and wasn't some asshole interested in ambience. "We don't need anything."

A few toughs shot billiards, and two very young kids were playing chess with plastic pieces and paper clips for pawns. Francis kibitzed but gave up soon, pronouncing both of them hopeless. He was absolutely blotto.

Across the lobby, through the glass, you could see the indoor pool. There is something about the green water here, the diving platform, the women in white caps, the stack of kickboards that always reminds me of putting my mother away in one dry dock or another, one cirrhosis way station after another. She eventually checked out for good in one of these wards. I listened to the echoing walls and mourned the ravages of her alchoholism. Some lonely teenager pounded a punching bag next to the row of vending machines.

"We close at nine, you know," the check-out girl called to us as we made our way toward the gym.

"We know," I said, and we went in.

Francis made a big deal of retying his shoelaces, fixing his socks, wrapping his keys and money in his coat, then trotted onto the waxy floor. Only the near side of the gym was lighted and two of the baskets were bent, so we played at center court. His stomach bounced, his glasses fogged with his first puff of breath. He scratched his gut and flopped around the court, stealing the ball from me to take a very old-fashioned running one-hander from the right corner—Francis' secret weapon when he played high school ball in the forties. Hank Lusetti and my junior varsity basketball coach used to shoot like this from all over the court, sort of a shot put with backspin and a lot of leg action, falling away.

Francis' one-hander was different from theirs in that his came nowhere near the basket, which was big and soft and had a wide board to pick up all the junk. Orange rims with brown cord: Thanksgiving decorations, late. I took some free throws, then some jumpers from the corner, not hitting too many of them. Francis floated along in the ooze of his own juices and couldn't move or dribble that well, but he passed the ball with real authority. He brought his whole massive chest into play, and the ball popped into your hands with zing on it. Long ago the Voice of KRCX had played the game, and what was surprising was that he didn't have traditional center skills. He had a small forward's moves: hook shots, and jumpers. Out of shape, he still knew how to shoot soft stuff that clung to the rim, but he didn't seem to know where the rebound would land. He definitely followed through on every attempt, sure sign of a shooter rather than a pivot man.

"Francis, what's the story? You play like a guard. Where are your George Mikan muscle moves?"

251

"Not me, my friend. I wanted no part of the elbow wars. Meet the original Mel Counts."

"Mel Counts, meet Double Bubble Biederman."

I took a quick series of jumpers across the key, making more of them, getting into a groove, reminding Francis of my glory years. "Okay," I said, "I guess you're ready."

"Ready," he said, nearly tripping when I missed badly and the ball ricocheted right at his feet.

"Ten–zip, your lead, that's what we agreed on. Winner's outs, clear it to the line." I dribbled inbounds from halfcourt to start the game.

"Twenty years ago I saw you play zone-breaker guard at Drake and, before that, Johnny Ack-Ack in high school. I hate to tell you this, but I thought you'd have held onto your game a lot better. I really don't need any handi—"

A rush of adrenaline erased my adulthood and connected me to the boy I was at sixteen in City Park Playground. When were you most heroic, when were you most alive? Sixteen in City Park.

I dribbled left, crossed over down the lane for a lay-up. I canned an eight-foot bank. I hit a jumper from top of the key.

"Just wait till I get my hands on the ball," the Voice of KRCX kept saying.

I felt my fingers finding the range, but shooting is even more in the legs. If you spring off your toes the way you want to and go up strong, it's almost impossible to shoot poorly. The ball travels down your spinal cord, opening everything up. I hit three twenty-footers in a row, a bunch from the left corner, off drives, off reverse spins. When you're hot the ball is the world, the court is a map of that world, and it's your kingdom.

I hadn't played in almost a year but was establishing my rhythm deeper and deeper, getting back a chunk of my youth by pushing a chunk of Francis' deeper into the distance. Memories poured out of every move of my body. I dribbled very fast straight at Francis, forcing him to cross-step, and he fell over with a flop onto the big cushion of his keister. I went up over him, dreaming I could dunk.

At 11–10 he sucked air and said, "You got me on fool's mate. It's yours, pal. I'm out of practice. Thirty years ago I would have stuck you in the popcorn machine."

"What the hell, Francis, you gave it a shot. You obviously once were really good. I wish I could have seen you play in high school."

"Hey, go fuck yourself in the ladies' room," he said, then looked for a water fountain in case he had to throw up.

The counter girl said, "You guys gotta be out of here in twenty minutes, you know," and returned to her TV program.

I collapsed against a rolled-up wrestling mat that had a huge Stallion emblem in the middle of it. When Francis returned, a weird silence obtained between the two of us. The viciousness I played with had humiliated him and surprised me. I told him about the time Bradley Gamble, who had moved to Cedar Falls and had always been Ethan Saunders' friend more than he was mine, revisited Des Moines. In a late-night five-on-five I kept taking it to Saunders, beating him and beating him and beating him to the bucket, trying to win back my old friend Bradley until it got too dark to play. I told Francis about the time Leo Handley said Jim Morrow would always be his best friend, though I might be his second-best friend. At Leo's backyard hoop I refused to stop scoring against him. Every bang of the ball off the garage door was another nail in his coffin until he said okay, maybe we could all be best friends.

The gym heater whirred. I didn't know what the point of these stories was. I said I was sorry. I said, "I guess I've always thought if I played basketball as hard as I could I'd keep my closest friends."

"Well, shut my mouth," Francis said, "the Man is here."

Walking across the court toward the blackened baskets at the other end, wearing his roan Stallion warm-ups and his Franklin jacket, palming a ball in one hand and an umbrella in the other, was Menkus. He stepped out of his sweats, then something absolutely primitive took over when he began dribbling. He wrapped the ball around his ankles and popped a number of little lean-ins from inside the key. If he recognized me or Francis against the wall, he didn't acknowledge us.

"I can't believe this," I said. "What an opportunity."

Francis dribbled the ball off his foot and chugged after it before it bounced across the darkness into Menkus' court.

"My shot's on," I said. "I'll bet him I can score once before he gets to ten. If I win, I get a real interview. I lose, I promise to leave him alone and write a puff piece. You want any side action?"

"Pretty heavy bet," Francis said. "By ones or twos?"

Menkus glided around the far basket in the half-light, and every six or eight seconds you'd hear the hard swish of the net at that end. Waves at night. The dark. Shooting, you own the world.

I was getting carried away, but I wasn't unconscious. "By ones," I said.

"You're on for another case of Johnnie Black."

I could see only the general shadow of Menkus' movements and could hear him buzzing words to himself, reminders Jumpin' Bean had probably tattooed onto his wrists. *Faster, faster. Hard off the dribble. Protect. Spin, spin. Softer.* You could hear the screech of his Nikes, the occasional clang of the iron, and the constant whipping, whistling sound of twine getting shredded. He was a beautiful pure shooter, and every clean shot of his, every lift of the net was an untangling of the knots of the cords, canceling my doubts about his past, all questions, all problems, all worries.

I crossed the time line, slapped the ball out of his hands, and went for a lay-up at the side basket.

"What you up to?" I said.

"Nothin'. Just tom-tommin' my originality." His voice sounded more than ever like Scottish bagpipes, with a lot of sudden pitch changes.

"You're a great shooter, but what are you working on your gunner moves for if you want to be Magic Johnson?"

"The moves you do alone don't hurt nobody."

"What's that, Menkus, a line they used to feed you at Franklin?"

"Hey, don't hit on Mr. Hoover. He's the Man. He made me, and you is who makes you." Quotations from Chairman Mao in ghetto jive. Because his black talk sounded so bogus, I had the sudden but false intuition that he was putting me on, that he could speak regular if he wanted to.

"Speak English, Menkus. This isn't the south side. This is River City."

He smiled his pirate's smile. Francis collapsed into a metal chair, and I felt closer to my fat friend than to this flimflammer dribbling in and out of his legs. The counter girl came in to say she was closing in ten minutes. You could practically hear *on and on and on and on and on* filling the gap between Menkus' ears. Not a thought in sight, just a lot of mumbo jumbo he'd picked up to snow people. I tried to steal the ball again, but he wrapped it behind his back and through his legs onto the right side.

"Tell me one thing," I said. "What does my wife do for you as your contact person?"

"Come on, man, you're too negative all the time, beatin' on everybody. Miss Biederman helps me what she can, learnin' English. Last week she was showin' me how to study sharper. I see why she says keep air space among me and you. She's a good lady."

"That's no lady," Francis said, struggling to his feet. "That's his wife."

I didn't know what to believe anymore about Deborah, but Menkus ticked me off and I challenged him to ten for the interview. I said, "I'm real curious, you know. I used to play a lot. You're not afraid, are you?"

My fantasy bloomed to life when he chuckled, stopped dribbling, and mock politely handed me the ball. I took it all the way to the other end of the gym, where the baskets were lit and at least I didn't have that disadvantage as well. I felt him out, pushing the ball through the key and around the horn.

Call me a two-year-old, Francis: it was ridiculously exciting to be on the same court with Menkus. His hands were down around his knees and he trailed me wherever I went, amused by my pep.

From the left side I made what I thought was a fairly quick move to the bucket. I cocked my elbow to protect the ball and hung as long as I could, double-clutching at the last possible instant. Menkus, who I could have sworn was standing at the free throw line, came from behind not simply to block it but forcibly to rip it out of my hands. He dribbled to the top of the circle and jumped so high that I felt the sole of his sneaker graze my stomach. I'm not kidding. He waited a three-count before even thinking about turning to look at the basket. I looked up, watching his squared shoulders, his full follow-through on a shot so sweet it could have been designed to test suction capacity on a new net.

Every year Bill Russell says over and over that basketball is horizontal, that it's mainly a matter of getting to certain spots on the floor and cutting off angles. If anyone should know, the bearded wonder should, but he's wrong. It's an altitude game played by stunt pilots. In 1891, when the sport was invented, someone had to sit in the balcony to take the ball out of the peach basket on made shots. A hundred years later high risers just go up and get it.

I took a couple steps forward to face Menkus on the next try. He didn't do anything different. He shot the same shot with the same squared shoulders, drained eyes, and straight back; the same jump, the same arc and spin on the ball; the same crashing swish, which this time took an odd bounce off the soft part of the floor and rolled toward Francis, who had deteriorated smack dab into the middle of the d.t.'s. He thought the basketball was a pumpkin and had trouble throwing it back.

"Get 'im, Belvyn," Francis said. "Go get 'im. Sink that stinker Bieder Meter."

After a while I didn't bother to rush at Menkus or throw up a hand. He kept taking and making exactly the same shot. Nine jumpers in a row from twenty-two feet, shot with total non-chalance. Laxadaisical, as the players say. Even I could make a few shots like this, but consistency is the key. He just kept making them. Bob Pettit plus panache.

At 9–zip he rocked on his left leg and took a mini-step with his right foot like he was going up one last time for the jumper. What the hell, I figured, I'll throw a final lunge at him. So much for the routine: when he lulled me to sleep he switched stations. That's another key. Don't be too predictable. He put the ball on the floor, took a few high, hard dribbles down the lane, and sprang.

Take a look sometime at fans' faces when a player is in midair on a dunk. Nothing can go wrong anymore. He's no longer aiming for the goal. He's in it. He is it. The net is his. Watch in particular the fans who are standing with their fists raised. They're watching themselves out there on the court as no one has ever seen them, before they lost their wings.

Menkus twisted 360, reverse-dunked with two hands, vibrating the rim and the basket support. I was in such awe of how long it took him to fall back to earth that I forgot to get out of the way. He tucked his legs and twisted to try to avoid me but landed with a thud on the side of my ankle. I yelped and Menkus unleashed a howl. It was the first time I'd ever seen him really out of control. We both tumbled toward the wall, where Francis cowered, afraid the whole backboard was going to come crashing down. For all I knew, he was seeing the spots on the ceiling as pink elephants. Please don't let Menkus' leg be broken. He tossed around the floor, wailing like a baby, massaging his right knee.

"Try to stand on it," Francis suggested.

"No, no," I said, "you're not supposed to move."

"Just to test it," Francis said.

Menkus, who trusted that drunk rather than me, tried to stand and fell right back down. My ankle was bad, but it was his right leg that was killing me. If it was his knee and it was torn, call it a night on this season, possibly his career, and my Milwaukee.   •

The TV girl came in to see what all the fuss was about. Francis told her to call an ambulance, then let Menkus lean on one side of him and me on the other and carried us into the lobby. Francis has powerful triceps from lifting so many gallon jugs. We sat near the vending machines for what felt like an hour. My ankle was puffing up already, so I fiddled with the socks and shoe on my left foot. Menkus couldn't straighten out his knee, which was swollen purple. He sang:

> A love supreme,
> A love supreme,
> A love supreme . . . ›

His knee was wet. He screamed, shaking his head hard back and forth like denial.

"I'm sorry," I kept saying. "It was my fault. You're a brilliant basketball player. I had no business being on the same floor with you. I'm so sorry. I think you're great. I hope you're going to be all right." I babbled on.

In the way athletes are supposed to be brave, he suddenly snapped out of it and said, "Did you see that 360?"

"I saw it," I said.

When the counter girl brought over a couple of Cokes she finally recognized Menkus and said, "My little brother'll kill me if I don't get your autograph."

Menkus wrote in reverse. Francis tried again to throw up in the sink but couldn't.

"Hey, I know," he said. "Fuck the ambulance. I'll drive us."

I wouldn't have let him in his condition drive us to the next parking space, and I told him no.

River State Clinics is only about half a mile up Burlington and over the bridge. Pretty soon we heard the siren; then the ambulance guys hopped out of the van, putting Menkus on a stretcher. A dim little light flickered outside the Rec building. I was going to go with Menkus to the hospital until I saw a needle in a box in the ambulance and remembered I hadn't given Barry his injection at eight.

Francis sat in front with the attendants. The counter girl unchained her bike. I was carrying my parka and my basketball. Menkus lay on a stretcher in the back of the ambulance, moaning, pleading with me and Francis not to tell Hinselwood how it had happened.

"Come on," one of the ambulance guys said to me. "Let's roll."

Barry's blood sugar was probably rising, making him sick to his stomach.

"Menkus," I said, standing on my right foot while they were closing the rear doors on him. "I'm sorry. You have to understand. My kid's a diabetic. I forgot to give him his shot. I'm going to drive home now, and I'll check on you at the hospital later tonight, okay? I'm sorry. Please forgive me."

He flipped me off as the ambulance pulled away, Klaxon twirling on Francis dozing in the front seat.

I hopped across the parking lot as fast I could, got in the car, slid over, engaged the gears with my throbbing left foot, and put pedal to metal. The streets were wet and fairly busy, but I went through two stop signs, a yellow light, and a red light, startling a number of pedestrians and putting a real crimp in a lot of the cross traffic around Clinton, until I got past the river and up Grand Avenue. I took a splashing left onto Melrose, heading out toward Westgate.

I have never been closer to wishing I had God to pray to. Fuck it, I'll pray to Him, anyway. I hadn't trusted Deborah; I hadn't trusted Menkus; I hadn't trusted anyone. I was weary of myself, sweaty in my cold car, all guilty ambition. Please, God, let Barry be okay and Menkus' knee be nothing. It hurt like hell to bear down on the clutch, but I had to get home as fast as I could. Every time the engine whined between gears it was saying: Change me. Make me well. Make everyone complete again.

I imagined Francis in the ambulance, vomiting into an oxygen mask, and Barry trembling on top of his covers, his skin hot and his breathing shallow. My ankle was really swelling up. The street was dark. I floored the accelerator.

I screeched around Westgate till it turned into our dead-end little court, then skidded past our unplanted front yard into our unfinished garage. I limped into the house and I ran, I actually ran on that goddamn ankle into Barry's room, which was lit only by his blue night-light. He was sound asleep and looked okay but was sweating lightly. I had to wake him up to make sure.

"Barry," I said. "Barry, talk to me. Are you all right?"

It took a while. It took a lot of shaking and tugging and finger snapping to drag him out of a deep sleep. His face was warm, his pajamas were wet, and his blankets were wrapped around his pudgy body like ropes.

"Turn out the lights, please," he said.

"Are you okay?"

"Will you please turn out the lights?"

"I forgot to give you your insulin," I said, disentangling the sheets and blankets, slapping him into new pajama bottoms.

"Oh, that's all right. Someone called and I didn't answer it, but it woke me up and I shot myself."

"You did?"

"Uh-huh."

"You promise you weren't dreaming? You really did?"

"Uh-huh," he said. "Will you please just turn—"

"You're fine, you're really okay?"

"Yeah, sure," he said, looking around for his favorite animal, a one-eyed koala named Alex. I found it under the bed and closed the window the last half-inch or so.

"Okay, then," I said. "Good night."

" 'Night."

I took two steps toward the door, hopped back, lifted him up, and squeezed the stuffing out of him. Putting him back in bed, I pressed full weight on my sprained ankle and let out a little groan. Please tell me it isn't your knee, Menkus, tell me it isn't bad.

"Am I getting too heavy for you?" Barry asked.

"No, it's okay. It's nothing. I twisted my ankle playing basketball tonight. You're amazing," I said, walking out of the room slowly, backwards. "I love you, do you know that? I think you're the greatest. A bowl of Sugar Crisp tomorrow morning for breakfast."

"Two bowls."

"Twelve. It doesn't matter. I love you," I said. "Do you understand what I'm saying? I'll never let you down again. I love you."

The pain pounding my left leg made me passionate, happy. Pure schmaltz, but I felt it: proud to be part of the whole human agony.

"Dad, somehow you really just gotta learn how to relax," he said. Holding Alex in his arms, he turned away from me, toward the hot blue light.

ELEVEN

RIVER State Clinics, like the rest of River City, was being renovated. A whole new wing was getting added, and the kidney dialysis ward was going to be named for Raeburn. Detours led to cyclone fences, cranes and dump trucks sat at the bottom of huge pits, scaffolds swayed in the wind, and signs all over said PARDON OUR PROGRESS. It was nearly impossible to get where you wanted. I just assumed Raeburn devised this maze to intensify my pain and keep me away from Menkus.

At the Emergency desk a nurse brandished her clipboard and asked what our problem was. Limping, dripping an ice pack, sweaty from not showering, I could see why she didn't believe me when I said I wasn't here for myself. Wheelchairs pushed by orderlies whizzed by, ambulance alerts sounded. I sat down in the waiting room, which was empty except for a television whose colors were scrambled. The nurse yielded to a resident, who said it was only a sprained ankle and recommended applying the rice treatment.

"Rice?"

"Rest, ice, compress, elevate."

"Oh, very clever," I told him. He was dressed in green pajamas to let you know he was busy saving humanity. "You can go now."

"Well, then, what are you here for?" the nurse asked, reducing the sound of the late news. Gray hair peeked out of her nurse's cap and her kind face forgave.

"I want to see Belvyn Menkus."

"You can't do that. Dr. Ridenour is examining him."

"How's he doing?"

"That I can't tell you, Mr. Biederman. He certainly didn't look very pretty when he arrived. He was traumatized and there were effusions."

"What does that mean?"

"His knee was a geyser," she said. "Fluid, blood."

Now every yowl I heard was Menkus' knee. I asked her to assure me it was all somehow going to be okay, but she wouldn't. I whacked the couch, which made the TV picture better and my ankle worse. My leg in sympathy with his. The TV had a doily on top of it in the shape of a Stallion.

"You're not a relative, are you?"

"No," I said, "we were just playing a game together. I'm his friend, I hope."

"So you were there when he was injured?"

"He fell on my ankle. It was completely my fault. I should have gotten out of the way."

"Accidents do happen," she said. "That's why there're hospitals."

Well, yes, I said, I guessed that was true. She took some more information from me about the collision, and it came out that Francis was with us.

"Oh, my, that's a funny man. He really had us roaring when he stumbled through here. That's a funny man. Is he also a friend of yours?"

I admitted he was.

"Is he that funny when he's sober?" she asked.

"When is he sober?"

"They took him to Detox. He'll be okay. They just wanted to give him some oxygen, let him lie down a little, sleep it off. You're sure you won't let us give you a new ice pack and wrap that ankle for you?"

"No."

"Then I would strongly suggest you do what the doctor told you and visit your friends tomorrow."

"But I need to see Menkus," I said. "He has to know I'm here."

"He may already be in surgery, Mr. Biederman. If you were his father, you wouldn't be allowed—"

"I have to see Menkus," I said for the last time and made a feint like I was going to break through the double doors into the operating room, but my ankle buckled under me. Down I went.

"Satisfied?" she asked, shaking her head and helping me up, then serving as my crutch into the living room. When I called from a pay phone the line remained busy, and I figured Deborah was dialing all over town, wondering where the hell I was.

I should have gone home. I should have elevated the ankle and wrapped it and packed it in ice. I should have tried to confirm Deborah's innocence. On the long dark night of my soul there were a lot of things I should have done that I didn't do. I had to touch bottom to see if I could come back to the surface, breathing, and I had to do it alone.

I bought two sixes of Molson Ale and a pack of pretzels at the Quik-Trip on Gilbert. Only a few blocks away stood an old motel called the Jefferson Davis. River City is comfortably above the Mason-Dixon line, but the background of the Vacancy sign was a confederate flag. The parking lot was mud and the motel office featured a stuffed squirrel, a rocking chair, and kids that looked like Walker Evans photographs. It was just the place to drink myself unconscious. Robert E. Lee took my check and made a general gesture toward a room.

Lying on the bed, moving through the Molson, I felt my hair curling into Menkus' phony Afro; I felt his gray sweat shirt hanging loose on my shoulders; I felt his bottomless green eyes opening into mine. I saw his behind-the-back pass against

Omaha, his dribbling exhibition before that game, his slam tap against Kansas, his lobs inside to Durland at Dayton, and then of course his reverse dunk at the Rec Center and his screaming knee. I saw these plays over and over again, like when I was fifteen and in love with most of the girls in my algebra class and couldn't get to sleep because I was putting their bodies through every position I could imagine and finally just wanted it to stop, only it wouldn't stop.

I got some ice for my ankle and came back and opened another bottle. All night long I was a fool for memory, a creature of my pathetic past. I thought about Beth, my elementary school and high school girl friend; and about my mother's descent; about Dicky, my West Des Moines backcourt mate who died under a forklift; about Mr. Ruiz telling us the Mexican people looked at death as a positive thing and reading to us from the Bible.

Dicky took too much out of us, though. We picked up the slack for a few games, then caved in, and by early February the team was a shambles. I had to be playmaker as well as scorer. Hogging the ball as much as I did, I attracted local attention. After we were easily eliminated in the state quarterfinals, a Drake scout approached me and said he had come to watch someone else but liked my enthusiasm. Not my shooting or passing. My enthusiasm. Projecting me as a zone breaker off the bench, he offered a tuition scholarship with books paid and he'd see what he could do about meal money. It was all very simple and straightforward. There wasn't the faintest whisper of any talk about cars or apartments or WATS lines or girls or jobs. Raeburn was surely right on target. These things were available in 1958. I just wasn't good enough. I would no more have thought of turning down the scout than he would have thought of upping the ante.

Beth and I had been going steady senior year, in a friendly, formal ritual that consisted of Saturday night passion plays in her car. My decision to accept the Drake scholarship was the "final blow" for her, since she had no intention of going to Drake just to be with me and I had nowhere near the grades to get into Carleton. The scholarship was the only way I could possibly have afforded college, since my mother was a full-time patient in a private sanitarium and Dad's only income was bouncing from club to club as a tennis instructor. Mom thought she had married Jack Kramer, and when she got a club pro, instead, she hustled houses and IV'd alcohol until Bombay Distilled started giving her more solace than lot space and two and a half baths, and then she plummeted. She went from distant to more distant to irrecoverable.

As a freshman I was the junior varsity's designated shooter, our gunner whenever we faced a zone, though Dad stopped showing up because when he wasn't club hopping he was visiting Mother at the institution in Lake Forest, an hour outside Chicago. Long-distance shooting had always been a way for me to perform the most immaculate feat in basketball, to stay outside where no one would hurt me. I'd hit four or five in a row, force the other team out of its zone, then sit down to contemplate my mother's transformation from a beautiful little bumblebee into a puffed-up pear. By the end of the year I was told for the millionth time in my life that I must learn to take the ball to the basket and mix it up with the big guys underneath. I didn't want to because I knew I couldn't. I already knew I was a full step slow.

During the summer Beth came back from Carleton and, out of desperation, flung her body at me one last time until it became too sad for both of us to continue the charade that we were still close, and my mother came home from the hospital and needed only a few days to show what a sick, vicious, uncontrollable drunk she was without professional supervision. Throughout the summer Doug Beacham, my old playground mentor, worked with me on my drives, and the first few non-conference games of my sophomore year I started at wing for the varsity. In the first quarter against Oklahoma State I got the ball at the top of the circle, faked left, picked up a screen right, and penetrated the lane. The defender stayed with me, and when I went up for my shot we were belly to belly. To go forward was an offensive foul, and backward was onto my ass.

I tried to corkscrew around him but couldn't pull off what Menkus does so well—change position in midair. The Oklahoma State guy's hip caught mine and I turned 180 degrees, landing on my leg. While Oklahoma State apologized, the referee said I was probably permanently crippled and called an ambulance. My left thigh tickled my right ear. I shouted curses until I passed out from the pain.

I had a broken femur and spent the winter in traction at Methodist Hospital, where Dad visited me most every night after giving tennis lessons, but Mom didn't come because she was confined to Belmont. One night Dad came in, looking down but not rock-bottom depressed, and said Mom passed out, hit her head on the sink, and expired. It was such a formal word, "expired," and it took its sweet time to imprint on me, like when Mr. Ruiz told us about Deeky. I was weirdly calm and quiet, as I was when Dad died fifteen years later. Honestly, my reaction to Mom dying was just sort of "Oh." She'd been gone so long, and now she was gone for good. But I will never get over my self-revulsion about how relieved and pleased Dad and I clearly were that we no longer had the alcoholic albatross of my mother hanging around our necks.

My doctor misread my X-rays, removing the body cast too early, so I had an aluminum rod planted next to the bone and wore a leg brace and swung crutches all year, preoccupied with my own minor injury. The rod's still in and vibrates when rain's threatening. It got me out of Vietnam in '63, but at the time what ate at me most was my shame over caring more about my broken leg than my mother's death.

The coach didn't believe in me enough even to red-shirt me, and when the brace came off that summer Beach tried to work with me to get back my wind and speed. He gave up when he saw my heart wasn't in it. Dad and I would just stay home, romanticizing Mom, watching the Cubs lose, watching tennis turn into a major sport the moment he left it. In fall basketball practice I wasn't fast enough or angry enough to play Biddy ball. A full step slow had become a step and a half, and a step and a half was curtains. Junior year I was ninth man on a ten-man team and kept a game journal, which evolved into a sports column for the *Drake Bulldog*. I soon realized I was better at describing basketball and analyzing it than playing it. Like thinking of witty repartee six hours after the party's over, I could concoct the perfect move only after the whistle had blown the ball dead. I'd finally found my water level. There is nothing sadder in my experience than understanding this is as far as your talent can take you and no further, *because you don't have all the gifts*. It's the lesson I finally learned and my father learned; and when my mother learned it about my father, she became a ginhead. In my column, I was savage on our mediocre team, and the coach called me *Ace*, as in Ace Reporter, since I was certainly not his star ballhawk. *Ace* also reminded me I wasn't as successful in basketball as my father was in tennis, and my father was a failure.

With Molson Ale coursing through my veins at the Jefferson Davis, all I could think about was my ability to shoot when left open and my inability to guard anyone quick or shake someone who hounded me tough. As a senior I fell into the most pathetic role: the guy with all the answers and explanations, the well-informed benchwarmer who knew how zones were supposed to work but had nothing to contribute. I became a fan.

I was an American History major and I did decently because I was actually semi-interested in the stuff, absolutely all of which I have forgotten with the exception of how Iowa reached statehood. I have no idea why these names and dates have stuck in my craw like Mississippi Valley Conference field goal percentages, but they have. Marquette and Joliet showed up in 1673 to greet the Winnebago Sioux. By 1682 Iowa belonged to France. In 1762 we were traded to Spain for a backup center to be named later. Dubuque, a French Canadian, got a fur trade going and in 1788 bought twenty miles from the Indians for his mining operations. In 1800 Iowa got traded back to France. In 1803 the United States picked us up on waivers. In 1804 Iowa was part of the Indiana Territory; 1805, Louisiana Territory; 1812, Missouri Territory; back to the U.S. in 1834. No one ever wanted Iowa. The Sioux refused to let white men work the mines on their land, and in 1832 *Black Hawk* v. *the United States* ended in: United States— 9,000 square miles; Black Hawk—zippo. Iowa was Michigan Territory in 1834 and Wisconsin Territory in 1836, finally separating from Wisconsin in 1838. Iowa was denied admission to the Union in 1840 and 1842 before finally being allowed in in 1846. Along about then Calvin Raeburn came clomping down the path in an ox cart.

I did well on exam questions if I could connect them up somehow with the Louisiana Purchase, but everything after the Civil War bored me to tears, and my real major senior year was journalism. My column became the most popular daily feature in the *Bulldog*, and from there it was cinchy to step up to sports editor. I was aware of what other college sports sections were doing, and I would send out my best pieces to critiquing services and newspaper writing contests, hoping to get taken on as a cub reporter. I was so ambitious because my basketball dream had ended, I felt alone in the world, and I needed something else to try to be as good at as I had once wanted to be at basketball.

It had become so routine for me never to get into games that I took to carrying a Bic pen in my sock. Once, I was called in during the last minute, was fouled, and I fell. The pen leaked throughout my shoe. When I crouched to shoot my first free throw, I heard the plastic crack and felt the ink squish. On the bench, I would write on my hand until I advanced to writing on a little pad I sat on. It was like I wasn't really even on the team anymore except during practice, where I was used as a blocking dummy, and Dad stopped showing up for the games altogether. He stayed home and brooded on the televisionization of tennis, too late to help him any.

The River State Indians came to town on a snowy, windy, below-freezing night in the middle of February, and for some reason the *River City Register* man didn't show up. I was always aware now of press row, and I had come to watch the reporters as carefully as I once did the players; the writers were my new heroes. So I kept especially good notes, wrote up the story, and called Mr. Reeves to see if he could use it. He said he could, though he wasn't as grateful as I thought he'd be, and he printed it without byline or a lot of fanfare. To me, what I'd just done was indistinguishable from nomination for a Pulitzer. My thread was that number thirteen on Drake scored thirteen points and had thirteen rebounds. Marty's lead was: "At midnight, Darryl Banks probably puts out saucers of milk for black cats and looks for ladders to walk under."

I loved that lead and desperately wanted to know the person who wrote it. I started covering all Drake sports events, getting a lot of bylines. Mr. Reeves was still formal on the phone, respectful, encouraging, kind. My first big assignment was covering the Drake Relays, where I ran around like a monkey tallying results, phoning them in, and getting the lead sports story, but a lot of the excitement was lost because I had no one to share my success with. Dad, away on a welter of exhibition dates, was impressed only by professional athletic excellence, anyway. My mother was dead, Beth was long gone, my college friends and girl friends were no longer tight with me once I left the jock fold, and I finally cried for my mom because I needed her now and was crying for myself.

When we had a return match at River State, I was walking off the court, trying to look disconsolate after we had lost by ten points to—as they were known then—the Indians. Someone came up and tapped me on the shoulder. I thought it would be a kid asking for an autograph, and I was looking forward to surprising him by already having a pen ready. It wasn't a kid, though he wasn't much bigger than a kid. It was Mr. Reeves. Standing on the court while he was on concrete, I was at least a foot taller than he was. This was almost twenty years ago. Rolling a homemade cigarette and spitting out the tobacco, he looked to me like a leprechaun that just got in from skeet shooting. He had a bounce to his step, which he lost in 1974 with the first fibrillations, and he had on a hunting hat and hiking boots and a Pendleton shirt and possessed the face of a man in effortless triumph from having just stalked a deer or outrun a jackal. There was a quality of energy he conveyed that was ecstatically athletic.

All he said was, "Hello, Albert. I'm Marty Reeves. I like your work a lot."

"Gosh, that's so good to hear, Mr. Reeves. I'm so happy to get assignments from you, but you haven't said too much about them and I was worried you weren't too pleased because you really hadn't said too much one way or the other." My mouth was running at 78 rpm and my mind was skipping most of its allotted synapses.

"You'll learn," he said, "that the highest compliment in this profession is when no one says anything. Like being an umpire. You've just reported what is there."

This seemed to me to be such an apotheosis of wisdom that I literally wrote it down in the notebook I was carrying. I got in trouble for returning late to the locker room, and I very nearly missed the team bus back to Des Moines because Mr. Reeves and I sat in the front row together and talked about my work and looked out at the court, which under the dimming lights was receding from my view as my future got filled in.

"I want you to come for an interview," he said.

I had thought of going on to get my master's in journalism at Drake, but this was an amazing opportunity. I'd go to River City for several years, move on to Chicago, and from there who knows? If in 1962 you had told me that in 1980 I would still be in River City, I would have laughed heartily.

Marty was small, compact, intense, strong, tough, and he looked the way kids look—like he could go anywhere. No foxhole was too small. No barbed wire was too tangled. Offering me an interview, he might as well have said he was knighting me. At the end of summer, as if under ether, I drove to River City and got dragged out of the *Register* office and over to Phil's, and then we started talking about a horse they had to shoot when it didn't make it over the jump in the final round of the Equestrians in Rome. . . .

Finishing the first six of Molson, I burped, napped, and told

271

myself I couldn't phone Deborah with Barry asleep, so I started in on the second six and suddenly wanted to file a piece on Menkus' accident. I walked over to the motel office and said, "I'm a journalist, and I was wondering if I could maybe borrow your typewriter."

"Yeah, you're a journalist and I'm Loretta Lynn," the owner's meaty wife said. "Why don't you just go back and sleep it off, okay, mister?"

I gave her a twenty. She shrugged, which I took to be a yes, so I carried down the hall her old manual, which felt like it hadn't been used since the Voting Rights Act. I tried to write just a regular article on Menkus and couldn't. I crawled into bed, trying to sleep, but my ankle was killing me until I realized what I needed to say.

> Every good sports story is about the same thing—bumping up against limits and going beyond them, being in trouble and living with that trouble. Menkus, my message to you is simple: don't come back until you're ready, but when you do return don't play scared. Because you're playing for me, my friend, you're playing for all of us.

I awoke to a garbage truck grinding gears and called a stringer to come get my piece. Then I stood like a stiff in the shower, trying to sober up.

I ate breakfast at Hamburg Hut on roan-and-gray plates. I had a ringing headache and galloping guilt about leaving Deborah in the dark, but she and Barry were already at school and I went right back to the hospital. The carpet was getting vacuumed, coffee-and-Danish trays were being pushed through the corridors, doctors chatted up RN's. People were buying magazines and papers, though not the *Register*, which wouldn't be out till noon. The place was well lit in the morning and allowed your recovery hopes half a chance to take. I asked a black nurse how Menkus was doing.

"Belvyn's in Ortho," she said.

"Sounds like the dentistry division," I said, just feeling combative.

She could barely believe how ignorant I was. "Ortho-pedics," she said, pronouncing every syllable slowly to make sure I caught it. I went around the hall to Ortho, where they told me Menkus was upstairs in Ambulatory.

"Come again."

"Post-op. He had emergency surgery last night, as I assume you're aware," said a man at the desk, one of this new breed of efficient male nurses. "You *are* family?"

"Of course. Micky Menkus. Stepbrother. Just got in. Where is he?"

"Fourth floor, last wing on your left. . . . There's such a wonderful little pun embedded in your last name."

Men kiss. Cute. I'd be sure to tell Francis.

The elevator didn't work, and I ran up the staircase and around the fourth floor until I found another desk and another nurse. This one looked like a freshman majoring in Patient Sympathy.

River State Clinics is a teaching hospital, which means there are always at least half a dozen medical students turning someone else's injury into a learning experience. When I finally found the right room, eager-beaver fledglings were recording every word a gray-haired windbag uttered while a nurse fluffed up pillows so all the interns could see Menkus' ravaged knee. Articular cartilage damage. Bucket handle tear. Torn menis-cus. Certain phrases the ancient eminence kept fondling because he liked the way they sounded. The wandering class-room finally wandered to the other side of the room and another exhibit. Menkus still hadn't said boo. He cowered be-neath a white sheet with his knee on a styrofoam pad the color of his eyes. A metal railing went all the way around the bed to keep him from falling onto the floor.

"Hey," I said.

He tried to give me a grin and said, "Hey, Albear, look, man, I—"

"Listen, Menkus," I said, taking his hand and squeezing it and staring down into those dead eyes of his, "I'm sure you've got the world's most comprehensive health insurance, but if it doesn't cover every red cent of this disaster you have my word: I'm good for it."

Shaking his head in a way that suggested Raeburn would take care of everything, he nevertheless looked hurt and scared. For the first time I saw him for what he was—a goofy, vulnerable kid I happened to worship. I promised myself I'd already done to him the last damage I would ever do. He lay under the sheet, drinking a soda, with his carved-up knee in a plastic splint.

"I guess you know I've been digging up this piece on your past. Well, I'm not going to do it anymore. I won't print it, I'll let it all go. Take me, my man, I'm yours," I said and laughed to make it sound lighter than it was.

I realized I was picking up some of his diction, and how patronizing that was. I couldn't help it, though.

Menkus snorted like he got soda caught in his nostrils and said, "I appreciate what you're tryin' to say, but don't be pullin' no hero number, man. You already tied."

"What do you mean?"

"The bet binds you, man. You lost ten–zip on the slam. You got to go hide if I want it that way. You got to write me up pretty in the paper. That deal already went down."

I hadn't thought of that. I honestly hadn't. But he was right. "I wrote kind of a combination fan letter-apology to you for today's paper."

"Don't be cryin' over my corpse, Bieder. It was only arthur scopy."

"What did they—"

"I got how they say a torn Menkus. They open it up, take a peekaboo, say lookee here, flick it out. I'll be back for league game *numero uno*: Champaign at Champaign."

"Torn meniscus," I said, like Deborah correcting the Bare's homework. "Arthroscopy."

"And who're you, head motherfucker of bone repair?"

He said this too loud. The medical team examining an old man's back glowered at us. The student-doctors were trying to talk the old man into turning on his side. He was afraid. They assured him it wasn't going to hurt too much. They needed to look at something or other in order to bring their anatomy books to life.

"They say it's only a bucket tear," Menkus said. "Come from hangin' above the bucket too long."

I loved the joke. It showed he still had all his faculties intact. I laughed my goddamn head off and he stared at me to say, Hey, man, it wasn't that funny.

"I heal like a bitch. I be recuperatin' but a short time. It ain't nothing more than a flesh wound," he went on, pinching his elbow skin.

Flesh wounds don't go to the bone, I needed to tell him, but I said, "You sure they had to cut?"

"Got to get to it quick. I laid here all night, not knowin' nothin'."

"They put you out?"

"Here to here," he said. His arms were long enough that he was able to point from his feet to his Afro without any problem. The knee looked like a split golf ball. "When I woke up, the guck was jetting and everything was unlocked. They say I'll be back for Champaign."

The Champaign game was only a month away, and I figured someone was feeding Menkus a line about being back so soon, to pump him up. He had Christmas vacation as a buffer, but knees are tricky. Cartilage damage isn't a sprained ankle. You can't just pop out of surgery and set up the offense.

"So how long will you have to wear this thing?" I asked, tapping the splint.

"I'm bookin' game time Saturday."

"Come on, man, you're not going to be able to play against St. Louis."

275

"I'll be there eagle-eyein' the opposition." Watching the pro scouts watching him, charting his recovery.

The medical team walked out of the room, leaving the old man like a beetle on his back, having to wait till they finished conferring in the corridor. His pecker peeked out of his ridiculous bib. I couldn't get over how white Menkus' face was, as if in draining his knee they'd gone ahead and emptied his expressions. His only gift in the world had just been cut out from under him by an idiot ex-jock who didn't have the sense to get the hell out of his way before he landed.

"I don't know how to tell you how sorry I am," I said. "How terrible I feel."

"Don't say nothin', man, 'cause it's already done. All I remember is skyin', double pumpin', hangin', then glidin' down and seein' you gazin' up, not doin' jackshit, just standin' there, like a post. You shoulda got outta the way, ass*hole*," he said, but it was clear them weren't fightin' words.

"I know."

"You shouldn'ta camped in the paint if you can't draw."

"I know," I said again, "I know. From here on in I hurt nobody. Even though I know about the GED's and SCTE night school and straight C's and Raeburn's loans and my wife being—"

"I already told you, man, not to hit no more on your lady. All she does is help me learn shit."

He talked some more about how bad he wanted to whip the team together this year, then stuck my hand on his knee and told me to apply pressure while he did straight leg raises. He was supposed to start these exercises tonight but wanted me to offer medium resistance now so he could see how it felt.

What the hell, I'll be honest. To be allowed to press on that knee, to hold on to the one I hurt, sent electrodes through my arm. His right leg was already a lot stronger than either of mine would ever be. I had trouble holding him down. Nine hours out of surgery, he grunted and lifted while I tried to resist until a woman from X-ray came in and said they needed to see what his knee looked like.

276

Though she had a stretcher and a burly orderly behind her, I said Menkus and I could manage it by ourselves. She popped the railings on his bed and moved the stretcher over.

"Come on, Menkus," I said. "Here we go."

Pain shot up my leg when I put all the pressure on my ankle to squat and slide him over, and when I slid him onto the stretcher I lost my balance for a second and fell on top of him. I kept going and gave him a hug around his high shoulders, clapping onto his gown.

I embarrassed him and he held back. However, he didn't really fight me off. He gave me a grudging little piece of himself, and that was all I ever asked for.

"Okay, man, okay, just leave the other stuff alone, and then you can write pretty again when I be back for Champaign."

"Ready, sweethearts?" asked the X-ray woman, buckling him in. "Can I tear you two away from each other long enough to get some pictures taken?"

Watching Menkus get wheeled down the corridor with his knee in a splint and his gown coming undone, I battled back water.

The old man in the far corner wanted to be turned onto his side. To hell with the medical team out in the hallway: I turned him over. He grumbled thanks. I said good-bye to the sympathy major at the front desk and went looking for the elevator. This was the second time Menkus had insisted Deborah was a Girl Scout. I was going to call her and clear things up once and for all. So who was standing in the elevator when the doors parted? Vicki. And what did she have to say? "Ooh, ooh, ooh, boy, are you in trouble!"

For someone who had so much homework to catch up on, she was doing a lot of chasing around. She was surrounded on both sides by specimen trays, then sat down all excited and out of breath on a bench. Various types of hums bombarded us: heater, vacuum, TV.

"What did I do now?" I asked.

"I've been trying to get you since nine last night. I finally reached Deborah an hour ago and she hung up on me. I'm almost sure she thought we'd been out together. Where were you?"

"With Menkus."

"You're kidding."

"Francis and I were shooting hoops at the Rec Center. Menkus came in, and I bet him I could get a bucket off him before he got ten off me. If I won, he'd give me a real interview. If I lost, I'd have to stay away."

"Oh, I see, so you snapped his knee in half to make sure you won."

Plastic plants were set in wooden barrels, paintings of sailboats were hung on the wall. I doubt there's a sailboat within twenty miles of River City.

"How did you hear about Menkus already?" I asked.

"It's out."

"Francis must have blabbed."

"I think KRCX did have it first."

"Jesus."

"Anyway, how is he?" Vicki said.

"Francis?"

"Menkus."

"They're telling him he'll be back in a month, but I don't see how, when he tore cartilage. He fell during our little bet. I'm responsible. It's all my fault. I left out my foot for him to fall on."

"Not intentionally."

"No, of course not, but I wasn't alert. Like Menkus said, I shouldn't—"

"You can't blame yourself."

"Sure, I can. I felt so guilty last night I checked into the Jefferson Davis and drank myself unconscious. So, anyway, what were you calling about?"

"The true journalist's nose sniffs meat," she said, moving around on the bench so she could look at me. "Larry Hutchins gave me some pretty amazing new dope on Menkus."

"I'm not interested," I said.

"What do you mean?"

"I don't want to go after any more dirt."

"Wait till you hear it," Vicki said. "Larry asked me out to dinner last night and I said no, so he said he'd treat and had a bit of information he wanted to share. I met him at Cats. His ex-girlfriend, who's still a 'good friend,' manages Menkus' apartment building, and she told Larry she never sees a check from Menkus. It comes straight from Raeburn's realty company."

"Gallery Homes."

"Right. Menkus' apartment is just a tiny studio way down on the thousand block of Washington, but inside he's supposedly got all kinds of goodies tucked away. Plus—I know this sounds too good to be true—she says Menkus leaves his key on the ledge above his door. No one else can reach that high. She sees it whenever she changes the hall light bulbs."

"Menkus' knee is wrapped in a splint, his career is in jeopardy, and you want to go burglarize his apartment. I can't believe you."

"So what time do you want to go over there?" Vicki said, fingering a leaf of the plastic plant hanging over her shoulder.

"No, Vicki. Really, don't say that. I just got through telling Menkus he could trust me. I want to see him recover. I'm only going to go after Raeburn from now on. And I also have to talk to Deborah."

"You sound confused."

"Because it doesn't make sense. Why would Hutchins tell you all of this?"

"He's bitter and lonely and wants to go to bed with me."

"Then why did his ex do what she did?"

"She wants him back."

"You've been studying too much psychology."

"Well, come on," she said. "Let's go over there while we have a chance. We'll just take a quick look around. We won't harm anything."

The single worst thing I've ever done in my life was let her drag me back into the elevator. "I promised Menkus I was on his side from now on," I said as we went down. "Five minutes ago I watched him get wheeled into X-ray, and I was practically crying."

"We're not the Red Cross, Albert, we're reporters."

I have a couple of feeble excuses centering on the facts that I was still hung over and my ankle was killing me. But the truth remains: I was damned deadly curious. My spine was made of shredded basketball nets. I had to tear off his flesh until only the skeleton remained, until I knew he no longer possessed me. At least this was the last step, the resolution one way or another, after which I was finished. No matter what we found out, I would use it only against Raeburn and not Menkus.

Two innocuous-looking brick buildings stood across from each other at 1011 Washington. A used Audi Fox was parked out front, but there was no proof it was Menkus' other than a batch of tube socks in the backseat. All four doors were locked. Now Vicki's hand was sweaty whereas I was relatively cool, doing what I had to do, filled with the simple need to know.

Each building had twelve apartments, every one with a square window, and at the bottom of both buildings were a washer and dryer and a bank of mailboxes tucked into an alcove. Neither of us had heard of any of the people who lived in Building A, but on the Building B mailbox Vicki noticed the name of the girl who was the manager and Hutchins' ex. There was also an anonymous slot that I figured for Menkus'. We went up one flight of stairs. The light was dismal and the carpet was ratty red stuff you find in bars where the pinball always tilts and the time is half an hour slow.

"I guess there's no way he could get over here," Vicki said.

"No," I said, "not very likely."

She had the shakes, so she played watchguard while I jumped up to get the key from the ledge, reaggravating my ankle. I fiddled with the lock to 2F until the door opened. It was a small enough place that you could tell immediately no one was home unless he was hiding in the shower. Vicki rattled the bathroom door and said, "Yoo hoo? Belvyn? It's Vicki Lynch. I just came over for an interview and the door was open. You in there?"

She was pretty scared. The toilet didn't answer. A stereo as large and complicated as a life-support system was on the floor, and I turned it on to provide cover. Even in River City Menkus had found a soul station. The kitchen and bedroom, both small, were barely set off from the living room, and the half-bath was in back. A Betamax had all the cable circuits and a rack of movie tapes. Menkus seemed to be a fan of Fred Williamson and Pam Greer.

"They must be a real visual family," Vicki said.

"What do you mean?"

"Raeburn bought off his parents with a Betamax, right? And now here's another Betamax. Maybe that's where Belvyn gets his peripheral vision."

"That jibes with his reading problems. Dyslexics sort of see things in 3-D." I took in the room and gestured. "This is how people operate when they think no one wants to stop them."

"You mean Menkus?"

"No," I said, "I mean Raeburn."

Vicki rewound Menkus' tape machine and played back the phone messages, which were mostly from Hinselwood and Ott to return their calls or from groupies to meet Menkus at the Silver Dollar for drinks. The rug in the living room was a huge pile of dirty laundry, and the only pieces of furniture, aside from Stallion gizmos, a sea-green couch, and a dilapidated desk, were stacks of music magazines and basketball magazines and sports sections, a couple of camera cases, cutout felt letters all over the floor for him to fondle.

I wandered around. The bathroom was awash in debris. The drain was clogged with hair; the shower curtain was torn and off the rack; toilet kits were spilled across the cracked linoleum, which was scummy with dirty towels and more hair and soap and shampoo. Afro combs and packs of Trojans lined

the counter. The mirror was shivered. What saved the bathroom were used tubes of Ben-Gay, whose smell returned me to
setting my legs on fire with that sweet white stuff, wearing it as
a badge of honor to tenth-grade homeroom the first few morn-
ings after the start of basketball workouts.

The kitchen was a disaster of junk food, unwashed dishes
and cups, open containers, empty grocery bags everywhere,
three weeks of garbage. It looked like the maid had forgotten
to come in since Columbus Day. The bedroom was cleaner
only because it had less in it. A lot of nice shirts and shoes were
thrown in the closet, and a portable weight machine was
pushed into the corner of the room. A couple more cameras,
Nikon and Olympus. Lying across the mattress was the fun-
niest bathrobe I've ever seen. It was so un-Menkus, a long
brown leather thing with a fluffy fur collar. I was just thinking
there weren't as many doodads as we'd been led to believe by
Hutchins' ex-girl friend—a Betamax here, a Soloflex there, a
camera collection, a few threads—when Vicki shouted from
the living room: "Eureka!"

She'd been clawing through the drawers of Menkus' "study
table," where under more magazines and an unopened pack
of binder paper were lecture notes for all his classes, including
Deborah's, so he could sleep late after grueling practices if he
needed to. Outlines for the whole semester in Rhetoric, Math,
General Science, and World Geography, though nothing in
Deb's handwriting.

"They pay TA's to do this kind of thing," Vicki explained.

We kept looking for deeper clues, but there weren't any,
only a pair of spelling primers which could have belonged to a
precocious kindergartener. Crib sheets were crib sheets. I
heard some commotion and stopped everything for a second. It
was just the people next door waking up late.

"We should copy everything and get out of here," Vicki
said.

"Relax. The smell of Ben-Gay is transporting me to the
gyms of my youth."

"Let's not make the same mistake we made at Sioux City."

"Which was?"

"Not coming away with the smoking pistol."

"You really think they would have let us do that?"

"We should write down who all the calls are from, what classes the notes are to, the serial number of the weight machine and the cameras and the Betamax. Everything."

"We're not copying everything down because we're not going after Menkus anymore. We're leaving him alone. I only want Raeburn. I thought I made that—"

"You're kidding me," she said, and I suddenly heard Menkus' stereo again, which had been on the whole time. I just hadn't been listening.

"I'm as serious as I can be."

"After all I went through to get us this, you don't even want to take notes on what's here?"

"To be honest, it's not as bad as I thought it'd be."

She nodded over to Menkus' desk, where his whole semester was summarized for him.

"Look," I said, "you didn't see him in the hospital. I promised I'd do what I could to help him bounce back, and that's a promise I intend to keep."

Hitting me, she hit hard. What we were really arguing about was why we'd both finally backed away from each other. Too much had happened and not happened in too short a time, and all the emotions were coming out raw.

"I thought we were a team," Vicki said. "We don't decide guys' guilt; we're just supposed to print what we find. We haven't done anything wrong."

"Of course we have."

"You're protecting Deborah as well as Belvyn."

"So what if I am?"

"Well, if you don't print it, I will."

"No, you won't, because if you do I'll get you on illegal entry."

"I would say you already did in Sioux City," she said, trying

283

to seduce me by alluding to Knights' Inn, but I was having none of it because I just wanted to clear things up. Though she was almost in tears, she still had her spunk, which was what I loved about her in the first place. She put on her coat to leave.

"Vicki, please," I said. "If we can get to Raeburn without destroying Menkus, fine, but this would ruin someone's career."

"No, it wouldn't."

"Yes, it would. I don't want to cause any more problems for him than I already have."

"You're like everyone else," she said. "You're as bad as Marty and Francis or my brothers, for that matter. You're not a journalist. You're just a fucking fan."

Trying to make a pun like hers to lighten things up, I took a basketball magazine and fanned it in front of her, but she didn't laugh, and when I tried to touch her she pushed me away.

She said, "If we publish our piece, I might get the *Globe-Democrat* thing, and for sure you'll get the Milwaukee job."

"I realize that."

"And you're still going to cop out?"

"I don't see what I'm doing as copping out."

"Okay, then, it's over," she announced, marching to the door. "I'm breaking up."

"Breaking up, what are you talking about?" I said, trying to stop her, but she already had on her gloves. If you suffered an argument, you broke up. If you discovered something, you printed it. She was that young. She told me to let go of her and say good-bye.

"Vicki, don't act so melodramatic about this. Let's talk."

She zipped her coat, put her pack over her shoulder, and slammed the door. I watched her run against the wind toward town, striding hard, pumping her arms, really letting out her kick until her entire perfect body was only fluid movement forward. She never looked back.

The Betamax. The Nikons. The Soloflex in the bedroom, the leather bathrobe. The cheat sheets under the unopened binder paper. I won't pretend I wasn't tempted to splash all this across the Weekend section of the *Register,* then fly to Milwaukee to sign my W-2 forms. But I couldn't help feeling something bad had died when Menkus tore his knee and maybe something better was about to be born. Putting Vicki's scarf in my coat pocket, leaping to place the key on the ledge, I went downstairs into day, bright and blustery.

TWELVE

I HEADED straight to the office and, working my ass off, cleared a tremendous amount of copy until the early edition arrived and I saw my Menkus piece wasn't printed. I went through Sports twice, then the whole paper, thinking maybe the story was given feature play, but that hadn't happened, either. I visited the bathroom, where I encountered Sabrina, who said she was only looking for a roll of paper towels. I studied the faces of people in Editorial, wondering who had wielded the scissors, since Marty never kills my stuff. I finally found him chasing his nitro tabs at the water cooler and asked him what had happened.

"What, did I cut myself shaving again?" he said, checking his chin in the little mirror above the water bottle. We were in Editorial, and I didn't like the looks we were getting from our resident geniuses, who wanted us to get out of their hair so they could talk about big topics like lunch.

"No, I mean didn't Jeff run my piece over to you in time for today?" Jeff's the stringer who came over to get the piece—a nice kid, fleet of foot, but endowed with an elevator that doesn't necessarily go all the way to the top.

"It got here, all right."

"Well, where is it?" I said, but saw what was coming.

Editorial decided to close the door and say, "Albert? Marty? Would you guys mind taking it outside? We're trying to finish the front page." Oh, the front page—NEW DOUGH-NUT SHOP OPENS ON CLINTON.

"I thought we'd save it," Marty said.

"Save it, for what? The whole point was I was there at a four-alarm fire. I lit the match."

"Look, Albert, I'm sorry Menkus got hurt, and it's too bad he fell on your foot. You were drunk, you felt guilty: fine, you got it out of your system. But that's no reason for us to run *True Confessions*. It would have been an embarrassment. It's already in Kill."

"Jesus, Marty, come on. We've known each other for nearly twenty years, and you've never—"

"That's all I want to hear about it," he said and handed me a list of wrestling results to set in agate, as it was giving him a migraine.

I slumped at my desk, sulking. Suddenly I was incapable of a decent column? Listen, Marty, you know what you can do with your wrestling agate. He was on the phone now, bargaining with his bookie. I looked up my piece in Kill copy. I read it. I looked around the room at people happily typing. I waved hi to Sabrina, who waved back a wad of paper towels. I started over and read it again. Marty can't write his way out of a paper bag, but give him something to edit and his pilot light goes on. He can spot Kill copy at a hundred yards. I saw what he meant. The column was subjective to the point of being insane, and the worst paragraph went:

> There are hollow victories and inspiring de-
> feats, trivial wins and important losses. The wis-
> dom in my head tonight is that the beer com-
> mercials are true: we only go around once in
> life and have to grab for all the gusto we can.
> When Menkus recovers, he will show us how to
> grab gusto without being selfish, how to give as
> well as receive.

Marty was off the phone and out buying bullets for his rifle. I put the cover on my typewriter and called it a day.

The English department is rarely the hottest spot on campus, but late Thursday afternoon during exam week it had all the appeal of a padded cell. Kids were either suffering through exams, preparing to flunk them, or exhausted from having barely survived them. I bumped into the crazy lady janitor whose red wig was askew, as always. A radio plug was jammed into her ear and she was saving old newspapers, even ones that had pieces I'd written. A journalist's heartthrob. She shuffled around outside the women's bathroom, banging her broom against the brick wall. I took the elevator to the third floor, then down the corridor under the bright fluorescents and past some scholars who looked like they'd just flunked junior year. The Philosophy department shares the building with English, and I ran into two of the Phil's contingent, Dobrinsky and Neikrans, who said they'd just left a congratulatory note in Deb's box. Adrienne kissed me congratulations on the cheek, and Tolliver, straight from central casting in a tweedy movie about Oxford dons, pumped my hand seriously, puffing his pipe. Mrs. Diehl, a Chaucer scholar and religious fanatic who is appropriately troll-like, gave me a little curtsy and newly respectful nod. Deborah must have had quite a night of it with Mr. Hemley.

I stood for a minute outside her office, watching through the open door, listening to her be a genius. I could see her brown slacks; her cork heels spilled on the linoleum with the ankle straps undone; her sweater, a black woolly thing I gave her for our fifth anniversary, draped over the chair; the shadow of a boy's shoulders. All her spread-out clothes came together in my mind as her, Deborah Jean Rasnick Biederman, this piece of person, this flesh, this body I knew. Chilly surprises ran through my pipes like a shot of love.

As her student left I asked him what kind of mood she was

in, and he replied, "Brutal." I walked in, saying, "Hello, Professor Biederman. I came by to congratulate you on your book and also to find out why you gave me a C in 101."

She didn't even pretend to laugh. She rearranged her stockinged feet on the rim of the garbage can.

"Please just hear me out," I said. "I couldn't face anybody last night. I had to check into the Jefferson Davis and get plastered until I thought things through. I didn't go off and marry the Queen of Sheba." She looked down and didn't say anything, which is the best interview technique there is. Stay silent while someone is preparing to hang himself, and he'll stop to tell you why he chose a particular type of rope. I did. "I take it everybody knows by now about Menkus' knee. I'll die if I've ruined his career."

Deborah got up to erase the chalkboard and push the erasers together, sending up a cloud between us. She walked across the room and stared out the window at the bridge and the river below, which was frozen.

"I called around midnight and it was busy," I said, "so I assumed you were home and Barry was fine. Come on, Deb, there have been times you stayed at the library until three or four and didn't even think of calling because you were so involved in your work. I accepted that. Can't you give me the same break?"

She shook her head.

"Okay, error number one: I shouldn't have left Barry alone. I'm sorry. A few minutes after Francis and I started playing, Menkus walked into the gym and I bet him interview/no interview I could score one basket off him before he got ten off me, which I would never have had to do if you hadn't concocted that crazy scheme of yours in the first place."

Deborah looked at the papers on her desk and spun around in her chair so her back was facing me.

"On the last play of our little game Menkus dunked. You know what a dunk is, don't you?"

It struck home how much my woman usually talked. I

missed the white noise of her mind. This silence game of hers was the cruelest trick; fucking up for twenty-four hours had rendered me invisible.

"He landed on my ankle, twisted his knee bad, and had to go straight to the hospital in an ambulance. I was going to go with him until I remembered I'd forgotten to give Barry his shot and rushed home with a sprained ankle."

"You remembered you forgot," she said, unable to restrain herself, then zipped her lip again.

"Barry was fine," I continued. "He'd given himself the shot, so I went to the hospital to check on Menkus. They wouldn't let me see him, but I knew he was in surgery. That's when I tried to call you. I should have come home then. I know that. I'm sorry, I was crazy, I felt hyper. My ankle was killing me. I checked in at the motel, got drunk and depressed, and then went back to the hospital this morning. He tore his cartilage. Supposedly it's a very clean tear, the type that heals quickly. They went in with that arthroscope thing and got all of it, and he says they're telling him he might be back in a month. Menkus forgave me, why can't you?"

She was just about to tell me when the phone rang. "Biederman, English," she said.

The other party said something, and Deborah said, "Yes, yes, it is."

The other party asked for something else, and Deborah said, "Yes, yes, I do."

The other party talked for quite a long while, the volume rising so I could tell it was a woman's voice and Deborah only said, "What?"

After a little while she said, "No, I didn't."

Then, "No."

"No," again.

Then, "Quite sure."

A long speech by the other party, high and whiny, and Deborah said, "Yes, I will, I certainly will do that."

Finally, "I'm terribly sorry. Please accept my apologies."

I had no idea what this conversation was about but hoped

she'd gotten in trouble for not turning her grades in on time, which might help melt the glacier. She sat in the wooden chair, tapping her pencil and looking at me, biting her gorgeous bottom lip, dialing numbers with the receiver in the cradle, idly pushing extension buttons. My ankle started acting up again.

"That was the registrar," she said with enough bitterness you could cut it with a bookmark, "asking me why Belvyn's transcripts haven't been returned yet."

"Oh, sweet Jesus, I forgot."

"You forgot? Like you forgot about Barry's insulin? What's got into you, Albert? What the hell were you doing with Belvyn's file?"

"Well, at the Rec Center he kept saying how much you were helping him out and—" I stopped pacing to sit down, and Deborah rolled up a piece of paper and meant to throw it into the garbage can but missed. I sank it cleanly from seven.

"And . . ."

"I was curious."

"Curious about what?"

"What your relationship was."

"We're sadomasochistic sexual partners, didn't you realize?"

"Come on, Deb. You don't have any right to be so sarcastic. I know."

"Know what?" she said.

"I know," I repeated. I didn't want to have to say. I didn't want it to be true.

"This isn't *Front Page*, Albert. Tell me what you mean."

"I know about Raeburn running interference for Menkus everywhere he goes. I know you're his contact person."

Standing up, she pushed the partition behind the desk and said, "Honey, you must have an incredibly grandiose idea of what a contact person is. The way you say it makes me sound like an alien. It's not that big a thing."

"One kid I talked to made the contact person out to be Santa Claus and the Easter Bunny rolled into one."

"Raeburn talked to me that day at his farm. All he said was

he'd appreciate it if I kept an eye out for Belvyn. It was very nebulous."

"How do you mean?"

"It wasn't a formal deal or anything. I gave Belvyn a few more hours of tutoring this week because of exams. That's all it amounted to."

"That, and outlining class for him."

"What are you talking about?" she said, visibly uncomfortable for the first time, and when I reached across the table to try to take her hand she pulled back. Her face clenched tight into ugliness. The heat in the office was on too high, and Deborah rearranged her hair, changing herself so what I said wouldn't be true.

"This morning Menkus asked me to pick up his radio, and I moseyed around his apartment, counting NCAA violations. There were cheat sheets in a desk drawer."

"My God, Albert, they aren't answers to anything, they're just outlines to give an LD student half a chance at comprehension. They're only my TA's lecture notes. It turns out I don't need Raeburn's help, anyway."

I cocked my head and raised my eyebrows, like Deborah does when she thinks I'm lying, but she would have none of it and went on: "I didn't get home until late last night myself. Mr. Hemley kept us up till eleven-thirty, twelve, going on about how much he liked the book, and if the rest of his readers like it as much as he does they'll probably print it this summer, which would—"

"How do you know Raeburn didn't arrange it all for you?"

"Albert, don't do that to me. I've worked on this thing for five years. Raeburn carries no weight with the Press. They're completely autonomous."

"Then why did you do it?"

"I want to get tenure, I want us to stay here. I thought it might help. Is that so awful?"

"I don't know," I said. "I guess not."

She walked around the room and I walked around the room in opposite directions, and when we met in the center she stood behind me and massaged my neck. "We're going to be okay," Deb said, "we really are. Everything is going to be good from here on in."

Frankly, this kind of talk terrifies me. The next thing you know is Skylab falls on your house or Three Mile Island engineers are hired to rebuild your sewage system. Deborah is intellectual, but she isn't idealistic. I'm not sure I'd ever admitted that to myself before. To get ahead, she did what the world demanded she do.

"I mean, my book is actually going to be published. I still can't fucking believe it."

Fucking meant she wanted to celebrate, but I was too tired and confused to do anything more than bob my head and try to smile. We'd cleared enough off the blackboard for one day. Deb had to give an essay test to her First Person seminar. She put on her shoes and sweater and gathered some mimeo sheets.

"We can deal with this if we work at it," she said, and we hugged gently, like glass rubbing glass.

Saturday morning, when I went to the hospital to see how Menkus was doing, he wasn't in his room. I thought I had the wrong floor or the wrong hall or that he had escaped. Then I saw him creaking down the corridor on crutches, followed by a Vietnamese nurse. He was wearing an oatmeal-colored gown and a wrap around his knee. His Afro was unraveled. He hadn't shaved or washed. He looked sixteen and smelled like a cesspool.

"Hey, that's great," I said, trying to be encouraging. "Already up and about. Before you know it, you'll be goaltending with those sticks."

"Snuff the happy shit, man."

"Pardon me if I'm pleased to see you walking around. I didn't expect you to be on your feet so soon."

"You a fish. My knee's swollen bad. It hurts, it hurts. And you dancin' around here like you just won Bingo."

The Vietnamese nurse nodded at me. Other nurses went by,

an old lady in a wheelchair, an empty stretcher. Menkus moved slowly but steadily toward his room.

"Come on, man, lighten up. I brought a picture of you as a sort of—"

Leaning on one crutch, he ripped the four-by-five-inch photo of him hanging in the air with both legs pulled to his chin as he looked right and passed left through Murphy's outstretched arms. The nurse collected the pieces on the floor.

"This ain't no fuckin' John Wayne flick, you dense motherfucker, nor neither no goddamn article in *Sports Illustrated*. My knee is fucked up. You fucked it up. I'm ascared it's fucked up for good, can you dig that?"

"I'm sorry, I was just trying to help. I brought along the picture as inspiration, something to work your way back to. I'm writing a really positive story on you now."

"No harm, no foul, huh, Bieds?"

"How do you mean?"

"No autopsy, no foul. I shoulda blowed the whistle on you a long time ago."

He stomped the last twenty yards to his room faster than I thought you could move on crutches. As he got into bed, his knee didn't look too puffed up, and there was only a little hole on the side of his leg near the calf. While the nurse got things ready for his sponge bath, I sat in the room, asking him when his parents were going to visit and whether he planned to watch the game this afternoon. He put on headphones. He wanted to take out his anger on me, so I left him with his bitterness and drum solo and scouted Ambulatory until I found a doctor, a young guy who had a thirty-dollar haircut and a burn on his neck. I asked him what was going on with Menkus.

"It's quite typical," he said. "Yesterday he was elated he wasn't hurt worse. Now he's returned to reality. He has to deal with Rehab. It's not an easy transition. Healing hurts and also takes time."

"So how's he doing?"

"Well, ideally, of course, he would never have been injured." The doctor had odd hand mannerisms. His gestures weren't in sync with his voice, like a politician reading idiot cards.

"How true. Look, Doc, ideally, we all wouldn't die. I didn't—"

"Put it this way: he won't be riding any Yamahas for a while."

"If I hear one more joke out of you," I said, "I'll implant your stethoscope in your urinary tract. I want to know how he is."

"Well, Belvyn has the best possible cartilage tear: anterior cruciate medial meniscus. Only one suture was required. And he has flat condyles and very round tibia, which can't hurt recovery time. Everything points to him being ready, quote-unquote, the middle of January."

"Which just happens to coincide with the start of the conference."

"Yes, it does." It was a business like anything else. "I'm sure you know, Mr. Biederman, as a sports reporter, that we feel a certain pressure to get him back in action. He'll be taking a calculated risk; that's the way this game is played. He'll make it, I'm confident he'll make it. But it's possible the knee won't hold up for him. There's always that chance."

The doctor babbled some more about medicine not being an exact science, then said, "The last thing you want to do is magnify the patient's perception of instability. The less tentative he is, the more likely he'll recover." For no real reason, he grabbed my elbow and squeezed. "This is an injury we can live with."

We? I suddenly knew why Menkus was pissed. "What's going to happen next?" I asked.

"The swelling should subside completely within ten days, then we can start light running and swimming. The following week—"

"I don't think he knows how to swim."

The doctor laughed. He hadn't considered that. He forgot that kids on the south side didn't have their own swimming pools. Eager to impress, he fed me more details about how neat and clean arthroscopy was until I wearied of technicalities, slapped him on the back, and said "Great" to get out of there and go take Barry to his first basketball game.

Hinselwood, striding hard, whizzed by, saw me, stopped, and pivoted to say eight words: "You'll pay through the nose for this, Biederman." Then he strode on, a man with a mission.

The St. Louis game was the end of the pre-Christmas part of the schedule, and the crowd was distinctly less than full capacity. Maybe it was my imagination or the weather, but it seemed like fans were jostling me as Barry and I worked our way through them to press row. The Stallion Battalion gave me an even ruder welcome than usual, unfurling a banner that said SEND THE SPORTSWRITER TO SIBERIA. It wasn't my imagination: I had single-handedly turned the warm barn into an ice palace. Mr. Ed and the Mares were, I thought, challenging me to a staring contest as the players and refs loosened up. The Spirits got caught in a snowstorm and had to ride a bus from Chicago, arriving forty minutes before tip-off, but they played like they'd spent the last three hours taking shooting practice. They zoomed ahead on 70 percent accuracy from the field, destroying the zone River State threw up to protect Peter Keil, Menkus' replacement. If the offense hadn't quite jelled with Menkus at point guard, without him it was what he called beating off by himself: a ragtag chaos of Black Stallion dribbling in circles; Tomlinson tossing prayers; Durland and Gault batting the ball back and forth until they were called for lane violations; and Keil, usually such a solid sub, panicking in the starter's role, fumbling frantically. Barry refused to feign any interest in any of this or even listen to my pointers. Instead, he fiddled with a miniature, magnetic chess set Francis sent him for Christmas.

At halftime the Pork Queen was crowned, which was the only reason my son was by my side. Seven of the eight candidates were introduced to the crowd, and of course the one Barry had the crush on was the one who didn't show, which sent him into hysterics. Laurel had refused to come to the game because she felt he should have a crush on her, and she was right. These girls were on the hefty side of pretty and apparently hadn't heard of smiling. Hardly anyone clapped for them, and the Stallion Battalion hissed en masse and threw paper cups. The mike squealed.

"How come people're booing them, Daddy?" Barry wanted to know. "They didn't do anything wrong."

"We're down fourteen. Fans get frustrated."

"I hate this place. Let's go, okay?"

"We can't do that. I gotta watch the rest of the game. If you really want to go, we can call Mommy or have a cab take you home. This wasn't a very good game to come to because the best player, that boy you met the day we went rowing, is injured, I injured him, and—"

"I need something to eat, Dad. I feel sorta out of it."

We scampered downstairs to the canteen, where we reaped the only benefit of such a small, lethargic crowd: waiting in line wasn't a major battle. I even got a cardboard box to hold our hot dogs, Cokes, and bags of peanuts. Still, Happy, who is always happy, made it clear with a clown's frown how unhappy he was with me. Fans who were never behind Menkus in the first place were suddenly defending him to the death within earshot of the sent-to-Siberia sportswriter. Barry and I had to retreat under a stairwell to be able to concentrate on our lunch. We talked about Iran announcing that it wanted twenty-three billion dollars in exchange for the hostages' release. I said Katie Koob alone was worth more than that, and Barry agreed.

In the second half Missouri State-St. Louis put on a man-to-man press and lobbed cross-court into the seam of the RSU's to go up fifteen with six minutes remaining. Three-quarters of the 8,800 who'd made the mistake of coming had already left by the time it was over. River State was able to get as close as eight only because St. Louis called off the dogs early and Tomlinson mopped up per usual against the reserves, making the final score semi-respectable.

Barry slept in his seat while I typed the story. Later, riding home, Barry said, "Promise never to take me to another game."

"Come on, Bare, this wasn't a fair test. You have to at least—"

"Never."

Tomorrow, the twenty-first, would be the shortest day of the year. Today, the twentieth, was only the bleakest, coldest, darkest, and most depressing.

"Okay," I said.

If our phone number wasn't unlisted, I'm afraid I would have been harangued mercilessly. As it was, I got plenty of poison pens at work and, while Christmas shopping in the mall, I seemed to be the beneficiary of a disproportionate number of cold shoulders. Had Hinselwood actually orchestrated this backlash? I seriously doubted he'd dare to stoop that low. By the same token, I told myself to let it all blow over by ignoring it.

On Christmas Eve Deborah and I sat under the mistletoe in the living room. Presents were spread a foot high around the tree, which was hung with popcorn, silver balls, and stars. The fire flickered. Barry was upstairs with Laurel, watching a *National Geographic* special about geese. Kissing Deb didn't stop her from continuing to go through her grade book to make sure she hadn't given out too many A's.

"So how did Menkus do?" I asked.

"Huh?"

"What did Menkus get?"

"I thought you'd stopped the grand inquisition into every crook and nanny."

"I was just asking."

"He got a C."

"The Sioux City express rolls right along."

"What's that supposed to mean?"

"It means—"

"I know what it means. He got what he deserved. He showed signs of real improvement on his final."

298

Piano music tinkled from Deb's kitchen radio.

"No one's rounding his grade up to the nearest letter or anything like that?"

"Honey," she said, pushing me off her lap, "that's insulting. What is this big obsession of yours with the purity of Belvyn's education? What's the big deal? When are you gonna let go?"

"I don't know," I said, staring into the fire, then at the presents and the tree and the grade book and Deborah. "I want to make sure he turns out okay. I don't want him to become another victim."

"I think it's some kind of weird displacement projection-fixation."

Christmas day was almost hot, in the low fifties. Iran broadcast a film of hostages walking around a balcony, eating and waving. Katie K. wasn't in any of the pictures. Everybody on local stations wondered where the hell she was.

We let Laurel give Barry the ant farm he wanted so bad, and he went bonkers. She also gave him a stuffed pig in compensation for the real one we didn't give him. She gave us butterscotch candies her parents always have out, and we gave her the paperback Audubon bird guide. Barry got a plastic farmhouse from us and a down jacket and wool shirts from Deb's folks, along with a card explaining that in these clothes he'd be wrapped warm enough to visit. Deborah gave me a pair of running shoes.

"Hint-hint. My body's falling apart: get back in shape."

"Barry picked them out," Deb said, squeezing my stomach.

I said to Barry, "Okay, bub, this means you and I are going running this afternoon, right?"

"No, I can't, 'cause I gotta listen to this record with Laurel."

I'd given him a record that had thumbnail sketches of a couple dozen animals and the noises they make.

Deborah was so busy handing out hot cider and gifts and fixing the tree that she got to her own presents last: twelve bottles of Liquid Paper from Laurel, a sweater and wool socks from her parents, spices and a calendar of the past year from Barry. From Adrienne an anthology about autobiography published by Princeton University Press, which struck me as a mean-spirited gift, but Deborah was delighted with it. From me a sheer black nightgown with red trim guaranteed to cause cardiac arrest in a blind dromedary. She looked at me, and I looked at her.

Throughout the Midwest, all prodigal sons and all prodigal daughters were calling their disappointed parents to make amends, so the lines were overloaded, but we finally got through and thanked Errol and Louise for the winter gear. Barry refused to get on until Deborah froze him with a look, and he was positively bubbling with holiday cheer for Grandpap. Deb promised to visit them sometime over the vacation. I thanked them three times for gloves and a knit cap. We gave them a weekend at a Rhinelander resort with sauna and whirlpool and indoor pool and Magic Fingers mattress, which I think they dreaded.

While Barry and Laurel played the animal-sounds record in the living room, Deb and I went upstairs to get our own animal sounds going. We made love the way you can only when you've been married too long. Sloppy romance, solid, serious fucking, slowly, almost unconsciously feeling for ourselves in the semi-dark at the end of the day. Our bodies fit perfectly. Space modules in control and circling to connect. Changing positions, giving pleasure. Body parts that knew by memory and instinct the other body parts. I was in deep and smiled, and Deb smiled, too, not sexy or sad but just contented, softly laughing. What it was was home, if I'd only let it be that. I thought about our move from a tumbledown duplex on the edge of the student ghetto to this Tinker Toy castle in the tracts and how, when the U-Haul guy asked how far I was going, I wanted to kneel on the curb and bawl when I said, "Four miles, maybe ten max, counting the return trip back here." She looked younger and tougher in her new nightgown and left it on while we were coming, wrapping it over my head

300

when we were through. Hilarious and lethargic. I love my wife in black on Christmas. I want to stay with her forever. A confession about the nine-year itch kept surfacing and diving back down.

"Honey?" Deb said.

"Yes," I said.

"Merry Christmas."

"Merry Christmas."

"*Je t'aime.*"

"What?"

"I love you," she said.

"I love you, too."

"I can't believe you stole Belvyn's transcripts."

"I can't believe you agreed to be his bodyguard."

"Well, we're both go-getters. We both want it too much."

"Want what?"

"Success. That's not the worst thing in the world."

When Deborah got up to start dinner, I went jogging in my new shoes. Laurel had gone home, so I dragged the Bare outside with me. It was still pretty warm and not yet totally dark. We weren't halfway down the street when he stopped to tie his shoes and said, "I'm kinda tired, Dad."

"Come on, Barry. We can make it at least once around the block."

"I feel faint. I gotta check my sugar."

Whenever he wants, he says that to get out of doing things. He's supposed to exercise more, but we can't push him beyond the limits he sets. At this rate, that's walking into the kitchen. Injuries we can live with. I let him go.

I loved my big blue shoes. I leapt from one soft cloud to another, heard thuds and snaps behind me and kept turning around, but nothing was gaining on me, only twigs cracking and the footfalls of early middle age trying to buy back time. Tomorrow, I told myself, I'll run around the block twice. It's a long block.

Dinner consisted of delicious chicken and conversation

about Barry's toys. Afterward, while I cleaned the dishes, Deborah studied the paper and decided we should see a movie called *The Electric Horseman,* since we missed it when it came through the last year. Which was fine with me. We sang Christmas songs in the car, the streets were empty, the night was warm as blood. All was well until, in the popcorn line at the Englert, we bumped into Vicki arm in arm with Hutchins. There were about fifty people in the whole theater, including sad, lonely Gail Lewis of the French department, and we stood next to Vicki and Hutchins. I hadn't seen or heard from her in a week, and she looked like the most desirable thing ever to get stuffed into denim. Hutchins looked like he just got laid. After saying Merry Christmas, I didn't know what else to do, so I introduced everybody.

"Deborah, this is Vicki Lynch, who works with me on the paper. She's one of our stringers. I think you guys talked to each other on the phone briefly, right? And this is Larry Hutchins, who used to be on the basketball team. Larry, Vicki, this is my wife, Deborah, and my son, Barry. Barry, no, no ice cream. Just popcorn and a Coke."

The line had moved up and he was trying to squander the family fortune.

"Hi," Vicki said, squeezing Hutchins' hand and so my heart. I missed her.

"Hi," said Deborah.

"Hi," said Hutchins.

"How did your psychology test go?" I asked Vicki.

"Just fine, thanks, Mr. Biederman." Really laying it on thick.

"The rest of your classes?"

"Big box of popcorn you got there," she said to Barry.

"Yep," he said, spilling his Coke until Deborah helped out. "Come on, you guys, the previews are starting."

"So I guess that story we were working on is pretty much finished," I said.

"Guess so," Vicki said, shrugging the hair out of her eyes.

"See you later, Mr. B.," Hutchins said. "Nice to meet all of you." *Kind of a prig for a black guy,* Vicki had called him, *not exactly my type.* Well, fuck them. They deserved each other, the new generation of cutthroat ladder climbers. Fuck them both.

At first I liked Robert Redford, ex-rodeo champion now huckstering breakfast cereal in Las Vegas. Then I liked Jane Fonda, TV reporter after a scoop. Barry was colossally bored until the movie got out into the country and the horse had a little elbow room to maneuver. I watched Barry, watched him get excited. I realized: who gives a shit about the reporter's scoop? What counted was grooming the horse back to health and then setting him free. Wild thing, you make my heart sing. Vicki and Hutchins cuddled in a corner, hardly watching. Deborah said she liked Jane Fonda's boots and wanted a pair.

When Rising Star joined the herd, they showed that animal in slow-mo isolation returning to the green hills. I was right with Barry, clapping and screaming my lungs out. Deborah told us to hush so she could catch the dialogue. Dialogue? The horse was galloping. Love him, you dumb fuck, I told myself, love him.

THIRTEEN

NEITHER Deborah nor Barry had classes to go to, though before leaving to visit her folks Deb met twice with Adrienne's Women's Studies coterie to help them get together an interdisciplinary curriculum which, so far as I could make out, meant that Emily Dickinson had to stop being given short shrift, even in social-science classes. Women firefighters, Susan B. Anthony coins, Title IX equality on the court, it was the rage all over and showed up everywhere and affected everything. What with the extra time on our hands, Deb and I tried to get deeper into serious bedding, but she made a big deal out of having foreplay until my lips were numb, and me giving her a backrub until she fell asleep and me putting in the diaphragm and me providing a running commentary, telling her how lovely and desirable she was. From my point of view, it was outstanding communication but boring sex.

Most of the high schools and colleges were taking a break, and my job was mainly just rewriting and setting AP pro summaries and holiday bowl stuff. Christmas vacation was supposedly time to gather loose ends, but Menkus refused to speak with me before or after his release from the hospital; Barry's ant farm fell to the floor and broke, all the ants scurrying about his room, which was probably what he wanted in the first place; and Deb whisked off for a long weekend in Wisconsin, Barry tearfully in tow.

The next big event of the vacation wasn't until the following Tuesday, when a benefit lunch was held before a night game against Northern Michigan. The benefit was a fundraiser for building a new sports complex five hundred yards from the field house on a hill overlooking Highway 218. What is this River City mania for renovation, of fearing what we have is never good enough? Per Hinselwood's request, the athletic department was relegating the field house to just a recreation building on the pretext that, when packed, it was a firetrap. At the benefit lunch they wanted to start raising twenty-one million bucks for the new arena.

In Danbrook Hall, where the jocks lived and ate and tore apart the furniture, the Varsity Club catered a lunch for the big buyers, backers, and boosters. Local pols, including Hizzoner the Mayor; hospital officials; Amana Colonies muckamucks; a guy from the Herbert Hoover Memorial; successful store owners; local presidents of Procter and Gamble, Montgomery Ward, K-Mart. They didn't have name tags, but they didn't need to: the dour cuss from the Hoover Memorial was a dead ringer for our illustrious thirty-first. As master of ceremonies, Francis was reduced to saying things like: "I've always lived by the philosophy 'Clean body, clean mind.'" Pause. "Take your pick." Gales of laughter like you've never heard. Raeburn sat at the head table in tux and tie, overseeing the operation since he'd be kicking in two or three million. He waved his cowboy hat at Francis and clapped people on the back, making sure they were having a great time, telling them to drink up.

What I felt coming toward me in waves from the crowd was a general antipathy held just in check by the snot-nosed civility of the occasion. Gail Lewis' one ex-boyfriend, head of Engineering, was here, as were heads of all departments, some of whom I recognized, some of whom I didn't. Tolliver, of course. Stacey, the American Studies man, Adrienne's boss. Beehler, Philosophy, a proud Prussian. The Comparative Literature *grande dame* and the American History king, Herbert Hoover's biographer. And all the deans and vice-deans and academic deans and undergraduate and graduate deans, all the guys who'd battled Deborah on everything from attendance lists to choice of books ever since she got here. Financial Investors, Inc., representatives, and even people from the governor's office were here to talk about twenty-one million for a gym when they couldn't find twenty-one thousand to pay Deborah a decent salary. Then again, Deborah can't double-reverse dunk.

Cold light bounced off the windows, good hot food and decent wine were placed on the tables, and Francis leaned on the podium, telling self-deprecating jokes about alcohol and coeds while introducing one bloodsucker after another. It tweaked the old heartstrings to see Drex making an idiot out of himself for nothing down, especially when "Dutch" was readying his inauguration speech. I pretended to be taking notes, but everyone Francis introduced had exactly the same message: give money. The story line wasn't overly complicated. And no one was getting out of here until the greenbacks grew wings.

A bank vice-president, a woman from Waterloo, sat next to me. She was wrapped in a purple outfit that looked to me like a bathrobe but was evidently high-fashion formal wear. She wore pearls, bracelets, rings, enough perfume to fell a horse, a face that had got stretched out of shape smiling at too many cocktail parties. "Whom do you represent?" she asked.

"What do you mean?"

"What company are you with?"

"The *Register*. I'm a reporter."

"Oh. You must—"

"What bank are you from?" I asked.

"We really must support the arena," she said, not answering my question.

"Why's that?"

"We must. It'll be a gathering point for the whole community, like the Parthenon. You've seen the blueprints, haven't you?"

I didn't want to see the blueprints. I wanted more red wine, and I wanted loathsome creatures to stop giving me the evil eye. Dinner salads were served. Drinking and half listening to Parthenon, I made a list of everything negative I knew or was pretty sure I knew about Menkus:

> You forged Belvyn Menkus' GED's for him.
> You bribed him and his parents with Betamaxes.
> You forged a C average for him at SCTE and paid his tuition.
> You recruited my wife to get him lecture notes.
> You pay his health insurance.
> You pay his rent.
> You make his Audi payments for him.
> You bought him a Soloflex, a leather bathrobe, movie tapes for the Betamax, a handful of Nikons.
> Etc.
> All of this is appearing in tomorrow's *Register*.
>   Love,
>   Double Bubble Biederman.

I folded the note into a paper airplane and asked one of the student waiters to bring it to Raeburn with the message, "Let's talk." I didn't expect anything to come of it, I honestly didn't, but I hated getting patronized by all these rich slobs and felt like it was my duty to try to shake things up a little. I figured the worst thing he could do was tear up the note in little pieces and return it to me as dessert.

Francis droned his way through more party jokes. About a dozen tycoons got up and talked about their commitment to student athletics, the ideal of excellence in scholarship in sport, a sane mind in a sound body, money for the arena. The preppy president of River State spoke eloquently, extemporaneously, *ad infinitum*.

Shortly before the turn of the century the waiter brought back a note that said, "Meet me in the men's room in ten minutes."

I'd hit Raeburn at just the right time. I'd played my one

hand perfectly, since the last thing he wanted as the arena campaign got launched was a diversionary rumble. Things were moving slowly at the podium. When Parthenon got the ball rolling with a pledge of five thousand dollars, she was greeted with a great round of applause and Raeburn stood to go, catching my eye. I nodded, waiting for him to leave, then followed him into the john.

There were only three urinals, and two mid-level executive types were on either side of Raeburn, discussing with him the importance of getting Amana Refrigeration more heavily involved as a major donor, so I sat in a stall and rolled toilet paper. It was too awkward for them to stand around waiting while he was still at the urinal. They left and I joined him, unzipping my fly.

"So," I said, "the arena campaign getting off to a pretty good start?"

"These kind of things are always slow at first, but I can make up for that," he said, smiling. I figured he'd already lost this round to me and was trying to cut his losses. With the kind of money he had, he was never going to lose the big war. His face was red, and he looked like he'd drunk more wine than I had.

"Local businesses pitching in much?"

"Not as much as they can. Come on, Biederman," he said, banging his hand on the pipes over the urinal, "what are we lookin' at here?"

What I was looking at was the wall. Standing next to him and pissing while he fiddled with his business, I couldn't help remembering the prostate problems Dad had the last years of his life. Raeburn was an old man with a ten-year-old tux and his cowboy hat on crooked and a mediocre cigar sticking out the side of his mouth, and I almost felt sorry for him.

"Barry had such a great time out at your place that day. He keeps talking about it. He rivals Francis in his admiration for you."

The chairman of the Chemistry department, a conservative, snippy beanbag named Sheridan, came in and pissed, and

Raeburn and I stood silent. I looked straight ahead, and he squinted at me, searching my face for clues. I didn't give him any. When Sheridan left, I said, "I just wanted to let you know what will be appearing in tomorrow's paper. I was hoping maybe to get a paragraph of reaction from you."

"Oh, you were, were you?"

"Yes, sir, I was."

He put his cigar on top of the urinal, dug my list of accusations out of his pants pocket, and said, "Well, here's my reaction." He had a time of it getting a grip again on the cigar, directing his dick to the piss pot, and holding the edge of my list, but what he was threatening to do was set the paper on fire.

"I know you wouldn't do that," I said.

"These trifles?" he said, waving the list of accusations in my face before just charring each corner of the paper.

He pretended to be trying to prevent himself from laughing, but he did laugh and I laughed a little, too. I didn't know what was so funny other than that he had a Tinkerbell laugh that was absurd. I was through pissing, so I flushed, and we stood side by side, staring at each other.

He lit the paper and held it close to his face, like he was trying to scrutinize it at the last minute, which he wasn't. "You think I'd let you run this nonsense in the *Reg*? You have nowhere to go with it except right down the toilet." He dropped the text into the bowl and drowned it with a full squirt.

"You don't own the *Register*."

"Try me," he said, "just try me, you punk kid."

The way he said this, with gravel in his tongue and his bushy eyebrows crawling, suggested he wasn't cemetery whistling. The trouble with playing my one hand was that I thought I had a full house, King high, and when he called my bluff all I had showing was a pair of eights.

"You motherfucker," I said and wanted to shove him, but the wine finally gravitated to his kidneys and his face portrayed the sheer relief of taking a delayed piss. I couldn't bring myself to hit him in the midst of such ecstasy.

"Correction: *The* motherfucker," he said. What was he planning to do next: pull down his pants to prove he had balls hanging down to his knees?

A student waiter came in to wash up and comb his hair, said he'd like to contribute ten dollars to the arena campaign. Raeburn thanked him and told him to run along now.

I had to ask: "You didn't get my wife's book accepted for her, did you?"

"I didn't even know she got it accepted." I tried hard to believe him. "Who's publishing it?"

"River State Press."

"Well, congratulations."

"She's hoping it'll get her tenure."

"Oh, she'll get tenure," he said, by which he meant either that getting a book published by a junior faculty member put a dead bolt on tenure or that he could guarantee her tenure, and I simply had no nerve to push it further. "I'm very fond of her. And your son. I'd be pretty fond of you, too, if you'd just relax a little bit, Biederman, and stop challenging our heroes to grudge matches."

Suddenly he was Joe Deferential, though he wasn't going out of his way to do me any favors. I was a little gnat one of his horses' tails swatted. I understood that I'd finally met, for all intents and purposes, the mayor of River City, but what I had trouble stomaching was that I was his garbage collector. The Rodney Dangerfield of River City had friends elsewhere who would give his complaint the respect only a 36 pt. headline can command.

"Why don't you become my friend like everyone else? Come on, let's shake," he said, and we shook—my right hand and his left since he was still concluding his piss. His cigar was out on top of the urinal. He needed a match. No, I didn't have one. I squeezed to kill, but that seventy-year-old farmer had the grip of a python.

"All along I have had only one simple desire," I said. "I just wanted the kids to get back their own game the way—"

"It is their game," he said, flushing, then moving over to the

310

sink to wash my germs off his hand, spraying the water all over. "I'm just bankrolling it." This was supposed to be a joke. I didn't laugh. "Now go on, get back out there, take notes like a good little boy, and mind your manners."

A whole clan of academics entered the restroom, and under their cover he returned to the arena auction. He thought he had me, but I had him: I still had Milwaukee. I went back to get my coat, downed the rest of my wine, shook Parthenon's hand, and left. Leaving, I saw Raeburn look at me and then at Francis, saw Francis look at me and then at Raeburn, felt a hundred pairs of eyes passing judgment. I crossed the quad and ran upstairs to the beautiful, archaic gym, spanking myself in the thigh.

While Hinselwood worked with Gault on his jumper, while Ott and Nagel showed Monroe Terry and Durland how to play a two-game, while Cliffie Davis and Rod Williams went at it one-on-one and everyone else practiced free throws for the game tonight and talked brave, Menkus jogged softly around the edge of the gym and I took notes:

> M. wearing an elastic brace, dragging his r. knee, moving slow. Dribbling, getting the feel of the ball, passing to himself, against the basket supports and bleachers. Timing off. His dribble died and on a behind-the-back pass the ball actually caught on his hip, a mistake I'd make. What would happen to him in game conditions? He's definitely favoring the r. leg, not jumping very strong on jumper. Limps when he pivots off bad knee. Feeling his way back, tiptoeing, caressing the ball. Rising Star sent back into the hills to regain his gait, stumbling. And am I actually going to play the Jane Fonda role—sell my soul for a scoop? I wish I'd left him alone from the beginning and watched from afar. Is D. never wrong? He's holding onto himself, staying within. The ball bounced away on a bad dribble

311

and he came over to pick it up, giving me one of those eighth-of-an-inch nods, a barely perceptible dip of the chin as he stroked his new goatee. Secret communication of the courts, grammar school machismo. His nod says forgiveness. My half-wave says from now on I'm just a fan in the cheap seats, taking notes. Liar. Hypocrite.

Northern Michigan was the farthest east of all of River State's pre-season opponents, the most blue-collar, the hardest-working, the most serious, the least rah-rah. Most of their kids come from Detroit, and Black Stallion, a Detroit native, knew half of them. They played a 3–2 match-up zone, which gave their defense all the double-teaming help of a zone with the intensity and pressure of man-to-man. Traditionally, they're one of the most unselfish teams in the league, and they had an odd high/low offense that featured a quick, baldheaded guard who penetrated to the hoop and rebounded well, along with a long-haired center who spent all his time outside, popping jumpers from the circle.

But Durland and Terry took turns harassing the center and Black Stallion played defense for once, constantly turning their little guard out into the wings where he could do no harm. Plus, Black Stallion played the point and ran the offense with more abandon and imagination than he'd ever shown. Tomlinson finally got beyond his solitary gunner role into the flow of the action, and even Keil didn't look so nervous anymore in a starter's role, reverting to his scrappy form. Hinselwood's patient strategy finally paid off. With Menkus out of the lineup, methodical pattern ball made sense.

The main thing was that everyone was hustling his heart out to fill Menkus' absence. You could tell they'd decided not to just sit on their hands until the hero returned. And yet they were playing essentially his game: Black Stallion ball handling, Tomlinson cutting, Gault going to the hoop, Keil dishing off,

Durland helping out on D, all playing together like West Des Moines the day Dicky died; only Menkus hadn't died.

He sat at the end of the bench, not wearing crutches or a brace but resting his right leg on a chair. He wasn't one to cheer or clap. He barely raised those enormous, green, dyslexic eyes of his and took it all in. Maybe the key was that he simply saw things at a slower speed and a different angle than anyone else. The ball was smaller, the hoop was bigger, the other players moved for him within the second sight of freeze frames. Ted Williams used to report having such experiences. In the pitch-dark ordinary eyes can see bright lights only by looking slightly off-center; I suspected Menkus' eyes and mind were doing something like this all the time. In order to get by, Menkus filled gaps before nondyslexics saw solids.

The Northern Michigan game did more for his rehabilitation program than any number of negative-only sessions on Nautilus. Black Stallion was posing a threat to Menkus' job and that had to accelerate the healing process, which I was then probably going to retard by getting him banned before he played his first Mississippi Valley Conference game.

What with the vacation and the rain and Menkus sidelined, there were even fewer fans here than for Missouri, and very little energy emanated from Mr. Ed, the cheerleaders, the Battalion, not even any animus directed at me. No one in the crowd knew how to react. We cheered almost tentatively, waiting for the good luck to run out. RSU bent but didn't break. They had huge lapses, and for a whole huge stretch at the start of the second half they looked really ragged, Cliffie and Keil whipping up a wild free-for-all on offense while Gault and Tomlinson played man-to-man defense and everyone else sat in a zone so flexible it self-destructed. Toward the end of the game they weren't playing any particular kind of ball other than holding on by their fingertips to a dwindling lead. The Stallions got the break they needed when Black Stallion drew a charge on Northern Michigan's baldheaded guard for his fifth foul. BS hit the free throws to put River State up by five with thirty seconds to go, and that was that. You had to be happy for the home team.

I went into the locker room to offer congratulations and found Menkus in the jacuzzi, doing isometrics against the wall of the tub.

"Hey," I said.

He nodded.

"They looked pretty good out there," I said.

No reply.

"I watched you gettin' the kinks out earlier today. How does it feel?"

"Stitches out, swellin' down. I'm runnin' this week, be playin' hoops by January first, no thanks to you."

"No swimmin'?"

"I don't know how," he said.

"I'll teach you."

"Don't want to know how from you, no how."

The room was hot, and more heat came up from the jacuzzi. Menkus looked uncomfortable in the blue bath. I was starting to say that everyone should know how to swim in case of emergency when Hinselwood bellowed, "Get the hell out of here, you miserable asshole. You want to break his other leg for us, too?"

"On my way. Good game, Coach. You didn't happen to send flyers to the good citizens of River City informing them to ostracize me, did you?"

"No, but I'll be sure to stick inserts in tomorrow's *Reg*. Please get out of my face, Biederman. I literally can't stand to look at you, and I have trouble believing you still have the gall to show up around here. You've already injured the kid. What more do you intend to do?"

"It was an accident," I said. "You can ask him."

Menkus did not bound to my defense.

"I want to talk to my players, if you don't mind."

I nodded. "Go ahead."

A half-hour later Tinseltan held a press conference to explain that all along he'd been building the team to peak now. Over the next several days came the inevitable reaction whenever a team plays better without its injured star: they're better off without him. The surprising part was that Francis and Vicki joined in the chorus. On his post-game show and again on *Stallion Standouts* Francis said River State was finally turned around but hadn't come together earlier, "as other pundits declared."

Due to Carol having too much Mary Kay bookwork to organize a party properly, Marty's hopes for a New Year's Eve shindig were dashed, so Deb and I went to Tolliver's party, where Deb told jokes about how provincial her Rhinelander parents were and I felt for the first time something like love for them. Tolliver toasted Deb repeatedly, and Adrienne and her pals from American Studies and Women's Studies broke plastic champagne glasses and howled at the moon, and the Chaucer lady, Diehl, and the Shakespeare man, Hirsch, rapped criticism while a few boys from the Composition program and I huddled in the corner of the Tollivers' rural-chic living room, watching the Bluebonnet Bowl on tape. I'm sure I seem to them like a parody of a sports reporter, but they do everything to remain academic cartoons to me. Though I feel I try to like them, I don't really take them seriously.

Vicki accomplished a pure and perfect piece of revenge. She wrote a column that said it was time to "stop looking for program saviors and just play ball." Menkus could be a part of it, she hoped, "but the Stallions jelled playing the way they've always played, without city ball or razzle-dazzle." Since the *Stallion* wasn't published during Christmas vacation, she sent it over my head to Marty, who printed it without my knowledge. I was home, having just finished watching the Cotton Bowl and Sugar Bowl and teases for the Rose Bowl, when the paper with Vicki's article landed on our welcome mat, and I immediately screamed bloody murder into the phone at Marty, who said, "It's an excellent piece, Albert, considering it was written by a college senior." The last clause opened up crawl space an inch wide, through which I slithered.

"I can't believe you did this to me. After all these years, Marty, I just can't believe it."

"You're on shaky ground, my friend, to be up in arms over anything. First I get a call from this Woolf character in Milwaukee who says you're up for a job at the *Journal*. Then Raeburn tells me you were threatening to publish some exposé piece here."

"What did you tell him?" I said. I'd been watching so many highlights and replays that I lost track what game I was watching and what was live, until Anthony Carter flashed his mug and I remembered I was watching UCLA–Michigan in Pasadena, where the weather was ninety-eight in the shade.

"What did I tell who?"

"Raeburn."

"The same thing I told you before you went to Chicago a month ago. The *Register* is a local paper for local people. We're not in the business of rumor mongering. We're a sports page. Root, root for the home team: that way you get to keep your job."

"What are you saying?"

"I'm saying the *Journal*'s always been very pro-Madison, and you better not be in the business of selling them fake scoops about how terrible River State is."

I said the only thing I could say: "You know me better than that. What did you tell Woolf?"

"I told him you're the best."

"Thanks, boss."

He felt bad about printing Vicki's story, so when I asked him for Friday off he said yes but added, "Do you really want to do this? Do you really want to leave this little paradise?"

"It's just exploratory."

"Like surgery."

"What?"

"Exploratory surgery."

"Yeah. Same word."

The man knew where to rub salt in the wound.

While watching the Orange Bowl, I called Ed Woolf to schedule an appointment and booked a flight from Cedar Rapids to Milwaukee with an hour layover at O'Hare.

I could have written the story the *Journal* wanted before the plane crossed the Mississippi, but comeback hopes weighed heavily against the lure of the scandal and all I was left with was a love letter from myself to the game. Swallowing the dirt tasted like shit. On the front page of the *Quad-Cities Times* Khomeini considered executing the hostages and Mary Tyler Moore got divorced. The world was going to hell in a hand basket, and I thought: why shouldn't I be in on the fun? I wrote up what was essentially an expansion of my note to Raeburn—the apparently invented GED scores; the Beta-maxes; the bogus C average at the bogus night school; the contact person (without mentioning Deb by name); Raeburn taking care of tuition, insurance, rent, cars, and also probably the weather for all I knew. I underlined certain phrases, circled others, drew arrows, made connections, added up debts. I had that list ready to go like a gun in my inside left coat pocket, right next to my heart.

At O'Hare I wandered down long white corridors of silvery reflections and checkpoints to the phone that's supposed to be the busiest in the world. I wanted to talk to Mrs. Menkus. She answered by saying: "Happy New Year."

"Hi," I said, "this is Albert Biederman. You sound in good spirits."

"Well, why shouldn't I be?"

"What happened?" My mind somersaulted. If Raeburn had just bought them a condo in West Palm Beach, I was Milwaukee's.

"The day after Christmas, Louie was lying in bed with a hangover and got a call from his supervisor at Greyhound. Lots of holiday travel, I guess. He's back at work, and we think it's permanent."

317

"Hey, that's great."

"I hear a lot of commotion in the background, Mr. Bieder-man. Where are you calling from?"

"O'Hare. I'm on my way to Milwaukee for a job interview at a newspaper up there." Which I will or won't get depending on whether I have the guts to tell the truth about your son. "I'm going to show them some of my articles on Belvyn, but I'd still like to write maybe one more piece on his recovery, since he seems to be coming along so nicely. A real thorough profile. Upbeat." I could barely say the words.

"Haven't you done quite enough?"

"What do you mean?"

"I feel awful about you being involved in the accident and you've already written so much about him," she said, sounding very tiny, distant. "Now he has to try to make good your kind words."

I heard second call for my flight and said, "Do you know what I've been dying to find out for the longest time?"

"No, what?"

"Where Belvyn got such an unusual name."

"Hasn't he ever told you that story? He was born at Chil-dren's Memorial Hospital, just off Belden Avenue on the north side, and Louie liked the name but Belvyn never learned to spell it right, not even in high school."

"That's fascinating."

"Well, it's better than Fullerton," she said. I loved the way she laughed shyly at her own corny jokes. "Listen, Albert, all kidding aside, I can't tell you how grateful we are to your wife and some of those other reading teachers for catching Belvyn's dyslexics. He might have gone through the rest of his life cross-eyed."

"I'll certainly tell her that. I've got a plane to catch, but listen, give my congratulations to Mr. Menkus on getting his job back."

"Good luck with the interview."

"Right. Happy New Year."

"Yes, sir, God's Son in '81."

"Good-bye now."

"Good-bye."

Though we barely discussed his injury, I had called her to try to talk myself out of destroying Menkus. Did I have it in me to blindside a kid who couldn't pronounce—let alone spell—his own name, the cross street where he was born cross-eyed?

The plane went straight up the back of the icy body of Lake Michigan, hovering just a few minutes, and in a jiffy we were already gliding over South Milwaukee, then angling for General Mitchell Field. General Mitchell, I learned almost immediately upon arriving, was a World War II flying ace whose squadron hailed mainly from Wisconsin. Life-size cardboard figures of him dominated the lobby, and one of his planes was parked out front.

I took a cab to the *Journal,* and the cabby had apparently been hired by the Milwaukee Historical Society to provide me with a running commentary. We took Howell Avenue past Kinnickinnic River; past St. Josaphat Basilica bearing cast-metal griffins; past an industrial valley with its grid of rail tracks, junkyards, foundries, tanneries, burning coal, roasting hops; past a cemetery whose headstones were all Polish names. We were now on the South Sixth Street Viaduct, overlooking the Menomonee Canal. Milwaukee, population 1.5 million, is the eleventh-largest city in the United States and has always had squeaky-clean government, cleaner streets, friendly citizens, and a nice mix of progress and tradition. There was once a sort of protest march against something or other from downtown to the river, and the demonstrators walked in place at all red lights.

I was freezing to death in the backseat of this talking head's taxicab. I empathized when he said people around here use brandy as antifreeze. The sky was brutally blue at degree zero. But even the cold and me being underdressed for it seemed part of the cityness. I wanted to learn how to live here. Beyond ramshackle houses at the edge of town, a tangle of electricity drew us into the central congestion of light and chrome and steel. Gray buildings with history and character got lost in the fog of the Milwaukee River. This was a city that hadn't tucked its past into a crypt. The War Memorial, Old World Third Street, and Teutonic Avenue told me that much. I wanted the job bad.

At Third and State, the *Journal* building filled the entire square block. A fleet of green trucks was just leaving to get the afternoon edition out to carriers. A huge compass graced the back of the building and in the front window were five clocks —the current time in Calcutta, Tokyo, Moscow, London, Milwaukee. Plus, gauges measuring wind direction and velocity, temperature, barometric pressure. They all pointed to the fact that it was incredibly cold outside. A wonderful old-fashioned green lantern hung above the front door, and when I opened my portfolio for the guard and gave him my name I had a stupid panic that he was going to arrest me. He sent me upstairs with a visitor's card.

The newsroom was encased totally in glass and some people were at typewriters or terminals, but no one looked especially busy since they'd just got the paper out. The reporters here seemed to dress a lot nicer than we did at the *Register*, which was the benefit of working for an employee-owned corporation. Your take-home was enough to allow you to buy new threads once in a while. The departments were divided only by the way the desks were arranged—all for one and one for all and all that. I asked someone where Ed Woolf was, and she pointed him out. After so much communication back and forth between him and me, so much time spent dreaming about Milwaukee and tailing Menkus, after the traveling and brooding I'd done today, talking to Mrs. Menkus and listening to the cabby's Chamber of Commerce speech, I was disappointed that, physically, Woolf was rather unprepossessing. He was older and tireder than I thought he'd be, and there was nothing athletic, ex-athletic, or potentially athletic to him. Medium height, scrawny build, fat ass. He seemed maddeningly familiar, but I couldn't place him until I caught sight of the University of

Madison pennants, binders, promotional material dotting Sports: with his buck teeth, tiny nervous eyes, and dark hair combed into an elaborate crosshatch on top of his head to cover a bald spot, he was a dead ringer for the Madison Badger mascot. Absolutely a dead ringer.

He gave me a classic wet noodle handshake and said, "You must be Albert Biederman."

"Yes," I said, "I must."

He gurgled a chuckle, though I didn't mean it to be that funny, and he said, "Well, welcome."

"Thank you. You've got a really beautiful building to work in here. The *Register* could probably fit in the washroom."

"That's why you're here, isn't it, to step up a little in class?"

"I guess that's right," I said, though I hate the word *class* used in this sense. I always think it means I have to start acting like F. Scott Fitzgerald.

"So how was your trip?"

"Good. Good. Interesting cabby. He must have thought I was paying him by the word."

"You got Ronnie. Hey, you guys, he got Ronnie coming in from Mitchell," he said, introducing me around on a rapid tour of the joint, and they all thought that was hilarious. I tried to gab with some of the guys, but it was clear it was his interview, and no one else seemed to know too much about me or be overly interested. Several older, vaguely European-looking guys with mustaches and vests, each with his own beat— Packers, Bucks, Brewers, Marquette, Madison, high school. Specialists. The high life. F. Scott Fitzgerald.

Then we sat at his overflowing desk, surrounded by copy and press releases and wire-service tear sheets. He offered me a drink.

"I'll have some coffee," I said, rubbing my hands.

"Drink enough of this and you'll forget about how cold it is."

"Okay, pour me a little."

He very much liked my acquiescence and pretended to ask my advice about some layout changes he was playing with, but

I didn't have much to say because I've always loved how airy the *Journal* looks, how they can throw in everything but the kitchen sink and still leave room for the page to breathe, how they set off pictures with black border.

"Your editor over there at Iowa had nothing but good things to say about you."

"Marty Reeves. We've been working together forever."

"What does he think of your contemplated move?" he asked, pouring me more Jim Beam despite the fact that I'd barely touched what I had.

"He doesn't see why I'd want to leave, but he's not doing anything to stop me. He accepts my, me, my, uh—" I suddenly felt like I'd left my tongue in the backseat of Ronnie's cab.

"Well, whatever he thinks, we think six times more so. We're very high on you. I think you have a major career ahead of yourself."

"Thank you," I said, "that's very nice," and to try to free up my hands I put my portfolio on the edge of his desk.

"What's that?"

"My portfolio."

"Oh, shit, Albert, we already know what you can do," he said, whipping through it. "Like that pre-season piece on the Mississippi Valley, is that in there? I thought that was great, the way you focused on first-year coaches and senior players and how that would create a lot of one-on-one play. That's really inventive."

"And I'm pretty sure it will prove out, aren't you?"

"Of course it will." There was a pause while he poured himself some more whiskey and made to pour me some more, but I hadn't drunk any so he leaned back and said, "Did you bring it?" He flared his badger teeth. I'd been played for a bumpkin.

"Bring what?"

"Your big investigation piece. You're a week late and a dollar short, but if that baby is tucked in this portfolio some-where we're still in business."

I opened my coat and reached for my list and kept going

down into the pocket and coming up empty. After about the third or fourth attempt to take it out, I knew I wasn't going to be able to take it out, and what kept passing through my head was being unable to mix it up in high school, never having the killer instinct even when I was very good, always settling for the soft jumper outside. Push come to shove, I got shoved. Vicki had me pegged: I was a hometown fan like everyone else.

"What's the matter?" he said.

I pulled out a map of Milwaukee, which didn't make a lot of sense, and he said, "I think I already know where County Stadium is."

"I don't have it," I said. "I've got a bunch of other good stories in my portfolio, but that one just didn't pan out."

In five minutes I could have logged the desired information on his processer, and I would have been paid twice as much to live in a city three times as interesting and write about events four times as exciting, and I couldn't do it. The least I owed Menkus was to bury the mess I'd made of his life.

"Hey, we've seen all the other stuff, Albert. What happened, it didn't materialize?"

"No," I said.

"Well, maybe you could just summarize it for me." Bar none, that is the least attractive request I've ever heard come out of a journalist's mouth.

"There isn't any article. They proved to be false leads. I'm trying to tell you, Mr. Woolf: nothing came of it. I had some crooked sources. I'm sorry. That's all I can say."

He leaned back and leafed through my portfolio one more time, but the tension had gone out of the interview; my brand-new leather ball had sprung a leak and was quickly deflating. "Well, it's all perfectly solid, of course, but you knew how much we were looking for the h-h-home run from you."

This was the first time he'd stuttered since I'd been here and it seemed to signal a definite stop to my forward motion, like he was uncomfortable and wanted me to leave. The conversation drifted to general sports gossip while some new computer information came up on the Green Bay Packers, who were having a horrendous year.

"How would you define a good sports writer?" he said.

"Just a well-informed fan in the bleachers, ga-ga for the game."

"I'm sorry, Albert, I wasn't concentrating."

"I said, 'Just a well-informed fan in the bleachers, ga-ga for the game.'"

He laughed till he coughed.

"What's the matter with that?" I said.

"You don't think that's a little hokey?"

"No, I don't, Mr. Woolf, not at all. Not anymore. I think what got me confused in the first place was thinking I was ever anything else. I'd like to get something straight here, if you don't mind. I don't see any dearth of U. Madison paraphernalia around here. You're a Badger fan. I'm a Stallion fan. You brought me up here to rat on River State, am I right?"

"I thought we cleared that up weeks ago. I've never pretended to be uninterested in a good juicy story."

"Well, let me put it to you this way. What if my investigation piece hadn't come up empty and was about a Madison or Marquette star? What then?"

"I would have evaluated it as a news story," he said, but the weird resemblance between him and the Badger doll on top of his file cabinet, like that between a dog and its owner, told me which way his evaluation would go.

He gave me another fast tour of the joint on the way out and I again tried to make conversation with some of the guys, but they seemed busy, and knowing that when I didn't deliver the dope the interview was over I didn't care to hang around that much longer. I wanted the job bad. Not that bad, though.

On the return flight, the Mississippi gleamed blue below, a distant beauty.

I worked at the office the next day nonstop, trying to avoid admitting where I was, but I felt like writing a compare/

contrast paper for Deborah. Saturday can be hectic at the *Register*, and it was even more oppressive than usual. All I felt was the humongous *Journal* building versus our cramped quarters; our hillbilly rags versus their upscale threads; their relaxed excellence versus our nervous incompetence; their co-operative versus our caste system; their top-of-the-line terminals and enclosed glass, our heavy-breathing hothouse. It was like River State versus the Milwaukee Bucks.

Marty interrupted my reveries by sitting on my desk and saying, "We're not trading you to Milwaukee, are we, Albert? Because, I mean, we can always extend your vacation, if that's what you need."

It was hard not to want to hug him or something. Woolf was a wolf in sheep's clothing; Marty was Marty in an over-sized sweater. "I don't think so," I said. "It didn't work out. I'm here for good."

"Lovely. Then I feel compelled to tell you to wrap up your piece on Menkus as a *profile* and forget about him. You've got to get back on the beam."

"Raeburn must have got on your case but good."

"It has nothing to do with him. It has to do with maintaining certain minimum professional standards."

"All right, Marty, all right. Don't give yourself chest pains."

"Raeburn has nothing to do with it."

He went back to work in a huff, and I did, too. I turned a three-inch stock of notes, only a month's work but my life's project, into an utterly innocuous profile and locked it into the terminal.

Around four I got a call from Vicki, who yelled into my ear, "Thank you, Albert Biederman!"

She spoke with such heavy enthusiasm that I just assumed she was being sarcastic.

"For what?" I tried.

"I got in, I can't believe it, I got in."

"Got in where?"

"Missouri J-school. For next year. Isn't that incredible? I'm getting out of Iowa. I just got the letter. You must have written a great rec. Thanks a million."

"Well, what can I say, Vicki? You're a good journalist. I didn't agree with your piece on Northern Michigan; it was a little shrill for my taste, but it was very well done."

Vicki isn't stupid. She isn't even in the ballpark of stupid. She picked up the bitter sound in my voice.

"Fine, Albert, good-bye, if that's the way you want to be about it. I thought you'd be happy for me."

"I am happy," I said, overjoyed. "I just think you have a lot of growing up to do. You have to realize there's such a thing as loyalty to—"

"I don't want to get plunged back into a big soul-searching morality session. I was just calling to give you the good news and thank you for everything. We're very different, I see that now."

"I'm glad you at least came around on Menkus."

"What's that supposed to mean?" she said.

"It means that it comforts me you finally saw the error of your ways."

"What it means is that I don't need the story anymore."

There are killer journalists and good-guy journalists, and it was pretty obvious now, if it wasn't before, who was who. My consolation was that I wasn't an asshole. And her consolation was that she got what she wanted.

"I've got your scarf. You left it that morning at Menkus'."

"Well, God, I'll be seeing you around. I'm still working at the *Reg*, aren't I?"

"Sure, I guess." Silence. Sabrina was interviewing the owner of a new floral shop, and Ira Barker, our historian, was combing the files for info on the different colors Johnston County fire hydrants had been painted. My fellow workers are sometimes nothing more than shades to me. "I thought you said Hutchins wasn't exactly your type."

"Maybe he isn't, I don't know. That was our first real date. I was bored Christmas night, so I went out with him. He is sorta stuffy. I miss you, Albert."

"I miss you, too."

"What are you doing tonight?" she said.

"Nothing much, but—"

"But what?"

"I'm trying to let the nine-year itch pass out of my system."

"That's all we were, an itch? Fuck you, then."

"You know what I meant. I'm trying to be married, since I'm stuck in River City for the duration. I didn't get the *Journal* job."

"Shit, I'm sorry, did you want it really bad?"

"Apparently not bad enough. I didn't give them what they wanted."

"And what was that?"

"The scoop on Menkus."

"You're kidding. That's all you had to do? The job was yours if you gave them the story and you didn't do it?"

"Pretty much."

"Well, you never really went after it from the start, just like you never really gave us a chance. You're happy here; you're happy where you are; you love your family."

"Vicki?"

"What?"

"Shut up, okay?" I said, though I said it so she could tell I wasn't angry at her, but myself.

"Albert?"

"Uh-huh."

"Can I tell you I think you're great, how much I admire you, how much I've learned from you?"

"Sure. Can I tell you the sky's your limit?"

She laughed because she couldn't handle the seriousness of what we were saying about ourselves and each other, and I laughed, too, because I couldn't handle it, either.

"Okay, Albert, okay, thanks," she said, then mumbled something about having to get off to call everyone else with her good news.

My favorite movie of all time is *It's a Wonderful Life*. My favorite moment is when Jimmy Stewart comes back down the stairs at the end to kiss the knob that never stays on at the bottom of the banister. I tried to have feelings like that; I tried to squeeze my cold typewriter and busted pencil sharpener and tried to embrace the assholes and mediocrities who work here and my wobbly desk, but it didn't happen. I felt only resentment and failure and a boxed-in quality. I concluded that those higher reconciliations are reserved for the movies.

On Wednesday I drove over to the field house and watched practice for an hour. To tell myself I was working, I carried my binoculars and notebook. I looked all over the court until I finally realized that Menkus was playing second string, wearing gray rather than roan. I was Iscariot in the house of the true believers—a couple of kids who had snuck in seemed to recognize me and make a point of scorning me. Menkus had shaved and his hair was flat, like he was chastening himself for the long haul ahead. Hinselwood blew his whistle every couple of minutes to talk about what Pittsburgh College would be doing Friday. It was impressive to me that three weeks after surgery Menkus was even out here, but his knee was wrapped and he moved slowly, protecting the leg. He looked a little lost, and Cottonwood ran play after play right at him, picking him off Gault's screen and sending Black Stallion backdoor on him, as if to say: This is my team now, pal.

Menkus hung in. Though limping, somehow he managed to play fairly solid D on Davis. He still had his eyes. He anticipated invisible openings and rallied the second team into putting up a good fight. It was terrible to see him reduced to this, because he might make it through college okay in second gear but he was never going to instill fear in the heart of Maurice Cheeks. In a strange way, though, it was a showcase of his skills. He couldn't just turn on the juice. He had to outhustle everyone in his head.

I put away my binox and left to go find Karl, the team trainer, who was puttering around the towel room. I asked if there were anything special about Menkus' body that enabled him to be back on the court so quickly, and I was in such a paranoid state that I had to be grateful to Karl for not acting diffident. He said, "Any normal person has no business even running yet. I tell you, Albert, this kid's ligaments are made of moon rocks. Beautiful bouncy knee joints, calves and thighs as tight as my fist. But we test him and we test him, and what I can't get over is his peripheral vision. Your wife has him working with a dyslexics teacher, and I read an article on the problem. Do you know what's wrong with dyslexics? They're ambidextrous in the brain. Multidirectional. You know how they used to try to shake dyslexics out of it? Have 'em do a lot of tumbling. I think this kid took one tumble too many. I tell you, Albert, he's not a normal person. It's almost inhuman what this kid can see. I would not be surprised to find out he's a Martian."

Between ambition and morality came Belvyn Menkus, whom I adored.

Before dinner Friday I turned on the Pittsburgh game. Deborah and Adrienne were in the kitchen, fixing tacos and talking up a storm. Francis was announcing the game and Marty was covering it for us, since I didn't care that much about a Menkus-less RSU beating up on one of the weakest teams west of the Ivy League and Marty wanted to visit some hunting friends outside Pittsburgh, anyway. Barry was bungling a blood test in the living room. I asked him whether he'd like to go to the first league game next week in Champaign, when Menkus would be trying to come back. I wanted Barry to appreciate the part of me that was still younger than he was.

"Nope," he said, "no way."

"Come on, Bare, you didn't really give it a chance at the Bloomington game. What you saw was—"

"A bummer." Laurel's language.

"This game here we're watching isn't any good, either, because Menkus isn't playing. They're winning despite themselves."

The Stallions took an early lead on a series of Pittsburgh gaffes. The women came in with tacos, peas, and Cokes, and Deborah said to Barry, "Honey, I overheard you turn down Daddy's invitation to the game. But I'm gonna go. I want to see how Belvyn does."

"You do?" Barry said.

"Yeah," Adrienne said, "you do? Since when did you become a sports person?"

"Listen, Adrienne," I said, "you're so into American Studies. You'd be a hell of a lot better off checking out the history of basketball than whisking off to Disneyland or interviewing hotrodders on the Coralville Strip. Basketball was invented in Springfield, Mass.; no other country plays it half as well as we do; and it's going down the tubes due to the corruption of drugs, money, and television. What could be more American? So how about it, Bare?" I said.

"How about what?"

"Going to the game with us."

"I'll have homework to do."

"I'm interested in cultural resonance, not empty ritual," Adrienne said, recovering too late.

"All right, you two," Deborah said to Adrienne and me. Then to Barry: "Come on, honey, there'll be great farmland all the way down there. The game's in Champaign."

"Does that mean all the players are going to be drunk?"

Barry knew Champaign was in Illinois, but he loved this kind of pun to show how precocious he was, and I liked it because now he'd be in a good mood to be talked into things. Adrienne thought Barry's line was so splendid she wrote it down in a little notebook she kept with her wherever she went.

The tacos were outstanding, and I made a strenuous effort not to monopolize them. Francis sent his cameras all over Menkus at every timeout to rub in his absence, which had already cost me a case of Johnnie Walker Black. Durland,

Gault, and Terry dominated both boards and tipped in what few shots Tomlinson missed from the outside and Black Stallion blew on breaks.

"Let's do it, Bare," I said. "The ride down'll be worth it even if you don't like the game. We'll see hogs and cattle and what all else south of Peoria."

"We'll stop?" he said.

"Sure, if we have time."

"Will we have time?"

Barry's nobody's fool. He was committing himself to no qualifications. His blood test dripped all over the table and onto his peas. After waiting a minute, he beamed because he was pretty certain it was high-normal.

"Yes," I said, "we'll definitely have time."

Barry wanted to know whether Beverly Little was going to be at Champaign. I didn't know who that was, and Deborah said it was Barry's favorite Pork Queen candidate, and, no, Beverly probably wasn't going to be there. Adrienne shook her head over Deborah's failure to correct Barry's burgeoning sexism. The Stallions were up eight at the half and should have been up twice that. Black Stallion had six assists. Durland had twelve boards. The Panther zone was a sieve and their offense was total anarchy.

Barry closed his blood kit and said, "Guess what I'm going to do for Show and Tell on Monday?"

"Give a talk on basketball?"

Adrienne flipped through Deb's magazines with greasy fingers and Deborah laughed, but she was on cloud nine on account of her book and was laughing at everything.

"Gonna do a whole show on diabetes."

I cringed and looked at Deborah, who said, "That's right. At Barry's checkup this week Dr. Price said it would be a great idea for two reasons: to inform the other kids in the class about it, and as a way to come to terms with some of the heavier issues."

It seemed gruesome for him to stand at the head of the class and mix sugar and blood and urine like some witch brewing up a caldron of trouble. I didn't want him making a case study out of himself, but he seemed eager to do it, and Deborah and Dr. Price were behind him. What did I know to argue? These were injuries we could live with, as the doctors were always telling us. Sure. They didn't have to live with them.

In the second half Black Stallion really took control, setting up Tomlinson and Keil for open fifteen-footers, keeping Durland busy, running the show. The Stallions pulled away from Pittsburgh. After dinner, Barry trooped off to bed and Adrienne left to go study architecture plans of Coralville fast-food joints. Deborah commenced to tell me how noble it was to bag the Menkus investigation and settle for a compromise.

"Compromise, nothing," I said. "I gave up the story and didn't get the job."

"You surrendered to what you loved. What more can you ask of yourself? You protected Belvyn. Christ, you protected me. I mean, what would we have done if you had got the Milwaukee job?"

I shrugged and said it didn't matter anymore.

"Truth to tell," Deborah said, "Barry and I had our fingers crossed against. It's no failure to find out where you belong and where you want to be. We are who we are, here, forever."

Deborah always had to be O Wise One, quoting something to make our lives sound significant. "What's that from?" I asked.

"Straight from the heart," she said and could see I was sulking, so she pulled me into the den, closing the door. We shivered, as the heating had yet to be installed. She undressed herself while undressing me and ended up sixty-nine on the floor. Socializing with lovelorn Adrienne made Deborah horny again. I liked being able to hear Francis' voice in the distance but not be able to make out what he was saying. I liked Deborah's mouth, usually so full of explanations, wrapped around me now with nothing to say, no more words, nothing to worry about. She told me to push myself back a bit on the carpet and lower my hips.

At the office Wednesday I called Menkus. I barely had the phone to my ear, expecting the blues as always. It rang and rang. I assumed he wasn't home and had forgotten to punch in his machine. I was about to hang up when a drowsy voice answered, "Yo."

"Menkus, is that you?"

"Yo," he said, a little irritated.

Danny and Earl from Cityside were cutting up around the coffee machine.

"I can't believe you actually answered the phone. After what Hinselwood said, I thought you had me permanently on hold."

He faked a laugh and said, "I do as I likes. What's cookin'?"

You could never really tell whether Menkus was being distant or friendly. It was just one big deception game to him. He was always playing point guard.

"How's the knee doin'?" I asked.

I felt like Danny and Earl were versions of myself ten years ago—having the time of their lives writing this and that, getting a paycheck, chasing skirts, hanging out. Nothing had really hit them yet.

"A little swole up after practice today, but it's comin' back."

"You looked pretty strong yesterday. Maybe seventy-five percent? You gonna give it a go against Champaign?"

"I just has to see how things feel in warm-ups."

Marty brought me a press release about the wrestling team that I was supposed to rewrite into English, and I watched Danny and Earl bring coffee to a new girl in Features, pushing for lunch, wanting it.

"You're not gonna start, then, you don't think?"

"No, man, I said I got to see how it feels, play it by the ears."

"Well, know that we're countin' on you," I said. "You'll be playin' for a lot of us out there on Saturday."

"Look, man, don't load your trip on me. I ain't playin' for nobody. I'm playin' to get my knee back."

"I got some tickets and sent them to your folks, your old Franklin coach, and Rita, trying to bring everyone together. I hope you don't mind. I thought you could use a few fans in your corner for your comeback. Maybe they'll drive down from Chicago to give you a boost."

"I don't need that shit. I don't want Rita stickin' her fuckin' tits in my face. How did you hear about her, anyways? That's past. Why can't you leave me alone?"

"Come on, Menkus. I'm just trying to lend a little moral support, show you you've got a few people behind you."

"I make it on my own."

"Come on, man, we're all in this thing together."

"I ain't in nothin' together with nobody. Coach is right: you're a *de*structive individual. You damn near fucked up the future of my life with your snoopin' nose. I'll be way better off if you leave me alone to do my shit. I got to go to class."

He said this last line straight, like he was really just about to stick his books in his backpack. Then he hung up. I looked for Danny and Earl and the new girl in Features, but they were already gone. Out of curiosity, I asked Gerry downstairs in Classifieds, and she said the three of them had gone out to lunch at Arturo's.

Throughout the week I called as many players as I could reach to get their opinions on how Menkus was going to do.

Monroe Terry: No comment, sir, but thank you very much for calling me.

Black Stallion: I can't foresee him comin' back for a long time yet. Not for real. We're winnin' without him, right? Right. I pick up the slack. He be back when he's back. He has to beat me out first for the point.

Gary Tomlinson: Well, you know, of course, Mr. Bieder-man, I miss the way Belvyn sets up the floor and me in particular, but then on the other hand he shouldn't rush back, only to hurt himself. Still and all, if he's ready we can use him. Then, too, Cliffie is playing well, so there are many variables to consider.

John Kendall: No comment, sir.

Jeff Kendall: I feel pretty much the same way as John, sir.

Norm Durland: He's been playing better each day in practice, getting stronger, regaining his confidence, though how do you know how well he'll do in a game? You don't. He's a good guy. He speaks funny, but I like him.

Rod Williams (phone machine): Shortcake lemonade fizz —what time it is!

Peter Keil: Gol, this is the first time since high school anyone's called me like this. It's been a real thrill to step in for such a great player, though it's nice to play a little, too. It's neat. I'd happily go back to being sixth man to get Belvyn back in the lineup, sure. He's a real gamer.

Hinselwood: No, I haven't told any of my players to steer clear of you. All I told them was that I hold you directly responsible for our shaky start. No, Biederman, I don't care to discuss it further over fudge sundaes.

Friday I finally realized all the Christmas decorations were down. They'd probably been down for two weeks. All car tires had chains. All trees were bare. Winter was entrenched. The mall finally had a roof over the whole structure and most of the walls up, so the construction crew would be able to work through the weather, finishing the project. Hard labor wouldn't have to freeze its ass off in February. It cheered my heart to see progress made on the white elephant. I didn't want it here, but I was going to be here for a while and it was, too; so okay, get it done with, get it built, have opening-day speeches with landing lights crisscrossing the sky.

Saturday morning I struck a deal with Barry. I promised to hoist him into the cab of a bulldozer on some nearby property and stop at every animal and machine on the way to Champaign if he'd jog with me now for a few minutes before we left.

"Okay," he said, but only with me dragging him out of the house. He wasn't wearing tennis shoes because he didn't have any. He's constantly throwing them out and saying he lost them.

"We both have to get back in shape," I said.

Barry was never going to get back in shape, but I let myself forget that because it was a sweet morning and I was tired of his whining. I really ran us. No stopping till we made three times around Westgate Court. Only then were we going to see the dozer. Barry wheezed, gagging for breath; we weren't stopping, though I wasn't exactly floating on air, either. My chest pounded, my side ached, my left leg tightened on me, and I could feel my ankle acting up again. We were starting on our last lap when Barry complained of dizziness and begged me to stop pushing him.

"We're doing good," I said. "We're stretching ourselves. It's gotta hurt a little. You gotta push yourself."

He pushed me and fell, scraping his knee, then screamed through a face full of tears: "You're trying to kill me, you asshole."

"Jesus, Bare, come on. You're okay. We'll have Mommy fix you up in no time if she can tear herself away from her corrections."

Barry skedaddled across the street and over lawns with a speed he hadn't shown a glimmer of on our court run. You never know what you've got cooking on the back burner until you're hungry.

"Come on, Bare," I shouted at him, but he was long gone. "We haven't even seen the dozer yet. Come on. I'll take you over there."

Game time.

FOURTEEN

B ARRY wasn't kidding. I had pushed him too hard. We weren't twenty miles east on 80 when he conked out cold, which proved to be a lucky break since we got a horrendously late start due to Deborah refusing to tear herself away from Hemley's corrections. We didn't have time now to stop and look at animals. Riding over the rickety bridge that threatened to throw you down the Mississippi, then off 80 to 74, past flat land getting richer in the gentle rain, past cows huddling, Deborah read the AAA guide to Illinois. So as not to wake Barry, she whispered some of the highlights. Moline is the farm implement capital of America. Carl Sandburg, a poet, was born and buried in Galesburg.

Only when we reached Champaign did Deb shake Barry awake and get his orange juice and graham crackers ready for him. "Yoo-hoo, we're here, honey."

"Did I miss the land?" he asked.

"Yes, but we have the first game of the Mississippi Valley—"

"I wanna go back," he said. "I wanna. You promised." The crankiness again, the exhausted bitchiness. The run had really worn him down. He was crying his ducts dry.

"Come on, Barry," Deborah said. "Look at the auditorium. It's a wonderful piece of architecture."

"No, no, no." He sounded genuinely desperate, trapped in

the car. "I wanna go back. I want Mommy to drive me back."

"Fine," I said, pissed. "I'll get a ride home with Francis."

"No," Deborah said. "We're here to see how Belvyn does. Let's give it a chance."

We gave it a chance.

The parking lot was immense and complicated, and the building was larger and even more monstrous. It was a white structure in the approximate shape of an egg, incredibly well lit, huge, clean. The seats were set far apart, way above the gleaming floor, and even the box seats were forty yards from the action. The gorgeous baskets were painted such a bright orange they looked like lacquered, lipsticked lips holding short skirts. We in general admission were out in Timbuktu. The arena equivalent of the Downtown Refurbishment Project. All the appeal of a cancer ward. I looked for Mr. and Mrs. Menkus, Mr. and Mrs. Jumpin' Bean, and Rita, but their tickets weren't together and I had no idea where to focus my binox. Half an hour before game time, the gym was filling slowly with the orange and blue of Marauder fans.

"What do you think of this place, pretty neat, huh, Bare? Like a great big barn," I said.

It was nothing like a great big barn. He sat silently, percolating, refusing to eat his graham crackers.

"Okay, honey," Deborah said to him, "let me try to explain it to you so maybe you'll enjoy the game more when it begins. See those two open cylinders at each end of the floor down there?" She jerked his head up and around when he tried to stare at the leather seat. She hadn't taught remedial English since 1974 for nothing. "Our team, in roan and gray, will try to toss the ball into one basket while the other team, the bad guys in orange and blue, will try to put the same ball into the other basket. Now when one team scores—"

"Come on, Deb, Barry went to the Missouri State game with me. He knows a few things. He's not a total beginner."

"Oh, well, then let me explain how a one-two-two offense can penetrate a three-two zone match-up from the high post," she said, just playing with jargon to have some fun and make

338

me happy and try to lighten up Barry, who at this point the editor of the *Farm Bureau Spokesman* couldn't have roused.

"Do you want something from the refreshment stand?" I asked him. "I'll go get us stuff."

"I wanna go home."

"Snap out of it," Deborah said.

"You guys made me miss the animals. You played a trick on me."

"You were sound asleep. You needed the rest."

" 'Cause you tired me out," he said. "You did it on purpose."

"Don't say that," I said. "I did not."

"I wanna see the Pork Queen."

"Hush up," Deborah said. "This isn't our backyard. We're visitors here."

At about twenty of eight, the crowd was near capacity. I noticed Vicki and Francis at opposite ends of press row and Raeburn settling into a reserved box, toting Chicago recruits. The three guys in the first balcony who looked like G-men were scouts. The cheerleaders and mascot from the University of Champaign kidded and traded somersaults with the cheerleaders and mascot from River State. Both teams were taking shooting practice. Menkus always avoided his teammates during warm-ups and it tended to take him a while to get out the stiffness, but now he looked practically arthritic and his isolation wasn't only self-imposed. They weren't talking to him. He wasn't getting the ball passed to him out top, and the Stallions weren't moving to make sure his knee didn't bump into theirs. Though not precisely tripping him as he went by, they certainly didn't seem to be going out of their way to ease him back into the lineup.

He definitely favored his right leg, but he hit his shots, jumping smoothly, controlling the ball off the dribble, staying within himself. I couldn't wait for the game to get under way. I wanted him to soar. Barry represented his protest by playing tic-tac-toe alone. Hinselwood went out on the court to talk to Menkus about something.

Not surprisingly, he didn't start. Champaign had five guys

as fast as brushfire, against whom River State's pass-pass-pass game plan did next to nothing. The Marauders were mostly from Chicago, high-rising risk takers who simply didn't have the patience to wait till late afternoon for RSU's motion offense to forge ahead. The Marauders stole the ball and ran it down the Stallions' noses. You can take kids out of the playground, but you can't take the knife out of their hands. During time-outs, Hinselwood got histrionic with Cliffie Davis, who wasn't making anything happen, and Menkus sent a lot of eye contact and goofy gestures in the direction of the Champaign bench.

When the first line tuckered out, Champaign just kept checking in more speed skaters, and beyond them they had even more guys who could run all night and shoot all day, never stopping to wonder where the water bottle went. Mincemeat for Menkus. Rod Williams replaced Keil and, on two successive possessions, got stripped of the ball and drew air. Terry came in for Durland and got called for goaltending. The Stallions were trying to play their own game by not matching the Marauders one-on-one, but Black Stallion continued to generate diddlyshit, and when he got frustrated he forced shots or sent the ball back around the horn to the weak side, grinding gears and throwing everyone off. Plus, the gung-ho refs weren't any help: fifteen thousand people were in the pavilion, and of these 14,700 were singing Marauder music while the River City contingent in the northwest corner was embarrassed into sullen silence. River State's defense, of course, off such sluggish offense was lazy, uninspired, and depressed. So what did Redwood do with three minutes left in the half, down by fourteen? Put in Menkus. And what could Menkus do in such a short time? Very little.

At first I thought that, based on what they'd done during warm-ups, the Stallions would keep the ball away from him, but that didn't carry over into the game. They were too far behind to carry a grudge. They looked to him immediately, forgetting what they'd learned during his absence. Too anxious to come back, they gave him the ball and then stood around, watching. He, frankly, wasn't up to it. He went at solid three-quarters speed, which would have beaten a lot of people easily. Against Champaign, though, it resembled reverse. He got beaten baseline for a dunk, had his shot blocked, fell to the floor, and on a break toward the end of the half threw the ball behind Norm Durland. Do you realize how hard it is to throw the ball behind Norm Durland on a break? I tried to tell myself Menkus was looking bad in a good way. He was just rusty and, if he was favoring his right leg a little, maybe that wasn't because he was a cripple but only afraid.

At halftime the houselights came up and Barry said, "Okay, it's finally over. Let's get out of here."

"It's only intermission," Deborah said.

Barry didn't look right. He looked tired and bored, but beyond that he looked totally worn out, like he'd been playing off-guard the last hour. His lips and tongue were wet and sweaty.

"Come on, Bare," Deb said, taking his hand and lifting him up into the aisle. She's amazingly strong when she has to be. "What do you say we do a little exploring and find you some food?"

"I'll stay here and study stats. Buy me a hot dog, okay?" I said, then in a whisper asked Deborah what she thought was going on with Barry. She said she hoped he just needed some fresh air. I said force-feed him if you have to.

"I'm not hungry," Barry said.

"We can still take a walk, can't we?" Deborah said.

I couldn't hear any more of their conversation as they wandered away. The halftime entertainment was a boys' gymnastic club doing impossible things with their unreal bodies, which plunged me back into the hottest summer of my life. While I was doing lay-up drills one day in July, racing up and down the court, two girls and a boy rode their bikes over to me, and the prettier girl took me aside and said the other girl, still pretty, needed a make-out partner. I recognized their faces but didn't know them. I was a virgin and fifteen, and here is how much I believed in basketball: I said, "Ride your bikes off my court. I have lay-up drills to do." I thought basketball would save my soul if I gave everything I had to it; sooner or later I would fall through the hoop to paradise, and the stunner now was realizing I hadn't changed. I hadn't given up that hope. If Menkus recovers, my life has possibility.

With my binoculars I looked again for the Menkuses, the Jumpin' Beans, and Rita, but couldn't find them. To be honest, I'm not sure how much I wanted to. The two couples would blame me for Menkus' injury, and his ex would blame me for not adding insult. This ridiculous game that was my youth.

Deborah and Barry didn't show up for tip-off and I figured either they're pigging out, they found something interesting to look at on their walk, or they've headed home. The last alternative was a possibility since they'd taken their coats.

Cedarwood commenced to make the first and only genius strategy move of his life. He let Menkus start the second half. Break the bank, caution to the wind, etc. "Got to go with the flow," as Menkus says. Champaign's guards dogged him all over the court. They took no prisoners, offered no special sympathy for the gimpy-legged motherfucker. In the first minute he showed he had no intention of playing tentatively. He didn't seem to be worried anymore about going down. He missed a couple shots and threw a pass over Durland's head, but they were solid shots and the pass was a good idea. He was trying to work himself out of a box.

The turnaround came with RSU ten points down and nine minutes left in the half, when he got the ball out front on a 2-2 break. This was it. Either he could still make something happen or he couldn't. He weaved to Tomlinson's side like he was only going to bounce a pass to him, set a screen, and let Tomlinson shoot his long ball. Tomlinson read Menkus' crazy green eyes and played the fake perfectly, taking one step behind Menkus, pretending to set up for the screen, then cutting hard for the hoop. Menkus led him with a soft hook pass. Tomlinson couldn't dunk in exchange for Fort Knox, but he put it in nicely, anyway.

The crucial thing to me was that a month ago Tomlinson's

entire grasp of basketball consisted of gunning from all angles, and now he knew there was more to it than that. Menkus made him better by passing the ball exactly when and where Tomlinson in his heart of hearts wanted to be, forcing him to recognize his own instincts. The next trip down the court Menkus cleared a side and buried a line-drive jumper over one of Champaign's innumerable waterbugs, and the time after that he worked a textbook backdoor, picking off Black Stallion's man with his—with Menkus'—bad leg and then hitting Cliffie for a freebie on the opposite side. RSU was down only four, the Marauder fans were trying to dam the tide with dumb chants, the Stallion contingent was blowing horns, I noticed Vicki and Francis looking alive, and Deborah and Barry were still not back yet.

When Champaign called a wise timeout I got up and walked through the corridor, checking bathrooms, but couldn't find my family anywhere. Maybe they'd left.

Pumping his fist, Hinselwood put Gault back in for Terry, and after the timeout Menkus played like he was almost daring his knee to buckle on him and if it didn't hold up at least he'd go out in a big way. But it did hold up, at least so far. Off a break he jump-stopped, putting full pressure on the knee and slamming the last dribble so the ball flew over the defender into Durland's hands for a dunk. Durland, a dunk? The pass was perfect.

Menkus took the best quality of each player on the team and made each player stretch that quality until it stretched no further, then made it stretch some more. Trying to get all his teammates to come together into a hallelujah chorus, he high-fived with Black Stallion, shouted at Tomlinson, patted Durland on his heavy ass, and argued with Gault. Menkus yelled out in hope, and when I yelled back *Menkus, Menkus, Menkus,* the hostile crowd surrounding me stared daggers and I thought I was back home. I saw Mr. and Mrs. Menkus in their Sunday best, standing up on the other side of the arena, clapping. Halfway between them and me, all alone, Jumpin' Bean bounced up and down, churning his hands like he was signaling *motion*. Raeburn beamed in his box. I figured Rita for a no-show.

The Champaign crowd was essentially silent. A bad case of the orange-and-blue grumps. Playing with him, playing through him, Menkus' teammates played better than they were ever capable of, and Menkus kept the pressure on. He faked a pass to Tomlinson, reverse-spun off his right leg to freeze his man, and snuck inside for an easy bank shot. He didn't seem to have lost more than a half-step in his move to the hoop, and even less than that on defense.

Is he okay, is he really okay? Can he regain that half-step, and if he can't is it the difference between playing and not playing pro ball? Luckily, I couldn't tell and wasn't up for asking the G-men scouts their opinion. He'd come back ten days earlier than expected. As well as he was wheeling, he was nowhere near full strength yet. I kept trying to get a half-wave from Vicki or the thumbs-up sign from Francis, who didn't see me because he was too busy following the action, announcing it, loving it. He and I are lonely old ghosts, watching our youths pass before us.

In a few days Katie Koob will be on her way home to Jessup, and "Dutch" will be perched on Pennsylvania Avenue. Sooner or later Marty will feel a big thump. Right now he is at the *Register* office, oiling his gun, listening to the game, and taking nitro pills when the pace gets too intense. Both my parents are dead. My mother and father are dead. Before long Barry will come to understand that each of us has a life span to contemplate and he has, in all likelihood, a much briefer one than the rest of us. Menkus' knee can buckle next play, next week, next season. I will feel the grief and guilt as sharp as his pain. What I want most I can never get back because we are all partners in time, caught between a hard place and Downtown Refurbishment. What matters is not getting beaten down and swallowed up, but resistance against, the sweetness of here and now. In the press conference after the game Menkus will say: "I didn't do nothin' special-like. The knee felt good. I just look for the open man down low and feeds him."

Deborah, here is my capsule autobiography: I have gone from a pure shooter to a hack playmaker. Menkus showed me how to give again. I can't do it alone. It's time to press the home court advantage.

See? See? I feel like buttonholing everyone around me and saying, See—I told you he'd pull us through this sloppy winter. Bringing his body back, he is showing the Regals who they are and how good they can be, and they are up eight with five minutes left. Before the crowd starts booing, the Marauder coach takes another timeout, and I hear my name over the PA system. *Albert Biederman, report to the main lobby immediately.*

I think I am hearing things and turn to ask my neighbor his opinion, but just before the timeout is over I hear it again, only now it's *Dr. Biederman, please report to the front lobby. This is an emergency.*

As I get up a new play develops. I know I should go straight to the lobby, but I don't. I watch Menkus and Black Stallion trap the ball, Menkus stealing it from behind, then directing traffic crosscourt. Going down the steps, I take my time, trying to catch the end of the play. I feel nimble. My bad leg, my sprained ankle, I can live with these injuries. But all about me I feel the gray fog that gets trapped in gymnasiums, the slow death of dusk descending, and I can't get this cloud out of my head. I stop once more at the first balcony and see that Black Stallion has been fouled, and I crave to see in slow-mo instant replay what just happened, how Menkus set him up. When I get to the lobby five or six cops are standing in a circle around Deborah, who is semi-hysterical though rational enough to say, "Barry's in shock. I can't get his mouth open. These guys won't do anything except wait for paramedics."

I hear the crowd getting whipped up, and I wonder why. They must be cheering a reversal of fortune, though maybe by now they've become Menkus fans. I don't know and suddenly don't care.

Trembling and sweaty, Barry's lying on the cold concrete with his head resting on a cop's leather jacket. All blood is drained from his face. His eyes dilate. Flesh of my flesh, low blood sugar of my blood, he needs something fast. His mouth is clenched tight, so Deborah sits on his legs to keep him from bouncing while I pry his lips apart with my index and middle fingers.

He is at least halfway into insulin shock, screaming madness: "You fucker, I'll hit you. I hate you. You hitter. I bite."

He does bite.

"I need sugar packs and cups of water," I say, and the cops hustle down some steps to get the stuff from a refreshment stand.

The only gratitude I get from Barry is teeth marks in my skin and socks to the chest, but at least I have his mouth open.

Deborah says, "I feel so embarrassed, Albert. I feel so bad, freaking out like this." I am looking at the beginning of the rest of our ambivalent life together. I am thinking, *30*, newspaper lingo for *Fade to black, 30, this baby's written.*

One of the cops says, "You sure you know what you're doing, buddy?"

Sure, I'm sure.

I mix the sugar and water and pour it carefully down Barry's throat at an angle so he doesn't gag, and I keep pouring. I watch his eyes narrow, and now the crowd is cheering us on. Maybe the momentum has shifted. Maybe it hasn't. It doesn't matter. What matters is that Menkus might make it back, Barry's choking but coming to. They each have an outside shot at the future. Barry's kicking and coughing. My only desire is to be his father. *I didn't do nothin' special-like. I just look for the open man down low and feeds him.*

"You fucker, I hate you," he says, hitting me, and it's almost as if he hates me for bringing him back from the dead.

"Come on, Bare, sit up."

"Laurel's away to play," he says.

My ears pound, Deborah tells the cops to stop smoking; and in her snappy anger, in the fierce fire in her eyes, I see what I have always longed to see: the loyalty of love.

"I hate you," Barry says again.

The crowd is going crazy, and most of the cops leave to find out what's happening.

"Just keep swallowing the sugar," I say.

"I'll hit you, fuckhead," he says, but this is his last curse. Every punch from here on in is him letting me know how strong he is, and when he takes a big breath you can literally see the blood flowing back into circulation, and Deborah and I squeeze him and each other so hard we practically cause a relapse.

"Can we go home now?" he asks.

"We are home," I say, "we're home for good," and Deborah catches my drift and my heart does a reverse spin toward hope.

About the Author

David Shields graduated, Phi Beta Kappa, from Brown University in 1978 and received his master of fine arts from the Iowa Writers' Workshop. He has held a National Endowment for the Arts grant, an Ingram Merrill award, a James Michener fellowship, and a James Phelan award. He was born in Los Angeles, where he currently lives.